WARRIOR'S MARK
DRAGONS
BOOK THREE

S.E. LOWER

Susan Lower Books

Language note: This book uses different Native American words to stand in for the shifters' ancient language, a tribute to the folklore and culture of the fictional people who gain animal spirit guides at their coming-of-age. The end of the book contains a pronunciation guide.

S.E. Lower

www.selower.com

ISBN: 978-1-945274-18-3

Marked by a Curse
Warrior's Mark: Dragons
SE Lower

Susan Lower Books

Glossary

Solanu – Mate

Bitatelo - mountain lion

Bodaway Achak – **firemaking spirit**

Hehewuti - warrior mother spirit. - One who could hold and bestow a spirit to anyone.

Mal'drathir - Shadow snatcher

Nimitqwa Ktelo - as you once were and will be again.

Ohunko - guardians whose dark hearts stain their spirits

Nituwe he - who are you?

Shólan - friend (Shoh-lahn)

Unahu - mate

Wakinyan - thunder/ thunder spirit

Wiyoya – Chosen one

One

Deep in Crag's Cliff, past the iron gate and into the mountain's gut, Aluk led the woman single file through the prison corridor. Stone scraped his shoulders in the narrow corridor, forcing him to glance back at her.

Her pale skin glowed in the firelight.

A psychiatrist sent by the State of New York, here to 'evaluate' their newest inmate. A young man not yet twenty, possessed by one of the ancient guardians, corrupt and dangerous.

The third time she bumped his back, she murmured an apology. Either she didn't sense the danger surrounding her, or she had nerves forged of steel.

She shouldn't be here, his dragon snarled, rising hot behind his eyes.

She'll be gone soon, he told it, forcing the ancient spirit within him down.

Her quiet steps slowed at each cell. Soft intake of breath. Scratch of pen on paper. He'd request her notes later to ensure no maps or confidential information left these walls.

Prisoners straightened. Others lifted their heads to stare. Aluk's chest rumbled; he choked the growl. No one spoke. They knew better.

Aluk wanted to refuse her descent upon arrival. Her scent of peaches lingered in his nostrils, stirring a part of him long dormant.

Bond-scent. Wrong. Impossible. His dragon snarled inside him, twisting as he fought to keep the beast in the cage of his mind.

He grunted with the effort. Once she saw the man in question, she'd leave.

Taran brought her up the mountain by human means. He ran off as soon as the door closed upon her arrival. He'd take her back himself if need be. This was no place for a woman.

The threat of the Fae hovered on the horizon. Their boundary around the mountain grew weak.

Protect. His dragon, at the edge of his consciousness, whispered. *Mate.*

His steps faltered. *Not possible, dragon.*

He had a mate, and then he lost her.

This woman's scent... peaches... imprinted on his soul. *It's not her.*

He paused before the isolated cell at the end of the hall. "Stay back."

Aluk moved close to the next cell and motioned for her to stand with him. Her hair flowed down her back, transforming to the color of ripe strawberries in the firelight.

Delicious, his dragon rumbled.

Heat shot through him. His nostrils flared as he barked, "Stand up. You've got a visitor."

A scrape of metal echoed in the back of the cell. His guest stiffened beside him.

A towering figure strolled forth from the darkness, halting inches from the cell's bars.

She gasped beside him, a soft sound he might not have heard without the silence embracing them.

The *ohunko,* a spirit of one of their ancient guardians, appeared in his human form. His dark, gleaming eyes revealed the bear spirit possessing the man.

She turned her head. "Is this necessary?"

"Necessary, Miss Everett?"

She waved her hand toward the prisoner's lack of clothing.

"I thought you understood this is a shifter prison. You're lucky he's in human form. Otherwise, he couldn't speak with you. If he does at all."

Her green eyes flashed. That pert little nose wrinkled. She reached into her bag and pulled out a folder with a state emblem.

"You're Scout Jameson."

When no answer came from the younger man, Aluk used his alpha authority and said, "Answer her."

A slow smile seeped from beneath those haunting eyes. "I am Gorak, chief brave and guardian of my brother bears."

"Okay," she said, flipping back her hair from her shoulder. "I'm looking for Scout Jameson."

"Gorak," Aluk informed her. "He went by the name of Scout before the bear guardian possessed him."

"Bear guardian?"

Gorak lifted his chin, moving closer to the bars. Aluk stepped between Ms. Everett and the bars.

"Why do you look for a boy, *winyan wanagi*? When a man stands before you." Gorak's lip curled.

She tilted her head, glanced over his body, lingering at his dangling manhood, then back up to his face. "Almost." She smiled. "Not quite."

A growl built in Aluk's throat before he could stop it. His dragon raged at her attention on another male. He swallowed it down, but his hands had curled into fists.

Her insult caused a flick of red in Gorak's eyes and his nostrils to flare. He grabbed the bars, and when she jumped back, Aluk's hand found the middle of her back to steady her.

An old itch spread across his palm; warmth seeped through the silk of her blouse to prickle in the blood of his veins. He snatched his hand away as if he had been burned.

Across from the young man stood Miss Everett. She appeared mid-twenties at most; he guessed from the youthfulness of her stride and the brave front she held beside him.

"I'm Dr. Everett. I'm here to help you return to your family, *Scout*. Would you like that?"

Aluk considered that an odd thing to say, but his brother, Conleth, spoke as a medical professional, clinical, and not like they were brothers.

"There is no *Scout*. I am Gorak, the greatest warrior of all the guardians." His shoulders rolled back, and his chest puffed out.

A low rumble of a growl came from Aluk's chest. Gorak tilted his head, eyeing Aluk, then looking back at Dr. Everett.

"Then tell me, Gorak, how long have you been a guardian?" Her eyes brightened, leaning slightly forward.

Aluk shifted his weight, angling himself between her and the bars. He watched Gorak's hands hover near the bars. The ore coating would burn him. Aluk's dragon spirit coaxed him closer, eager for Gorak to test the bars and feel the ore's punishment.

The young man relaxed; his hands slid back from the bars between them. "For many centuries."

Dr. Everett didn't bat an eyelash at Gorak's proclamation. She pulled out a pen and made a note in her folder. "Right then. Do you wish for me to help you return to your tribe? Do you understand why I have come?"

Gorak's eyes darkened. Aluk's blood turned to ice. He placed his arm in front of Dr. Everett to push her back. She bristled, planted her feet, refusing to budge. A lock of hair fell over Gorak's forehead. His voice dropped to a whisper that somehow filled the hollow space. "*Nimitawa ktelo,* Dr. Everett. As you once were and will be again.*"

The words hit Aluk like a physical blow. His heart hammered against his ribs. His dragon surged, recognition blazing through every nerve. *No, it couldn't be.*

Dr. Everett frowned. "What does that mean?"

Gorak smiled, stepping back into the shadows of his cell.

"I think our little visit is over." Aluk crowded Dr. Everett back down the hall from the *ohunko*'s cell. Aluk grasped her, pivoting her, then propelled her in the direction they had originated, despite her protest. With no choice but to go forward, she marched ahead. Her spine stiffened under the pressure of his hand.

As they passed, one of the spirit hunters stood next to his bars. His head bent, but Aluk could feel the man's stare on Dr. Everett. He growled, his eyes burning with dragon-sight as he glared at the prisoner. The man slunk back. Aluk blinked, his pupils adjusting from dragon to human.

Within the upper halls, Aluk rested his palm near her lower back. Even through the silk of her blouse, heat radiated from her skin into his palm. His dragon purred. The urge to pull her closer, to shelter her completely, nearly overwhelmed him.

Her shoulders pulled back in her suit jacket, her pencil skirt a matching black, and her shoes' short little heels made a clip-clop sound down the stone hall.

She didn't pull away from his hand, but her spine had gone rigid. Was she afraid? Angry? He couldn't tell, and that unsettled him more than it should.

Aluk's hand remained at her back, fingers tense. He tracked every shadow, every doorway they passed. He paused at the entrance, gesturing for her to enter. "After you."

Heat spread through his chest as she crossed the threshold.

When the door closed, she confronted him. "Did I hear you growl at a prisoner, Mr. Vasumen?"

He grimaced and then moved toward the shelf on the distant wall, where he stored glasses and scotch. Knowing it would not affect him, pouring himself a drink gave him something to occupy his hands. "Can I get you a drink?"

"Do you always drink when you're on duty?"

"I do when I'm always on duty." Aluk held up the glass, took a swig of scotch, and let it slide down his throat nice and smooth. "Are you sure I can't get you anything?"

Her satchel swinging at her side, she crossed her arms. "Relocate Scout Jameson from that cell to quarters suitable for his treatment."

Aluk sat his glass down. "Despite what you may have been told, Ms. Everett. This isn't a medical facility. It's a prison."

"A correctional institution." She tilted her chin up, those sharp green eyes leveling with him. For a second, she sounded exactly like Naomi. The same steel in her voice. The same tilt of her chin. His chest constricted. He turned away, reaching for the scotch to hide the expression he couldn't control.

Since returning higher on the mountain, closer to the core of the spirits, his dragon's spirit had urged him to find her, and the grief of his loss worsened.

"Call it what you wish. Scout Jameson no longer exists, and the *ohunko* inside his body is dangerous. He stays where he is. And now that you've seen him, you can write your report and return to the government."

Aluk's chest tightened. Decades had passed since he lost his mate, but the wound still ached fresh.

Dr. Everett clutched the strap of her satchel. "I'm afraid you won't be getting rid of me that easily, Mr. Vasumen. I have been assigned to Sentinel Peak until Scout is rehabilitated."

His brother failed to share this information with him upon delivering Dr. Everett to Crag's Cliff. She reached into her satchel and held out the papers. Government authority held zero sway on the mountain. Long ago, boundaries defined Sentinel Peak, protecting the shifters' refuge from the outside world. Before they could take the papers from Dr. Everett, it appeared the choice had been taken from them.

He scanned the papers. His jaw tightened with each line. Known descendant. Mandatory relocation. His fist crumpled the edge of the page. "You share the blood of the ancestors?"

Instead of the mountain becoming a haven to their people, the government used it as a dumping ground. How many Fae worked within the human government agencies to manipulate the state to act in their favor?

She chewed her lip. Her gaze flicked away for a split second. When she looked back, her expression was carefully neutral. "If you are implying I was forced to come here, I was not."

"Then you are free to leave whenever you wish?" Aluk's question hung in the air like a heavy weight, his gaze boring into her. Her brow furrowed for a heartbeat before smoothing. If he'd blinked, he would have missed it.

Her shoulders tensed. "There is still the matter of rehabilitation for Scout Jameson and returning him to his parents."

Aluk stepped back and placed the papers on his desk behind him. He ran his hand down through his long beard. The primal instincts of his dragon spirit refused to allow her to leave their sight. His chest burned at the thought of developing feelings for another. It was best to send this female away than risk losing himself or his dragon spirit from enduring the torment of another mate.

He needed to get her off the mountain before she became another casualty of the curse. His dragon extended its claws, racking his mind for one excruciating second.

"There is no return from a place like this," he grunted.

"I am very good at my job, Mr. Vasumen."

"Alpha."

"Excuse me?"

"I'm the alpha of the mountain tribes, Dr. Everett. I suggest you get used to calling me Alpha or Aluk, will do. We're less formal here atop the mountain."

"And you're not my alpha. I believe the state..."

"Nothing!" He slammed his fist on the desk. The room seemed to shake, and she froze.

She held his gaze, chin lifted, though her fingers had gone white on the strap.

She won't break. His dragon rumbled.

Aluk clenched his fist and cleared his throat. "The state has no jurisdiction here. You're in my territory now, which makes you my responsibility."

A shatter of ice erupted in the glitter of gold in her green eyes. "I am ruled by no man." She stepped closer. "I will work with you on this, but don't mistake cooperation for submission. Now, if you would kindly direct me to suitable lodging and provide a space more suitable for communicating and treating my charge, we can get started."

He gazed at her for what seemed like minutes, never blinking, unwilling to yield. Alpha or no alpha, the incredible sensation of proving his dominance ran through him hot as a live wire. No female ever challenged him since Naomi.

Let her try, his dragon spirit reasoned. *We must keep her close.*

"The only lodging you'll find here are rooms in the north tower. Otherwise, the resort offers lodging at Avalanche Ridge."

"And my charge?" A spark lit in her eyes.

Her scent—peaches and cream—wrapped around him like a drug. *Claim her mouth. Silence her.*

She deserves better.

He needed her to submit, to acknowledge his authority, but not with possession. "Jameson stays right where he is."

She studied him for a long moment, her jaw working.

"Then the north tower it is."

His dragon spirit lunged forward, seizing control. His hand shot out—and stopped, trembling, an inch from her throat. Not to harm. To touch. To feel her pulse hammering beneath his fingers. To tilt her chin up and taste those defiant lips.

Her breath caught. Her eyes widened, but she didn't retreat.

For one suspended heartbeat, the only sound was their breathing.

Then Aluk snatched his hand back as if burned. His chest heaved with the effort of restraint. His dragon roared in his head.

He moved toward the entry, expecting her to follow. As he led her from his office, Gorak's words echoed in his mind: *As you were and will be again.*

His dragon recognized her the moment she arrived, and that terrified him more than any Fae curse.

Two

After dragging her luggage up three flights of stairs, Palisade glared at the high and mighty alpha standing at the top of the north tower. He appeared bored, and didn't offer to lift a hand to help her.

Those dark, stormy eyes tracked her progress. Not impatient. Wary. Guarded. Her existence presented a problem he hadn't yet solved.

He was mistaken if he believed this would cause her to abort her mission. He didn't intimidate her. No matter how her stomach clenched at the sight of him. She wasn't leaving here until she had completed her task.

Palisade fought to catch her breath as she neared the last step. A sheen of sweat broke out on her neck and arms. She pasted on a forced smile, not going to give Aluk, 'Alpha,' Vasumen the pleasure of her discomfort.

"Isn't this the landing pad for a helicopter?"

"At the top of the tower. You're one floor below." He turned and walked down the hall, not bothering to offer to assist her. She expected much, given he left her near those steps, offering no assistance with her luggage.

"What an ass," Palisade muttered under her breath and grabbed the handle of her suitcase. She tugged it along with the other, but it didn't stop her gaze from traveling down his backside. Brute or not, the way he filled out those black cargo pants caused additional sweat to trickle down between her breasts. It was always the hot ones.

Palisade blew a strand of hair out of her eye and caught him glancing back at her before he jerked his gaze forward. His shoulders had gone rigid, spine straight.

Interesting. The mighty alpha wasn't as unaffected as he wanted her to believe.

Too bad for him she didn't come here looking to tango, especially with brutes like Aluk Vasumen.

The hallway stretched before them, lined with heavy wooden doors. Her suitcase wheels clattered against the stone floor as she followed him.

He stopped near a door. "This is your room, Dr. Everett. You'll find my chambers next door down."

She hadn't anticipated his room being this close to hers. Did he suspect her true cause? Something in the way his eyes assessed her said the mighty mountain alpha didn't trust anyone.

"My room is next to yours?"

He didn't answer, just gestured for her to enter.

Inside the room, the dry air enveloped her. Palisade trembled; not from the chill transitioning to warmth, but from relief. Finally, the stairs ceased torment. A sizable bed, a tiny desk, plus a window facing untamed wilderness, greeted her.

She assumed he lived somewhere else, perhaps in a village, since the town was further south. The sole indication of civilization nearby. A shiver ran down her spine. Trapped. In the middle of nowhere. In a prison full of dangerous shifter bloods. With a man she barely knew. *Perfect.*

She lost her grip on her small suitcase. It tumbled down over the other and landed at his feet. So professional and ladylike of her.

The thought of being so close to him, of sharing a hallway with him, filled her with unease. Her orders hadn't involved the alpha, not directly, but he posed a challenge to accomplishing her task.

He might not want her here, but Palisade needed to complete her task without delay. She could pretend the young man lost to the *ohunko* needed her help to live out the rest of his day in peace and harmony as long as it kept the gates for Palisade to access Crag's Cliff open.

Alpha Vasumen cleared his throat; lines formed between his brows. "You are my responsibility while you are here. Therefore, you'll stay in my section of the tower."

"Is that a suggestion or an order?"

His tone had implied she was a child, and he was scolding her for asking a stupid question.

"Do all the residents here think they're an ancient spirit of some sort?"

He ignored her question.

Over the centuries, the increasing recorded incidents of people shifting from human to animal caused the state to draw boundaries and create precautions to keep both parties safe. It also kept the shifter bloods herded onto the mountain under the hold of the curse. She knew their wrath when provoked very well, having trained with Fae comrades.

Her hand trembled, the shaking spreading up to her wrist. She rubbed it against her side, willing the tremor to stop. One dose left. One more week if she was lucky, maybe two if her body cooperated. Not that it ever did. She was fine one day and bedridden the next.

First, the headaches would return. Then the weakness of her muscles turned to water until even climbing the stairs became torture.

Finally, the fever that never broke, burning her from the inside while she shivered with cold.

The Fae healers had never named what was killing her. They'd only shaken their head, told her she had a rare condition, progressive, and without their medicine–fatal.

She'd lasted this long through sheer stubbornness and their antidotes. Yet, the medicine only slowed the dying, didn't stop it. Only a cure could do that. Her Fae benefactor had the means to get the cure, and completing this last mission was their price to extend it to her.

Traveling up the mountain had taken more energy and exertion than she had expected. Here, the air became thinner. Colder. A giant fortress sat embedded in the mountain. It blended in with the terrain. Without the ranger Taran, she may not have found it.

"I'll leave you to settle in. There is less oxygen outside the fortress because of our elevation. I would discourage you if you're inclined to explore the landing above us. Should you pass out from lack of ability to breathe, I cannot ensure your safety, Dr. Everett."

The warning came out gruff, almost annoyed. His eyes lingered on her face, searching. Checking for...what? Understanding? Signs of weakness? Or genuine concern he didn't want to admit?

"Noted." Palisade pulled her suitcase to pass him. As she sat it down inside the door, she reached and picked up her fallen one. Straightening, she paused at the depths of his dark eyes. They intrigued her. She met his gaze, holding his stare.

She didn't dare look away.

Lines formed across his brow, and his lips formed a tight line. The longer she looked at him, the more hypnotizing his eyes became. Dark as storm clouds, but beneath the hostility, something other than his dragon spirit lurked. Something raw. Grief, maybe? Or loss?

For a heartbeat, he looked like a man haunted.

A trickle of sweat rolled down her face. Everything inside her screamed to look away. Would he consider her level gaze a challenge?

You're not here to fight him.

Pulling up to her full height, she searched for any signs of vulnerability. Her benefactor always warned to avoid looking a target in the eye. So, she did, matching their stare, and watching their life fade.

Somehow, she got the feeling Alpha Vasumen teetered on that line.

Palisade took a step back. Enough. She hadn't come here to analyze the alpha.

He towered over her, standing over her average human height. She came just under his chin. "You may call me Palisade if you wish. Especially since it looks like we'll be neighbors."

Before he could respond, she bent and grabbed her small suitcase. She shut the door, but not before seeing the flicker of amber in his eyes as she severed their connection.

Not anger. Not annoyance.

Hunger.

Her breath caught. She pressed her back against the closed door, heart hammering. Whatever that look meant, it wasn't simple dislike.

It was far more dangerous.

Once she got the tremble in her legs under control, Palisade tossed her suitcase on the dark green coverlet of the bed. She'd packed only what she couldn't live without, not knowing if the state would lift their penance of the blooded ones.

She turned slowly, taking in her new accommodations. Unfortunately, from what she'd seen, the entire fortress lacked modern conveniences. The fire burned to provide light inside a crease in the wall, casting dancing shadows across the stone floor. A large tapestry of a landscape hung on the wall by the door. The overall atmosphere of the room gave her austere and masculine vibes.

A pleasant sensation warmed her as she sat on the corner of the bed, whispering of familiarity like a best friend. With Déjà vu resting on her shoulder, a chilled prickle skated across her skin.

She'd felt it ever since her first introduction to Aluk Vasumen. Like she'd known him all her life. Impossible. She'd never been to Crag's Cliff or the Endless Mountains until now. Palisade brushed aside the unusual sensation and went to peek in the small bathroom.

Though her accommodations may not have been those of a luxury hotel, the bed held fresh linens. Inside the bathroom, she discovered updated fixtures, not at all what she'd have guessed from the hall.

Good. At least she could shower and work in relative comfort.

She slipped off her heeled shoes and paced across the fur rug. Time to document everything while it was fresh. She should have written more notes, but she imprinted them in her memory files. Palisade found her tablet, pulled out the device, and activated the talk-to-text app.

"Scout Jameson. Early twenties. He thinks he is a centuries-old guardian named Gorak. Bear spirit."

Another chill raced up her arms. Her mind returned to the cold, dark depths of the dungeon. Yes, a dungeon. A crudely fashioned prison created out of something from old history books. Not a castle, she shook her head, trying to release the image in her recent memories — a fortress built high in the mountains, high enough to give an average human a nosebleed.

The prison's warden, a rough, burly man whose eyes went dark as smoke and looked like he rose from the bowels of hell. A killer, she'd bet. She knew the signs, the controlled movements, and the constant awareness. The way he positioned himself between her and every potential threat in the dungeon.

She understood killers appeared in two categories: those who enjoyed killing, and those compelled to kill. Aluk Vasumen was the latter. She'd stake her life on it.

A little nagging voice in her mind whispered to stay clear of him. The intensity of his stare threatened to see right through her, and that baritone voice had the power to command the strongest of men. Yet, she recognized a kindred spirit, another who carried the weight of impossible choices.

Then there was Scout. The report filed by the state department stating that a human officer witnessed his capture during his vacation in the state park provided her with an insight into the mountain. Now, she needed to fulfill her end of the bargain and get what she needed before her Fae employers made their next move against the shifter-bloods.

She rubbed her temples. Too many variables. Too many unknowns. Focus on what you can control.

Not the alpha.

Naked. She almost laughed aloud when the random thought popped into her head. Not the alpha. But she had a feeling he was far more impressive than Scout in his birthday suit.

And Scout hadn't shocked her so much as his blunt display of dominance startled her. She made a mental note of the prisoners' lack of clothing to include in her report. Too bad the report was fake. Had the guardian taken her hint about fulfilling his purpose?

It had been cold in the dungeon with no visible heat source.

Good thing shifter blood ran hot. Too bad she didn't have any to chase away the ice filling her veins.

Palisade pulled out the file again on Scout Jameson. Aluk considered the young man dangerous. He had no idea. Part of her ached for the guy. No one knew how much time they had on this earth. Not

Scout, trapped in his own body, and not her, dying slowly without a cure. Releasing Gorak from his host, would give was her only option for the Fae to grant her the cure. Not another temporary antidote, but the actual cure that would save her life.

The cost? Scout Jameson would die.

Her stomach twisted. She'd killed before–targets who'd chosen their path, who'd known the risks. But Scout? He was an innocent young man possessed by an ancient guardian spirit. He had chosen none of this.

Neither had she.

Palisade pressed her palm against her chest to ease the rattle in her lungs that the mountain air couldn't quite erase. One life for another. This was the trade.

She was running out of time to decide whether she could live with it.

In the meantime, she wrote him up as having a personality disorder for the sake of his family and to appease the state. It worked to get her into the prison fortress. However, her benefactor required results, not reports.

With the alpha keeping close watch over her, freeing Scout and Gorak may be more challenging than expected.

Since arriving, the mountain called to her. The sacred forest and endless peaks cleansed her lungs. For the first time in years, she breathed without coughing. The bite of the fresh mountain air cleared her lungs.

Palisade placed a hand over her heart.

Once the government opened the Endless Mountain Reserve to the public, her survival became dependent on another's death. Her benefactor had given her a deadline.

One innocent life for hers.

Nausea swelled inside her, the vile taste like a sour lemon. *What is your life worth, Palisade?* The tremor in her fingers from earlier faded, and she returned her focus to her work, continuing her assessment.

"Aluk Vasumen. Alpha. He claims to be a leader of his people. Observation: His roughness precludes his position. Protective..." She thought back to the encounter with Scout.

"I bet he's one of those men who likes to be in control." She paused, reconsidering. No—not likes. Needs. There was a difference. Men who enjoyed control in her experience did so to guard themselves, hide their emotions, or evade facing traumatic situations.

What are you protecting, Alpha Vasumen?

Or what are you afraid of?

She clicked off the recording and set the tablet aside. An audible rumble emerged from her stomach, reverberating in the stone chamber.

The journey to the mountains left her hungry, and the fruit smoothie from her breakfast had long worn off. Her stomach cramped and grumbled at the lack of food. She should have asked about meals. Other choice words lingered on her tongue for the man and held her from asking.

Turning off her device, she slipped on a pair of tennis shoes and prepared to explore her new surroundings.

If she could locate the dining hall within the fortress maze, she might find food and intel on the number of guards, prisoners, and escape routes.

Palisade descended the tower stairs, her footsteps echoing in the stairwell. On the second landing, she found a man in black cargo pants headed her way. He stood a little taller than most men, all long lines and quiet strength. Not the heavy, broad presence of an alpha. His eyes caught the light and pulled warm color from it, shades that made her think of hazelnuts and lattes. Heart curled in her stomach. She shut her eyes, willing her brain to stop comparing the stranger's face to a cafe menu. She closed her eyes for a moment, trying to get food off her mind for a moment.

She grinned and opened her eyes. Did they all breed tall, dark, and handsome?

His head lifted, chin up, nostrils flared. Sniffing?

She ignored the urge to check for body odor.

The big bad alpha of the mountain hadn't told her anything about staying away from the guards, and since she wasn't a prisoner, she intended to explore her surroundings. "Excuse me."

His eyes widened slightly, then a slow smile spread across his face. "Headed to dinner?"

"You don't think I'm trying to escape, do you?" she asked.

His grin broadened, displaying the dimples in his cheeks. "Women are rare in this place."

She admired his dark hair, cut short and shaved on the sides, not long and tangled like his alpha's. Having looked at him too long, his eyes swept over her.

"Dinner it is. Either way, you caught me."

She could have sworn she heard him mutter, "Nice."

When his eyes returned to her face, he licked his lips. "There are not many places you can wander in a place like this alone."

"I don't suppose there is. I'm Dr. Palisade Everett, but please call me Palisade." She fluttered her lashes.

"Trace."

She slipped her fingers around his offered arm. "It's a pleasure to meet you, Trace. I suspect we will become good friends." *The best of friends*, she grinned, spotting the keys hooked at his waist.

Three

Aluk paused outside the staff dining room.

Her scent still lingered in the hallway. She sat with Trace and two of the other wolf shifter guards. His skin prickled at the soft sound of her voice. At her laugh.

"Hungry, alpha?"

Aluk looked over at Pinto approaching from down the hall. "Report?"

The older shifter with gray streaks in his cropped hair stopped a few feet from him. "There's a woman in the dining hall. Several of my guards have spotted her."

"Yes." Aluk glanced back into the dining hall. Dr. Everett tilted a glass to her lips.

"I'm told her escort departed. Are you taking her back to the village or further to town?" Pinto followed Aluk's gaze.

None of the guards here had mates. What Pinto didn't say in words, Aluk read in his eyes.

His dragon didn't like the way she had leaned against Trace.

"No. She stays in the north tower with me for now. She won't be here long. Let your guards know to keep out of my tower and not to allow her access to any of the cells without my presence."

"Of course." Pinto motioned for Aluk to go ahead of him.

He sat with Pinto, their meals brought out from the kitchen staff. Thick steak and garlic mashed potatoes steamed under his nose.

Trace leaned closer to Palisade. Aluk's breath stopped, his chest locking. Whatever the wolf shifter said made Palisade tilt her head back and laugh again.

His dragon roared in his head.

He pushed back from the table and headed for his tower.

"Alpha," Pinto got to his feet.

Aluk waved for him to stay.

He'd wanted...no, he needed... her to leave.

Aluk's strides lengthened. His dragon threatened to burst forth if he didn't make it outside in time. *Soon, his brothers would have to protect their people without him.* The darkness edged into his vision. *Mine.*

Your mate is gone. Accept it. Aluk stared at the stars outside his tower. He inhaled the crisp mountain air. Its icy sting hitting his throat. The burn held back the beat inside him.

The moon greeted him from behind a snowcapped peak. He shed his clothes, allowing his human form to dissolve like mist. Scales unfurled across his skin in the moonlight. His muscles bulged, his frame broadening as his dragon spirit solidified. He stepped back into the darkness but stayed at the edge of consciousness. While the beast pushed for dominance, Aluk held on to a single strand of control.

You claimed the female, and I let you, his dragon growled. *Now it is my turn to pick from amongst the females. She is the* wíyoyá. *The chosen one.*

Aluk didn't argue. He couldn't risk another hibernation, not with the Fae to keep them enslaved in the curse. He needed to stay present. His family depended on it. The mountain depended on it.

The beast tilted its head back and spread its wings. *She* was here. Issabrie. At the heart of the mountain, trapped for eternity.

While fate brought him Naomi, the mountain took her, too. The dragon never accepted her.

The dragon soared through the air and circled the peaks.

His father warned him. *Choose wrong, and you'll lose yourself.*

He chose Naomi.

The dragon chose Issabrie.

A void in his chest burned.

We can't release her. Not ever.

The dragon craved Issabrie. Aluk's duty demanded he protect his people. The war between them never ceased.

She came to him at night. He sensed her in the phantom warmth against his scales. The whisper of her voice. The soft promises they'd made to each other.

His gut twisted. Spreading out his wings, the dragon dove through the night, burning off his human's restraint.

He flew and swooped around the mountain peaks. His eyes tracked across the forest and rocky slopes, seeking a hidden cave or sheltered crevice to claim. Every shadow, every movement in the forest below came into sharp focus.

The lair under Avalanche Ridge reeked of his brothers' mates. The scent drove his dragon mad with territorial fury. Another lair existed, hidden deep in the mountain. Ancient vows held the Fae queen within. Issabrie.

No, he wouldn't revisit his dragon's memories.

He spread his wings and dove through the night. The wind screamed past him as he burned off the rage of being trapped in human form. A cave hid among the cliffs, its entrance concealed by rock and bushes. He caught a faint scent from within. Familiar. Achingly familiar. *Issabrie...*

His wings stirred the foliage as he descended. A faint glimmer of light escaped from a crack in the stone. The blood seal glowed faintly in the crack. Magic hummed against his scales, pulling him to the entrance. His dragon's heart hammered against his ribs.

He angled toward the cave entrance. Then–strawberry-tinted hair. Emerald eyes. The vision slammed into him.

Aluk jerked up, racing up the mountain as though pursued. He circled the peak, weaving through the mountains or shooting up through the clouds. Ms. Everett's face haunted every thought. He couldn't escape her scent.

No, doctor. Dr. Palisade Everett.

Mate.

His dragon breathed out a long stream of fire toward the peaks. The soul warrior inside him pulled toward the keep. Toward her. A recognition he couldn't deny, couldn't fight.

The others had come: the *hehewuti* and the Fae queen's blood, but this one, this *wíyoyá*, smelled entirely human.

He must keep her close. Protect her. Deep in the mountains, his dragon sensed the pull back toward Crag's Cliff. He flew around her peak–always her peak–before returning. Protect. Even if it destroyed him.

Palisade stood near the edge atop the northern tower, looking out at the mountains. Moonlight illuminated her pale skin in a soft glow. Her hair fell spilled over her shoulders and down her back. The scent of summer orchids, ripe and exotic, hit him as he glided toward the landing. She wore a long nightgown, and a robe knotted at the waist. As he landed, her breath caught, soft, but he heard it. His dragon lowered its head in submission, a gesture of peace.

Her eyes rounded. Her fear rolled off of her in waves, souring her sweet scent.

He warned her. Told her to stay inside.

Her scent turned sour with fear and sweet with excitement. She took several steps back, giving him room to curl his tail in her direction.

Foolish woman. She'd pass out up here.

Forcing the dragon aside, he became human again.

The fear on her face melted. Her eyes widened, lips parting.

His chest rumbled. Aluk reached down and grabbed his pants. He carried them as he approached her. "What are you doing up here?"

Her gaze fell to his manhood, standing at attention. His dragon blood still ran hot from the flight–from her scent.

Just biology. That's all. Nothing more.

He took his time pulling on the rough jeans, clearing his throat to force her gaze to meet his.

"Fresh air," she croaked. "It's stiff down there..." She shook her head. "Stuffy. I mean, it's stuffy down there."

"I warned you to stay inside."

She nodded, breaking eye contact. He swallowed the chuckle gathering in his chest.

"This prison is full of shifter-bloods, unless you enjoy watching a man before and after he shifts."

Her cheeks turned deep red.

As long as she isn't looking at anyone else but us.

She wasn't his mate. She couldn't be his mate.

His mate was dead.

But mine is not, his dragon snarled.

Her scent intensified the fire in his blood. This body, this smell, didn't belong to the one he loved. Peaches. He'd crave them from now on because of her.

Aluk grabbed her arm, hauling her toward the trapdoor leading back inside. She struggled against his grip, her face flushed, brows drawn together.

"What do you think you're doing? Let me go," she demanded, her voice rising with indignation.

Heat surged through his veins. He clenched his jaw and ignored her protests. His gaze fixed on the trapdoor, and he held his breath to avoid inhaling her scent.

Not ours. No matter how she smells.

As he pulled her closer, their bodies brushed. A jolt of electricity shot through him, loosening his grip before he regained control. Liar. The temptation swelled. He wanted more than just getting her inside.

She's turning blue. Get her inside.

"Do I scare you, *Doctor*?"

"You are a dragon."

Ah, so the dragon entranced her, not his physique. A chuckle escaped him. His dragon spirit purred inside him as her eyes widened with understanding.

Before she could protest more, he swept her in his arms and jumped down through the trapdoor. She screamed, wrapping her arms around him. His dragon rumbled approval, purring again as he held her close.

His grip tightened as his feet hit the stone floor. As soon as he set her on her feet, she jerked away, pulling her robe tighter. Her heart drummed in his ears, fast and irregular. The beat was irregular. He narrowed his eyes.

Something's wrong. Her heartbeat...it's not right.

He reached out through their blood bond. *Conleth, I need you up at Crag's Cliff in the morning.*

Conleth's response through their blood link was immediate. Battle strategy or Band-Aid?

The Fae made them all wary. Aluk grunted.

Both. See you in the morning.

"I should go." Static lifted strands of Palisade's hair. Her hand twitched as she held onto her robe.

He swore in his head.

Control. He still had some.

Frighten her, yes. Make her leave. Yes. See her perish. No.

"You don't have to fear me." He put his jeans back on, leaving them unbuttoned at the fly. Her gaze jerked down to his hand, held at the zipper. Slowly, he adjusted himself before closing his pants.

Caught staring at him, she brushed her hair back over her shoulder. "Is this what this was all about?" She motioned with her hand. "A demonstration of your strength? I'm well aware of male rituals to show dominance. You don't scare me."

Her flushed cheeks, wild hair, and glistening eyes said otherwise. He could have said 'boo' and sent her skittering off like a little mouse. He should. One word and she'd run. His dragon growled, igniting a flame in his chest.

She wasn't their mate.

She wasn't Fae.

It wasn't safe for humans. He and his brothers had captured the ohunkos. The Fae would come in search of Conleth's mate, Trinity. The Fae needed her to release the queen. His dragon spirit snarled, twisting inside him. He wrestled the dragon down, forcing it back inside. Peaches!

The spirit stilled.

"Are you all right?"

He curled and uncurled his fists, counting backwards until the dragon spirit settled.

They couldn't afford more deaths on the mountain.

If anything happened to her, the state would retaliate. They had enough enemies without adding another.

Aluk reached toward her, causing her to retreat and tremble. The fires burning in the wall trays radiated more light than heat. He motioned for her to walk ahead. She needed blankets and a hearth. This high up, the snow remained while the rest of the mountain had thawed.

"It's not me you need to fear." His eyes shifted, his human pupils turning to slits. His dragon wanted to look at her. He appeased the dragon. Man and beast warred more frequently now. The Fae conflict forced him to stay human more often.

Palisade gasped but stood her ground. Blue crept across her lips, and color drained from her cheeks.

Aluk grabbed her by the belt of her robe, yanking her toward him. He tilted his head, her mouth mere inches away. His nostrils flared. Peaches. He squeezed his eyes shut, unwilling to let his dragon spirit peer at her. She wasn't theirs to mark.

She stilled against him.

His eyes opened, and the dragon came forward.

He rubbed his nose against hers. His dragon spirit purred in his chest as it greeted her, their *Wíyoyá*.

No... not his mate. Not Naomi.

Her eyes drifted shut. Her face tilted up.

Blinking, Aluk pushed his spirit dragon back. He yanked on her robe ties. Her eyes snapped open. Her hands flew up to grab his, but

Aluk turned and pulled her behind him. He gritted his teeth, fighting the furious beast raging inside him.

In front of her door, he turned, catching her gaze. The brilliance in her eyes dimmed to jade. Before she could protest, he flung open the door to her room.

"Do not go up there again."

"I am not one of your prisoners," she said.

"I cannot guarantee your safety if you insist on disobeying my orders."

"Because you're a dragon," she challenged, her blue lips pressed thin. With her head held high, she looked him in the eye.

"Because I am a man."

He waited until she had closed the door between them. His dragon snarled. Walking away took every ounce of his strength when he wanted to pull her close.

"Let this be a lesson," he murmured, more to himself than his dragon.

Inside the sanctuary of his chambers, Aluk fell back on his bed. A slow burn ignited again in his chest. He tried to warn his brothers that this woman sent from the state would bring them nothing more than trouble. Taran and Conleth insisted on working with the state to ensure their people's safety. As alpha, his people's protection always came first.

The spirit of his dragon carried the pain of that responsibility. After hundreds of years, it festered. Feral madness crept through his dragon's thoughts.

This woman, this doctor of healing broken minds, complicated everything. What she learned from the state was nothing compared to the war his people faced. They needed fewer humans on the mountain, and their boundaries closed off again.

Conleth's mate, Trinity, was working on it. Until recently, the Fae had their people running the PPI–Paranormal Phenomena Investigations–along with the spirit hunters.

His dragon spirit pushing against his instinct to rid them of this woman. It would rather keep her close. Claim her.

She was nothing of his Naomi.

Nor did she possess any magic to compel his spirit.

Her luminous, untainted gaze concealed her soul. For a moment, he saw it lingering deep down inside her. He scented fear along with something else. Beyond the fear and the succulent scent of peaches, something reeked of rot.

He hoped for her sake she wasn't something more. Little kept him from falling into the darkness. He needed what remained of his strength to protect his people when the Fae came.

Unable to rest, he stood guard outside her door, ensuring Dr. Everett didn't go sleepwalking.

Four

Palisade got a late start in the morning. Staying one step ahead of Alpha Vasumen was her only option. She had learned nothing important at dinner, and last night's adventure up atop the tower confirmed what she'd been told.

All three Vasumen brothers had dragon-shifter blood. She needed to be careful around the alpha, wary of him if she wanted to fulfill her end of the deal.

Palisade caught herself staring at the tower window again. She'd barely slept, replaying the moment he'd pulled her back from the edge, the way his breath had caught when he—.

She reached for her hairbrush. *Focus.*

He presented the greatest threat to her, along with her objective. Alpha. Dragon. Or Man. She needed to survive first and think about the future later.

And not one with *him.*

Even if he invaded her dreams at night.

Failure is not an option. If she didn't accomplish her task, no antidote. No antidote, no life.

She had to produce results soon. Her benefactor had lost patience after one unsuccessful mission some months before.

Dressed in her crisp black slacks and sapphire blouse, she twisted up her hair in a gold clip. Satisfied with her polished, professional appearance; she made her way toward the stairs to the dungeon. A guard with dark skin and hazel eyes stood at attention near the entrance, his posture military-straight. He glanced at her, curious but not hostile, though he didn't say a word as she walked down the hall.

The twist in her stomach tightened upon spotting Alpha Vasumen. He blocked the way forward.

She straightened her spine, lifting her chin. She wouldn't let him intimidate her. Not today. "Good morning."

He moved, obstructing passage. "Dr. Everett."

"Are you always this formal?"

"You'd wish for us to become better acquainted?" His dark eyebrow rose.

Alpha Vasumen's beard was untamed this morning. His dark, near-black eyes evaluated her, urging her to look away.

After last night, she'd half-expected him to avoid her entirely. Instead, here he stood, blocking her path. Watching her like she was a puzzle he couldn't quite solve.

Lowering her eyes, she observed the black-laced military stock boots, the black cargo pants, and the pistol strapped to his hip. A working man's clothes. Practical. Ready for anything.

She'd seen his dragon last night. She should have been terrified, should have run. Instead, she'd felt... safe? No, that was ridiculous. Wasn't it?

She should have been more surprised to see the beast, but seeing it reaffirmed the information her benefactor provided. According to her benefactor, no one else had the ability to succeed. They'd chosen her, the weakest one on the team. Where she lacked physical strength, she made up for it with intelligence.

Yet, nothing prepared her for the brutal alpha who one moment shut her out and the next sparked a fire inside her.

She glanced toward the dungeon entrance. Trace had been easy. A few smiles, some shared drinks, and he'd talked freely about guard shifts and supply runs. Surface intel.

Vasumen, though. The alpha didn't trust easily. Yet, atop the tower that evening, something changed. The way he'd steadied her, his breath catching when—

No. Focus on the mission. Get him to talk. Free Scout. Obtain the antidote. Simple.

The air changed before she saw him.

Brimstone threaded with bergamot and a sharp twist of citrus cut through the cold like a spark striking flint. It filled her lungs, hot and biting, until her knees softened beneath the weight of it. Alpha Vasumen. The fortress walls, the noise, the ache in her chest—everything dulled. She exhaled slowly, shoulders lowering as if her body remembered something her mind refused to name. It shouldn't have felt like peace. But it did.

Her eyes traveled up his chest, over those muscular arms, to his dark, straggly hair, then dropped back to his lips. She caught herself before imagining what lay beneath that beard. "Uncivilized," she muttered.

His lips twitched, and he must have heard. "You're headed to speak with the boy?"

She blinked. Was that...amusement? The hint of a smile softened the hard line of his jaw, making him look younger. Less like the intimidating alpha and more like—.

She caught herself. More like what? A man she could talk to?

Dangerous.

"Scout Jameson is an adult by human standards."

"Of course."

A flutter caught beneath her ribs, and she pressed a hand to her chest. How could she when she had answers to seek? Deep down, the dark part inside her, which refused to reveal itself, had whispered Scout Jameson would lead her to those answers when she first agreed to come. Heat spread across her skin, causing her flesh to tingle.

The natives of this mountain, the guardians of the animal spirits, the ones the state referred to as 'shifter bloods,' believed in love at first sight. They professed to locate their mates this way. But Palisade reminded herself that love didn't happen at first sight.

Her stomach dropped, something fierce coiling tight in her core.

She saw his dragon.

Palisade tore her gaze away, nails biting into her palms.

The mission. Scout Jameson. Answers.

Not him.

Not why she came.

She had one antidote left and time running against her.

"I'll go with you."

"That really won't be necessary..."

By the tilt of his hips and the straightening of his back, she doubted he would let her pass any other way.

"I see. Well, then. Lead the way."

Like before, she followed Alpha Vasumen down the curved stairs into the dark dampness. Several flights later, they came to the bowels of the fortress. The clip-clop of her shoes sounded on the stones beneath her feet. Alpha Vasumen paused and glanced back over his shoulder at her, a brow arched, but he moved on. She shifted her weight, trying to muffle each step. Of all the shoes in her closet, she would have chosen the French heels she favored.

She could hear those still snoring. Somewhere behind them, a low whistle and up ahead, the sobs coming from a cell scratched at her chest. The sobs came from the last block of isolated cells. Scout Jameson.

"Front and center," Alpha Vasumen barked.

She bit back a retort. Eyes gleamed at her from their shadow-blanketed cells. The boy's head rose. Palisade ignored Alpha Vasumen's hand to keep her back and moved closer to the bars. "Scout?"

Slowly, the boy turned his head at the sound of her voice. A tremor ran through his shoulders. His eyes widened.

Vasumen's hand pressed against her hip. Tingles scattered across her side where his palm rested. "Don't."

His voice made her freeze with a warning she couldn't decode. His body went rigid behind her. Heat poured off him in waves.

Wide, bright eyes blinked as the boy stood. His shining black eyes glinted. Scout's mouth curved into a lazy grin. He sauntered up to the bars, and she stepped back against the solid wall of Alpha Vasumen's chest.

Palisade tilted up her chin. "How are you today, Scout?"

"Gorak," he corrected her. "*Winyan wanagi*, I am caged, but you will set me free."

"Your parents miss you, Scout." Heat radiated from her back while another prisoner leaned near their bars. *Liberate Scout. Getting him out.* She noted they had come down the same way as on her previous visit.

"And you, *winyan wanagi*, do you miss me?"

"How can I miss someone I have just met?" She reached for her bag. Nothing. Her hand closed on empty air. She pressed her eyes shut and dragged in a breath. She looked at Scout.

"Your mind may not tell you who I am, but your heart has drawn you to me. Soon, you will remember." His voice dropped lower, possessive. "And when you do, *winyan wanagi*, you will be mine. As you were always meant to be."

Scout's black eyes slid past her to lock onto Alpha Vasumen.

Conflicting emotions washed across Scout's face. A whisper came from the cell nearest them. Scout's face contorted. Pain laced through her temple. She winced. Her hand shot to her head.

Her breath caught. Cold flooded her veins.

The antidote should have held for another month. She still had a week. The pain drilled deeper.

Unless it had been altered. Unless her condition had progressed faster than predicted.

We expect progress, my dear. Your condition is manageable only as long as you remain useful.

The Fae dealt in contracts and consequences. She'd signed hers in desperation, and now she was bound to deliver results or die trying.

She couldn't fall apart in front of them. Not now. Now, she with nothing to show for her time here. *72 hours. You can do this.*

"I think our visit is over." Alpha Vasumen turned her by the shoulders to steer her away.

Palisade shook her head. Pain shot through her left eye. She bit her lip. A groan died in her throat. She needed to return to her room, where she'd left the antidote. The antidote. She had to get the antidote. Alpha Vasumen's gaze narrowed. She pushed a breath through her teeth and straightened. Her legs shook, but she locked her knees. He didn't take his gaze off her.

"It does not matter where you take her, Firebird. I will always find her." Scout's black eyes slid past them toward the shadows of another cell and snapped back.

"She's mine. She was always mine." Scout called out as Alpha Vasumen nudged her down the hall to the stairs leading them back up out of the dungeon.

Palisade squinted and focused on the path ahead.

A noise scraped from another cell. She glanced over. A man stood in the shadows, rising from his cot. Even in the dim light, he looked gaunt. Skin stretched over bone, eyes sunken, but those eyes burned too bright for his skeletal frame. No—not his eyes. Like Scout, another presence looked through them.

Their eyes locked. Recognition slammed into her. A knowing. A warning she couldn't name.

Pain erupted in her temples and tore through her skull. She swayed. Drums pounded inside her skull, matching her racing pulse. She groaned, pressing her palm harder against her temple.

Two dark eyes, blacker than the shadows of the dungeon, met hers. The drumming intensified, or pulled her closer? She couldn't—.

Her chest tightened. A burn ignited within her middle, cold spreading through her veins like ice water. Not like Vasumen's heat. This was different. Deeper. Like roots pushing through frozen ground, seeking...

The man's lips didn't move, but a whisper echoed through her bones. *Yes.*

Palisade didn't breathe.

Her vision darkened at the edges. Arms locked around her from behind, lifting her off her feet. He swung her up in a bridal hold and moved with surprising care, despite his urgency.

"I can walk," she mumbled, even as her head spun.

"No, you can't."

She wanted to argue, but darkness threatened the edges of her vision. She hated him for being right.

Pain throbbed in her temple. She buried her head in his neck, cheek against his shoulder. Warmth seeped through his clothing and soaked into her chilled body. His scent hit her. Pine and Smoke. Wild mountain air.

Color flashed behind her eyelids. White light seared. She squeezed her eyes shut. The burn spread across her eyelids. She dragged in breath after breath. Nausea churned. Cushions gave beneath her. A couch. She jerked, looking up. Light stabbed into her eyes. She threw up a hand. She leaned back. His hands slid down her legs and gripped her knees. "Stay here. Don't move."

"I need my bag from my room. Please." She leaned forward, elbows on knees. She dug her fingers into her hair at the base of her neck and breathed. In. Out. Bile rose in her throat.

Twenty-four hours here, and she had nothing. The Fae wanted a map of the interior, the weaknesses behind the fortress walls, and Scout Jameson freed.

How could she betray people who showed more concern for her than her benefactor ever had? No, she couldn't think like that. Sentiment wouldn't save her life.

"Does this occur often?" His eyes flashed red.

"I need my bag. Please. I have... I have medicine I need to take." Palisade hadn't had a splitting migraine like this one in months.

She groaned, kneading her fingers into the base of her head, trying to keep her muscles from knotting. *Relax.* It helped if she relaxed.

Footsteps echoed. Each one was a hammer against her skull. She tilted her head and squinted. A man kneeled beside her. Long dark hair fell over his shoulder, almost brushing her arm as he leaned in. He shared the same native features as the Alpha, but was leaner. Where Alpha Vasumen was raw power, this man was controlled precision.

Antiseptic cut through the mountain air and pine scent.

His voice was lighter, quieter than the alpha's. "Where does it hurt?"

"Migraine," she mumbled. "I just need to take my medication and rest."

His hand covered hers at the base of her neck. Gentle, but clinical.

"Is the pain here?" He took his other hand and touched her right temple. "Or here?"

Despite the throbbing in her skull, her mouth twitched.

A low growl rumbled nearby.

"It started at her temple," Alpha Vasumen's voice rang out from the other side of her, close, closer than she expected. She trembled as the nausea set in.

"It'll go away as soon as I take my medicine. My bag, please."

She heard the quick snap. Cool pressure settled on her neck. She sighed at the instant relief. "Please, I'd like to go back to my room."

"Do you get migraines like this often?" The other man's voice deepened, light concern giving way to professionalism.

She could have lied, but that would gain her nothing. Not when she'd need help to her room to get the antidote. The headache might go away without taking the antidote. The pain, however, would work its way through her body and make her too ill to complete her task in return for the next vial of antidote.

She hated the weakness inside her for putting her in this position. "Yes."

"I should document this. Any medical episodes involving insiders—"

She sensed his hesitation. The same calculation she'd seen in others.

"The state requires reports of all interactions with non-residents. Just to be on the safe side."

"She's our guest, not a case file for bureaucrats who don't understand what happens on this mountain."

"No."

A hand touched her knee — Vasumen's hand.

His touch sent warmth racing up her leg. She shifted, struggling to pry her eyes open. What had brought it on so suddenly? So much for a warning this time.

"They're already watching us closely since the hiker incidents. If something happens to her–"

She dismissed the hiker's remark. Right now, her head wanted to explode.

The doctor back in New York promised the headaches would only become worse as her illness progressed without the proper treatments. No human doctors had an explanation for it, but her benefactor did.

"Nothing will happen to her." Alpha Vasumen's hand still rested on her knee. "Not on my watch."

She needed that antidote until she discovered its true cause and cure.

Fat tears rolled down her cheeks as a man's face came into focus. The leaner one watched her with an intensity that reminded her that these men were predators beneath their human skin. Recognition flashed through her mind and vanished before she could grasp it.

"What were you doing when the migraine hit?"

Palisade sensed him piecing it together.

"She was down in the dungeon with Gorak," Alpha Vasumen didn't mention she'd stopped near another cell. She hadn't swayed until she looked at the other prisoner.

"You let her go down there?" Not a challenge, as she understood the hierarchy system enough, but his concern touched her.

"Not alone. I was with her," Alpha Vasumen growled.

The other man's eyebrows arched, and despite her pain, Palisade caught them exchanging a look. Something between exasperation and knowing amusement. "That proved effective."

Palisade squinted as the pain eased to a dull throb. She reached up to hold the icepack in place, her fingers brushing the alpha's. His hand slipped away as she took its place.

"You'll bring him up to me then?" He directed the question at Alpha Vasumen, but it sounded more like an order than a request.

The alpha rumbled. Slowly, she glanced between the two men, careful to keep the pain behind her eyes at bay.

Brothers. Her intuition clicked into place. Both voices carried the same baritone.

What had Scout Jameson said to her? *Your mind may not tell you who I am, but your heart has drawn you to me. Soon, you will remember.*

Had he done this to her? Did the natives, with their powers to control animal spirits, have other supernatural skills her benefactor hadn't mentioned?

"Get her a glass of water, will you?"

She glanced then at the alpha's brother. Really seeing him for the first time as her vision cleared. His dark eyes studied her. "Do I know you?"

His eyes shifted from pupil to narrow slits before returning to normal. The transformation was so quick she might have imagined it if not for the dragon she'd already seen on the tower. It didn't surprise her, but confirmed her suspicions. "Have you been to Avalanche Ridge?"

"No."

Alpha Vasumen held out a glass of water in front of her face.

"Here, drink as much of the water as you can." The alpha's brother held out two small, round white pills.

"What's this?" Common medication didn't help for long. She needed what was in her room.

"Conleth is the medic at Avalanche Ridge and the clinic in Sentinel Peak."

She heard the pride in Alpha Vasumen's rough voice.

"You are brothers." She accepted the pills and the glass of water, hoping to appease so he could escape back to her room.

"You met our other brother, Taran. He's the one who dropped you off here." Conleth's hair swept forward as he tilted his head.

"Yes. He represents your people, the ranger."

"They'll ease the pain and make you drowsy for a few hours." Conleth kept his professional mask firmly in place. "But if you're having episodes like this regularly, we need to talk about the underlying cause."

She didn't know how she would manage the stairs, let alone become drugged. If she collapsed on the stairs, would he carry her up them, too? Remembering his body pressed against her, his arms holding her tight, shouldn't have comforted her. But it did.

"I'll see Dr. Everett to her room. Then I'll meet you back inside the library," Aluk's voice left no room for argument.

Conleth stared at his brother for a long moment. Their eyes glazed. A strange, distant look passed between them. Alpha Vasumen lifted his chin. Conleth's mouth curved as if he'd won some unspoken point before he strode out.

She swallowed the pills, finished her water, and dabbed at her tears. The embarrassment of breaking down in front of them burned hotter than the migraine. "I'm sorry," she whispered. "I didn't mean to–"

"Don't." Alpha Vasumen held up a hand. "You're in pain. Nothing to apologize for."

She looked up, surprised by the lack of judgement in his dark eyes. She'd expected impatience, maybe annoyance. Instead, he just looked...concerned.

When was the last time someone looked at her like that? Like she mattered beyond what they believed she'd come here to do.

Alpha Vasumen reached out as she tried to stand. "Can you walk? Or I can carry you again."

Temptation and pride warred inside her. Palisade took a deep breath; the air stung her lungs. Holding the ice pack that slipped from her neck, Palisade took Alpha Vasumen's arm, her fingers trembling slightly. She fought to let go, but a little voice whispered to hold tight.

He scooped her off her feet and carried her toward the north tower. "Relax, Peaches, I've got you."

Peaches?

Through the fog of pain, the nickname snagged her attention. So at odds with the gruff, intimidating alpha who barked orders and prowled his fortress like a dragon guarding his hoard.

She wanted to ask why, but the darkness pulled at her, and his steady footsteps were oddly soothing. Warmth radiated from him. Her eyes drifted closed.

He was a predator, a dragon, an alpha.

So why did he feel safe?

Peaches, he'd called her. She didn't understand it. Didn't understand him. Didn't know why her body relaxed against his when every logical part of her brain screamed this was dangerous.

The Fae wouldn't approve. Her mission depended on staying detached.

But as the darkness finally claimed her, she stopped fighting the urge to lean into this strength.

Just this once.

"Stay with me," he murmured, and for a moment, she could have sworn his voice gentled.

Must be the pain playing tricks on her.

Five

"You called Taran?"

Inside the private library of the fortress, Aluk found Conleth and his mate, Trinity, flipping through the old texts Trinity retrieved from her grandfather's estate. Trinity kept her eyes on the text. "He'll be here soon."

Aluk reached out through their blood bond and confirmed. His brother flew in dragon form, the invisible thread of their connection glowing brighter in his mind. Within the farthest recesses, another faint light lingered. Thinking he'd severed that connection long ago, Aluk ignored it, but its presence nagged at him.

"There's no mention of the Mist Forest, the Great Hunter, or even the curse in this one either." Trinity huffed. She piled the book on top of a stack of others. "Are there more books somewhere else? Something that goes further back in your family's history?"

"I didn't realize you would bring her with you." Aluk's fingers tightened on the doorframe. Conleth's hand rested on Trinity's lower back, a gesture so simple, so unconscious. Inside, his dragon clawed at his ribs.

Conleth scoffed. "As if I'd let her out of my sight. We may have stopped *Prezi*, the mountain lion *ohunko,* from taking her, but the Fae don't give up easily. Until the curse is broken, she's not safe."

"No one is safe." Aluk's chest rumbled. "I haven't forgotten what dangers lie around us. We don't need to add any more humans to the death toll and give them reason to rise against us."

The library door opened. Taran filled the doorway. The scent of wind and high altitude announced his arrival. "That's why I brought her."

He closed the door with a deliberate snick.

Aluk reached through their bond. His brother's dragon remained agitated after the flight.

"There are Fae bloods amongst the humans, and they've gained positions within the state government. You know they're going to come after us, so why not keep them close?"

Sound logic. Yet his pulse hammered against his throat at the thought of Palisade being anywhere near danger.

Trinity closed another volume with a frustrated sigh and passed it to Conleth. He set it on the growing stack of useless texts, then fixed his gaze on Aluk. "How do we know this woman isn't one of them?"

"I would have sensed if she were," Trinity said, looking at Conleth. A moment of silent communication passed between the two mates. Conleth lowered his chin. Her lips turned down.

Aluk paced back and forth. His brothers' gazes followed him across the room. He'd seen those looks before. Their careful assessment and hopeful glances at the arrival of a new female.

The old wound in his chest throbbed, a phantom pain that never fully healed. His hands trembled, and he fisted them.

His dragon chose Palisade, just as he had chosen Naomi.

Fate was cruel.

Neither he nor his dragon could survive another blow to their heart.

Taran picked a book off the table pile, flipping its pages. "Where is Dr. Everett?" he asked, his voice more casual than usual.

"If you're that worried, why aren't you keeping an eye on her?" Aluk replied, his tone sharp.

Taran's eyebrows wiggled.

Aluk's fists tightened. Heat crawled up his spine. The tower. Was she still in the tower? Alone? His feet shifted toward the door before he caught himself.

"She's not well." Conleth pulled Trinity onto his lap.

Taran's smug expression faded. "You should take her with you to the clinic," he suggested. "She can recover there."

Aluk's nails bit into his palms. He uncurled them slowly, one finger at a time. The clinic. Where others would tend her. Touch her. The thought sent his dragon into a snarl that rattled his teeth.

She wasn't theirs to protect.

"You're right. She needs to go to the clinic. Take her."

"No!" Trinity's hand flew over her mouth. Her eyes widened with gold rushing in to flood out her natural violet hue.

Conleth wrapped an arm around Trinity. "I don't think that's a good idea. We don't know why she's here. The Fae have people working in the government. They sent Trinity. They could send others."

"They sent me to die," she reminded him quietly.

The thought of his late wife sent guilt stabbing through him. He'd loved Naomi. Cared for her deeply. Chosen her when his people needed an alpha's heir, and his dragon remained stubborn.

His dragon had been obsessed with Issabrie for centuries. *Centuries.* His father warned him about the madness lurking in his bloodline. *You must let the dragon choose.*

With Naomi, he'd been the one doing the choosing. The one in control. He'd courted her properly, asked her father's permission, married her in the traditional ceremony with all their people watching.

And his dragon had tolerated it. Allowed it. But never accepted her.

The bond between them had been a choice of mind and duty, not soul and fate.

Now, his dragon spirit was doing it again. Fixating. Obsessing. Claiming another woman was *Mate* with the same fervent certainty it claimed Issabrie.

How was Palisade different from the woman trapped in the mountain? Both had walked into his life uninvited. Both carried secrets and danger. Both made his dragon feral with want.

His dragon spirit snarled. *Different. She is ours.*

You said that about Issabrie, Aluk repented in his mind. *You've been saying it for two hundred years.*

This one. Mate.

Convenient.

"No one's dying," Conleth declared, pressing his face into Trinity's neck and inhaling.

She looked at Aluk. "Alpha?"

Her golden Fae eyes shimmered like a time glass waiting to cut into the depths of the secrets he carried. He looked away, pacing around the table. The stack of books and scattered papers offered false comfort. Beyond these doors, dangerous criminals filled the fortress. Some were shifters. Others were the hunters who'd murdered their people and stolen their spirits.

"No one's going to die," Aluk repeated, done arguing with his dragon spirit.

The image of strawberry-colored hair spread across white pillows flashed through his mind. His feet turned toward the door again. He planted them firmly.

He warned Trace to keep away from his section of the fortress. The scent of wolf blood near her sweet peach aroma sent his fingers curling into fists again. "As the alpha, it's my duty to protect everyone on this mountain."

Including Dr. Everett.

"Keep her here." Conleth pressed his face against Trinity's neck. "Until we know what's wrong with her."

Trinity relaxed in Conleth's hold.

"And the curse?" Aluk's eyes narrowed.

"We need more information. Ben and I have been searching for the key to breaking the curse." Conleth and Trinity exchanged a glance.

"We're close." Trinity looked at Aluk.

Inside him, the dragon stilled, suddenly alert.

What last thread must they sever to break the curse?

Not what... Who.

Aluk smoothed his features into neutrality, but his pulse thundered in his ears.

It started with Taran's mate Gwen, and Aluk's dragon refused to acknowledge the change in the mountain. The harsh year-round winters ceased, and the rains brought floods and people back to Sentinel Peak. The Fae knew this, too. They sent Trinity, intending to sacrifice her, and seal the curse again. They failed. The Fae wouldn't give up. Neither would Aluk. His dragon pulled back into the darkness of his mind, alert and conflicted.

"We need to know the source of the curse." Trinity slipped off Conleth and walked toward him. "Your dragon knows."

Aluk's eyes narrowed. Trinity took another step. He held up his hand. "Stay out of my head, Trinity." His dragon growled in his mind, desperate to guard its secrets about the curse.

"I warned you." Dread coiled inside his soul, and his dragon's power forced his silence.

"While my spirit is the eldest, Ben's spirit retains the guardian's knowledge. We don't know fully why the guardians turned against their people." Although Aluk's dragon did. The arrogant beast inside him refused to unlock all his memories. *This information is irrelevant now,* his dragon said. *The guardians can do no more harm.*

Aluk picked up a book. Its leather binding worn with age. He traced the thick rawhide stitches, but his thoughts climbed the tower stairs. Strawberry hair. Green eyes filled with confusion and pain. He blinked, dragging his focus back to the ancient leather.

His dragon roared. The sound reverberated through his bones. The beast wanted to protect the people. Wanted to protect *her.* Both. Aluk's chest tightened at the impossibility. Heat flooded through him. Protective. Possessive. Wrong.

He shoved it down, but it rose again like a tide.

Just another face to join Naomi's in the darkness.

His jaw clenched until his teeth ached. The dragon's instincts. His own resistance. Two forces tore him in opposite directions.

His grip tightened on the volume until the binding creaked. Centuries of his people's history lined these shelves—births, deaths, wars, treaties. None of them held the secrets his dragon guarded. He set the book down with deliberate care and turned to his brothers.

For centuries, his dragon spirit had let its human choose a companion without marking her.

Without the mark, he survived the loss of Naomi.

His gaze lifted to the ceiling. The tower room lay directly above. One floor. A few dozen steps. His muscles coiled to move. What if Dr. Everett wasn't who she claimed? What if she was...more?

She belongs to us now.

No more innocent lives, he said to his dragon.

What would prevent the Fae from returning? From seeking other means to restore the curse?

"The Fae Queen wanted to control our people."

His dragon rose inside him. *Don't.*

The leather binding of the book creaked under his grip. "Our ancestors fled here to escape the Fae realm." His throat burned. "Then the alpha trapped her."

Trinity leaned forward. "And?"

"She intended to use the mate bond to rule over us." The words tasted like ash. "So he imprisoned her in the mountain."

The beast within him snarled. Memories of flames and shadows flickered in his mind, but the dragon's grip tightened, silencing his tongue. Centuries of secrets pressed down.

Issabrie...

Whenever he tried to reach those memories, all he saw was Issabrie's silhouette. Then pain. Searing. Soul-deep. Shutting him out.

Silence settled over the library. Therefore, he couldn't trust the dragon spirit to guide him.

Conleth stood, pulling Trinity back against him. He rested his head on her shoulder. Her hair spilled across her face. She puffed to clear the strands from her eyes.

She blew to keep the strands out of her face.

Taran stared at the book behind Aluk's desk.

Aluk's gaze drifted to the ceiling, tracking upward through stone and timber to where Dr. Everett rested in his tower.

That's all they need to know. All his dragon allowed him to say. It seethed inside him, and he let it.

His dragon clamped down, forcing his silence.

Dr. Everett came from a world of laboratories and textbooks. What could she understand of warrior spirits and ancient gifts? Of sacrifices made in blood and fire?

If his brothers were right about her... His hands flexed. Far more dangerous prisoners had occupied these cells.

His dragon demanded he check on her, but other threats came first.

Trinity's voice cut through his distraction. "What if they didn't use the old burial grounds? What if they went somewhere to reach the spirit realm?"

"What do you mean?" Aluk leaned against the corner of the table. Books and notes spread across the surface from weeks of searching for burial grounds where old bloodlines remained and shadow spirits dwelled. They knew of only two: the portal site and the life tree outside the village. Both places held sacred meaning to their people.

Trinity's hand moved to her throat. The *bileto ohunko* had nearly killed her several weeks ago. She came to find the missing agent, who led hunters to them. Then she too became the hunted. One of the Great Hunter's guardians tried to eliminate her to save them from the curse.

Now she saw a connection between the Fae and their Great Hunter.

Aluk couldn't refute it. His dragon spirit slunk back into the dark of his mind like a cobra ready to strike.

How much of what she speaks is truth?

A headache formed behind his eyes. His skin stretched too tight; his dragon spirit wanted to burst free. The spirit inside him growled, heat boiling under his skin.

Tell me, dragon.

The dragon spirit snarled.

So, Trinity wasn't far off in her assumption.

The Fae queen hadn't come seeking to control them; she wanted to reclaim what they had lost. *Why not hunt the shadow spirits?*

"We've searched all the burial sites known and marked for the past two centuries and have found nothing." She tapped her finger on her lips for a moment. "It has to be an unmarked location."

Aluk spirit dragon coiled tight.

"Warriors denied proper burial—" Conleth scratched his chin. "—spirits with nowhere to go."

"No bloodlines to return." Taran broke the silence.

"Trinity believes the life tree, and the trapped spirits, link to the Mist Forest in the Fae realm." Conleth sat beside his mate, giving Aluk a long, hard look, his forehead creasing with concern.

Aluk met his brother's diagnostic stare. "I'm fine."

Conleth's frown deepened. He opened his mouth, then closed it.

The beast refused to merge with his soul. Losing Naomi widened the space between spirit and soul. His dragon chose Dr. Everett, separating them further. His father warned him about sharing the burden with his brothers. Other dragons in the past had tried to challenge the alpha.

Taran's temperamental dragon spirit might try, hothead that he was. Admitting his grief might give them reason to challenge him for alpha. His dragon's claws sprouted at the thought.

Conleth nodded curtly.

Aluk scratched his beard, wrestling control back from the beast. He turned his attention to the external threat. "It's possible."

Conleth's mate sensed things others couldn't. One of the rare female shamans of their people, she sat back in her chair. Her gaze probed Aluk.

He shifted away. Under Trinity's knowing stare, his chest tightened. Naomi's face flashed behind his eyes. Her laugh. The way she'd touched his face. Gone.

His hand moved unconsciously to his chest, pressing against the hollow space where warmth used to live. The dragon stirred again, turning his thoughts to peaches and strawberry hair. He shoved the image away violently. Betrayal tasted like ash on his tongue.

A pang of guilt and grief swelled, pressing at his lungs.

"I can't go back to Aeron's estate. The new lord made that clear." She pushed back a strand of her silver-white hair.

"And the PPI?"

"They've locked me out."

"How long before they send someone else?"

"To investigate the deaths?" Trinity met his eyes. "Not long."

"Or send a woman to check on a human possessed by a spirit guardian," Taran muttered.

Ice flooded Aluk's veins. Dr. Everett. Beautiful. Intelligent. Perfectly positioned. His dragon roared in denial, but his mind raced through the possibilities. A spy. She could be a spy. Guilt followed, urging him to put his fist through the wall. He gripped the table's edge instead, knuckles white. "We need to be careful. The Fae are waiting for an opening. We have to stay ahead of them if we're going to break this curse and heal our people."

Trinity's expression fell. "I'm sorry, Aluk. I should have thought this through more."

"No." Aluk held up his hand. Trinity flinched, and he softened his voice. "Not your fault."

The fault lay in the fracture between him and his beast. A true alpha would have sensed the changes and protected his people before blood spilled. His jaw worked. Never again. He'd shield them all—Trinity, his brothers, the humans who came here. Even Dr. Everett. This time, the Fae would discover no weaknesses in his defenses.

His feet pivoted toward the door. The stairs. The tower. He could be there in seconds. Make sure she was—.

He forced himself still, boots planted on the stone floor.

Trinity's eyes softened. "How does your visitor fare?"

Aluk's shoulders went rigid. He searched Trinity's face for the distant look she got when she slipped into someone's mind. But her eyes remained present, merely concerned. His muscles relaxed slightly.

"She's resting in her room."

Conleth leaned down and whispered in Trinity's ear. Her lips curved into a smile. Then he straightened and said, "Her symptoms suggest more than migraines."

Aluk narrowed his eyes, his dragon rising, alert. "What do you mean?"

Conleth hesitated for a moment. "I need to run some tests to rule a few things out first."

Aluk's arms crossed over his chest. His hands shook. He pressed them harder against his sides until the trembling stopped. Naomi's pale face on that day. The way her hand had gone cold in his. *Not again.* His knuckles went white.

"What things?"

"It might be her heritage or an ailment," Conleth admitted, wrinkling his nose. "Her scent is off."

Fire erupted in Aluk's chest. His brother. Leaning close to Dr. Everett. Breathing in her scent. His vision tunneled, tinged red at the edges. A growl built in his throat before he could stop it. "You won't scent her again."

Conleth raised an eyebrow. The twitch of his lips irked Aluk's dragon spirit further. Conleth stayed silent in their bond for Trinity's sake. Trinity's mate bond with Conleth didn't extend their mental communications to the rest of them.

"Is it because she's human?" Taran asked.

Aluk caught the glance that passed between his brothers. His eyes narrowed. They were hiding something. The irony wasn't lost on him. He kept the deepest secrets of all, but it burned.

"What does a human smell like?" Trinity scrunched her nose.

"Not Fae," Conleth said.

"She smells like peaches" He shouldn't have admitted it to his brothers. Shouldn't have let them see how thoroughly she'd gotten under his skin. But Trinity had asked, and the truth had slipped out before he could cage it.

She smells of peaches.

Bond-scent. The unique fragrance that only a true mate carried. Shifters could go their entire lives without encountering it, some never finding the one person whose scent called to both man and beast.

Aluk had never scented it on Naomi. Not even once.

He'd convinced himself bond-scent was a myth. A romantic fantasy his people clung to. The reality of their dwindling numbers meant practical matches, chosen for compatibility and bloodlines, not mystical connections that might never come.

And yet.

Peaches. Sweet and sun-warmed and utterly, devastatingly her. The scent wound through his senses like silk, found every hollow place inside him and filled it with warmth.

His dragon had smelled it the moment she had walked into the prison. Had recognized it, even when Aluk's human mind was still cataloging threats and defensive strategies.

Mate. Mind. OURS.

Taran snorted, crossing his arms and placing a hand over his mouth. His younger brother knew better than to provoke the beast inside him.

He checked himself, the connection between brothers, to ensure none of his thoughts slipped through to them. He was the alpha, and he didn't need them to have any more excuses to consider him weak.

Trinity and Conleth exchanged looks, Trinity's lips twitching. Aluk growled, and Conleth held up a hand. "I'm just saying this is a good opportunity to find out where she comes from."

Aluk's teeth ground together. Fae blood would mean his brothers would start their matchmaking again. The hopeful comments. The pitying looks. Worse, if she carried Fae blood... His dragon spirit conjured an image of Dr. Everett locked in the mountain's depths, like the queen his ancestor imprisoned. The dragon was confused. He couldn't have two mates, let alone three, considering his deceased wife.

Aluk left them to their research. His feet carried him toward the tower before his mind could argue.

No, not because the bond pulled. He needed to prove something.

His dragon had fixated on Issabrie for centuries. Had nearly driven them to madness trying to reach her through the mountain's seal. Had refused every potential mate his human side suggested, waiting for *her*.

And now? Now it claimed *this* woman was their true mate?

His dragon was lying. Or deluded. Either way, Aluk would prove it.

He'd go up there, look at Dr. Evertt sleeping, and feel... nothing. Concern for a guest, maybe. Protectiveness of someone under his care. But not this bone-deep certainty his dragon kept insisting on.

He'd prove the bond-scent was imagination. Prove the pull was just his dragon's latest obsession, and he was still in control.

The dragon spirit within him huffed.

His feet carried him toward the tower. The stairs took longer than usual to climb, or maybe he wanted to take his time getting there. At her door, he paused. Pressed his palm against the wood. Inside, her heartbeat echoed through his heightened senses.

His dragon pressed against his eyes. Eager bastard.

He should leave and not give the dragon spirit the satisfaction of seeing her. His brothers needed his help to plan their next move against the Fae. First though, he had a point to make.

And every plan he'd had shattered the moment the door opened.

Six

The mighty alpha himself stood at Palisade's door when she opened it. His amber eyes softened at the sight of her, easing her tight muscles. "Feeling better, Dr. Everett?"

The alpha's brother checked on her twice during the day. He drew blood once, brought tea another time. He'd shown her how to pinch between her thumb and finger, which eased her throbbing head for her to rest. Surprisingly, the trick Conleth showed her worked, but for how long, she didn't know.

She kept quiet about consuming her last antidote. By the time he discovered her rare illness, she'd be long gone.

Her stomach rumbled from staying in her room all day. Thanks to the antidote, the pain in her temples eased. But pressure lingered behind her eyes, stronger and more persistent than before.

"Much. Thank you for checking on me."

"Are you hungry? I can bring you something, or you may join me and my brothers for dinner."

She tried to imagine him delivering her meal to her door. Her spine stiffened at the way he looked at her, shoulders back, chin jutting with arrogance. She could already picture him deciding for her, controlling her every move. Another red flag that she couldn't ignore. The thought chilled her—being under another man's thumb, losing her independence. She'd have to play this safe if she wanted to free Scout.

She planned to see him again in the morning. No doubt the alpha would insist on going with her. She needed to talk with the *ohunko* without the alpha watching her every move.

"Do you mind waiting a moment while I change?" She looked down at her yoga pants. The alpha's gaze swept over her curves. As his gaze traveled over her, warmth crept up her neck. His attraction became her advantage. A tool. Nothing more.

"You look fine the way you are," Alpha Vasumen said, clearing his throat. Palisade's heart fluttered at the compliment. *Stop it.* Palisade laughed to deflect the compliment. Pain flared in her temples. She pressed a finger to the area, easing the pressure. Why now? Why did this have to happen in front of him, of all people?

"Are you okay? Do you need me to call Conleth again?" His voice carried genuine concern, which only made her irritation worse.

She forced a smile and shook her head slowly, masking the throbbing pain with an air of calm she didn't feel.

"Dinner in your room, then?"

The idea had merit. Palisade took a deep breath. He already thought her weak. Her cheeks flushed, thinking of how he had carried her to her room. The warmth of his arms lingered in her memory, bringing longing and frustration in equal measure.

She hated anyone thinking of her as fragile, a burden. Her past had taught her to take care of herself, to never show weakness. She'd survived this far, hadn't she? The thought gnawed at her. What if she grew too sick to free Scout? Too weak to fulfill her bargain and get the cure? Her health declined. Her emotions warred between fear and anger. The cycle fed itself.

His concern moments ago reminded her why she didn't get close to others. She wouldn't allow anyone to pity her. Not him. Not anyone.

She caught him staring, waiting for her answer. "A change of scenery might be nice."

Alpha Vasumen's eyes sparked with a burst of red like a dark flame, and his nostrils flared. "You don't need to change to join us."

His voice dropped lower, huskier. Her breath caught. She tilted her head and caught his gaze. A little zing of excitement raced along her skin as she recognized the hunger in his gaze. "I think I do."

"Don't feel you have to wait. I can find the dining area on my own." She stepped back and grabbed the door to close it.

"I'll wait."

She closed the door and leaned back against it, her head throbbing in sync with her racing heart. How long should she make him wait? Her stomach cramped in complaint, and she decided not to keep him long. They wouldn't be alone, but she should still dress for dinner. Her head pounded more fiercely, and she cursed her body's reaction.

Her body quivered. Heat flashed through her. She grabbed a notebook off her bed and fanned herself. Her stomach went from cramping to queasy. With a hand on her stomach, she waited for it to pass. Taking deep breaths, she tried not to panic. Not now. *Not again.* The antidote needed more time to work.

Leaning her head against the door, she bit her lip to keep from screaming in frustration. On the other side of the door, Alpha Vasumen waited.

She survived the thin mountain air, survived standing on that tower. Her body, however, had other plans. "I can do this," she whispered. Her body begged to differ. She moaned as another wave of heat washed over her.

"Dr. Everett? Palisade?" Alpha Vasumen called through the door.

Sweat broke out on her forehead. *He'll see you as weak.* She chewed her lip. Her stomach cramped again, but pride fueled her resolve.

She couldn't afford to let him think she was anything but strong, or could she? The man, after all, wasn't her ally, but another part of her whispered he wasn't completely her enemy either.

Opening the door again, she tried not to grimace. "I'm sorry. I don't think I'll be leaving my room this evening."

"I'll get Conleth," Alpha Vasumen said but didn't move. His eyes dulled and darkened. For a moment, his focus shifted inward. Palisade's vision blurred around the edges, and a wave of dizziness crashed over her. Panic tightened in her chest. This was new. Her knees went weak. The thought of fainting terrified her. Yet, the more time she spent with the medic, the more likely he might diagnose her illness.

One diagnosis and the alpha would banish her. Her chance of freedom from this illness would disappear.

"No." Her hand shot out and grabbed his thick arm. "Please." She couldn't see the medic again tonight. Trying to buy time, she said, "I just need to rest."

His hand covered hers. Warm. Gentle. She closed her eyes, fighting the heat pulsing from deep within. It raced through her veins. Her stomach clenched harder.

Two strong hands wrapped around her arms. "Let me help you get to bed."

She stiffened, her headache pulsing again.

"I don't want you to fall," Alpha Vasumen said, carrying her inside her room. Pressure built in her head. It had never been this intense before. She released him to grip both sides of her head. As soon as she reached the bed, she curled up.

"Don't move. I'll get you some water," he said, like she had a choice.

Silence echoed like a scream in her head. She curled up tighter. Light flickered. Darkness pressed like a hard weight against her closed eyelids. She never heard the door open, much less close.

Something cool touched her lips. A woman whispered near her ear. Then, a hand closed around hers, sharp and electric. Her body jerked, and the world slipped.

Color shattered across her vision, a wild spill of light that bled into a single blinding wash. Then everything drained away, leaving only fog and shifting shadows.

"Daughter..."

Palisade turned toward the voice. A shadow stepped out of the fog — the outline of a warrior. His headdress flared around him, feathers shifting like living things. One brushed her arm, cold tickling across her skin.

"Who are you supposed to be?"

Panic scraped up her throat. What if her benefactor had slipped her something else, not the antidote? Maybe she'd swallowed one of their vile spells. This had to be a magic-induced dream.

"I'm not your daughter." Her breath stuttered. "I knew my father. You are not him."

The man dipped his chin, his gaze heavy with something she couldn't name. "She's coming. Fight for what belongs to you."

He turned away. A staff appeared in his hand, and he struck it against the ground. The sound cracked through the fog.

A second figure emerged. Bone armor clung to his chest. Black and red paint slashed across his cheekbones. His eyes pinned her in place. Before she could move, he seized her arm and shoved her to her knees. A rock bit into her flesh, and she cried out. He fisted her hair and wrenched her head back.

She grabbed his wrist, fighting to ease the pull. His painted face hovered over hers. "Let go of me," she rasped.

Her scalp burned. Needles of pain crawled across her skull. Painted shapes and ancient symbols blurred together, swirling across her vision.

The stone. A cave. Heavy air pressing at her ribs with each breath.

She panted, her lungs tight. Her heartbeat slammed against her chest, threatening to burst. The gleam of a bone knife flickered before her, sharp enough to steal the air from her throat.

Nausea rolled through her.

On a ledge deep within the cavern, the knife waited, glowing faintly. Moist heat gathered around her, thick as breath. "Please," she breathed. "Let me go. I'm going to die, anyway."

A tear slid off her cheek and vanished into the dark.

The warrior's breath warmed her ear. "Your mate can't save you. Fight. Become the first."

A searing pain tore through her skull. She screamed, the pressure swelling until it stole her breath. Her body curled in on itself as the vision ruptured around her.

The crushing grip vanished. Warm, steady hands gripped her arms, pulling her backward. The fog broke. A familiar chest pressed against her back, solid as stone. "I've got you."

She sighed at the scent of clove and ashes and ... Aluk Vasumen.

His hand rubbed down her back.

Someone murmured. A woman. She'd worry about the other female later. Her eyelids refused to open. She sank against the alpha, his heartbeat steady and calming. Being here, against him, felt right.

"She's burning up," Conleth murmured.

"You will be the first." She clung to the words.

Alpha Vasumen stiffened behind her. "What does she mean?"

"I don't know," the woman said, confusion roughening her voice. "It must have been something from the vision she had when I touched her."

The chest against her back rumbled, a comfort to her racing mind. She tried to process what had happened. A shiver slipped down her spine, slow and cold, as the woman's words sank in.

Her stomach tightened. Seeing the past or future... Her pulse jumped, caught between fear and hope.

What if the woman's gift led her to her biological family? What if her condition was hereditary? Maybe she'd find a cure without paying her benefactor's price.

"I didn't see all of it. When the Great Hunter turned, he shoved me out of the vision."

Great Hunter. Was that the man with many feathers? Who was the other? Heat rose throughout her body. Her stomach lurched, rising hard into her throat, and a moan clawed out of her before she could stop it.

Strong hands turned her to the side. She groaned. Hands cooler than her flesh brushed her neck as they held her hair away while she heaved.

"Are there any other rooms on this floor?"

"Just this one," Alpha Aluk told the woman. "Take my room tonight, and I'll stay here."

Palisade realized the woman must be Conleth's mate.

"Put her in your room, Aluk. I'll get fresh sheets. These are soaked."

"Should we move her?" Alpha Aluk asked.

Heat flooded her cheeks the moment she heard the woman's voice. If vanishing were a gift, she would have taken it now, sinking straight through the mattress and into the stone beneath.

One thing she hated most about her illness–the inability to control her body functions.

Someone shuffled, fetching sheets. Guilt weighed on her chest. Their kindness scraped against every lie she'd trained herself to believe. She didn't deserve their hands on her, steady and gentle. Her plans would destroy their trust.

His concern brushed against her like a bruise, tender and unwelcome. Why was he worried about her? Palisade tried to lift her head. His hand pressed against the side of her face. Her muscles locked, a sharp jolt shooting through her chest before she could breathe. He ran his hand down her hair, and she relaxed.

"Would you rather she stayed in this mess?" The woman snapped.

"But only until the room's ready," Alpha Vasumen said.

Palisade groaned as he lifted her.

"Careful," the woman said.

Alpha Vasumen's movements sent her head spinning. She cracked her eyes open, then gave up, letting the sickness consume her.

Seven

Her skin looked too pale against his.

Aluk laid her on his bed and pulled the blankets up to her chin, smoothing them once... then again. He straightened and crossed the room. He yanked the drapes tighter, blocking the draft. The fire burned low. He dropped another log on it, maybe harder than he meant. The wood cracked against the grate.

A part of him still braced for the past to repeat, for her to slip away like Naomi had, dying before he could reach her.

Dr. Everett moved under the covers. A faint moan escaped her.

He moved toward her in a rush, hand outstretched. His fingers hovered above her shoulder. Heat poured off her skin. The dragon clawed inside him. He forced his hand back.

Behind him, the log caught with a sharp pop. Light flashed gold across her flushed face.

His hip clipped the dresser beside the bed. The washbasin rattled against its rim. The noise punched through the haze. Pain bloomed along his side. He pressed a hand to it. Better than thinking about how badly his control had slipped.

Dr. Everett shivered again. Her brow creased.

He stepped back, putting himself between the bed and the door. Heat spread through his chest.

He'd been imagining her in his bed last night.

The dragon coiled around his ribs with a low, possessive hum.

It's temporary.

She stays.

Trace came to his room. "Is she okay?"

A snarl rose from his dragon. Aluk clenched his jaw, then forced it to relax. He didn't want the wolf shifter guard anywhere near Palisade. Didn't want him in this room. Not now. Not when she was vulnerable.

Stand still. Think. Breathe. The dragon ignored him, pulling him half a step toward the bed.

"Migraines." He glanced over his shoulder. She lay curled on the bed, face pale and drawn. Her hair tangled, clothes wrinkled. Even unconscious, her jaw stayed tight.

"I will tend her."

She was under his protection.

The dragon hissed. *Mine. No other males.*

Trace's brows rose. Aluk huffed. He'd shown too much interest in Dr. Everett. He learned to look for hidden motives. Naomi had taught him that lesson. He had to stay sharp, think like the enemy. Even when that enemy might lie in his bed.

"My cousin's mate suffers from them. They are worse when she hasn't eaten." Trace frowned. "If I have your permission, I'll go down to the dining hall and bring her some food. I smelled stew coming from the kitchen earlier."

"Do that." Aluk crossed his arms and turned, blocking the doorway. He kept both Palisade and Trace in his line of sight.

"If you'd allow me to switch posts with Rob this evening, I could sit with her to give you a break."

A growl tore from Aluk's chest.

Trace froze.

The dragon clawed behind his sternum, threatening to tear through.

Trace lifted his chin, holding his ground. Bold as always.

The dragon snarled. *Challenge me?*

Aluk's jaw locked. "Permission. Denied."

Trace leaned and looked around to the woman in Aluk's bed, then back at Aluk. "Are you planning to mark her, Alpha?"

"Do you think she's your mate?" Aluk's eyes flared with heat.

"Her scent last evening suggested she would not be opposed."

The dragon slammed against his ribs. His vision sparked.

Trace's nostrils flared. He'd scented the shift inside Aluk. "Taran mentioned keeping her on the mountain. I could take her to Sentinel Peak when she's able to travel again. My rotation is almost done."

The dragon lunged. *Challenge. Mine!*

Aluk's hands trembled. He tucked them under his arms.

"If you don't intend to mark her, then I'd like to spend time with her."

Trace had that right.

Aluk vowed never to mark a mate. He closed his eyes. The beast poured into his veins, demanding the shift. Heat rolled off him in waves. The air shimmered.

"Back off," he muttered. His control was slipping.

It snarled and paced; the claws digging into his soul. When he looked at the other man, Trace lowered his gaze.

Mine.

She didn't belong to them. He shoved the thought to the dragon.

The dragon rumbled. Liar.

"She is free to choose." Aluk slammed the spirit into a cage inside his mind. It wouldn't hold long. "You will not cross the threshold of my private chambers."

Dr. Everett stirred. A sound caught in her throat.

Aluk dragged in a breath.

Trace eased back a step. "I would never."

Aluk nodded, and Trace spun on his heel.

They needed females. The Fae's curse had seen to fewer births, fewer opportunities to pair. Aluk understood Trace's hunger for a mate.

He raised his voice. "Return to your duty. Don't come into this section of the fortress without my permission."

Trace's scent faded down the hall. Aluk found Trinity and Conleth in the spare room next to his, stripping the bed.

"You've settled her, then?" Conleth asked.

"I tucked her into my bed. Trace offered to sit with her." His dragon spirit slammed against its cage.

"That is not wise," Trinity said, tossing the soiled bedding onto a pile near the door.

"What did you see when you touched her?" Trinity had pulled back from Palisade's memories. She stopped before making her worse.

Conleth went to the closet and took out new sheets.

Dr. Everrett's luggage sat untouched in the corner. Her peach scent had faded, replaced by his brother's musk, Trinity's lavender, and the sour tang of illness.

Trinity bit her lip. Her silver hair sat in a messy bun.

"Do you always have visions when you touch others?" Aluk kept his distance from his brother's mate. Trinity's ability to touch the living essence of a person and recall memories had saved a man's life months ago. It helped them track the ohunko trying to harm her, and she'd read from his memories.

"I can't always control it."

"Tell him what you saw." Conleth dumped the sheets on the bed.

Trinity hesitated. "It wasn't a memory. More like a dream."

She grabbed the fitted sheet and tossed a corner to Conleth. Inside, Aluk's dragon spirit settled. His brother touching Palisade's bed didn't bother him with Trinity there. The beast rumbled. *Our room. Our bed.*

He could move her things now. Her luggage sat right there. *No*, he curled and uncurled his fingers into his palms.

"Then what did you see?" Aluk asked.

"Two men approached her. One called her daughter." Trinity glanced at Conleth and shook her head. "I can't tell you more. I pulled back when I realized I had invaded her privacy."

Aluk snorted. It hadn't stopped her in the past. "Then how do you know it was a dream, not a memory?"

"Because it took me to a forest, and the man had a full headdress of feathers, and the other had a stripe of black and red painted across his face. No one runs around like that on the mountain anymore unless it's for a ceremonial purpose." Trinity smoothed the sheet, avoiding his gaze.

A vision of the Great Hunter? Of the ancient ones who once roamed the mountain? "You're not telling me everything."

Perhaps it was a warning, a sign of what was to come.

His dragon spirit chuffed.

What is it then?

"There's no more to tell," Trinity said.

"He called her daughter?" Aluk's brows drew together in deep thought. His dragon spirit didn't so much as stir. "Who do you think she is?"

Grabbing a pillowcase, Trinity turned away from Aluk. "You know who she is."

Mine. The dragon spirit surged inside him.

"Dr. Palisade Everett. She's an outsider sent by the state to interfere in our tribes' business," Aluk said with a growl.

Trinity took the pillows and put them on the bed. "She is more to you than to us. You know who she is."

Conleth shook his head, his eyes dulled as he spoke through the bond to his mate. She glowered at him in return. Aluk watched the silent exchange, a pang of envy shooting through him. Without marking a mate, he couldn't communicate.

Now, watching Conleth and Trinity, Aluk, bitterness twisting in his chest. Loneliness cut through him. His dragon extended its claws, restless and wanting.

"I don't know who she is, and that's why she'll stay here until we figure out her purpose. If she needs to go to the clinic, I'll bring her there. Enemy or not, I won't have another human dying on the mountain for the government to send another Fae blood to investigate." He looked directly at Trinity.

Not her fault. She didn't cause the curse.

No, an alpha long before his time had done that. Aluk said nothing. Conleth took the hint and kept to the main topic of Aluk's new ward. That's all she could be. Anything else would feed the dragon's delusion.

"I don't believe her headaches are physical." Conleth helped Trinity finish making the bed. "They're only a symptom of the problem. I'll have a better idea once I get the results from the blood samples. Stress and trauma often cause headaches. Or suppressed memories."

"Or she may suffer from migraines, like some humans do." Trinity said, coming around the bed beside Conleth. She put her hand on Conleth's arm. "She can't unlock what she doesn't know."

He wanted to check on her—needed to. It annoyed him. His dragon spirit paced. *Check on her. Now.*

"You'll tell me when you figure it out."

"You may be the one to figure it out before I do," Conleth said.

"We don't know for sure she's human," Trinity said, leaning closer to Conleth. "If I am the key to the curse, Gwen is the mother of spirits, and we haven't broken the curse, then we're missing something."

Or someone. But Aluk kept silent.

Trinity's expression softened. "I know you don't want to hear this, Aluk, but if my death seals the curse, then maybe we need to free the queen from the mountain."

"No," Aluk roared, his dragon demanding the shift. His eyes blazed. Scales rippled across his skin.

Conleth shoved Trinity behind him. His chest swelled, dragon rising. *Touch my mate, and you die.*

Aluk's dragon snarled back. He grabbed his head and fell to his knees. The shift pulled at him, vibrating through his bones, and yanking at his soul. His dragon bellowed through their bond. *You challenge me?*

You threatened my mate.

You threaten the entire mountain. Stay away from my queen.

The revelation struck. *Queen?* The dragon retreated, plunging into the depths of his mind. Aluk swayed. He dragged in breath after breath. Conleth and Trinity hadn't moved. They stayed back. Conleth's eyes glowed bright red. He stumbled to his feet. "I need to check on my ward."

"Aluk, wait," Trinity stepped toward him. Conleth's arm shot out, blocking her.

"I would never hurt your mate." He'd kept her alive. He'd sent the *ohunko* back to the Great Hunter. Hadn't he? He headed for the door.

Conleth's voice dropped. "You're going to fly?"

"Keep her in my room. Leave when I return. I'm going to calm my dragon."

"What part of this mountain calms your dragon spirit, Alpha?" Trinity asked.

Aluk's hand went to his neck. "Who said it's a place? Maybe I just need to fly."

"I've seen your memories," Trinity's voice gentled. "Your dragon takes you to a place in the mountain. She's trapped somewhere only your dragon knows. The spirit inside you needs to let go, Aluk. We can end this curse and bring life back to the mountain. It's good Dr. Everrett has come."

"What does Dr. Everett have to do with this?" Aluk's dragon circled in his soul, restless.

"She's your mate," Trinity said.

"My mate is dead." But the dragon inside him disagreed.

"If the Great Hunter can grant spirits to his warriors, why can't a soul not be reborn?" Trinity asked.

Conleth frowned. "Only spirits move on to the next life. When we die, we never return to this world. We remain with the Great Hunter."

"The Fae believe that when we die, we fade, return to the earth, and become one with nature. Don't your books discuss spirit walkers? Fate entwining two souls to find each other?"

"Your mate has been reading too many of our ancestors' scribblings." Aluk moved again to leave. "You should spend more time in your lair than my library before the Fae invade again."

"Spirit walkers are lost souls," Conleth said.

"Some believed they cursed themselves." Fire burned in Aluk's chest. "I've told you before. My mate is dead. There is no one else. Not in this life."

"I've seen her before. In visions of the future. She's your mate."

Naomi wasn't his mate. She was his wife. Dragon and man wanted different things. It ripped a void between them. Her death still did.

Aluk grabbed a nearby chair and hurled it against the stone wall. "Enough. Do not speak of this to me again. She's not my wife." His hands shook. Aluk curled them into fists.

"She is not Naomi." Trinity remained calm. "She will never be the one you lost, but she is the one you need."

Aluk had heard enough. He turned and went next door.

Palisade lay exactly as he'd left her hours ago, one hand curled near her cheek, the other resting on her stomach. Her breathing remained deep and even, the fever finally broken. Color had returned to her cheeks, chasing away the deathly pallor that had stopped his heart earlier.

In sleep, the sharp edges that defined her softened. The wariness that shadowed her eyes was gone. The tension that coiled through her shoulders released. She looked...young. Vulnerable. Human.

His fingers curled against his thigh, fighting the urge to brush back the strand of hair that had fallen across her face.

The scent of peaches wrapped around him, filling his lungs with every breath. Richer now that the fever had broken. Sweeter. His dragon practically wallowed in it, a rumbling purr building in his chest that he had to physically swallow it down.

No. No, this was — This was exactly what his dragon wanted him to feel. What it had *made* him feel about Issabrie. A trick. A compulsion born of ancient magic and draconian obsession.

He'd survived Naomi's death because his dragon had never allowed him to bond with her. The pain had been bearable. Human grief, not soul-shattering loss.

But this?

When had he ever felt this? This bone-deep rightness?

Never. Not with Naomi. Not from the phantom of a woman from his dragon obsessed over.

And he wouldn't. The dragon had no right to choose this for him.

If he let himself believe this was real, if he cared for this woman and the dragon refused him the right to mark her...

Aluk headed for the roof. His dragon needed a reminder of the last woman he had tried to claim. Once out in the cold air, he stripped and let the dragon come forth. Wings spread. He launched into the sky, circling the mountain.

Eight

When Palisade woke later in the night, a dark figure sat in a chair out of reach. Her heart raced, pounding painfully in her chest. Fear coiled in her stomach like a living thing. She tried to move, but her head throbbed sharply as if she rested against a bed of needles.

She fought to focus on the figure.

His eyes shone red like rubies in the dark. Chills spiraled down her spine. Palisade swallowed hard, trying to suppress the climbing unease, and stared into those eyes. Familiar eyes. Ones that pushed warmth into her chest, easing her grip on the blankets.

The eyes of a particular alpha.

What was he doing in her room?

She remembered him laying her on his bed, and her eyes fluttered at his smoke and masculine scent on the blankets and sheets.

Her skin no longer burned to the touch.

No fire crackled along the walls as it did everywhere else.

Cool air touched her skin.

The mattress dipped beneath the alpha's weight. The slight movement sent the room spinning, and she winced against the wave of dizziness.

His hand cradled the back of her head, grounding her and gently lifting her face toward the glass pressed to her lips. "Drink."

She kept her eyes closed. His deep voice radiated through her like a ripple in a pond. Her hand slid over his to hold the glass. He didn't let up when she tried to pull away.

"Drink it all."

She coughed; the chalky liquid tickled in her throat.

"What is it?" She balked at the taste.

Her tongue was bitter with the flavor of the drug she willingly consumed. Her heart sped again, but then the heaviness set in, and her head ceased its pounding.

He eased her back down. "Sleep."

And as she gave in to his second command, she swore his fingers pushed back her hair and the brush of his lips against the center of her forehead.

She tracked time by meals. A tray of stew and fresh bread marked the difference between night and day. Twice, she inquired about the wolf shifter guard, Trace. Each time, the alpha's eyes narrowed without a response.

Palisade needed to befriend Trace, earn his trust, and then take his keys when the time came.

The alpha's silence sent her pulse racing, but she couldn't afford to show her hand in the delicate game of deception she played with him. Every move counted.

"Feeling better?" Alpha Vasumen's dark eyes searched hers.

Sleep tugged at her. The enormous bed was too comfortable to resist. She groaned softly. "How long have I been asleep?"

Palisade stretched as the remnants of her illness receded.

"Three days."

For three days she'd taken over his bed. Guilt mixed with a strange giddiness at waking in his bed. She regretted not staying awake to snoop when he left. An opportunity she would not waste again.

"I apologize," she murmured. "I did not mean to overstay my welcome."

"Don't worry about it. You needed the rest." Alpha Vasumen carefully arranged the pillows behind her as she sat up. His kindness complicated things. She needed to stay guarded.

"I don't get migraines often, but when they slam me, they wipe me out." Which is why she should have seen it coming. It had been several months since her last one. They seemed to become more frequent and more painful as she aged. The antidote kept them at bay, or it had until this one.

"One of the guards also has a mate who suffers from them. She lives at the lodge in Sentinel Peak. When you are well enough to travel, I'll take you to the clinic there. Conleth will want to check on your condition."

She knew of the shifter town at the base of the mountain. Increasing snowslides threatened the population, so residents had to abandon the town. Recently, the state had redrawn boundaries and included the town in the mountain's reservation.

Despite the unpredictable avalanches, those of the blood had no choice but to take refuge in the little village of Avalanche Ridge or the lodge. Over the past few months, her benefactors provided her with a file of information to familiarize her with the mountain and its people. Her primary target wasn't the shifter bloods, but to free the guardian locked away in the belly of the dragon's fortress.

"Has the medical facility been established, or has the state continued to grant permission for residents to travel across the boundary?" The state allowed few exceptions for shifters to leave the mountain. She suspected more than the state acknowledged lived among the humans without the gifts of their animal spirits.

Time pressed against her. Each passing day brought more urgent. For her plan to succeed, the government's policy on boundary crossings had to remain lenient. She needed to ensure she could travel out of the area with no shifter bloods hunting her. Her survival depended on completing her mission and vanishing.

"You're familiar with the town?"

"I know it's been closed because of the avalanches, and recently, residents have moved back since the thaw this past spring," she said. None of that was classified information.

"It will take time to regain what was lost." His careful phrasing didn't escape her notice. "Conleth runs the clinic. You are in good hands with him." He handed her a piece of bread. His hand lingered when she reached for it. Her gaze fell to his large fingers.

His eyelids lowered, and the red gleam faded from his dark eyes. Did he want her? Or was it something else? Kindness without a price always came due.

Alpha Vasumen dipped bread in the stew on the tray beside the bed. "Why are you here, Dr. Everett?"

Palisade took another piece of the stew-soaked bread. The muscles in her neck tightened as a dull ache formed at the base. "I'm here on behalf of the state to treat and rehabilitate Scout Jameson."

"Then you should report to the state that he's a prisoner of the mountain, and it's a life sentence for his crime. He's not leaving here. Neither are you." His eyes burned brighter, his voice roughened, and she held his gaze. What he said sank deep into her chest. Heavy. Cold.

"And what are our crimes? There are laws in place by the state. This mountain resides within its boundaries." Stew dripped from the bread onto her fingers. She brought her hand to her mouth, licking the savory liquid from her skin. Her gaze lifted, and she caught him watching her, his lashes lowered, looking almost predatory. She forgot to taste the stew, forgot the words she had been forming, as his gaze darkened.

Palisade opened her mouth to continue and had to stop. The argument scattered, and a tug formed deep within her, sharp enough to steal her breath. Silence stretched between them.

"Scout Jameson was caught attacking a woman while hunting spirits in the state park near the borders. Even if a spirit didn't possess him, his crime is punishable by life in prison. To steal one's spirit animal is to take their life, Dr. Everett."

Palisade stilled. She read the same information in his file. "And me? What have I done?"

Alpha Vasumen nudged her hand to take another bite of bread. "You saw my dragon."

His fingers brushed her skin, and her thoughts slipped out of order. She hesitated, the bread hovering between them. Was there something in the food?

Each bite made it harder to remember why she needed to stay guarded.

"And that's a crime?" she asked, curling her fingers in the blanket. She held his gaze, careful not to name what she knew.

"No one outside the mountain knows my dragon exists," he said.

"You're afraid I'll share your secret? I assure you I won't." The words came out too fast.

Her benefactor's warning about dragons stirred. Palisade pressed her lips together, the truth pressing just as hard.

"I know you won't," Alpha Vasumen smirked. "From this day forward, Dr. Everrett, you'll not leave this fortress without me at your side."

Her pulse jumped anyway, traitorous, her breath catching on the wrong side of fear.

"Then you should call me Palisade if we are to become close acquaintances." Her knuckles whitened as her grip tightened on the blankets. She had already given him her name once. Giving it again carried a risk she was a fool to take. Among the Fae, names were never just names. How long before he too demanded his due?

She had been placed here, whether or not she liked it.

His constant presence was both a shield and a shackle. Him watching her every move posed a complication to her mission. Not that she'd come up with a fail proof plan yet.

Her body noticed him long before her judgement caught up. She met many Fae and human men, none of whom got under her skin, however, none ever disrupted her this way.

She shut the thought down as soon as it surfaced. This was not the moment for attachment. Each moment he insisted on staying close to her increased her risks.

When this was over, he would hunt her down, imprison her, or worse. Some days she wondered if fighting to live another day brought any more peace than going somewhere to die in truth.

She crushed the pity as it surfaced. Her life depended on Scout's release. There was no room for doubt. Only leverage.

Not long after she finished her stew, he made an excuse and left. She rose from the bed and crossed the room. Her luggage sat in the corner of the room. Her satchel hung from the back of an elegant chaise, oversized enough for two or one enormous man. The image of the mighty Alpha Vasumen lounging there almost made her smile. Its deep red fabric clashed with the dark gray walls and black metal bed frame.

She didn't remember agreeing to stay in his room at all. She pressed a hand to her stomach; it lurched unexpectedly. Did he expect her to sleep with him? She pulled her files and tablet from her satchel.

Everything remained untouched. She searched through her luggage piece by piece. All the contents remained, except for her outfits, tucked back inside more neatly than she had packed them.

Her hand brushed across the inner seam of her smaller case. The crystal remained embedded in the suitcase lining.

The dim light of the alpha's room took the pressure off her eyes. She moved slowly, careful not to flood the room with light.

A soft glow radiated from the walls.

When the alpha left, flames reignited in the stone pockets set into the walls.

She pulled on a long skirt and tunic, then slid into her favorite leather flats.

She heard a whisper near the window and moved closer. Wind scraped against the fortress walls outside. The room held a single wide window. She leaned closer to the glass. The drop below stretched far too long. Without wings, she'd have plummeted to her death.

The glass didn't flex beneath her fingers. Thick against her palm, the cold of the outside never reached her. One escape route checked off her list of exits.

A shadow fell over her. She stepped away, expecting the alpha. The shadow stepped back with her.

The silhouette wavered at the edge of the light. She spun around. The shape was soft, curved like a woman. Was it hers?

It didn't move the way her shadow should have. "Is someone here?"

She turned again, heart hammering.

Yes.

The voice might have come from the shadow. It might have come from her.

Recognition stirred where none should have been.

She moved closer to the woman-shaped shadow. "Who are you?"

Who are you? The words returned, not in her voice.

"What kind of game is this?" Palisade stepped forward. The shadow slid aside.

Leave before it's too late.

"Before what is too late?" She blinked. Darkness swallowed the edges of the woman-shaped shadow.

Mate.

"Whose mate?"

The dream surfaced, fractured. She had spoken of a mate.

Pressure bloomed behind her eyes as she reached for the memory. A sharp pulse flared at her temple. Then another. No. Not again. This could not happen now. If it took her now, she would be helpless.

He comes.

"Who? What?" She staggered back as the door flung open. Light poured in from the hallway. She recoiled.

Alpha Vasumen's massive body stepped inside, blocking the light behind him. He filled the doorway — shadow and muscle and intent.

"Oh!" Palisade threw up a hand against the sudden light and turned back toward the shadow woman. Only Alpha Vasumen's shadow stretched far enough to touch hers against the stone. She caught a woman's name in the air, soft and unmistakable.

His grip anchored her where she stood. "Are you okay?"

She tore herself from his grasp. "How dare you come barging in on us like this?"

"Us?" Alpha Vasumen glanced around the room. "There is no one here but you."

"Of course, there is me, and if you'd given me a moment, I'd be able to introduce you to..." She turned slowly. "Where did she go?"

A deep rumble came from Alpha Vasumen's chest. "Where did who go?"

Palisade backed away. Her gaze swept the room. Her throat worked.

The room offered no answers.

"I don't know."

Nothing in her training accounted for this. Spirits were theories in books. Not this.

The back of her legs bumped the bed, and she sat.

"What do you mean? Was someone in here with you?"

"I don't know." She pressed her fingers to her temple. A dull ache pulsed beneath her fingers, stubborn and unrelenting. The antidote had never failed her.

Dragon magic soaked the stone walls of the fortress, designed to snuff out other magic. The fire in the stone pressed back at her.

"You're back faster than I expected." She clasped her hands in front of her. Stay focused. Stay sharp. Her thoughts refused to settle.

Alpha Vasumen raked his hand through his beard. "Add me to one of your case files if you'd like, Peaches, but I can sense when my mate is near."

Peaches. He called her that before.

"It's Palisade."

"You smell like peaches. Get used to it."

She'd argue with him over his ridiculous nickname later. She didn't even *like* peaches!

The ache behind her eyes eased when Vasumen came near.

He drew her in, close enough that stepping back took effort. Those muscular arms beckoned her to step into them and let him wrap them around her. *He's coming.*

"Are you saying you think I'm your mate?" Her voice betrayed her.

The idea might work to her advantage and offer a layer of protection should things go south. But the thought also twisted something deep within her. Being Alpha Vasumen's mate would compromise her position.

Relationships never ended well for her.

In the end, she wanted a clean break. A new life.

A life. Period.

Another tug pulled at her. More insistent this time.

The bond threatened the one thing she had never been allowed to keep. Freedom. Life. Don't get attached. Her survival and the success of her mission depended on her keeping a clear head. He crowded her thoughts. His eyes followed her, unbidden, tangled with the memory of the shadow woman.

"My mate is dead." His expression hardened.

"I see." A sharp sting struck her at his loss. Palisade kept her face neutral, masking the turmoil inside. This explained so much. Her therapist brain kicked in. Not a setback. An opportunity. She smiled. Oh, she'd add him to her case files. Alpha Vasumen's past intrigued her.

"No, you don't." His hand cupped the side of her face, tilting it toward him. "You're not her. My dragon doesn't get to choose. The choice is mine."

"Okay," she breathed. Best not to push. The ache in her temples faded. His touch, maybe the distraction. His gaze burned, possessive.

He was fighting his dragon. She could see it. Shifters didn't survive losing their mates. The bond shattered and disconnected the spirit. So how was he still standing?

She whispered, "I'm not here to replace what you lost." Deep inside her, a chasm cracked. She wished things could be different. But they weren't.

Palisade placed her hand over his heart. Steady. Strong.

He growled.

Alpha Vasumen stepped away and paced the room. He checked the closet, under the desk, and pressed his hands against the wall near the window. He stopped at the window and stared through the glass. His shoulders stayed rigid. His eyes glowed red. She eased back, one step at a time, edging toward the door.

Her heart hammered. Each step took her closer to the door. Just a few more steps. She could slip out before—.

"Where are you going?" He turned his head to look at her. Those red eyes blazed.

"I should return to my room. Thank you for taking care of me when I was sick. I'm sorry you're grieving."

She turned and walked down the hall toward her old room. His gaze burned into her back. She'd almost made it to her old room when Alpha Vasumen spoke. She stopped.

"You returning to my room calms my dragon and helps a great deal."

That couldn't have been easy to say. Palisade glanced back at him. The paid on his face cracked something inside her. She forced a lighter tone. "Do you expect me to pet the dragon?"

His eyes glinted. "Only if you like playing with fire."

He wasn't talking about the hearth. Was he flirting? Or was she reading too much into it?

She turned back toward his room. Her cheeks heated.

The thought jolted her. She'd almost forgotten why she was really here.

Nine

The door opened.

Palisade woke with a sharp inhale, her body already bracing before her mind caught up. Cold air swept across her bare skin, raising gooseflesh along her arms and legs. She shivered and dragged the blanket higher, heart thudding as the memory flooded back.

Alpha Vasumen's bed.

She squeezed her eyes shut, but it didn't banish the images of broad shoulders, steady heat, the way his presence had wrapped around her like something solid and immovable.

You returning to my room calms my dragon and helps a great deal.

Her pulse skipped. His truth should have irritated her. Should have sounded like an excuse. Yet, it stirred something reckless and soft beneath her ribs.

Maybe she did like to play with fire.

She pushed herself upright. The sheet sliding lower than she liked. This was a mistake. Letting herself rest here. Letting her guard down.

Someone cleared their throat.

Palisade gasped and clutched the blanket to her chest, heat rushing to her face as she twisted toward the sound.

Conleth Vasumen stood at the foot of the bed, a tray balanced in his hands. Tea steamed beside a plate of toast.

"Good morning."

She forced her breathing to steady, lifting her chin even as embarrassment prickled her skin.

"I see your color has returned," Conleth observed as he set the tray on the bedside table.

She swallowed. "Where is Alpha Vasumen?"

Probably not the best question after the dream she'd had about him.

Conleth tilted his head, studying her with the same dark eyes as his brother. "I wanted to check on you before returning to my clinic. Is your head still bothering you?"

"No. The headache's gone." She rolled her neck from side to side. The familiar pressure was gone, but something tighter had taken its place. "I thought you'd have left by now. I don't want to detain you from your other patients."

"My mate is in the library. Aluk's allowing her to take some of our ancestors' record books home. I have some time before she leaves. If you'd like, I can take you to meet her."

His mate.

She pushed the reaction down and let curiosity take its place. "What does she do?"

"She works in government relations. Research. Artifacts." Conleth moved toward the door. "I'll return in an hour to check your vitals."

Palisade watched him go.

Government ties. Research access. Conleth's confirmation matched what her benefactor had told her. The Vasumens wanted this curse broken, while the Fae fought to gain the advantage. What information Conleth's mate gathered, they'd protect. None of it mattered once Palisade fulfilled her part of the bargain.

Not by choice.

She understood more than most the strength to keep going another day. The Fae hunted Conleth's mate. Aluk struggled with the loss of his mate. Time had run out for them. It also reminded her why she never allowed herself to want anyone. Bonds had leverage. And leverage got people killed.

Palisade stepped into the alpha's bathroom and paused. The shower was built for a dragon shifter. Stone walls rose higher than she could reach, and the spray came down hard and relentlessly. She twisted the handle anyway. Hot water slammed into her shoulders and neck, stealing her breath. She braced a hand against the wall and let it happen. The ache in her muscles eased first. The tight coil in her chest followed more slowly, loosening one inch at a time.

She stayed longer than necessary. Long enough for the steam to blur her thoughts. Long enough to pretend the night hadn't happened.

She drank the tea while toweling off; the warmth settled her stomach. When she dressed, she chose the coral-colored dress without over-thinking it. Soft. Unassuming. Hair loose, nothing pinned or hidden.

She checked her reflection once and then turned away.

In her luggage, her fingers slid into the lining and closed around the crystal. It was cool and familiar against her skin. Waiting. Always waiting.

Once activation and everything would change.

She withdrew her hand and closed the bag.

The boots came next. Tall. Sturdy. Her dagger was still back at The Manor, and the absence of its weight tugged at her awareness like a missing limb.

She didn't linger after that.

The door opened, and she nearly collided with the man standing just beyond it.

Trace froze, color flooding his neck and ears.

She smiled before she thought better of it. "Hello there."

He ducked his head. "Hello, Dr. Everett. I hope you are well today."

"Much better," she said lightly, and stepped just close enough to make his shoulders tense. "Have you come to escort me again? I thought Medic Vasumen was coming."

Trace swallowed hard. For a moment, he looked as if he hadn't expected to be asked anything at all.

"Conleth didn't send me. Neither did the alpha. I was on duty last night. I stayed out here in case you came out. Or in case there was news."

He'd waited. All night.

"I'm so sorry," she said, softer than she intended. "Did you knock? I was in the shower after the medic left."

She kept the titles in place. Medic. Alpha. They weren't her friends, and she wasn't here to get comfortable around them.

"Ah... no." He glanced toward the stairway. "Alpha Aluk doesn't want me in his room."

"Oh." She recovered quickly, but not quickly enough to miss the flicker in his eyes. "He doesn't, does he?"

Bitterness tasted unfamiliar on her tongue.

He made it clear he didn't have any interest in her. It stung a bit, but the man had lost someone, and the fact he lived was a miracle in itself. Too bad she didn't have time to stick around to help him work through the grief.

Illness or execution. Those were the only endings waiting for her. There was no space in either for lingering, for healing, for helping a man grieve his way back to himself.

And yet.

The desire lingered anyway, stubborn and inconvenient. Something had taken root when he'd given her his room without being asked.

Why had he done that?

Last night, her heart had raced in a different rhythm. The memory refused to fade. He had to have felt it too.

She scrubbed a hand through her damp hair and straightened, letting resolve snap into place.

"I'll be moving back into my room," she said. "You're welcome to visit me when the door is open."

"I don't want to cause trouble. As the alpha, I must respect his order and will remain in the hall or see you in the break room, dining hall, or library." Trace turned and headed away.

"Are these places accessible to the prisoners, too?" She needed to get Scout Jameson and his possessed guardian spirit out of that cell. Fast. She had no idea how long the antidote would hold this time before wearing off.

"A few can access the dining hall," he said, leaning in, eyes bright with the hope of being useful. "There's also an exercise room, where they fight most often." His voice dipped, and he shared a private secret just with her. "The other areas are staff-only."

"No going outside," she muttered, leaning in slightly with an encouraging smile. In another life, maybe they could have become friends.

Aside from Diaden, she'd considered no one close enough for that title, and even he lived more in the *fae* column than the friend one.

"Thank you," she said, letting appreciation warm her tone, hoping to coax out more information.

"The elevation is hard on the lungs, and it would pose an escape risk," Trace said.

"We certainly wouldn't want that," she said, her tone more thoughtful than sarcastic. "Do you know where the alpha is? I still need to see my patient and sort out my living arrangements here. He doesn't get to decide who I visit, when, or where."

Her gaze drifted over Trace. He wore a long-sleeved T-shirt, cargo pants, and boots.

She stepped closer. His breath hitched, and a small smile curved on her lips. She slid a finger onto his chest, testing his reaction. When he didn't pull away, she traced a slow line down over his heart, across his abs, and toward the set of keys clipped to his belt.

"You can find him in the den on the second floor," Trace said, his gaze fixed on her fingertip as it halted just shy of his waist.

She withdrew her hand. "Can I see you later?"

"I'd like that." He grinned, gesturing down the hall. "I'll show you to his office before heading to my room."

As they descended to the second floor, their hands swung too close enough to brush. His arm grazed hers in a light, accidental sweep. Trace kept his gaze pinned forward with each fleeting contact, but she caught the tension in his jaw and smirked at his attempt to hide how much he enjoyed their nearness.

Too bad his touch didn't heat her skin or spark anything close to what Alpha Vasumen stirred in her. Conflicting thoughts crowded her mind. Each step brought her closer to the alpha's office and further into feelings she didn't want to acknowledge. Using Trace for his keys and information tugged at her conscience, a discomfort she'd never encountered in her line of work.

She stole a glance at him. He was kind, and the genuine interest he showed her made her wish there were another way to complete her task without deceiving him.

"May I see you before dinner?" Trace asked as they reached the door. "My shift goes through the night again."

Outside the alpha's door, nervousness bubbled up, mixed with a strange excitement she couldn't quite quell. Guilt tangled with the adrenaline running through her at the thought of leading Trace on while wanting to see the alpha. She drew a steady breath and nodded. "I'd like that."

Palisade lowered her lashes. She hoped he couldn't sense the turmoil rolling inside her. Shifter bloods had enhanced senses of sight and hearing. He would hear the beat of her heartbeat for sure.

"Then I'll leave you to Alpha Aluk. Good luck."

She watched Trace disappear down the hallway. Before her resolve could falter, Palisade pushed into the alpha's office. She wasn't afraid. She just needed the two of them to stay enemies. Emotions got people killed in her line of work.

Alpha Vasumen didn't look up from the book open on his desk.

She clenched her fist. *Breathe in... breathe out.* She waited. Still, he refused to acknowledge her. A tactic of control. Well, it wouldn't work on her.

Palisade strode to the desk and tapped her fingernails against the wood. "I would like to have a word with you."

"Alpha."

"What?" Her palm pressed flat on the rich mahogany.

"If you wish to address me," he said calmly, "you will call me *Alpha*."

Palisade pressed the inside of her cheek between her teeth. After the way he'd held her, brought her food, and stayed with her through the night, she'd hoped for a conversation that was... less formal. Brute. She drew a slow breath, trying to choke back the irritation needling under her skin. Chin tipped high, she looked down her nose at him and at the map lines stretched across the pages of his book. A queasy flutter rolled through her stomach.

She bit her cheek again and said, "We may have had a misunderstanding. I appreciate you sharing your room, but who I spend my time with is my business. I'll be returning to my previous accommodations."

"The only ones relocating are my guards in a few days. The new ones will arrive shortly, and you will go nowhere."

Palisade fought not to flinch at his curtness. What a fool she'd been to think anything had changed between them after last night. Her body pulsed. A thousand little needles prickled beneath her ribs. "You have no authority over me."

He looked up at her, his eyes dark and glinting. "We've been over this. You're in my prison, which makes you my ward. I have every right."

"You are. Not. My alpha. And I am. Not. Yours. To command." She curled her hands into the fabric of her dress, afraid she might plant her fist in his face as he rose to his feet.

She blinked hard, willing the tears back. What was wrong with her? A storm of emotions crashed through her—anger at his arrogance, guilt over why she was here, fear of being controlled. Or was it fear of what he'd do once he learned the real reason she'd come?

The muscles in his neck tightened. She noticed his control slipping, the beast beneath his skin stirring. "You will remain in my room and away from the prison cells and guards unless I escort you."

"I can't do my job from inside your room. I assure you I'm well enough to proceed, thank you."

"I am trying to protect you!" He slammed his fist onto the book. His eyes flashed a deeper amber.

"I don't need your protection. I've taken care of myself all my life. I don't need you."

His face softened right as her tears finally broke free. She turned away before he could see how she hated this weakness. The pounding headaches that had dogged her for days frayed her control.

"Save your tears, Peaches. They don't work on me." His eyes narrowed, sending a chaotic flutter through her chest.

"Recheck your eyesight. For a man who stayed with me through the night, you're a brute in the daylight. Is this a dragon thing?"—she swept her hand over him—"or a man thing? I can assure you, any tears I shed aren't for you."

"Careful. You'll give my dragon the wrong impression."

She forced her fingers to uncurl and put on a smile. "Perhaps I will visit the library for a bit. It will allow me to meet your brother's mate and review my notes on my patient. Later, I expect to see Jameson again.

"No," Alpha Vasumen said. "I ordered my guards not to let you through the dungeons alone."

"Are those the same instructions for not allowing Trace inside your room?" she shot back. "It's territorial and primitive, even for you. I'm nothing to you. If you'd back off and let me do my job, I can leave. You won't have to deal with me anymore, I promise."

Alpha Vasumen leaned back in his chair, a predatory calm settling over his features. "My family's safety relies on the ignorance of the outside world to our spirits. You possess dangerous knowledge."

"All knowledge is dangerous. It depends on what you do with it."

Head held high, she turned and walked toward the door.

Ten

Inside the dungeon, Gorak sat in the dark. The spirit of the bear and the ancestor who once walked the earth waited. Possessing the body of a hunter, the old spirit listened. The bear within snorted as the white wolf padded past his cell, circling back in a pattern. He rested, letting the man reclaim enough control of his feeble mind to move their shared body.

Huddled near the bars, he watched and counted each time the guard in wolf form passed. Soon, the other would come—the one who carried the scent of his future mate.

Gorak shared memories with the man, flooding the man's heart with the old spirit's longing to find solace for past wounds and filling the man's heart with Gorak's desire to seek solace for the past from his ancestors and his destiny.

In the darkness, the man lifted his head, his eyes as black and glossy as the bear staring out from behind them. Too long had Gorak wandered the shadows in search of the next guardian. This one was weaker than the last, younger and far less willing. Fear clung to him. He wanted to go home.

The man's vision filled with a memory: a hunt, an older man teaching him to shoot a rifle. A longing for acceptance washed over him, but Gorak wiped the memory away and replaced it with one of a female with strawberry-blonde hair and emerald green eyes.

The firebird would soon pay.

Gorak became more eager to see the female called Dr. Everett.

Her scent lingered in his memory, a sweet echo of warm summer days. He yearned to find out if her lips tasted as sweet as her scent, his desire for her growing stronger with each passing moment. She was his to claim. The queen promised him a mate. He'd wait no more.

As the moment ticked by, the wolf did not come back. Gorak settled. The man rested his head back against the cold stone.

He watched for the next guard to come.

Alpha Vasumen's refusal to let her see Scout Jameson alone complicated Palisade's task. The man was infuriating. She couldn't risk going against his orders directly, but she needed to get down in that prison without the alpha breathing down her neck.

She found Trace leaning against a stone wall, deep in conversation with another guard. Seeing him gave her a sense of reassurance, a tool she could use to her advantage. Palisade smiled and approached the pair. Trace excused himself from the guard, a wide grin spreading across his face.

"Were you waiting for me?" Palisade's lips curved into a smirk.

"Perhaps I was," Trace replied, with a playful glint in his eyes.

The guard beside him grunted. Palisade acknowledged the other wolf shifter with dark hair and a scar on his chin. "I'm sorry if I interrupted something. I wasn't expecting to see you again until close to dinnertime."

"There's not much to do here besides be on guard duty or sleep," Trace said. "May I walk you somewhere?"

"Umm. The library." She glanced back, sensing Alpha Vasumen's stare on her back. He wasn't there, but she suspected that, like any other shifter, he might hear or sense her movements around this place. "Can you show me how to get there?"

The guard beside Trace looked at her oddly, but Trace's smile broadened. "This way, my lady?" He held out a hand, indicating for her to go left down a hall she'd momentarily passed.

Palisade created a map in her head. At every turn and open stairway, a guard stood, or a wolf prowled. She stuck close to Trace, her arm brushing his, and the wolf shifter gave her a reassuring smile. "You're safe, Dr. Everett. None of the prisoners can escape the dungeon."

"Has anyone ever?" She kept her question light as they headed for the fortress library. Conleth's mate, Trinity, awaited to have tea with her there. She never refused a good cup of tea and an opportunity to gain information. With her degrees in social work and psychology, people opened up naturally around her.

"Not within my lifetime," Trace motioned at the walls. "As you can see, there is no way out of here. My ancestors built this keep to protect those inside and, in doing so, also worked to our advantage to keep our prisoners from escaping."

"And if they did?" she asked, a quiver in her voice.

Trace's gaze softened. "They'd never survive. As you discovered, the only way up or down from this place is to use snowmobiles or fly—if you can find the location. The fortress is built into the side of the mountain. Few outside the mountain can find it because of its natural camouflage."

"I see." She chewed her lip and hated pointing out the obvious. "But if I climbed up here, would not a shifter or other powerful being be able to do the same? You didn't climb to get here or fly, did you? Does your animal not take over in the wild?"

"My wolf often does, yes, but we're not that uncivilized. I have full control over when I shift." He stopped abruptly, grabbing her arm to keep her from walking past him. In a curt tone, he said, "The only way into the library is through here." He motioned to another narrow hallway close to the alpha's office. She needed to try harder to get him to warm up to her, not insult him.

Glancing at the hallway, she cringed. Not that she had anything against dark and narrow spaces. "It's not lit."

"The flames imbibed into the stone will flare when the magic senses you near to light the way as long as your intentions are pure."

She snapped her head around to gaze at him. Her heart paused. No one said anything about magical flames. What if it sensed her intentions?

"Whoa," Trace held up his hands. A playful grin spread across his face. "I was joking. You don't like dark spaces, do you?"

She laughed nervously. "I've never been one for small spaces, and the darkness makes it even more uncomfortable. You said the magic senses you?"

Trace grinned. "Body heat." His gaze flickered over her, those baby blues turning steel gray, and a sudden heat spread through her cheeks. She averted her gaze, her heart pounding, not because of his bold gaze, but because her plan was working.

As they descended the narrow, winding hallway, the darkness seemed to close in around them. Palisade clutched Trace's arm. His head turned, looking at where she held him. When she went to pull away, afraid she'd done something inappropriate, he placed his hand over hers and squeezed it gently. She learned a few things about men in the past several years, having trained and lived at The Mansion with those her benefactor referred to as her brothers. No fondness came to mind thinking of the others who learned to deceive and destroy alongside her. Using Trace's kindness to her advantage twisted her gut. Normally, manipulating others got her top scores. Today, it left her stomach sour.

The flames flickered and danced to life within the stone walls, casting eerie shadows, causing her to second-guess her motives.

Finally, they reached the end of the hallway and emerged into a small, dimly lit room. A warm, inviting aroma filled the air, the scent of freshly brewed tea. Sitting at a small square table with a stack of books piled on the floor was a purple-haired woman, her eyes a different shade of purple, looking perplexed and relieved at the same time.

"Dr. Everett, I'm glad you came. I wasn't sure Conleth would remember to ask you, and I didn't want to impose again upon you. I'm Trinity."

"Please call me Palisade." She turned, taking in all the high bookshelves and the largeness of the room. She hadn't expected such a well-stocked library in a prison housing feral shifters and other paranormal beings. She'd imagined dusty tomes and crumbling parchment in some small nook of the fortress or in a room in a tower. But this was a sanctuary, peaceful and well kept. The tables gleamed with polish and smelled of books and melted wax.

"It's rather remarkable, isn't it? This used to be a family stronghold long before...well... a long time ago." Trinity motioned to the chair across from her. "Join me for tea? I hope you're feeling better."

"Much better, thank you." Palisade's gaze fixed on the steaming cup of tea that Trinity held. After adding a drop of honey, she took a cautious sip. Unfamiliar flavors washed across her tongue. The warmth spread through her body, offering a fleeting sense of comfort. She took another sip, this time slower, as she tried to discern the odd taste. Paranoia or caution—she couldn't tell which was more justified. Still, she maintained a composed exterior, masking the tug on her senses.

"It's a blend of chamomile, peppermint bark, and clove. All natural and grown on the mountain," Trinity said, gesturing to the tea.

"Fae berries."

Trinity grinned. "Right. You're familiar with them?"

"Palisade blew on the steam rising from the liquid. "High tea with a mad duchess a few years back." She wouldn't include the details of distracting the older woman while a colleague searched the house and eliminated the duke at her benefactor's request.

"You don't need honey with a Fae berry in the pot. I have a thing for tea; I'm sure you'll soon discover after we've hung out long enough. I do hope you were able to assist the duchess. I understand you're here trying to help Scout. An admirable task."

She was anything but admirable. Palisade took another sip of the tea. Fae berries came from another realm. Traveling Fae sold them at the local farmer's market to make coin to fit in with the human's currency exchange. They brewed excellent tea, which contained many health benefits.

Palisade's gaze flicked back to where Trace had been, to realize he had slipped away without her noticing.

"Trace is gone," she murmured. Trace's presence gave her a steady anchor. If she were a lesser-trained woman, his absence might have left her feeling adrift. Imagining him with Alpha Vasumen having a conversation about her filled her with unease. She'd have to be more cunning to keep up her game. Her next move involved needing a set of keys hooked on the belt of a particular wolf shifter.

"It wouldn't be wise for him to linger." Trinity pushed a plate of muffins in Palisade's direction. "They're from the bakery in town. I had Conleth fetch them as soon as they opened."

"That's a long way." Palisade didn't want to let go of her tea. She loved the warmth and comfortable feeling spreading through her. Fae berries were not known to drug a person. Just the opposite, they boosted immune systems and promoted healing. It would be rude to ask for more, and the muffins smelled too good.

"Perks of having a dragon at your disposal," Trinity frowned and set her tea aside. "I wanted to apologize for touching you the other day. Normally, I can control it. When I touched you the vision just sprang. I'm sorry. I did not intend to cause you further pain or send you into an old memory or pry without permission."

"I don't believe I'm following you." Palisade tilted her head, peeling off the wrapping around the muffin. She brought it close to her face and inhaled its yummy goodness. Satisfied she smelled nothing foul, she broke off a piece to plop in her mouth. It melted in her mouth, and she nearly moaned.

"Good, right?" Trinity's eyes twinkled.

"I'll take apology muffins any day," Palisade grinned back.

Trinity mirrored her grin. "I'll remember that the next time I touch you, you have unusual dreams."

Palisade put down her muffin. Fragments of her dream lingered in her memory. "You have a gift? You're a shifter blood? I didn't think anyone possessed such a powerful gift?"

"I'm Fae," Trinity admitted. "I work for the Paranormal Phenomenon Investigation Unit of the government. They're the same ones who sent you about Scout Jameson."

Palisade didn't bother to correct her. If believing they worked for the same agency helped keep her positioned here, she'd let the misunderstanding slip. The image of the two warriors, their fierce expressions, and the bone knife remained vivid in her mind. She wanted to close her eyes and try to recall more of the details. The curiosity etched on Trinity's face stopped Palisade and made her wonder what the significance of her dream meant. Something important tugged at her. Something she needed to remember. Her mate couldn't save her. From what?

Not wanting to dwell on it, she said, "Yes. I know the special abilities some possess living here on the mountain and in surrounding communities." Palisade chose her words carefully not to reveal too much of her knowledge and promptly shifted the conversation back to the issue in question. "I had a bizarre dream. I never dream, not even when I'm amid a headache. You caused it?"

Trinity nodded, a subtle smile curving her lips. "My gift is looking into one's memories. I can recall the past or the future. When I touched you, it was to do neither, but sometimes it happens accidentally."

"I see." Palisade pondered this while she took another sip of her tea. She studied Trinity, noting the pride in the woman's voice.

Palisade sat in silence, the weight of what Trinity revealed settling in her mind. The implications weighed heavily. If Trinity could access memories, then she might have the ability to reveal what was truly ailing Palisade. Something that eluded even the most skilled healers. The possibility of discovering the truth was tantalizing, but it came with a dark shadow of doubt.

"Do you remember the dream?" Trinity leaned forward, her expression reserved and kind.

Palisade sipped her tea. She trusted the woman to tell her the truth about the tea, but did she trust her enough to risk her life based on a stranger's moment of kindness? Trust no one.

This was no different.

What happened beyond Palisade completing her task wasn't her business.

The painted face of the warrior popped into her mind, sending a shiver through her.

Maybe she'd send the woman a message to warn her, but the relief to her conscience wasn't much. It would have to suffice. She would have to suffice to follow through. No remorse. No guilt. No looking back. She was raised to live by that code.

"Mostly," Palisade smiled. She found herself drawn to Trinity. She seemed kind and intelligent and possessed a certain ethereal beauty unique to the Fae born. Maybe because she'd been raised at The Manor amongst such diversity, it helped her be at ease around the other women. In different circumstances, they may have become friends. Palisade discovered long ago that friendships come at a cost.

"May I ask what you dreamed? I saw a man with a headdress and another in a meadow, or was it a forest with you?"

"You didn't evoke it, but invaded my dream?" Palisade's eyes narrowed as she shot a glare at Trinity. Her heart raced, pounding against her ribs like a caged animal. She had spent her life dancing through a web of deceit and mistrust, always anticipating the next betrayal. The woman was more of a mastermind than Palisade expected, caught off guard.

A moment ago, she might have asked for help and given her a warning about her life being in danger. What game was this? Palisade waited for her to make the next move.

"Only what I said. If anything happened after, I retreated to protect your privacy. I can help, though. If you tell me what you saw, we can determine if it was past or future," Trinity sounded sincere, her eyes unwavering. Sincerity was a mask Palisade had seen many times before.

Palisade smiled for the woman's benefit. "That's normally my job."

Should she trust Trinity? Could she afford not to?

Deciding it couldn't hurt, Palisade recalled the dream for Trinity, watching for any reaction from the Fae woman. She listened and nodded as Palisade finished telling her.

"And he said, you'd be the first?" Trinity tapped her lip in thought. "The first what?"

"I don't know." *To die?* The sinking sensation in the pit of her stomach deepened, having left out that part from what she shared with Trinity. "Whatever it is, my mate can't save me. Seeing that I don't have a mate, I'm most likely doomed, aren't I?" Palisade knew better than to wave off a vision or dream. The Fae believed in powerful gifts and premonitions. She came here to survive.

"You're not doomed. I am the doomed one." Trinity said quietly. Pain filled her expression.

"You believe you're doomed?" Palisade's mind raced, unable to speak aloud her suspicions. "So, we'll face doom together."

She tried to lessen the impact of the knowledge. Once more, fate took away her chance at friendship. She didn't wish harm to this beautiful and kind woman. Inside her mind, she wanted to scream at Trinity to run. Her task made her an accomplice, even if she wasn't contracted to do it. Suddenly, her stomach turned. *Get a grip!*

"I'd like that. Not the doomed part," Trinity assured her with a faint smile. "I have too few female friends, and we girls need to stick together on this mountain."

"We do indeed." Palisade picked up her tea and finished it.

"Have you told Aluk?" Trinity played with a crystal shard around her neck, drawing it up out of her blouse and rubbing her fingers over it. It was not much different from the one Palisade hid. Was she working for someone too?

"Alpha Vasumen?" Palisade paused midway through, setting her cup down. Around her, the air warmed significantly.

"Is that what he told you to call him?" Trinity shook her head. "You should tell him. It's important for him to know this. You may be in danger."

Throughout her entire life, she'd been in danger. At The Manor, they promised her one day at a time, and she lived to see the next. She fought and trained. She excelled at her lessons, and the illness that plagued her became a bigger threat than those who raised her.

"I will should the opportunity should it arise, if only to ease your mind." This will buy her more time to figure out a plan to free Scout, aka Gorak, from his prison cell. She opened her mouth to warn Trinity, and then a wave of dizziness hit her. She blinked, and it was gone, along with the memory of what she'd wanted to say.

Eleven

Rather than return to her room, Palisade wandered through the main floor of the stone fortress. Another day had passed, and a sense of unease gnawed at her. She couldn't shake the feeling that she had forgotten something crucial. A man stepped in front of her, interrupting her thoughts and blocking her path.

"Can I help you with something?" the guard asked, his tone more stern than hostile.

"We seem to keep running into each other, don't we?" Trace said.

She turned, finding him behind her. His presence was immediately welcome. The corners of his eyes crinkled. Palisade managed a small smile. "I don't mind, but don't you need to rest before your shift?"

"Not if it means I keep running into beautiful ladies. They're a rarity here."

"Trace," she whispered, feeling wretched for having to play on his affections toward her.

"You can't blame a man for trying," Trace shrugged.

Her gaze fell to his hip, where keys dangled from his belt. Now might be her best chance. "Actually, I can't. I hate to ask, but I was hoping you might help me."

"Everything alright?" Trace asked.

In front of her, the guard remained silent, the glow of his wolf spirit shining through his eyes. Palisade assessed the guard. She couldn't afford to let him interfere with her plans. She needed to neutralize him peacefully, should he interfere with her mission? "I'd like to see Scout Jameson. The one who calls himself Gorak. It's been several days since I wasn't feeling well, and I need to check in with him. I want to make sure I can complete my report and fulfill my duty here."

Trace hesitated, his brow furrowed. "I'm not sure that's a good idea. Vasumen's orders were pretty clear. He doesn't want you to go down there. I would have to agree. It's not really a place for a lady to venture down through the levels to reach his cell."

"I'm not as fragile as I look. I won't break, and I'm much better since my last visit, I assure you." She resisted touching her forehead with the memory of the awful headache that had launched her into Alpha Vasumen's bed for days. "I promise. If I feel afraid or see any signs of a headache, we can turn back."

Trace glanced at the other guard, who shrugged. "You could check with Alpha Vasumen. He said she could go down, but not alone." The man rubbed the scar on his chin, regarding her.

Palisade's heart raced. This was it. If she could get to Scout, she might figure out how to help the ohunko escape. Too many factors worked against her, starting with the fortress walls embedded with dragon fire and magic to keep the shifter's animal spirits from taking form. *One entrance in...one entrance out.*

"I suppose I can take you down," Trace said.

"Just keep an eye on her," the other guard said gruffly.

Palisade resisted narrowing her eyes at the older guard. Streaks of gray filtered through his dark hair, but he assessed her like a common criminal. She almost snorted, but covered it with a cough. Trace frowned. She placed a hand on his arm. A small part of her wished Alpha Vasumen watched them. If the alpha saw her and Trace together, perhaps his dragon might give him a push to consider her more than a ward. A shiver of excitement raced through her. Her heart fluttered at remembering he claimed she calmed his dragon by staying in his room, but the thought of another man thinking she belonged to them lit a different fire inside her.

Thoughts of gaining his favor wove deep inside her, and she broke the threads, swearing to never pine her hopes on someone wanting her for more than knowledge and skills.

However, manipulating Trace made her no better than her Fae benefactor. She understood all too well what it meant to have someone see you as a tool rather than a person. Palisade was aware Trace had grown fond of her, but her life depended on the outcome of her task.

The guard raised a brow. Trace gave the guard a punch in the arm. "Keep your post, Jax. Let the alpha know where she is when he comes looking."

Palisade bristled at his remark, but took it for a win. He led her to the door, pulling out his keys and unlocking the bars to give her access to the stone stairs leading down into the many levels of the dungeons lined with cells below.

As they passed the hall leading down to the stairs of the dungeon, Palisade bit the inside of her lip in thought. Alpha Vasumen would insist on accompanying her if she directly made the request to him. She needed to see Scout alone, and because that would not happen, hopefully Trace would give her some space when she got down to Scout's cell to communicate with the ohunko.

She needed to act now before her illness returned or someone tried to prevent her.

"Are you sure you want to be going down to see him now?" Trace asked, tense as he walked her further down toward the cells.

Palisade licked her lips and said, "I don't want him to think I have abandoned him." She placed her hand on his arm. "If you were a young man struggling with Scout's issues, wouldn't you want to know someone still cared for you?" And if she didn't need to press it further, she said, "We're friends, right? I am probably the only friend he feels he has right now."

Trace's brow furrowed. "Scout is more dangerous than our other prisoners. He's human with a guardian spirit living inside him. The spirit has overtaken his soul. The man doesn't exist anymore. His mind is gone."

"Are you sure? Sometimes one's mind can be restored."

"Not in this case. The *ohunko* across from him is proof. You should ask Alpha Vasumen about the other prisoner down there."

"I'd rather you told me." A dangerous warmth spread through her at the thought of once more going near Alpha Vasumen. She had to be careful. Every word, every gesture, could potentially expose her true intentions. Alpha Vasumen had a way of making her tongue want to slip and clouding her judgement.

Trace's shoulders sagged slightly. "It's a tragic story, but the human understood the consequences of his choice. He wanted to protect others, and I find that admirable."

"How so?" Palisade asked, curious.

"Wasting illness. It's like a drug addict going through withdrawal, except it kills you in the end. Without a spirit, the body craves power, and without the hit of power to tap into, the body shuts down and wastes away."

"That sounds horrible." Palisade shuddered. She'd never heard of such a thing. It was a cruel fate, a slow, agonizing death. She pitied those afflicted with the wasting illness. To lose one's spirit, to become a mere shell of a person, was a terrible fate indeed.

She imagined herself weakening day by day until there was nothing left but an empty husk. How much time did she have before the illness took its toll? The headaches, the fevers, and the tremors became worse with each episode. Shifters needed a spirit first, didn't they, before getting wasting illness?

"It can be. I can't say he didn't deserve it. Until recently, we've kept humans off the mountain and reduced the threat of spirit hunters. They prey on our people to steal our heritage. I'd say your Scout Jameson does not differ from this man, but Peter knew his life was ending. There's no cure for wasting illness. So he took the wolf *ohunko*, Asigwani, into him and allowed it to fill his soul. Peter was the brother of Taran's mate, Gwen.

Perhaps that is what you want to believe, but I've seen him. The man is still there, and while he is, don't you think he deserves to know he's not alone in his suffering and has a right to find peace in this situation? He has a mother who worries about him, Trace. Does your mother worry about you?"

She moved closer, gazing into his eyes and frowning.

Trace huffed. "Five minutes, no more."

She jumped up on her tiptoes and kissed his cheek. "Thank you!"

Trace peeled her off gently. He avoided her eyes again, and she noticed his face was redder than she'd seen him before. Angry or embarrassed, she couldn't be sure. Did he know she wasn't being sincere? Did his wolf spirit sense her emotions?

She swallowed hard, trying to maintain her composure as she searched his expression for any sign of his true feelings. His gaze fixed somewhere ahead, and she couldn't shake the worry that he knew what she was up to.

Palisade followed him further into the dungeon. As they walked down the aisle, Trace hunched. Tiny hairs on her arms rose as she glanced at both sides of the cells. Inside one, a man wearing nothing but shorts peered out. His eyes followed her. An uncomfortable sensation entwined around her spine the further they went.

A few men called out, their voices echoing through the stone corridor. Some growled, their animalistic instincts taking over. Trace growled back, his eyes glinting with a deep shade of dark metal. A prisoner flinched and glared back. Those in cells stared boldly at them, not like when she'd come with Alpha Vasumen. The prisoners slunk back further away as she passed with the alpha. With Trace, they made their presence known.

Her fingers itched for the invisible weapons she had to leave back at The Manor, in her old room.

Trace held out his hand to hold her back. "Stop," he commanded, his voice low and menacing.

She stilled. Her muscles tensed at his command, and adrenaline flooded her veins.

Trace raised his chin and inhaled, his nostrils flaring.

"What's wrong?"

Trace gave her a nudge; his gaze directed ahead of them. "Back up now." He kept his body in front of her, shielding her from the unseen threat. She forced herself to move slowly, at a disadvantage from his keen shifter senses.

"Trace?" She tried to push him out of the way to see, but he held her firmly in place.

"Turn around and run straight to the stairs, and don't stop until you're back in your room."

Ahead of him, something dark moved at a speed that blurred it. It darted away from them, and Palisade sucked in a breath. What was he doing here?

Trace didn't take the time to strip out of his clothes. His body contorted, his muscles rippling and shifting. A primal energy pulsed through him. She'd witnessed this before when Alpha Vasumen shifted from dragon to man. But this time, it was different.

She swung her leg out. The movement was instinctual, a reflex that she couldn't control. She watched in disbelief as her foot connected with Trace's leg, sending him crashing to the ground. A surge of guilt washed over her. She didn't want to hurt him, but her body seemed to have a mind of its own.

He hit the floor with a grunt, and his eyes glinted darkly, a snarl ripping from his lips. He lunged at her. His claws extended from his fingers. Palisade instinctively raised her arm to block the attack, but her body betrayed her. She kicked out, her foot landing against his head. He stumbled backward. His eyes filled with a mixture of surprise and anger.

"I'm sorry," she cried. She didn't want to fight him, but something within her was taking control, something dark twisting in her mind's eye.

She gritted her teeth against the invasion. Her body became like a puppet with an invisible master pulling the strings.

Trace lunged at her again, his movements quick. She tried to defend herself, but he was too strong. Too fast. He pinned her to the ground, his weight pressing down on her. "You don't want to fight me."

Palisade's heart pounded in her chest as she struggled against Trace's grip. "I don't have a choice."

She wrapped her legs around his waist, her fingers digging into his flesh. He snarled in response. Fur sprouted down his arms, his wolf emerging. Her hand clasped his neck tighter, and his eyes rolled back a minute later. His large body went limp. He collapsed on top of her.

For a moment, she lay there, breathless and terrified. She almost killed him. The thought filled her with horror.

A form in the shadows pulled him away.

"Diaden." One of the men she'd lived with at The Manor became visible. Those narrow eyes and sharp, angled cheekbones made her stomach roll.

Palisade reached to Trace's belt and unhooked the keys. "How did you get in here?"

His white teeth flashed in the dim shadows of the dungeon. "I followed you."

He snatched the keys, but Palisade held onto them. His facial features hardened in the dim light. "Let go, Sade."

Her hand released the keys abruptly. He was the only one who ever called her that. "You're compelling me."

"Should have paid more attention to Yarron's lessons." He moved fast for a half-blood Fae.

She glanced back at Trace. He lay unconscious, his body sprawled out on the cold, hard floor. This is no time to feel guilty. If Diaden released Scout and took the credit, she could say goodbye to the cure she needed.

Palisade rushed after him, her pulse thrumming with adrenaline. She subdued Trace, but more guards would come.

"Did Yarron send you?" She had no idea what had happened outside, no idea if anyone had seen what she had done. Now, she stood trapped in this labyrinthine fortress with no clear escape path. For all she discovered, there was one way in and one way out.

"Wait!" she hissed at him. "Trace may have already alerted the others." Wolf shifters communicated through a mental link with their pack.

Diaden ignored her, his eyes fixed on the prize.

She sprinted to keep up, her boots and heels clicking against the stone.

Diaden tossed a set of keys to another, shorter Fae male, Bolt. The door lock clicked, and they descended another layer, disappearing into the darkness. A sense of dread washed over her. A voice in the back of her head whispered to abort.

"This isn't a competition, Diaden," she whispered viciously. She rushed down the stairs, stumbling in the flickering firelight on the walls. At the bottom of the stairs, Diaden paused long enough to draw more shadows around him and Bolt. "Do you still have the crystal Yarron gave you?"

"Of course," she said, pulling her shoulders back.

Tilting his head down, his eyes glowed gold, and he whispered the words to activate the crystal's magic. Her shoulders tensed, but nothing happened. Maybe it was too far away in the North Tower to open the portal to Yarron's estate. Trace wasn't kidding when he said this place was protected and magic didn't work inside the fortress.

"You're too slow," Diaden said, his voice dripping with arrogance. "Yarron sent us to ensure the mission didn't fail. Thanks for the keys."

Up ahead, Bolt jiggled the keys. His stoic expression said Diaden dragged him along.

Palisade couldn't help rolling her eyes. Typical Diaden. She knew he followed her, hoping to steal the glory of accomplishing this mission to gain more favor with Yarron. But this time, the reward belonged to her.

"This wasn't Yarron's doing. It was yours," she retorted. "Couldn't stand his sending me, could you?"

Diaden's expression turned sour. He hated when she challenged him, especially since she was human. He should have learned by now not to underestimate her.

Bolt stood awkwardly to the side. She ignored any sympathy for him. He'd always been a pawn in Diaden's games. Too inexperienced for other assignments. Diaden chose him for this kind of work.

As they approached Scout's cell, the air grew tense. Scout walked forward. He tilted his head. A lock of hair fell over one of his eyes. A deep rumble came from his chest, and Palisade tried to ignore how the guardian shifter stared at her, almost hungry.

He looked at her with wilderness in his gaze, glowing with each passing second. She forced herself to remain calm. But deep down, the beast within the man terrified her. That look made her blood turn cold. The glint of lust she recognized chilled her to the bone.

Backing away, forcing her gaze toward Diaden. Without enough time to form a plan, she was at his mercy. She doubted she'd get as much from Alpha Vasumen.

"No, Sade. You wanted your cure, and now you're going to get it." Diaden's eyes flashed, but he looked away before she caught the emotion in them.

"Then why are you here?"

"To ensure you get it."

Her job was to release the guardian to finish the mission of the guardians the Fae compelled them with long ago. Having met Trinity, Palisade didn't want the woman dead. She seemed kind. No one had ever apologized to her before like Trinity, for fear of invading her privacy. Trinity had given her a gift with that vision. Something that gave her a hint of her past and her future, a future she desperately wanted. The man said she'd be the first female. To do what?

The cell door swung open, and Palisade stumbled backward as Bolt shoved her forward. She twisted away, her back hitting stone close to another barred cell door. The air became thicker, warmer around her.

Scout Jameson, aka Gorak, walked out of the cell. His eyes appeared blacker than the shadows; his gaze remained fixed on her with a wicked grin.

Frozen in place by the sheer terror racing through her system, she watched as Scout turned his gaze toward the door.

"There's no way out," she told them, her voice trembling.

"For you, but for those of us with the right blood, we can walk through shadows." Diaden tilted his head toward the man. "Too bad, you're human."

A growl vibrated through the darkness. It slammed into Diaden, and the Fae disappeared into nothing more than air. She gasped as Scout grabbed her and yanked her off her feet. "MINE."

Shouts came from the top of the stairs.

"Consider her a gift from the queen. Now take her so we can go. I have no wish to encounter the dragon," Bolt said.

Gorak shook his head. "You have the keys? Release me."

"The fortress is protected. Your gifts shouldn't work here." Palisade glanced down the narrow hallway and then at Gorak as he presented his hands to Bolt. After several tries of keys, Gorak wrenched them from Bolt and tossed them inside the cell. "You're useless, Fae. Get these off now, or I'll feed you to the dragon myself."

Palisade's heart thrummed. She heard the pounding of feet followed by the *umph* of a body slamming against the stones. "They're coming."

"I can't call on gifts with these cuffs on," Gorak said, stalking toward Bolt and snarling. Diaden stepped in, his hands grasping the cuffs. "Think of the one who put them on you."

A moment later, Diaden's form reappeared, and he became the image of Aluk. She gasped. "How are you using your gifts?"

"The crystal," Bolt said, leaning to watch as the shadows changed and the alpha stepped into the hallway.

"Halt!" someone shouted.

The cuffs clicked off.

Bolt reached for his waist and pulled out a dagger. He crouched, ready to fight. "Diaden, we need to go. Guardian, possess the girl and get us out of here."

An arm came out and hooked around her waist. Hot breath hit her neck. "Mine."

"Palisade?" Alpha Vasumen's voice rang out as he stepped into the shadows. His eyes blazed red. Behind him, two wolves hunched and growled.

"Does this place go lower?" Diaden asked.

She answered against her will and glowered at Diaden. "I don't know."

"What do you know?" Diaden said harshly.

She was going to die. She knew she was going to die.

"*Wakinyan*! *Bodaway Achak!*" Hot breath followed by teeth grazed her cheek as Scout shouted. "What was yours is now mine, fire spirit. Betrayer!"

"You want the woman." Alpha Vasumen said, his voice dripping with contempt. "Get back in your cell, and she's yours."

His words hit her like a bucket of ice water. Alpha Vasumen didn't blink at sacrificing her to appease Scout. So much for being his ward and responsibility. She hated emotions. Yarron told her not to care. Diaden had been her first mistake, and Alpha Vasumen almost her second.

This is why she would never trust anyone.

"She is already mine." Scout gripped her by the neck. She held his wrist as he tilted her head back. "I have waited over a century for this moment."

"Possess her," Diaden urged. "I don't have enough energy to take you both. You need to merge now."

"No!" Palisade shouted, panic clawing inside her.

"You knew what you signed up for," Diaden said.

Alpha Vasumen walked forward, the wolves nipping from behind. The hallway was too narrow for their big forms to get around him.

Palisade struggled as Diaden dragged her back into the dark mist. "Let me go! This isn't what we agreed!"

"Silence, woman," Diaden commanded, and Palisade could shout no more.

Gorak's voice was harsh in her ear. "It is not your soul I wish to possess, woman. Shall I take you here in front of them? Would you like it if your Alpha watched?"

Palisade shuddered, imagining his intentions. Bile rose in her throat. Frantically, she shook her head. She stared at Alpha Vasumen, but his face remained an angry mask. Her gaze drifted to where they'd left Trace limp and unresponsive in the distance.

There had to be another way. She'd been taught not to take sides. *You take a job. You finish the job. You take your reward.* She didn't know what awaited them, but she knew she needed to do whatever it took to survive and protect the people who'd been kind to her.

"Get on with it, guardian," Diaden murmured, and the cooling air swirled around them. The shadows grew, and the other Fae stepped up to Scout as darkness engulfed them.

Alpha Vasumen roared as he lunged toward them.

She whimpered as the hand tightened around her throat.

"Back off, dragon," Gorak said with an inhuman growl.

Fury radiated from Alpha Vasumen in heat waves. His chest expanded, and the wolves all took several steps back. Both arms around her sprouted fur, and claws cut into her clothing. The bear made a low, grunting sound before it squeezed her. It squeezed her so hard that Palisade couldn't breathe.

An invisible band wrapped around her chest like a lasso, pulled taunt.

Steam came from Alpha Vasumen's nose, and he opened his mouth. Scout turned, trading her for the other Fae male. The fire hit the Bolt.

Diaden grabbed her, swearing in his native language. Pain exploded through her chest—not physical, but worse. Rage. Terror. Grief poured through her. A dragon roared in her head.

"I'm sorry," she tried to scream, but the shadows swallowed her whole.

With her head pounding and nausea swelling her throat, Palisade rolled over and threw up.

The last thing she remembered was the dragon roaring in her head, and the tug of the invisible rope trying to hold on to her with nothing but will.

It hadn't been enough.

She opened her eyes at the sound of birds chirping. She shivered, her body trembling uncontrollably.

Diaden held his head and shook it before getting to his feet.

Palisade tried to take a few deep breaths. Beneath her palms, moss pressed against her flesh, and trees reached for the sky all around her. Sunlight filtered between the limbs, dancing across fallen branches and large rocks.

Not far from her, a dark shadow curled out from around a tree. The shadow resembled a giant bear, which stood on its hind legs.

Scrambling to put more distance between it and herself, Palisade's back hit a tree.

Diaden approached her side cautiously. "Here is your body, guardian. Take her. What are you waiting for? Without a warrior to aid you in your quest, your task is incomplete."

Palisade slid up the tree, keeping her back pressed to it. "There's no magic inside the fortress walls. The crystal Yarron gave me was a beacon."

"Correct." Diaden looked at her, a deep scowl on his face. She held on to the tree to steady her legs. One hand pressed to her stomach.

"The cuffs keep the shifters from taking their animal forms, but those invited inside may use their magic without the cuffs, and a guardian without his cuffs can pull back into the ether of shadows like I can. The crystal was a beacon, but it gave my gifts a boost to portal out. Our guardian friend is more powerful than anticipated."

Palisade glanced at the bear's shadow. Its eyes gleamed as it fell to all fours and approached them. "A shadow spirit can teleport."

"Listen and you learn," Diaden quoted their master Yarron. A good spy always listened and learned as much as possible. "While you lie in the alpha's bed, some of us gathered the needed information."

"I can't control when the illness hits." She grimaced as the bear shadow wavered in the light and moved back into the patch of shadows closest to her. Her entire body quaked with the guardian's shadow spirit lurking near her. "Yarron promised me a cure. This isn't a cure."

"Your time is running out, Sade. Yarron knew it and has been keeping you alive for this moment. We need to hasten. The guardian disappears, and you break your deal with Yarron. You won't live much longer, not without the gift of the guardian's spirit to fill your soul." Diaden's expression softened, a flicker of something akin to regret crossing his features. Quickly, his cold, calculating mask slid back in place.

"Yarron promised me the final vial of antidote; it will give me more time. " Palisade approached him, staring him eye to eye.

"You mean the vial that allows any Fae to compel you?" Diaden grinned. "You're too gullible, Sade. You never would have made it this far without my watching your back. The Fae has many gifts and medicines, but what ails you is fate, and that can't be reversed. Call the guardian, invite it into your soul."

"No." A wave of despair washed over her.

Diaden's eyes softened, and her lungs closed.

"The guardian possesses me and takes my soul, and I die just like the man's body left behind in the prison. Only those of the same blood can merge and become one. It was all a lie to get me to comply," she choked, anger burning in her lungs.

"Would you rather I compelled you? Invite the guardian spirit inside you, Sade."

All these years she had worked to appease her benefactor. She trained. She went to school. She survived. Any dreams or hopes she once held in her youth, she gave up on when her illness shattered her visions of the future. She turned away, tired of fighting, tired of the constant struggle for survival.

The bear growled, standing again on its hind legs. Diaden laughed. "I think it decided to claim you. Have her, guardian. She's all yours."

A second later, the giant bear leaped toward her, and she froze. The shadow passed around her and slammed into Diaden. His eyes widened, and screaming, he gripped his chest like he was having a heart attack. Palisade stepped further and further away. Diaden gasped, and then his eyes turned black. "If you run, *Wiyoyá*, my chosen one, I will catch you."

Twelve

Aluk roared, his vision turning fiery red. At his feet, Scout's dead body lay. "Goark!" he bellowed, his voice echoing through the fortress.

His dragon spirit surged within him, trying to take control. The spirit within him sensed Palisade was missing. Her scent lingered faint within the vortex of the guardian's shadow mist. Not far from Scout's body, the crisp remains of a Fae male soiled his prison.

The dragon raged from within. It clawed at his mind, its thoughts and emotions seeping into his consciousness. His dragon's longing burned in his heart.

An image of Palisade flashed through his mind, her face etched with fear and desperation. The dragon's instincts took over. His arms rippled with scales. The battle with his dragon spirit intensified. Its power grew stronger, filling his veins. His tattoo against his heart burned as he roared, fighting back.

The wolf shifter guards backed away from him.

He strained against the creature's relentless assault. For decades, he fought it and tried to hold it at bay, but in the end, Aluk's human body was no match. The dragon spirit took control. Aluk's body shuddered, his muscles tensing as the alpha dragon surged from his soul. His eyes stung as Aluk fell back into the cage of darkness of his mind and the dragon won, taking over his human form.

Wobanaki Oska, the alpha of the mountain, leader of dragons, and the first to merge into this world, filled his lungs with air and rolled back his shoulders.

"Alpha," Pinto, Aluk's second in command of the fortress, approached him with caution. "They couldn't have teleported out of the fortress."

Oska blinked, letting his eyes adjust and his senses accumulate to this new human form. Thoughtfully, staring at the empty cell, he said, "A normal blood, no, but a guardian's blood is stronger. They come directly from the Great Hunter. Gorak is gone, and he has my *Wíyoyá*. He could not have teleported far."

Pinto's eyes opened wider, his wolf spirit glowing for a flash before retreating. He cleared his throat. "I sent Mateo and Zele to see to Trace. There are men on each floor securing the fortress. Do you want me to send out a search squad or alert the packs in Avalanche Ridge and Sentinel Peak?"

Aluk lay in the darkness, listening to his dragon spirit order his guards and waiting for his chance to push back at the dragon.

"No. I caught him once. I'll do it again."

Pinto lowered his chin and kept his gaze averted. "And the bodies?"

"Wrap them up, make sure the prisoners see them and then deliver them to the border. My brother's mate may inform the authorities where to find them," the dragon commanded. "Let it be known to the hunters and the Unseelie Court that this is our territory."

And with that, Oska turned, and his gaze met the wolf, Asigwani. He tilted his head, holding the wolf guardian's gaze far longer than any should without challenging the alpha.

"*Wakinyan*."

"Guardian," Oska said with a growl. "You have all forgotten your purpose."

"You turned your back on your people." Asigwani crossed his arms. His stare locked with Oska.

The dragon spirit snarled, more scales rippling down over his flesh. "I protected the people."

"You protected yourself!" Asigwani growled, stepping toward Oska. "You think you are the strongest, but you are weak. Why else do you take over your human than merge and give him strength? Soon, you will be the one to live as a shadow and become forgotten."

"Why do you linger here, guardian? What keeps you behind these bars and in that body?"

"*Sylnaros.*"

Oska's breath hitched, his heart pounding with a mix of anger and sorrow. *The one who completes me.* Memories stirred he tried to bury long ago, when their spirits called to each other. A torrent of emotions surged within him, and Aluk rattled the bars in his mind. Oska caught the slip of his control and slapped a padlock on the vault before his human gained access.

"Palisade is my *Wíyoyá.*" He growled. "Where would Gorak take her?"

"Did he?" The wolf guardian smiled sadly. "Are you sure she chooses you?"

Oska curled his lip in disdain. He took off up the hall, shoving the wolf shifter guards against the stone walls and rushing through the forest. His muscles stretched as soon as he reached the top of the north tower, and his body transformed into a dragon. His wings flapped powerfully, powerful gusts of wind sending pebbles and dust swirling around him. He took flight, searching for signs of Goark, bloodlust fueling his movements.

It would be harder to spot the shadow without a body. He tapped into his senses, seeking the guardian spirit's signature through his alpha connection to every living thing on the mountain.

Oska's thoughts went to Palisade as he soared through the sky. The wolf guardian's words echoed in his mind, and a nagging doubt gnawed at him. He flew for hours, scanning the vast expanse of the mountains. Each time, his flight veered closer to his old lair, and the woman trapped within. *She's not our priority. Find Palisade.*

As the sun set, casting long shadows across the land, Oska landed on a rocky outcrop. He gazed out at the vast expanse of the wilderness, his heart heavy with worry. He had to find her; he knew it. His destiny included her, and he would not stop until he brought her home.

Home...

If *Gorak* touched her... the Great Hunter save them all.

"Go," Diaden shouted.

He was buying her time, fighting the bear guardian trying to possess him. Her heart took off in a wild beat way before her legs got the message. In normal circumstances, she didn't stand a chance against the Fae assassin. He was quicker than she was in every way. Weak human. It kept her legs moving down the mountain. They found themselves in the South. The dragon ranger who brought her was smart to take her in many ways and confuse her path.

Behind her, Diaden screamed in agony; he could resist the bear guardian. Couldn't he? But it needed a body to fulfill its duty. She gasped, scrambling down a cropping of rocks and zigzagging through the trees.

Diaden intended to leave her behind. Bolt was the body. An honorable sacrifice for the cause of the Fae. With Bolt gone, Diaden expected it to be her. It should have been her, but the guardian didn't want her. Not in that way. It wanted her. Sweat covered her skin. The pounding of her heart blocked out any other sound. Sliding down a slope on her side, she caught her dress caught against the dead branches of a fallen tree. It clawed at her leg. The burn was not nearly as painful as the landing when a rock jutting out of the ground flipped her in motion. She landed on stomach.

Palisade scrambled to get back on her feet, her heart slamming hard in her chest. The sound of broken branches caused her to freeze. She whirled around. Diaden stood looking down his nose at her. His eyes were black, devoid of any life or emotion. A dark aura surrounded him, a sinister energy that brushed against her skin as she tried to step further away from him.

"Diaden." Sadness rushed forth unexpectedly. He challenged her, yes. Always the one to point out her human weaknesses and drive her to strive to prove him wrong. As much as he irritated her, he didn't deserve to have his light go out this way.

"Your brother in arms has interesting gifts. If not for these strengths, I might rip his soul apart for the thoughts he holds for you."

Whatever that meant, she didn't want to know. Diaden had never seen her as more than competition and weak at best. She pressed a hand to her heart, trying to buy some time. "Did you kill him?"

"Would it sadden you, *Wiyoyá?*" He tilted his head; on the slope of the hill, he towered over her. The shadow stretching behind him didn't match his shape. It was a giant bear.

"I can't say," because she didn't know. Miss him? Maybe like a thorn in one's side. Mourn for him? More than she'd ever admit, especially if any part of him remained to hear her.

"As much as I have enjoyed this chase, *Wakinyan*, the alpha dragon, will be hunting for you. I have waited a long time for this moment to come."

"And what moment is that?" she asked, out of breath and panting. Her hands slid down to her hips, and she bent slightly forward to open her lungs for more air.

"When I take his *Wakina* as mine."

"Me?" She straightened and pointed between the valley of her heaving breasts.

Those dark eyes smoldered.

She tried to keep her voice steady, her tone calm. "Oh no. I'm nothing to him. You mistake me for someone else. I have released you from captivity. Use Diaden's gift and portal us back to The Manor." She needed to find Yarron. Her blood sang with anticipation of confronting him, but her body ached to leave this place. It tugged at her center like a lasso trying to yank her back to a place she didn't know.

She hoped the spirit within Diaden could see reason. Deep down, it was a long shot. Gorak was driven by instinct and his unfulfilled purpose. Like the alpha, he would use her as bait. For a moment she thought she had a chance, but then Gorak's eyes narrowed. "Interesting. You are not what I would have suspected *Wakinyan* to choose for his alpha mate. What ails you, female?"

She ignored his last question. "I'm not the alpha's mate."

"No, *Wíyoyá*. You. Are. Mine."

Before she calculated another attempt to escape him, Gaork rushed her with Diaden's gift of speed. He tossed her over his shoulder and shifted into a giant brown bear.

* * *

Aluk existed within the confinement of his mind. His dragon blocked him from all senses but thought.

He stood in a sun-dappled meadow, the warmth of the summer sun on his face. A gentle breeze rustled through the tall grasses, carrying with it the sweet scent of wildflowers. Before him, Naomi danced, her laughter echoing through the field. She beamed; her smile radiated bright as the sun itself.

Aluk watched her, his heart filled with a bittersweet longing. He remembered this day so vividly that he never wanted it to end. They spent hours in this meadow talking, laughing, and dancing.

Naomi turned to face him, her eyes sparkling with joy. "Do you love me?" she asked in her gentle voice.

Aluk hesitated, his heart pounding in his chest. Her dark hair cascaded over her shoulders. He ran a strand of her silky hair through his fingers. He needed an heir to pass on his dragon spirit, and Naomi had been the perfect choice. She worked at her aunt's clothing shop in the village and dreamed of a large family.

"I do." The words weren't a lie; he came to care about her deeply. But he couldn't give her what she wanted.

She pulled him down onto the blanket and straddled his lap. "Mark me."

"I can't," he admitted, his voice a hoarse whisper. They fought about it often.

Naomi's face fell, her smile fading. "You don't love me," she said, trembling.

"I choose you." Aluk's heart ached with profound sadness. Her words only deepened the chasm of frustration within him. He wanted to mark her, to brand her with the emblem of his dragon, binding their souls in an unbreakable bond. But the fire, the searing heat necessary to forge the mark, never came. His dragon spirit lay dormant and unyielding.

"You need an heir." She pulled away, and as much as it pained him, he let her go. Admitting the truth would only make things worse.

"I need you." The weight of his failure pressed heavily upon him. He saw the longing in her eyes, the desperate hope for him to fulfill the rite of mates, hurt him more than she could know. She deserved to be honored as his mate, yet he was powerless against the spirit within him.

Tears welled up in Naomi's eyes. She leaned in, kissed him ever so softly on his cheek, and slid off his lap.

"Naomi."

"She's waiting for you," Naomi said, vanishing.

Aluk remained alone in the meadow. The sun set, casting long shadows across the field. A silhouette of a dragon spied on him. He stood staring back at it for a long time.

"You took her from me."

The darkness closed in around him.

Find her.

Thirteen

Gorak burst from the forest, his powerful legs carrying Palisade through the undergrowth. She clung to his back, her fingers digging into his fur, her heart pounding in her chest. The wind whipped through her hair, and the scent of pine needles filled her nostrils.

As they came to the edge of a clearing, Palisade's heart slowed. An array of elegant tents that seemed to shimmer under the rays of sunlight, each adorned with intricate designs of the Unseelie court's crest, comprised the camp they set up there. The air thickened as they approached. An otherworldly aura surrounded them. A faint glow emanated from the runes etched into the ground around the camp's perimeter. She learned long ago to recognize the rough scrapes in the earth and the fallen pattern of rocks and twigs.

The distinct scent of enchanted herbs wafted through the air as they crossed the runes. A circle of armed Fae warriors closed in on them. Her gaze shifted to the men and women standing tall and poised. Their hands on their weapons, ready to pull when necessary. She recognized their dark green leather pants, brown boots, and matching earthen-toned shirts. Unless this was a gathering of sorts, Gorak ran them straight into a Fae training camp.

Anger flared, and fear flooded her system. By the black symbol of a moon wrapped with thorns, she concluded they'd come from the

Unseelie side of the realm. These weren't all soldiers from The Manor, these were court soldiers from the sovereign's army.

Diaden never lied. Fae don't lie, but they manipulate, and here she was, enraged in a war she wanted no part of, being used as a tool in their grand scheme. The awe of entering one of their camps vanished with the cruel reminder of her role in coming here. Every tent, every pointed-ear warrior, only underscored how deeply enmeshed she was in their plans.

Suddenly, the warriors drew their weapons, stalking towards them, narrowing the circle. Palisade's fingers dug into the Gorak's fur. Her eyes met those of her benefactor.

"Stop!" Yarron commanded, stepping into view. His short blonde hair appeared bleached in the rays of sunlight. Dressed like the others, he lifted his chin and held his stance, blocking Gorak from passing through the camp.

Betrayal soured the taste in her mouth. She knew better than to trust him. Trust anyone. Yet, in all the years he trained her, raised her, she believed in him, and he'd used her. She admired him, striving to please him to stay alive. She knew better and should have heeded his warning–trust no one. He meant himself.

Gorak slowed, waved its head, and then stopped. Power radiated from Yarron, and she clutched the bear's fur tighter. Gorak grunted, but she held on, trying to decide if it was better to dismount or stick with her kidnapper. Although to be fair, she'd been the one to help him escape.

"Sade," Yarron held his hand up to show the power radiating from his palms. He used her nickname, and for once, it made her uneasy to hear him say it. She had seen the dark side of his ambition, the lengths he would go, including letting her die. Did he think she would trust him now?

"Dismount and join me," he said, more an order than a request.

A chill ran down her spine. Her best bet lies with the ohunko.

"And our deal?" she asked, unable to forget Diaden's revelation. Would he compel her to if she refused him? She frowned, not wanting to turn into their puppet again. The ache in her muscles and the pull on her energy protested against the idea.

"I have your payment as discussed." Yarron beckoned her with a flick of his fingers.

Gorak went down on his front legs as she slid off him. Palisade stumbled as Gorak unceremoniously dumped her onto the cold, hard ground. The air changed as Gorak shifted from a bear to a human. An arm came around her waist, hoisting her up and pulling her against him. "This female is mine."

Glancing at the ohunko face, Diaden's face, sent a mixture of fear and disgust washing over her.

She belonged to no one. Those dark, empty eyes of the man holding her reminded her how fragile and short life could be. Trapped, whether in the ohunko's arms, Yarron's deception, or the Alpha's prison, she'd die soon. Unable to control when death took her, she had the choice of where or with whom she perished.

Since escaping the prison, she hated failing to see the truth of Yarron's intentions. The Fae and the shifters lived years beyond humans. Yarron molded her and waited. She learned to mess with people's minds, read their body language and strike at the optimal time.

Even if she got away from Yarron again, Alpha Vasumen and Gorak would hunt her. Palisade's heart burned with the thought. It should be the alpha's arms around her instead of the tainted guardian inside Diaden. Her heart ached more for her rival and brother at The Manor. He'd been her first kiss and hated her after. He told her to take what she wanted, and she'd stolen a kiss. Their brothers training alongside them laughed, but Diaden's mood darkened that day towards her.

Yarron stared at the man behind her, his nostrils flaring. He had to sense Diaden was gone. All regrets aside, she prayed to the Great Hunter to help protect and keep Diaden alive. Despite their differences, freeing him from the ohunko might help keep Trinity alive. The Fae couldn't touch her. They needed a guardian to fulfill the rite. Diaden's gift included portals. All she needed was to get him across the gates into the Fae realm first.

Trinity had been kind to her. Conleth, her mate, helped Palisade and to keep her alive through one of her episodes. She intended to return the favor, and in doing so, sabotage Yarron for deceiving her.

She smiled. A terrible nervous habit the master trainer punished her for often during her years of training with him. "Diaden. Where is Bolt?"

"Dead," Palisade answered when Goark stuck his face into her hair and inhaled deeply. She never took her eyes off Yarron. "The alpha turned him to ash. My payment?" She forced her legs to remain steady after so many hours of riding on the back of the giant bear. Holding out her hand, she tried to move forward, but Goark growled from behind her.

"What is going on here?" Yarron swept his hand, indicating the Gorak's hold on her. His scowl darkened. From that look, she knew they would be in worse trouble. He warned them long ago not to create relationships within The Manor. To defy Yarron meant exile for Diaden and death for Palisade. In the past she might have trembled, but death awaited her now. And she needed to use what little time he had left to extract her revenge against Yarron.

A small piece of her still cared what Alpha Vasumen thought of her. Dying in the flames of an angry dragon wasn't nearly as appealing as having his arms around her. She shook the thought, Gorak breathing heavily down her neck.

"This isn't Diaden." He had been so full of ambition, so desperate for power. She shuddered to think what would have happened if the guardian had chosen her instead.

Understanding deepened the lines on Yarron's face. He stared for a long moment, the lump in his throat bobbing. She had never seen their benefactor show emotion other than anger. His ageless eyes filled with a moment's grief. It struck her in the heart, another reminder of the lengths Diaden would go. That he tried to give her a head start to gain her freedom.

"You need to let me go." She tried to step out of his hold. The arm around her pulled tighter, cutting off some of her ability to breathe.

"You'll leave the woman here with us," Yarron said, lifting his chin. "Once you fulfill your part of the bargain, guardian, I'll see if she is returned to you."

She caught the glint in his eyes. The curl of his fingers. He was lying. Yarron was a cunning strategist. He had no intention of returning her to Gorak.

"You should give me my payment now so he knows you will keep your word."

Yarron glanced around him as the warriors with him spread out around them in a circle. There were two dozen, some with swords, a few with bows, and all with the markings of the false king on their shoulder.

She felt the weight of their stares, the way their hands hovered near their weapons. Her mind raced. If they attacked now, could she fend them off? Images flooded her imagination: arrows raining down, the sickening thud of blades meeting flesh, and the chaotic whirl of violence from the battle. She forced herself to focus, to steady her breath.

She scanned the circle, calculating the odds. If she could delay them...

The warriors tensed around them.

She could almost hear a voice in her mind, a deep rumble of fury. She steeled herself, her gaze locking onto Yarron. A tug in her gut pulled her away, but Palisade didn't move. The rumble of fury grew loud enough to make her want to wince. Her nails bit into her palms. *He won't win.* Not here. Not while she was still alive to stop him.

"She goes with me," Gorak said, lifting his face from brushing his nose against her neck. His hot breath made her want to cringe. She didn't belong in this world or in the Fae's dangerous game to maintain their power. There was no way she intended to go with him. She had a better chance of survival away from him.

Leaving and going further away from Alpha Vasumen felt wrong. She longed for the safety and security of his tower. She missed his grumpy expression and the smell of his sheets while she occupied his bed. Her heartache increased.

There was no place for her in this world. She belonged in the human world, where she could live a normal life for as long as she had breath. How long could she feign compliance, biding her time until she found an opportunity to slip away? The thought of playing along with Yarron's scheme made her skin crawl, but it might be her best chance. How long until her illness made her immobile again?

Fourteen

A quick survey of the warriors' faces showed no signs of an ally amongst them. What she needed was a diversion–something big enough to cause chaos and give her a chance to flee. The thought of being caught and facing either Yarron's wrath or Alpha Vasumen was almost paralyzing. Her gut told her to chance it with Alpha Vasumen, and she hated that her heart agreed.

Yarron approached Gorak. His eyes fixed on the bear shifter with respect and reasonable suspicion. "You want to put your female in danger?" Yarron asked.

Palisade bristled at the mention of 'your female.' His female? She opened her mouth to protest, then realized that as long as Yarron thought she belonged to Gorak, it might gain her some time to find a way to escape them both.

Gorak growled, and the tension grew within the circle.

Her heart raced with anger, wanting to challenge Yarron, but she didn't want to encourage anymore displays of dominance from Gorak.

"There is no cure for the taint of your blood. You should be grateful I've kept you alive all this time," Yarron said, his voice deepening with agitation. With Gorak between them, her benefactor would not be wise to lash out at her. She tensed just the same in anticipation of the invisible strike. Knowing all this time Yarron used her and never cared about her struck a chord inside her. How many times had she done that to others to accomplish her tasks, and with what outcome? It hadn't been worth it. Trace treated her with more respect than most men in her life, and she'd betrayed his trust. He would not have believed her if she had said she was compelled.

She patted his arm. "It's okay. I can stay with them until you're finished with your errand."

Or until she got the opportunity to escape them. She'd met Trinity for only hours, but the wrongness of taking her life radiated deep inside her. Running was no longer an option. Yarron and the sovereign king of the Unseelie couldn't seal the curse if they couldn't complete the spell used so very long ago.

Her head throbbed at the thought. "There was never an antidote, was there?"

She knew Yarron heard her. His eyes narrowed, but his lips pressed tight. Rather than lie, he said nothing. A fresh cut sliced into her already bruised heart.

As the Fae warriors tightened their circle around them, Palisade took in each warrior, stance, and chosen weapon. Yarron reached for the pouch on his belt, and Gorak thrust her behind him. Confusion mingled with the defiance in her heart. *Does he think he can use me as leverage?*

She slammed up against the very bare backside of Diaden's human form, possessed by one of the ancient guardian shifters, an *ohunko*. The shock of contact sent a surge of adrenaline through her.

The distinction blurred in her mind between the man she grew up training with and the guardian spirit possessing Diaden's body. The heat of his skin, the solidity of his form only blocked her physically from Yarron and the others. Disappointment hit her in an unexpected swoop of her stomach that the man standing between her and a swarm of Fae warriors wasn't Alpha Vasumen.

"Diaden?" Yarron asked.

Fear, confusion, and an unexplainable pang of longing for the dragon alpha's presence churned within her. She wanted to escape while Gorak distracted Yarron, but she knew running now would be suicide. Too many Fae warriors surrounded them, and they moved faster than her human limitations. They would catch her before she took ten steps.

"Only Gorak."

Gorak's presence, solid and imposing, kept the warriors at bay for now. His temporary buffer might be her only chance to wait for a better opportunity. Yarron still saw her as useful, at least he thought her good leverage to control the guardian. She had been under his roof and command for enough time to understand a little of the way he strategized.

"Diaden's soul remains intact?"

There must have been something there to make Yarron question the man holding her against him. In her mind, she understood Diaden was no longer with them. It grieved her and peeved her at the same time. How could he have been so stupid? How could she?

Gorak lifted his chin. "There is no Diaden. Only Gorak."

Palisade's resolve hardened. What little help Diaden offered her vanished with his soul. Her hope plummeted for his sake. Playing along was the only option to keep her alive now. For however long fate graced her before her illness swept her away forever this time. She knew how to bide her time, and strike when least expected.

Yarron held up a vial. "Your female need this, guardian. Without it, she dies. Go complete your end of the bargain, and I'll see she is well when you return."

"Is it the antidote or just another potion to keep me under your command?" she asked, trying to step to the side around Gorak.

He growled and glanced over at her. Keeping himself in the position to glance at her and watch the others. "What have you done to her?"

"I have done nothing. You should thank me for keeping her alive," Yarron said.

"Will that cure me?"

Yarron lifted a brow like he did when she spoke out of turn during training sessions. Instinctively, she stepped back and stopped herself from retreating.

"This is the only thing that will keep her alive. Her fate is in your hands." Yarron wiggled the vial.

"Or control me," she spat. "I don't want your compulsion juice. You promised me a cure."

"There is no cure for the taint of your blood," Yarron said, his words laced with bitter truth. "You should be grateful I've kept you alive all this time."

His accusation of a taint in her blood cut deep. She needed the vial of serum. The potion was the only thing that could keep her alive long enough to protect Trinity and thwart the Fae's plans. Without it, her chances of surviving more than a month were slim.

Her gaze flickered to Gorak. He stood between her and Yarron. Her benefactor would not be wise to lash out at her. She tensed just the same in anticipation of the invisible strike.

"He speaks the truth." It wasn't a question. Even Gorak recognized Fae couldn't lie. "You are dying?"

A lump formed in her throat, making it hard to speak. She nodded.

Gorak's gaze seemed to bore straight through her. His eyes narrowed, and she bit her lip while keeping her eyes trained on the Fae warriors and Yarron. She tilted her head, listening for any attempts to approach her from behind. Gorak's mouth slanted in a sly smile, one Diaden used when he knew something she didn't. Her heart sank a little further. It never ended up with anything good for her.

"What do you think I am going to do?" Gorak asked, a hint of Diaden's accent merging with his voice.

"The sacrifice is not complete. Finish it," Yarron said.

"This is not the bargain I made." Gorak pulled back his shoulders, tightening those back muscles against her cheek. She tried to lean away. "The Wíyoyá is mine."

"You'll do as the queen demands." Yarron said, "Come, Sade. I'll keep her alive, but your time is running out if you wish to enjoy your reward while she lives."

He promised her an antidote. Would she get her chance to stop Yarron and the plot to hurt Trinity if the dragon alpha got to her first?

She might never get the cure to extend her life. Stopping Yarron and keeping Trinity alive mattered more. The Fae needed to learn they couldn't mess with other people's lives. Human, shifter, or otherwise, none of them deserved to become tools for the Fae's greater gain. To break the curse, to have their control over others' lives taken away was worth the price she'd have to pay with her life. Yarron taught her to die with honor, to do everything with purpose and precision.

Whether she liked it or not, she needed that vial. It might keep her alive long enough to help save Trinity and free the mountain residents from the Fae's hold. She shivered, not liking the risk of having Yarron or another Fae use her like a puppet. How much of the vial's liquid could she consume? A lick? A taste? The entire thing? Before the spell sank deeper into her blood and let it take hold of her actions?

Her stomach twisted. Perhaps Diaden wanting to leave her was more merciful than she suspected. Remembering this body belonged to Diaden, Palisade leaned her forehead against his back and whispered to him to stay strong. If one could stay strong, one could stay alive, he'd taught her that much.

Gorak's stance stiffened. "I'll not be betrayed again by your kind, fairy."

Palisade sucked in a breath at the *ohunko's* insult to Yarron and the warriors surrounding them. He growled, fur sprouting along his spine. A shadow swept over them. Her heart lurched. She dared to look up, her breath catching in her throat. The clouds darkened in the form of a dragon sweeping above the tree line. Its wings blocked out the sun.

Alpha Vasumen found them.

Deep inside her, a voice whispered in a language she didn't understand. She steadied her breath. The duality of relief expanding her lungs and dread chilling her bones made her dizzy. What would Yarron do to her if Gorak did not comply?

A roar echoed through the trees. The sound was like thunder, shaking the very foundations of the earth, causing her stomach to flip with anticipation. The Fae warriors fell silent, their eyes wide with fear. Yarron held his hand up to signal for them to stay.

From the shadows, a figure emerged. Alpha Vasumen. Her heart pounded, unable to tear her gaze away from him.

His eyes glowed with an unnatural light, his muscles rippling beneath his skin. The sight shouldn't have excited her as much as it did. There was something about him — an energy surrounding him that felt dark and feral.

"You have no place here on my mountain, Fae, be gone."

"It won't be your mountain for long, dragon," Yarron smirked.

"Leave, or I will send back your ashes for your king to spread across the dark forests of your realm," Alpha Vasumen said with a snarl.

Fifteen

"It will be you who returns to the Great Hunter's forest in disgrace." Gorak continued to block Palisade from going around him. She glared at the guardian, those emerald green eyes sharp enough to cut down the largest of men. Protectiveness swelled, and Oska growled. His nostrils flared as fire ignited in his core. "I'm not the one who betrayed my people."

He circled around the guardian, ensuring his female remained unharmed. *She's not ours to claim, dragon. Capture the ohunko.* Aluk said in his mind.

Are you even too weak to feel the bond of our chosen? He should have heeded my warning the first time.

Inside the cage, he placed the human; confusion filled him. He growled at the distraction.

Gorak turned with him, continuing to block his female from his view. His human pressed against the cage of his mind, but Oska enforced the cage. Aluk, the man, failed to prove a strong enough leader. Oska moved slowly, assessing the guardian who turned on their people and the Great Hunter's blessing." You'll see the Great Hunter before I will."

In this body, the Fae abilities of the guardian posed a greater challenge. The primal instincts within him surged. Fury ignited in his chest. "Release the woman."

Gorak lunged, leaving his female open. The ohunko's claws extended, aiming for Oska. The dragon alpha moved to dodge the attack. A spark of anger lit within him as the sting of the guardian's claws tore his shirt and scraped across his human skin.

Palisade sucked in a quick breath and stumbled back.

"No one touches my *Wiyoyá*!" He reached for her, not taking his eyes from Gorak. A Fae warrior with short hair and the fading light of age in his eyes tried to help steady her.

"By the trees. It's safer there," he urged.

Oska growled as the warrior touched her. She was *his*, and no one else should touch her. He gritted his teeth; a muscle in his jaw ticked. He allowed the seasoned warrior to lead her away, but kept his gaze locked on Gorak. He would deal with the warrior later. He would deal with them all!

Inside his mind, a sense of relief allowed his muscles to relax. The human, Aluk, eased in his attempts to escape his mind cage. Gorak's eyes glinted with menace. His attention was half on Oska's female.

As Palisade disappeared behind the large oak tree, the air crackled with tension.

Several of the Fae warriors, their swords and bows at the ready, formed a defensive line around the older Fae and Palisade. Their wary gazes fixed on Oska. He fought his instinct to shift. With one fluid movement of his tail or breath of fire, they would go down. To shift was to risk weakening his human's cage in his mind until he had time to accumulate to taking both forms. Instead, he grunted, allowing his human muscles to ripple, and his scales to prickle over his arms and shield his neck and shoulders.

He and Goark circled each other. With a roar, Goark charged, his claws outstretched. Oska met the attack with a counterstrike, willing his talons to extend from his human fingers. Their bodies collided.

Goark's claws raked across Oska's human chest, leaving deep, bleeding wounds. Shock rippled along with the pain. His human skin sliced open with the ease of sliding a knife through butter. Oska snarled. His human's mind laced with the brunt of the pain. Fire licked up his throat.

Fight like a human or shift.

Oska grunted. This body is too weak and vulnerable without the protection of his dragon scales. The wound in his abdomen refused to seal. Gorak danced around him, claws ready for another swipe. Until now, Oska had been playing with the *ohunko*, but the wounds of his flesh enraged him. Gorak's form surged, a blur of movement, aiming for Oska's throat.

With a swift motion, Oska delivered a powerful kick to Gorak's gut, sending him reeling back. Gorak roared, his eyes filled with feral intensity. Oska needed to keep the *ohunko* from shifting. He was upon the guardian in a blink. His weak human flesh screamed as he rained down a flurry of punches on the ohunko's face. Each strike landed more powerfully than the last.

Beneath him, the *ohunko* bucked and twisted, its form shifting and changing. Using quick force, he tossed Oska to the side. Pain shot through his side, and Oska rolled further away before the *ohunko* had time to take another swipe at his vulnerable flesh.

His body grew tired.

We'll bleed to death if you don't end this, his human warned.

Oska slammed the human back further into the recesses of his mind. The human, not Oska, was the weak one. The movement of one of the Fae warriors caught his eye. Panting with exertion, he glanced toward the tree, his sight locked on his female. Her face was pale, her eyes alert, and her body tense. Deep down in the essence of his being, she evoked a feeling long forgotten and stirred a sensation both of longing and bewilderment. But he pushed those feelings aside; lingering on them brought neither him nor his human any good.

His moment of distraction was enough to give Gorak the opportunity to jab his claws and catch Oska off guard. The claws slid through his flesh, between his ribs before Oska kicked the *ohunko* in the upper thigh and punched the guardian beneath the chin. Gorak flew back and landed on his back.

Don't stomp! Aluk shouted in his mind. You're not a dragon. Let me finish him.

Instead, Oska tackled Gorak. Steam poured from his nostrils as the guardian attempted to gain his feet. *You are too weak.*

Oska struck Gorak, knocking the guardian down to his knees. Shaking his head and growling, Gorak rose. Around him, the air constricted, and the *ohunko* shifted back into a bear.

He stood on his hind legs and roared before falling back on his feet and taking off between the Fae. They scattered, their fear turning into a stampede as they fled away from the guardian. Fickle, weak creatures. Oska snarled at them, more smoke than steam releasing through his human nostrils. He inhaled deeply, gathering the fire from his belly, and cursed at the human locked in his mind.

Aluk slammed against the mental cage. *You want fire to burn his ass? Shift! Don't let him escape!*

There is no place he can go that I will not find him. Oska chuckled darkly. Letting the *ohunko* run, he turned his gaze on Fae closest to Palisade. "Release my female, Fae-blood, and take this message to your sovereign. The creatures of the mist shall never again be under the rule of your kind. This mountain is *mine.*"

His gaze landed on Palisade. "And what lies within its heart?"

A rush of memories burned fresh in his mind. Issabrie....

You can't have them both.

He hissed, searing pain flooding through the muscles of his human body and his life soaking into the cloth covering his flesh. He wrapped an arm around his side. Why was it not fusing and healing?

"You have it wrong, dragon. It is my queen who will rule this mountain, and you." The Fae male grabbed Palisade.

A surge of primal rage erupted within Oska. His blood boiled. His muscles tensed. A growl rumbled in his chest. "Don't touch her," he snarled.

The Fae quirked a brow, his fingers curled around Palisade's wrist. A dangerous gleam in the seasoned Fae's light eyes.

Oska's throat burned in response to the frustration pulling at his anger. He lacked the ability to burn the arrogant Fae-blood where he stood. A shudder of fear laced through his female. Her fear wafted strongly through the smoke he released.

You'll burn them both and kill us if you don't shift.

"Your hold on this side of the realm is weakening," Oska frowned, refusing to acknowledge his human's protest in his head.

"You'll know your place once more," the Fae male shot back.

"Yarron," Palisade said, her tone sharp like a bite.

Oska stalked towards the insolent Fae, changing his mind about letting him live. Yarron backed away, tugging at Palisade. About to step in, Oska's pride in his chosen's strength swelled. She twisted out of Yarron's hold. "We made a deal."

Inside him, Aluk leaned against the invisible bars of his mental cage.

"That we did," Yarron grinned. He reached into his pouch and pulled out a vial of blue liquid.

Sixteen

Her heart soared at the sight. It wasn't a liquid cure, but it would buy her more time.

Palisade stepped toward it, her hand outstretched. Yarron tossed the vial. At the same moment, Alpha Vasumen leaped, and she lunged. Their bodies collided.

Palisade cried out.

The vial smashed on the rocky ground.

Her hopes, her grand scheme of redemption, shattered like the vial.

She landed on her knees, picking up a piece of glass. The precious liquid–the key to her prolonged survival–splashed across the unforgiving stone. She pressed her fingers against the wet surface, bringing a touch to her lips.

Alpha Vasumen caught her by the wrist. "You'll cut your tongue."

She flinched, pulling her hand away. His voice was too deep and rough for the man she met in the prison.

"There are worse fates," she whispered, thinking of her imminent death. How much more time would this have bought her? Enough to stop Yarron and keep Trinity alive?

Her heart seized painfully. Regret stretched far before her like a shadow. She avoided looking at the dragon alpha. Something inside her woke and stretched like a dormant muscle at this nearness. She refused to allow her hurt and frustration to escape in the form of tears.

He kneeled down before her, shocking her by taking her hand in his and sniffing the residue of the liquid. She sucked in a breath as sparks danced between their fingertips.

"It's Fae berry and sparkling water. Nothing to cry about."

"How would you know?" she sputtered, trying to hold all the pieces of her crumbling reality together.

His eyes lost the flicker of flames. They blinked, and if she guessed correctly, her dragon alpha appeared in great agony. "I've been around long enough, Wyion, to know the taste. Have you not tried the tea my brother's Fae mate brews?"

He spoke of Trinity.

"I needed that!" she exclaimed, her voice rising. "Do you have any idea what this means!" Fury and frustration burst from her with another hit to her broken reality.

"Fae Berry can speed the healing process and take your pain away for a time. My brother can give you something stronger and more effective than what lies broken here."

Her eyes brimmed with tears. She had no choice but to face the fact that her time would come soon. Sweat broke out across her forehead.

"My female. I'm so sorry I couldn't get here sooner," he said, shocking her. He didn't sound angry with her. He winced as he asked, "Did he..."

For the longest time, she took him in. Her gaze drifted over his face, taking in the dirt and grim, the cuts and bruises that marred his perfect features. Blinking, she said, "No, but I suppose this means you'll lock me away."

Palisade's vision blurred with tears. His concern touched her, but his deeper voice and those dark red eyes still alarmed her. Confused by his actions, she said, "Thank you for coming for me."

He pulled her into his arms, holding her tightly. She felt safe in his embrace, protected from the darkness that surrounded them. And as she listened to the sound of his heartbeat, she knew that no matter what happened, she would fight to ensure those on the mountain remained free from the Fae.

Seventeen

The alpha growled. His female's sweet scent of peaches filled his senses. Under the tears on his shirt, his blood continued to seep from his wounds. A bead of sweat trickled down his temple. He scanned the area, aware that the Fae warriors remained scattered throughout the camp.

"You're unwell," he murmured, his voice barely a whisper. He slipped his arm under her legs and back, trying to lift her. A burning sensation seared across his ribs, and he grunted. Oska staggered, attempting to rise with her. She gasped, her eyes widening in horror. Slipping from his grasp. Her feet hit the ground. Her hands trembling, she touched the gaping wounds.

His *wíyoyá* tried to stem the bleeding. She reached for the hem of her shirt, and he growled. Her gaze flew to meet his. "You will not disrobe in front of all these males."

"You're bleeding!"

"I am a shifter. I will heal." Yet, the mortality of his human body brought him doubts.

Shift, his human shouted in his head.

"You need to shift," she urged, echoing his human in his mind. "You'll heal faster."

But the alpha shook his head. "I'm fine."

"You don't look fine." His skin lightened from its normal bronze hue. The fire in his eyes barely flickered, causing her chest to close in tight.

"We'll rest when we reach my lair." He reached for her again. She glanced around, all too aware of Yarron and his men regrouping. Without his strength, neither of them would escape if he didn't shift soon. The back of her neck prickled with the awareness of the danger surrounding them.

Unable to run off without him. Palisade changed tactics and tried to encourage him. Leaving here without him wasn't a choice. He may hate her later, but she'd die before letting the Fae strip Alpha Vasumen of his dragon. "Will you fly me there?"

He grunted as he leaned heavily on her. "Give me a moment. I need to…"

Palisade grasped him, trying to hold him steady. "Perhaps you should sit for a moment." Although, by the crackling in the air around them, she doubted they had much time. Glancing around, she noticed the waviness in the air in the distance. She bit her lip, needing to make a quick decision. Fae shields kept others from finding their camps. She believed without Fae blood one might go through the enchantment, or she hoped since Gorak ran off. Diaden's Fae blood brought them into this mess, and her alpha dragon couldn't fly.

"He took you from me." She could see the fear in his eyes and reached out to touch him, but he pulled away. The sudden movement caused him to collapse. She went to her knees along with him.

Placing her hand against his cheek, she looked up. Several archers stood close to the trees. Their swords held at sides, tips pointed down, but their eyes trained on Alpha Vasumen.

"Alpha Vasumen. ... Aluk."

"You can call me Alpha or Oska."

"Where is Aluk? Alpha Vasumen?"

"Aluk is too weak."

She'd deal with the dragon and figure out how to recover the man later. Twice today, she'd lost someone to the possession of a spirit animal. Keeping Alpha Aluk alive needed to come first.

Something moved, and Palisade sucked in a breath. "We need to get out of here now." She watched several Fae warriors step out from around the trees. This wasn't part of their mountain forest. The Fae would never build their camp in plain sight. With Diaden's power, Gorak brought them past the invisible shield hiding the camp from others. The alpha came from above. The shield wasn't a dome. Someone wasn't smart enough to consider a dragon flying by, but Palisade swallowed. Yarron came back into view, with a glint in his eye, and the scent of magic in the air.

To take the alpha back as a prize might gain him greater favor with the Queen's brother. The sovereign king might prolong any punishment for their failing to seal the curse again.

That blasted curse and deadly illness doomed her either way. With a shuddering breath, she looked into the alpha's eyes. "Get up. We have to get out of their camp now. Shift. Fly out of here!"

Yarron held out his hands; the glow of his fingertips cinched her gut. In the distance, howls filled the forest. Trace's unconscious form lying in the prison flashed before her eyes.

"Did you send out the pack?" she whispered. The fear that hunted her made her pulse jump. Every howl tightened an invisible noose around her neck.

"The best enforcers," he grunted, color slowly draining from his complexion. Uncertainty gnawed at her, mingling with the dread, creating a volatile storm of emotions she worked hard to keep contained. Seeing his life drain away spiked the terror inside her.

She knew the wolves would not easily forgive or forget. Yarron didn't so much as flinch at the sound of their howls. The shield separated them. Nothing got through without Fae blood. Unless they were a dragon dropping from the sky.

No matter which side of the shield she chose, her fate wouldn't change. It didn't mean she wanted Alpha Vasumen to die. The way he swooped down, defending her against Gorak, had caught her off guard. He protected her, caring for her welfare. But why?

Yarron's men hung back, their eyes flickering to him for a signal. Her benefactor smirked. "You have served your purpose well."

Alpha Vasumen growled, he slipped his hand around her arm. His grip trembled. She glanced down at him. The fleeting fear in his eyes cut deep within her soul. "Shift! You're not healing."

In calming her emotions, she locked eyes with Yarron. She needed time for the wolves to arrive.

"Do you think the guardian will complete his task when he discovers you can't fulfill your end of the bargain?" Her heart raced, each beat a reminder of the time slipping away from them. What could she offer Yarron that would ensure Alpha Colen's safety? The Fae liked to make deals. *Think Palisade!* She also knew Yarron valued ancient artifacts and knowledge. Perhaps the promise of such treasure could stall him.

But would it be enough?

"The guardian will get what he was promised long ago when the task is complete. You will matter little to him. Not like you do to the alpha." Yarron's grin revealed misplaced knowledge.

"I mean nothing to this beast," she snorted. Yet, doubt crept in. The memory of Alpha Vasumen telling her she calmed his beast flitted through her mind. Is that why Gorak chose her and refused to possess her?

"Perhaps if not dead," Yarron said.

"What if I could offer something more valuable?" she asked. The Fae knew how to twist words and manipulate to their advantage. "Something the guardian has long sought."

Yarron's eyes narrowed, curiosity piqued. "And what might that be?"

"A relic from the old Fae wars," she said, trying hard to keep her voice from changing pitch. Any indication she might be lying would set Yarron off. "Hidden away, known only to a few."

Intrigue smoothed out his flawless features. "You think you can bargain with me, girl?"

"I know how you like a good bargain, and don't you always add a memento to your collection of treasures from your greatest coups?"

His eyes glittered with pride she recognized so few of the times. "I always knew you had a strong mind. You've done better than I hoped within your short life span."

"Do you want to hear my deal or not?" Warning bells rang in her mind. She had to ensure she left no loopholes for Yarron to exploit. Where were the wolves? Why hadn't they howled again?

One wrong word, wrong move, and she could bring doom for both her and Alpha Vasumen.

Yarron's wicked grin widened. "With the guardian free and the alpha within our grasp, what other treasure can you offer me?"

"Trinity," Palisade bit down on her lip, praying the wolves reached them soon.

Yarron tilted his head, and she explained. "I can lure her to the heart of the mountain for the guardian."

Could she? Yes. Would she?

Alpha Vasumen snarled at her, and she glanced at him. Trust me, she wanted to say. His eyes widened slightly, his body slumping more heavily against her, causing her to shift her stance.

"Do this, and there shall be a reward waiting for you," Yarron said.

The Fae had a twisted sense of rewards.

"By giving me more healing potions and false hope?" She tugged at the alpha's arm as he struggled to regain his footing. He growled, putting almost all his weight against her.

"Since you smashed the last one, I'm guessing it wasn't very valuable. No thanks." Her hand pressed against the alpha's heart. Its faint beat brought some reassurance. Now to get him on the other side of the shield.

"We can get another," Yarron held his hand out to her. "There may not be a cure, but you have a better chance of survival with me."

"How long?" she challenged. "How long will it take to make another vial?"

Once upon a time she might have believed him, but the sting of betrayal twisted in her heart.

"A week at most." Yarron's men closed in, their numbers more than she first suspected.

His offer tugged at the part of her that still yearned for his guidance and reassurance.

Against her, the alpha grunted, sweat dampening his brow with the effort to stand. Helping hold him up, she glanced at Alpha Vasumen, her heart aching with the weight of her decision. The choice was simple, yet agonizing.

"And will it cure me or only prolong my symptoms?" The pressure in her head returned. Where were those wolves? *Shift*, she pleaded silently.

The alpha lowered his chin. The glow in his eyes went dim. "I hear you," he whispered. "I am stronger."

"Not if you don't shift!" she hissed at him. "Please. Fly us out of here."

But he moaned, his eyes rolling back. Not yet! She needed him able to move!

"And what if I want something else?" she blurted to Yarron. "I give you Trinity and lock down the curse. You let me leave here with the Alpha unharmed."

"And why would I allow that?" Yarron spread his hands out. She held her breath. Waiting. *Where were the wolves?!*

"Because without him, Trinity will never follow me into the mountain."

"Ah, I see." Yarron glanced at his men around them. Looking at Palisade, his eyes turning gold, he said, "You give me Trinity and I let you leave with the King's dragon. I think not. You'll have to come up with a better deal than this."

Palisade's head pounded fiercely.

When Yarron's fingers glowed, and his expression sobered, she counted down from three. Two. One. She yanked back on the alpha, propelling him toward the nearest space in the shield. Golden light flowed from Yarron's fingertips as he bellowed and waved his hands toward them.

"Move." She shoved Alpha Vasumen in a zigzag. He stumbled, leaning on her. She pulled on him, his skin pale against hers.

"If you can't shift and fly, then you need to run," she gasped. Don't let his power touch you. Just a few feet or we're both dead."

The alpha snarled, then moaned, his feet moving and her straining to keep his upper body from crushing down.

"If you die," she said through clenched teeth, "that golden light will trap your spirit like a prison."

Yarron darted after them.

Arrows drew back on bows, releasing with a sharp twang. She dropped with the alpha, forcing his body to roll with hers. Arrows hissed overhead as they tumbled across the ground, barely clearing the invisible edge of the shield.

From the trees, a pack of wolves emerged from the shadows, their eyes glowing.

The arrows didn't come past the shield. Yarron halted on the other side, his magic pressing against the shield. To anyone without Fae blood, the forest remained unchanged.

Her muscles locked, every nerve screamed as she waited for the strike that did not come. The air rippled. Pressure snapped tight around her waist, stealing her breath. She cried out, collapsing forward as pain speared through her core.

No. No, no, no

She clawed at the ground, fighting the cramp tearing through her body.

"Alpha." Her hands fisted in his tunic.

She'd turned her back on Yarron. On the chance of extending her life.

The cramp tore deeper, locking her muscles as Alpha Vasumen lay unconscious beside her. Her breath came in shallow and fast, her heart battering against her ribs.

This is the price, she wept. And she would pay it.

The wolves circled around them, their eyes glowing red.

Her pulse stumbled when one stepped closer than the others. Black, white, and gray mottled his fur. His gaze fixed on the fallen alpha.

When he shifted, the air swirled, and a cloud collected around him. Bones cracked. Breath tore from his chest in rough grunts. A moment later, he stood naked and human, the forest steam curling around him.

"He's hurt badly. His ribs are bleeding, and he refuses to shift and heal," she said. The man's one brown eye and one green unsettled her. "We need to get him out of here now."

He glanced at the others. Five wolves waited, bodies taut, ears flattened, and ready to tear or flee on command.

He nodded once.

The gray wolf with white paws broke from the circle and vanished into the forest.

She glanced over her shoulder at the spot where she'd torn through the shield. The air still crackled there. Her breath hitched when she caught the shimmer again.

Beyond it waited the Fae.

She didn't need to see them to feel them. Arrows nocked. Magic coiled. A small army with time on its side.

"If you don't want to face every Fae in that camp," she said, shifting to block Alpha Vasumen's body from the Fae's view, "you'll help me move him."

He glanced up and frowned, his expression unreadable.

"It's a shield. You can't see them on the other side. They could step out at any moment. The longer we linger, the more they will gather and surround us if they aren't already slipping through the trees."

He crouched beside the alpha, who lay unconscious beside her. Sometime between the falling and rolling, he'd passed out.

She leaned closer. "Did you hear me?"

She hissed as another wave of cramps hit her core. Her knees nearly buckled. She bit down hard on her lip, choking back a groan as a sickening pull tugged at her spine.

The air crackled at her back.

If she fell back through it, Yarron's warriors would show no mercy. Not to the wolves, and certainly not to her. They didn't want her. They wanted the dragon alpha spirit inside Alpha Vasumen.

Her hands shook.

"Did you hear me?"

The lead wolf shifter peeled back his lip, a low warning rumble vibrating through his chest as he tipped his head toward the others.

"We don't have time." Blood slicked her palms. "We're going to lose him!"

Tears burned hot behind her eyes. Her chest tightened as a deep, spreading heat licked toward her heart.

The wolves paced restlessly, paws digging into the earth, eyes tracking every sound. None of them looked at her for long. Their attention kept snapping back to the alpha.

To the blood.

She forced herself to look too. A cold knot formed in her stomach.

She stood facing the wolves on the side nearest to the shield and pointed. "You're only a few feet from the shield."

Her pulse roared in her ears.

He's not going to die here.

Shift.

Please shift

Her gaze flicked back to the empty stretch of forest where the shield shimmered just out of sight. The wolves couldn't see it.

They were waiting.

Waiting for him to die.

Her breath stuttered. Would the wolves turn on her once it happened?

Her head throbbed.

Yarron wanted the alpha's spirit dragon. Her gaze landed on Alpha Aluk. He didn't need to cross the protection of the shield while another Fae pulled the spirit through and captured the dragon within to bind the spirit within their magical hold.

She gritted her teeth. Her fingers pressed more tightly to stop the blood from seeping from Alpha Aluk's wounds.

"No," she whispered, pressing herself closer to him. "You don't get him."

The Fae had always been patient. Always willing to let others do the dying.

"Did you hear me?" Her voice climbed despite her efforts to control it as she turned on the wolves.

A low growl rippled through the clearing.

Two of them shifted. Bones cracked. Flesh folded and reformed. Within seconds, men stood where wolves had been. They picked up the alpha, slinging one of his arms around each of their shoulders and dragging him between them.

The wolf leader motioned for her to follow.

His silent command cut through her paralyzing fear, and she swallowed hard, pushing past the ice forming in her chest. An invisible lasso yanked at her, insistent she stay close to Alpha Vasumen.

As she followed, the remaining wolves closed ranks around her, backing away from the shimmer she could feel but they could not see. The forest seemed to tighten, branches pressing in, shadows stretching long and thin.

Her breath tore in and out of her chest. Each step demanded more from her legs than the last.

Pain threaded through her temples. The world tilted, and she stumbled. Fur brushed her sides, heat and muscle hemming her in.

She glanced over her shoulder again. Her heart refused to slow, hammering so hard it drowned out everything else. Branches rustled overhead. Each whisper of leaves became louder than the last, feeding the crawling sense that they were being followed.

Palisade fought to steady her breath, but pain throbbed behind her eyes and her muscles burned with fatigue. Yarron's gaze flashed in her mind, cold and knowing. She saw it too clearly. Fae warriors stepping from behind thick trunks. Bows lifting. Magic flaring. Alpha Vasumen pinned, his spirit torn free while she stood helpless.

A swift yank on an invisible cord sent another cramp spreading through her.

The wolf leader walked beside her, unconcerned about his nudity. She lowered her chin, tracking the bare legs of the men carrying Alpha Aluk. "They're watching."

"The guardian?" he asked.

She shook her head. "Took off after they fought."

"Coward," the man muttered, a growl slipping through the word.

"Is there any way to get help sooner? I don't think he'll last if he doesn't shift. Those claw marks are deep." Her stomach rolled as her heart beat wildly.

She needed him alive. No matter that his dragon and Vasumen had different perspectives of her. She wanted him whole. Breathing.

If the Fae captured his dragon spirit, the mountain fell with him. They'd use his dragon spirit to twist these people into slaves of the Fae.

She had wanted to live. Clung to it. Bargained for it.

Wanting her own life had blinded her to how many others stood to lose theirs.

Not again.

She glanced at the wolves, willing them to move faster.

The blood darkened the cloth beneath his ribs. A strange pull tugged low in her chest, like a thread yanked tight, the small fibers snapping. She couldn't tell if it was her life or his unraveling with it.

If he didn't shift. If they didn't reach help—

No, he's too grumpy and a brute to go out this way.

"Please," she whispered, her voice barely audible over the rustling leaves. "He has to live."

She aimed her plea at the backs of the wolves carrying him, at the Great Hunter who watched over them.

"Our medic is on his way," the wolf leader said without slowing. "If what you say is true, we need to put distance between us and the Fae. I believe a few are tracking us."

Distance mattered only if Alpha Vasumen held on long enough to reach it.

She lengthened her stride, testing the space between them. The wolf leader marched at her pace.

She bit her lip, wanting to ask about Trace. The question pressed hard against her tongue, but she swallowed it down. To do so might give her away. She couldn't afford to have them see her as a threat and eliminate her.

Palisade didn't know if these wolves came from the prison or somewhere else. With little time left in her lifespan, she hoped Trace understood she hadn't wanted to hurt him.

The forest closed in around them, branches knitting together overhead. The wolf leader kept glancing at the sky.

She opened her mouth, about to warn him about the danger Trinity was in and the task Yarron had assigned the guardian, then pain lanced through her skull. The words danced on the edge of her tongue, tantalizingly close but frustratingly out of reach. She blinked, trying to grasp the thought before it slipped away. It dissolved anyway.

The sky darkened.

A rush of wind tore through the canopy as a massive dragon swept down.

The two men carrying the alpha laid him down and stepped away. The dragon, a huge black and red creature, lifted the alpha into its clutches and took back to the sky with him.

As she watched him fly off, the wolf leader stepped behind her and dragged her arms behind her back.

"What are you doing? Let me go!" She kicked back and struggled against his hold. He growled, his hot breath against her neck. "No one takes down a member of my pack and walks away."

Trace. Did that mean... Pain exploded in the side of her head and the world went black.

Eighteen

When next Palisade woke, she lay on the cold stone of a cell. Her head throbbed with a dull, persistent ache. She rubbed her temple, wincing as her fingers brushed against the stickiness of blood in her hair. The metallic scent lingered, nauseating her.

Using the wall as a guide against her back, she rose to her feet slowly. A wave of dizziness washed over her. Palisade tried to steady herself against the relentless pounding in her skull. Her vision wavered, and pain laced down her neck. She reached for the bars, wrapping her hands around them. She tugged on them and hissed at the burning sensation against her palms. Panic surged through her. Her breath came in shorter pants, confined within the unforgiving constraints of her chest.

Spotting the cot, she sank onto it. Her predicament twisted her insides. Her lungs burned, and she pressed back trying to breathe. *What did you expect, Palisade? You're dead.* Diaden claimed her human genes made her weak, and he often tried to talk Yarron into setting her out on the curb. Yarron always said he had grand plans for her. He paid for her schooling and trained her to take the missions best suited for a woman. She didn't need a degree in psychology to know she'd come to the end of her life expectancy.

But those grand plans always remained shrouded in secrecy, each missing piece pushing her closer to the edge. Palisade had been groomed for infiltrating the shifter prison to get into the minds of their enemies. She knew the risks, understood the stakes.

Trying to regulate her breathing, Palisade wrapped her arms around herself. Would they believe her when she tried to explain she didn't want to hurt Trace? She might have knocked him out for the keys had she not been used like a puppet. Alarm filled her. How long was Diaden or any others able to control her against her will? *Try explaining that.* Would they even give her the chance to explain?

She worried about Alpha Vasumen. His dragon spirit took over his body and acted like she were important to him. Her head throbbed with the thought, but something deep inside made her feel a sense of belonging. What if she never got the chance to explain everything?

She stared into the darkness beyond the cell door, listening for footsteps. The silence pressed in. Cold from the stone leached through her clothes. If she died here, no one would know how hard she had tried. Her chest tightened at the thought, at the thin, stubborn hope that the alpha might still see her as more than a liability.

Pain throbbed behind her eyes. She pressed her hand to her head and breathed through it. She needed time. Time to stop Yarron and the Fae before they reached Trinity.

That meant getting out.

She drifted in and out of consciousness. There was something she wanted to do. Something she needed to tell Alpha Vasumen. The thought slipped when she reached for it, pain spiking behind her eyes.

The Fae hadn't stepped past their invisible barrier. Why?

Yarron wanted the alpha.

Wolves against dozens of Fae.

She moaned and rolled over on her side.

"Ah, daughter, you wake."

The voice slid out of the darkness.

She pushed herself upright, blinking against the gloom as pain pulsed behind her eyes. "Who are you?"

She rose and edged closer to the cell door, scanning the dim corridor. Shadows shifted beyond the bars. *Daughter?*

"Asigwani," the voice said. "Guardian of the wolf packs."

"Show yourself."

"I am here."

She tilted her head. The voice came from the far side of the hall, just out of sight. "You said guardian, not guard. You're the other *ohunko*."

A growl came from the darkness.

"I mean no offense." *Way to go,* Palisade, antagonizing *the thing that might be your only way out.*

Silence stretched.

"You called me daughter," she said finally. "Why?"

She leaned closer to the bars without touching them. Her fingers still stung from before.

"You are a female of my blood."

"The guardian bloodlines are extinct." She leaned back against the stone closest to the voice. "You were cast into the shadows after the war."

"You're educated. Someone has shared our history with you. The Fae?"

"They raised me, but I'm human." She rarely spoke of The Manor. Of the long halls and locked doors. Of waiting. As a child, she remembered the hospital bed and the kind nurses. No one was coming back for her. They'd left her there to die.

Then Yarron appeared and offered a little blue vial to make her better. He paid for her schooling. Trained her the same as one of his elite warriors. She learned early on that gratitude and loyal kept her alive. She owed him for rescuing her from a premature death.

She closed her eyes, wanting to block out the past. "How can you know we're related?"

"Do you not feel the pull between us? It is like a bright light in a long tunnel of darkness."

The familiar sensation stirred. She felt it. A mix of fear and realization washed over her. How was this possible?

"If I am as you say, then why did you never come to find me?" A little later, she huffed, the truth of her realization settling in her mind.

"When the Fae entered our lands, we hid our families to protect our bloodlines, but they found them and we had no choice but to make a bargain to keep the next generation safe."

"The guardians died during the war." She released one of the very guardians, their bloodlines extinct, and possessing any man to serve their purpose. Diaden chose his path, but the knowledge didn't gnaw any gentler on her conscience.

"Our warriors were slain along with the dragons. Our spirits have lived in the shadows of the forest ever since." His voice sounded regretful. "But you are here now, daughter. I have waited too long for someone strong and healthy to emerge from my bloodline."

"I am sorry to disappoint you, Asigwani. I am neither strong nor healthy any more than I am of your blood. I'm a human."

"I know what you are."

Palisade tried to recall everything she knew about the old guardians. They were sent by the Great Hunter to protect the various tribes who welcomed them on the mountain. Each different spirit had a bloodline; without it, the human lost their soul to the spirit, and the spirit possessed the body for a limited time. Had Asigwani persisted beyond the death of a bloodline?

"Is the man's body you possess not of your blood?"

"No," Asigwani said, then growled. "You are unwell?"

A sheen of sweat broke out on her skin. "I..."

"He comes," Asigwani warned.

Her breath caught as the wolf shifter with the two different colored eyes came into view.

"Step back and hold out your hands," the guard commanded Asigwani, his voice low and menacing.

A growl vibrated through the space between them. Palisade tensed, angling to watch.

Power emanated from the guardian, turning the air thicker, warmer, and more stifling. Energy crackled between the guard and Asigwani. A sudden headache shot through her head, a sharp pain that brought her to her knees and made her press her hands to her temples. Trying to breathe through the pain, she squeezed her eyes shut. "Please stop."

"She's unwell. You must help her," Asigwani urged. "We must help her."

"You need to step back, *ohunko*. I've got a special pair of bracelets. A gift from the alpha."

Another set of footsteps echoed down the corridor.

Palisade forced her eyes open, blinking through the pain. The world wavered, then steadied just enough for her to see him.

"Trace."

Relief flooded her so fast a sob caught in her throat.

He looked at her.

Pain flashed in his gaze before his expression hardened.

"I'm sorry. I didn't want to do it."

He turned away from her and reached for the wooden box.

"I hear they are the latest fashion." Sarcasm laced the guard's words.

She whimpered and folded in on herself, drawing her legs close and pressing her forehead to her knees. Everything spun, sound and shadow blurring together, and she clung to the stone beneath her.

"Then you should wear them." Asigwani said, sounding far away. "They're not my style."

Palisade turned her head, forcing her vision to clear long enough to find Trace again. His broad back was rigid, his attention fixed on the cell just out of her sight.

Any hope of him helping her ended with another stab of pain, this time behind her eyes. She didn't have much time. Trinity. Yarron. If she didn't stop them, the Fae would take over the mountain.

Bile rose in her throat, and she moaned. "Not again."

"She needs help."

"She'll survive," Trace said. She deserved his animosity.

"No. She won't," Asigwani's growl vibrated through the corridor. "What will your alpha do when he finds out you let her die?"

Anger flared through the pain. Curse Yarron. Curse Diaden. Curse all of them for hoarding gifts they used to break people instead of healing them. Tears slipped from the corners of her eyes, tracking down into her hair. Why her? Why had Alpha Vasumen's dragon chosen *her*?

"She's lying to get your attention," Trace's voice drew nearer. "She's trying to escape her fate."

A broken laugh caught in her chest and dissolved into a sob. Her head felt like it might split apart. The pressure was becoming unbearable. She pressed her palms to the floor, shaking.

"Help her," Asigwani demanded.

"Put the cuffs on," the wolf guard ordered.

"You think trapping me in this form will prevent me from escaping? If I wanted to escape, I could have months ago," Asigwani said.

Silence answered him.

Palisade interlocked her fingers over her head. Her skull wanted to split apart. Heat flashed through her, then cold, then heat again, her body caught in a relentless cycle she couldn't stop.

"If you do not help her. I will," Asigwani's voice rose.

Something tugged in her chest.

"He's coming."

She sensed him coming near. A sob tore free, and she squeezed her eyes shut, dismissing the sensation as nothing more than the sickness tightening its grip.

"Leave that cell, *ohunko* and I'll trap you in the forest beneath the mist, where even the Great Hunter can't release you." Alpha Vasumen's voice rang out.

Palisade's heart skipped a beat. *He's here.* Relief flared so fiercely it burned through the pain in her head. If he was healed, he shifted, and maybe Alpha Vasumen was back.

Slowly, she lifted her head and rested her chin on her knees. Her vision wavered, swimming in shadows and red light. Glowing eyes stared back at her.

Alpha Vasumen remained out of reach.

"Please," she whispered, meeting his gaze. "End it. No more pain."

"She deserves pain." Trace snapped the lid of the wooden box shut. The crack of it made Palisade flinch. A heartbeat later, the box splintered against the stone wall. The impact sent another burst of agony through her head.

She clenched her teeth, fighting to stay conscious.

"I'm sorry."

Trace grunted. His legs swept out from under him. The air whooshed from Trace's lungs as he hit the ground.

The wolf leader didn't move. He lifted his chin, the wolf inside him coming to the surface, shining through his eyes. "She attacked one of your guards."

"She saved me from capture by the Fae." Oska's voice dripped with authority. The dragon remained in control of Alpha Vasumen. "Take your pack and return home, Pinto. I've brought fresh recruits with me to lock down the fortress."

She braced for his next command. Oska stood between her and them.

Pinto's fist clenched. His green eye turned brighter than the blue one.

"No disrespect, Alpha, but I have run this prison for decades. Even in your absence."

"And never before," Oska stepped over Trace, "have you dared to take what is mine and lock it away."

A key slipped into the cell door. Palisade's heart pounded as Oska approached. He crouched in front of her. His red eyes scanned her face, her skin, and searched her for injuries. His gaze softened. A spark of appreciation lay beneath the crease in his brow.

What was he doing?

"You're healed?"

"Enough."

He framed her face with her hands. The calloused roughness of his palms against her skin sent a shiver through her. The knot in her chest loosened, and before she could stop herself, she leaned into his touch.

"You are in greater pain than I, wíyoyá."

His thumb brushed her cheek. Then, without warning, his arms slid beneath her legs and back. Her arms went around his neck, clinging to him as the world tilted and she struggled to keep her wit.

He growled as he passed the wolf shifters. The space around them closed in. For the first time since the forest, a sense of calm filled her.

She lifted her head and looked at him. His gaze had narrowed, fixed on the man behind the bars. Her muscles ached at the sight of the man over Oska's shoulder. Asigwani's sober expression mirrored the turmoil inside her. She searched his eyes for answers she could not form. He lowered his chin as they passed.

As Oska carried her away, she rested her head against his shoulder. The pounding in her skull eased slightly. "Where are you taking me?"

Her stomach twisted with thoughts of another cell. She almost opened her mouth to ask if he would take her to Conleth, hoping to see Trinity. The thought turned murky and drifted away. Why did it matter?

The answer hovered just beyond her grasp. Anger burned there. The harder she tried to seize it, the more her thoughts scattered. She bit her lip.

Oska's warmth anchored her. The strength of his hold kept her from falling apart. His nearness pulled her back from the edge of the spinning haze.

"You shall see."

Trace rose to his feet again. His eyes gleamed in the low light.

Pinto gathered the splintered remains of the box.

She turned her face into the curve of Alpha Vasumen's shoulder, breathing him in. Smoke and pine. Stone and heat. The ache in her head eased another fraction, and she held on the small mercy.

Nineteen

Palisade lay motionless on the bed. Her breaths came shallow, uneven. Her skin had gone ashen; her lips tinged blue.

The dragon spirit refused to release control.

Oska stood at her side, hands clenched at his back. Fire coiled beneath his skin, restless, furious with the woman who came into his fortress and helped one of the most dangerous *ohunko* escape. Then turned around and put herself in front of danger to save him.

Pinto locked her in the escaped ohunko's cell. A necessity his head guard saw to keeping her contained. Protecting this mountain. Protecting his alpha prime. His chest burned still working to heal his wounds. She weakened him.

She's a betrayer. Aluk snarled from the cage in his mind. *She belongs in the* dungeon.

She. Is. Mine.

"It's worsening," Oska said. "Why aren't you doing anything to heal her?"

"Because I can't," Conleth kept his eyes averted. "She has shifter blood."

Palisade's lips parted, but no sound emerged. He heard her heart beating faintly.

His eyes narrowed. "Shifters don't get sick."

"All her symptoms suggest wasting illness." Conleth tucked her hands under the blanket.

Conleth's mate, Trinity, sat on the edge of the bed. She reached to help cover Palisade.

"Do not touch her," Oska said.

"How is that possible? I have shifter blood?" Palisade asked, awake.

Conleth shoved his hands in his jeans pockets and rocked back.

"Humans can get wasting illness. It happens when they have used the spirits of a shifter and sucked the spirit's power within them. It's like a drug hit, and you get addicted. They get wasting illness from the withdrawal of the loss of the spirit, like a shifter does when our spirit is taken from us."

"I'm human," Palisade whispered. "My parents were human." Her eyes slid shut. "I was sick. They traded me for a healthier one."

Aluk surged against the cage. *She lies.*

Oska growled low in his chest. *No.*

Through their bond, he sensed the truth. Her fear. Her exhaustion. The old ache of abandonment that never healed.

Fire stirred beneath Oska's skin. When they finished with the Fae, he would find the humans who cast her aside. He'd lock them in his prison for the rest of their days.

She's a master of lies, Aluk warned.

Oska searched Palisade's face. The tremor in her hands was beneath the blanket. The strain in her breathing.

There are *no* deceptions *here. Only a woman who has learned to survive too long on her own*

"I sensed something was off before, but thought it was your illness," Conleth said.

"It may be the stronghold of a compulsion spell. I'd have to touch you and go into some of your memories to be sure," Trinity said.

Oska's lip curled up.

Trinity looked at him, then at Conleth.

Palisade licked her lips. Her hand twitched as she pulled it from under the blanket. "Touch me," she whispered to Trinity. "See the truth."

In two strides, Oska blocked Trinity from her. Conleth's mate rose to her feet, and his brother moved in close, stopping inches away.

Their eyes locked. With all of his mental strength focused on keeping his human side caged, the dragon spirit held Conleth's stare.

Then Palisade's fingers brushed his hand.

He jerked his head around and raised a hand toward Trinity's back. She had a habit of slipping into memories uninvited.

Palisade's grip tightened, but was still weak. His hand lowered.

Her fingers were ice cold against the fire raging beneath his palms.

"I need to know," she said, "I'm dying."

His gaze cut to Conleth. *Why do her memories matter?*

Let them break the compulsion. Aluk urged from within his mind cage. *The Fae will lose their hold on you.*

He was torn between the need to protect her and breaking the Fae's hold on him. They'd use her again to get to him. She was his mate.

But Issabrie...

We need to know the truth, Aluk urged.

Oska exhaled slowly, forcing the fire in his chest to settle. "We can't let them have control." His thumb brushed her knuckles, grounding him in the feel of her. "But your safety matters more."

"I have never been safe. I grew up with the Fae. At a place called The Manor. Yarron gave me a home. He sent me to school."

The Manor.

Oska's palms heated. The Manor was no refuge. It was where the Unseelie raised their bloodhounds, boys and girls trained to hunt in the Mist Forest for his kind. They feasted upon them to strengthen their power.

He forced his breathing to steady. His human recoiled at the knowledge he kept buried for the sake of peace. What had they trained her to do?

"And he sent you to your death, like my grandfather sent me," Trinity said, her mouth tightening.

He schooled her to hunt us, Aluk snarled inside his mind. *He taught her to manipulate as they do. You cannot trust her.*

I do. Oska growled back. *Survival is not betrayal. No one lives through The Manor without learning how to endure.*

Aluk slammed against the cage. *Or she lies.*

Oska snarled, tossing Aluk back into the darkness. *Your grief jades you. Think with your heart and feel with your soul instead of your pride.* He stared over at Palisade. *You are no stronger than she, but at least she fights to survive.*

"I've known I've been dying for a long time. Yarron promised me the cure if I completed my task. The cure was too expensive otherwise," Palisade said.

Oska's hands curled into fists.

"The cure he smashed? The one of Fae berries?"

She had lived on borrowed hope, all while her life slipped away. She suffered, believing Yarron's lies. One of the wounds on his side flared with pain. He hissed and pressed his hand there.

"They tricked you," Trinity said.

Oska glanced at Conleth. "You must save her."

His human's grief hit him like a punch in the gut. *Now we're even, dragon.*

His focus returned to Palisade and the shallow rise of her chest.

Not by a long shot, human. She was never yours to lose.

"There was never a cure, was there?"

Aluk heard her question, muffled behind the cage of his mind.

Palisade's eyes grew watery. The dragon's attention sharpened, dragging Aluk with it as she wilted like a plucked rose. Still beautiful. Still dangerous. Even as her petals darkened, the threat of her thorns curled deep in his gut.

Aluk huffed, forced to wait. At some point the dragon would weaken, and he would claw his way back into control. Even now, the spirit's emotions bled through him, and he felt something shift.

"There's no cure for it, unless you count getting your spirit animal to return. We'd need to find out what happened to yours. I can try to unlock the memories. It might help us find your spirit animal," Trinity said.

Aluk snorted. He couldn't let her die, and yet, he could neither hunt down Gorak nor stay with her at the same time.

His dragon spirit refused to leave her, drawn like a moth to a flame.

We need her.

If she gained a spirit animal, then he'd have no choice but to keep her locked in this prison. She'd turned on her own people. She attacked one of his guards.

She's no better than one of the ohunkos.

Would not you have done the same to survive?

"There's something I need to remember, but every time it think I'm about to know what it is, I get a headache and it's gone again," Palisade whispered.

"They've been controlling you. Aaron held me under his compulsion spell for years," Trinity said.

"So that's how she took down a wolf shifter. I wondered," Conleth said.

Compulsion. Control. A body made obedient against its will.

Blood had spilled. Trust shattered.

His dragon fidgeted, heat rolling through the cage of his mind. Not anger. Something closer to recognition. *To lose control of one's actions is a fate worse than death.*

Aluk went still.

He remembered the blur of fire and blood after Naomi died. The hours he could not account for. The wreckage left behind after his dragon acted on his anger and grief. He had woken surrounded by ash and silence, his hands clean and his soul stained, told only later when he had done.

No choice. No voice. No stopping it.

His gaze dragged back to Palisade. Pale. Shaking. Fighting for clarity that slipped through her fingers the moment she reached for it.

We escaped the Fae and their cruel acts, the dragon continued, quieter now. *The Great Hunter* sacrificed *himself to save us.*

The memory of breath caught in his chest, even though he no longer had use of his lungs to draw it.

If she had been controlled, bent, compelled into obedience, then she had not chosen the blood on her hands anymore than he had chosen the destruction left in the wake of his grief.

We cannot lose her, the dragon pressed.

Aluk recoiled. Keeping her alive meant keeping her contained. Keeping her contained meant binding her to them in a way his dragon had always denied him.

She's not Issabrie.

She's not Naomi.

We'll have to mark her.

Then you will be the one to mate with her.

The dragon never allowed it. Not for Naomi. Not for anyone.

Heat surged through the prison walls of his thoughts. The want and desire for a mate returned, but the taste of his own failure with Naomi turned bitter.

Palisade's peach scent taunted him.

He needed her like his next breath.

Naomi should have been the one he marked. He'd chosen *her*.

The tear between his dragon spirit and his soul grew wider over the years. Then Palisade appeared at his prison and awakened that part of him again.

Chosen.

Fated.

His dragon growled in his head.

Fated or not, she'd helped the Fae try to destroy them.

"She must have stolen a spirit animal. There's no way she could have inherited one," Conleth said.

The dragon's certainty unnerved him.

A thin golden thread shimmered in the darkness of Aluk's mind, stretching toward Palisade. It pulsed once.

The dragon believed in her.

Aluk pressed against the edges of the cage, wary. Belief had cost him before. She had helped the Fae. Whatever her reasons, the truth did not vanish because the dragon wished it away.

"I don't steal," Palisade said, resolute despite the visible pain pulling at her features.

He wanted to trust her. Wanted to follow that fragile gold strand and see where it led.

He'd seen nothing like it, not from within him. Not even with Naomi.

Mine.

The growl rolled through his mind, possessive and absolute.

Did the beast even understand what it was claiming?

"You stole my prisoner."

Shock rippled through him. The dragon spoke his thought aloud.

Pressure built inside the cage, something loosened, something dangerous. If he pushed too hard, the dragon spirit would shove him back into the dark. If he hesitated—

"I'm trained to gather information and to kill, when necessary," Palisade whispered.

All the muscles in his body tensed- *Trained to kil*l. His dragon chose a trained soldier. Warrior. Assassin.

"Who sent you?" Aluk asked, gaining confidence with the sound of his words coming from his human mouth.

"Yarron."

"Are you even a psychologist?" Conleth asked.

Palisade tried to nod and hissed softly in pain. "Yes. Yarron paid for my education."

Conleth looked at him. "She won't last much longer. The illness has taken on at an aggressive rate."

"My memories. My choice." Palisade turned her head toward him. Exhaustion hollowed her eyes. The plea there struck him deeper than Aluk expected.

Naomi had looked at him that way once.

The memory store through him.

Her hand slipped from the dragon's grasp. The chill on her fingertips lingered on his skin.

The dragon turned away from her. The spirit's thoughts whirled. Emotions churned through the dragon spirit in a violent spiral. Possession. Fear. Want.

The bond between the dragon and Palisade pulled tight, strained by the separation of body and spirit. Aluk's grief drove a wedge between them.

The dragon turned away, exhaled to relieve the tension building in his shoulders.

What harm is it? Aluk pressed, testing the edges of his influence. *Or do you fear what her memories might reveal?*

Then, with a wave of his hand, the dragon yielded. "See what you must."

The effort left Aluk reeling.

Her memories might prove valuable in their fight against the Fae and in proving to his dragon spirit her true intentions. Or condemn her.

Because truth or no truth. She had deceived them.

As he suspected—

She had not acted alone.

"Yarron doesn't work for free." The dragon said, "I want to know who is paying him?"

A dark shadow of a man with pointed ears and a bear skin draped over him appeared in his mind's eye.

The image sent a cold ripple through him.

Aluk's soul cracked. Light slipped through, dragging the past forward.

The memory rushed at him.

A woman who was far too beautiful looked at him with her golden eyes. Her gaze was far too cold to hold genuine warmth. A subtle glimmer inside them became like a trance. It sank into him, pulled at him, wrong.

Then the vision vanished.

Heat slammed into him as the dragon spirit coiled tight, fire burning in a ring around his consciousness.

You don't control me. Aluk braced, his will alone holding against the fire. It burned hotter against him. He focused on Naomi. On his brothers—Conleth and Taran. On protecting his people. And Palisade.

Slowly, the flames receded, leaving the echo of her golden gaze behind.

"Some of her memories are blocked. I think it might be the compulsion spell," Trinity said, bringing Aluk's focus back on Palisade.

"What do you mean?" the dragon asked.

They defend her because they believe she was more to Aluk than the key to unlocking the curse.

A spark of anger ignited inside him. Good. His dragon needed to get angry with the woman instead of wanting to protect her.

Aluk couldn't allow himself to be swayed by his dragon's impulsive decisions.

She's a pawn. The dragon snarled in his mind. *A tool in a war that never ended.*

She was not the key.

His dragon spirit snarled. *She is fate. She is my chosen.*

Then merge with me, Aluk pressed, forcing the thought forward. *Let me feel what you are feel.*

If the dragon spirit opened itself, even for a breath, it might falter. A single crack was all Aluk needed.

You are too weak.

The dragon's thought cut through him. *The choices you and your blood have made are why we are here.*

The rebuke carried centuries of accusation.

Desire to claim this woman and protect her flooded the fragile golden thread tethering him to Palisade.

Aluk seized it.

If she is yours, he challenged, *then mark her.*

The dragon spirit stilled. Just like he knew it would.

To mark was to claim. To bind soul to soul. The dragon spirit belonged to the woman imprisoned in the mountain, the one with the golden eyes.

The one he couldn't release and his dragon couldn't abandon.

Why claim one when you want another?

You are not ready to understand.

"Aluk?"

Conleth stepped into the dragon's line of sight.

From the bed he heard, Palisade said, "Alpha."

"Yes, Alpha."

The dragon glared at Conleth.

"Do not forget your place, brother."

Conleth moved aside. A tick in Conleth's jaw and the flash in his brother's eyes turned red as the dragon reasserted control.

He tried to push his thoughts toward Conleth.

No response. The dragon spirit kept him from communicating.

His gaze settled on Palisade. She forfeited her life the moment she helped release Gorak from his cell. Mercy had no place here. His dragon spirit's distress over this woman gnawed at him. There was only one fated mate for them. Was that not Issabrie?

And still—

Palisade Everett pulled at him in a way he couldn't explain. Her scent of peaches filtered through to his memory, filling him with strength.

Aluk burrowed deeper in his mind, forcing himself inward. If he had to split open his soul and either merge with the spirit inherited by his father or die trying he wasn't going down without a fight.

Silence continued to stretch through the room. Conleth stayed near Trinity, protective of his mate. The dragon moved closer to Palisade. His gaze locked on Trinity. He stayed between the two.

"Tell me, what blocks her memories?" the dragon demanded. "Truth, woman. Spare us the charades."

Fingers brushed his wrist.

His dragon spirit flattered for a moment. Eyes closing. A hum vibrated through his chest. Palisade slipped her fingers between his. The contact sent a shock through him, splitting sensation from thought.

The dragon's attention whipped around. Her red hair burned against the white pillow. Green eyes met his, clouded and dull.

There is no going back for what she has done.

His legs gave way. The dragon sank onto the edge of the bed. One touch from this woman cracked him open. His lungs burned. His soul fractured, widening the fault already splitting him apart.

Answers rushed in.

"Aluk?" Conleth's voice sounded too far away.

Palisade's fingers slid along his palm. Their fingers entwined. His heartbeat thundered.

"What's happening?" Trinity's voice rang out against his fading reality.

The cage shattered.

Aluk dove.

"He's still hurt," Palisade whispered.

His body collapsed against her, driving the breath from her lungs. Darkness closed in as his soul shattered with the plunge.

Twenty

Aluk stood on a precipice. The wind whipped at his face.

"You must choose," a man with bronze skin and war paint on his face commanded. "The fate of this world rests in your hands."

Issabrie.

She was not the innocent woman she'd portrayed. For a blink of time, her glamor slipped, just enough. Long enough for truth to pierce him like ice driven beneath the skin.

She was the new queen of the Unseelie.

His dragon slammed against the cage in his mind, roaring, clawing, fire scorching the edges of his thoughts.

He had missed it. All of it. Her betrayal washed over him.

The warmth. The softness. The lie threaded through every touch. Without the guardian of his Thunder standing before him before him now, he might never have seen it at all.

"What will you do?" the dragon guardian asked, his eyes dark with empathy.

The wind howled louder, tugging at his cloak, as if the mountain itself waited.

Whatever he chose would never leave him. His dragon would carry this moment forever.

His chest burned with decision. One part of him, the dragon spirit, reached for her, for the promise of connection and love. The other, his human side, demanded obedience no matter the cost, and he'd pay with the price of his mate. Issabrie.

His dragon spirit roared, the force of it knocking him off balance. A hand closed around his arm to steady him.

Dark eyes met his.

"She's coming."

He nodded once. The duty to his people settled heavily on his chest. The breeze wrapped around him, sharp and cool. Even in the mountain's heart, it carried with it the faint scent of earth and wild flower.

He'd chosen this place. The mouth of his dragon's lair yawned behind him. Stone carved into the heart of the mountain itself.

No! His dragon spirit seethed. *Do this, and I will rip myself from your soul. You will never have a true mate.*

"She's not our mate."

A tremble seized his taunt muscles. He turned to the guardian standing nearby. His gaze locked onto the man before him. The guardian's dark hair was bound at the nape of his neck, revealing sharp cheekbones and eyes filled with wisdom and age. A faint shimmer lingered in his gaze, the quiet presence of his dragon spirit watching.

His throat burned. The bond with her pulled hard, deep.

A lie so righteous as the truth.

"You know this for sure."

The guardian inclined his head. "I saw her cast the spell upon you myself. I would not lie to you, Alpha."

"I know." It didn't make his task any easier.

"It is my duty and honor to protect you and our people." The guardian's gaze met his. "Does not it trouble you that one of their kind came here after we fled and claimed such closeness?"

His dragon spirit snarled, coiling tighter, heat building beneath his ribs.

A peace offering.

Her voice whispered through him. *Two enemies united.*

His dragon preened at the memory, the heat turning heady, almost sweet. For a breath, the fury ebbed.

His jaw tightened. His fist clenched until knuckles ached.

"She made my dragon forget. This mountain is a refuge."

Fire stirred under his skin.

"Our people were here long before the spirits crossed worlds," he continued. "The Fae have no claim on this land."

The dragon repositioned inside him, pain laced the fury.

If he chose wrong, it would cost him his heart and split his soul with the dragon spirit who chose him. If he chose nothing, it would cost them all.

An ache radiated deep in his chest. "If she's not our mate, then she is our enemy."

The dragon slammed against him. *You can't do this.*

The guardian did not flinch. "We must stop her. For your sake, and for my people."

"The other guardians are aware they are coming?" Pain flared behind his eyes.

The guardian nodded.

He turned toward the lair's mouth. The passage wide open, breathing shadow and heat, the stone walls swallowing the light. Cold brushed his skin. The fine hairs along his arm rose.

Movement stirred below.

A woman stepped into view, glowing as if the mountain itself bent toward her.

He looked away.

Mate! His dragon cried.

His jaw locked. His people needed him to stay strong. Long before him, his ancestors made a promise to protect the spirits who took refuge here. In return, the spirits shared their gifts with their warriors.

This will soon be over, dragon, and you will see the truth in time.

"They have taken their families to safety," the guardian said. "They prepare."

Retaliate. He felt it coming like pressure before a storm. He drew his shoulders back. Heat rolled through his chest.

"This is the only way to protect the mountain."

"It will give us leverage," the guardian said quietly.

He exhaled through his nose. "Then may the Great Hunter give us strength."

The guardian lowered his head. His gaze slipped toward the lair.

His dragon spirit stilled. The tiny threads of the woman's hold on his spirit infiltrated his senses.

She did not own his will, but her magic had found his dragon, and it was sinking deeper, winding closer to the place where bond and soul became one.

The moment his tongue heated and his mark bloomed on her flesh, dread cut through the fire. His tattoo burned in answer. A pulling ache. His dragon spirit leaned toward her without his permission, eager to please, eager to finish the bond.

Something slipped inside him. Quiet as a splinter beneath skin.

Her magic brushed his dragon, warm and intimate, and his breath caught. The sensation slid deeper, settling where instinct and bond intertwined. It felt almost right.

Almost.

Then the dragon guardian had sought him.

She. Is. Ours.

No.

She was not fate's gift. She had come with a purpose hidden behind her beauty and lies dressed as devotion. She had crossed into this realm and across his lands. She reached into his spirit without his consent.

"Are you certain we can't send her back and seal the gate between worlds?" he asked.

"We can't unless you wish to end her life and bury her at the base of the life tree." The guardian's eyes darkened, red bleeding through the brown as his dragon rose.

When the mountain natives discovered the spirits living within the forests of the land, they chose their warriors and blessed them with the abilities to protect themselves from the outside world. The first merging determined the bloodline of their next generation to inherit their spirit.

And now that bond burned inside him, waiting for him to choose.

Without the people, the spirits withered on this side of the veil.

Without the spirits, the natives may have lost their land in the battles to defend their territory and freedom. The balance demanded sacrifice.

"We can't kill her." He marked her. Unfinished, the bond anchored his dragon to her. Losing her now would rip the spirit from him and leave him as ash. No one survived a shattered soul.

The guardian's expression did not soften. "To send her back through the gates is futile."

She called to him.

With a pull. With the heat beneath his skin that answered before thought could intervene. His dragon surged toward the sound of her presence like a tide drawn by the moon.

He lifted his chin. "Then gather the others. I cannot do this alone."

"She does not come alone. The gate is open."

Deep in his chest, his dragon went still. The air itself paused. Both he and the guardian's dragons sensed the subtle tearing where the gate opened to the Fae realm.

Pain shafted through his chest, stealing his breath.

"She's not wasting any time," he muttered.

He curled his fists and drove the dragon deeper into the dark. The spirit swelled in protest, battering his ribs from the inside. Betrayal rang through both flesh and soul.

"You will not harm her," the dragon spirit commanded.

No.

But neither would he allow her to own him while he still drew breath.

She emerged from the path, light catching her like a blessing. The sight of her loosened his hold on his dragon spirit. Warmth spilled through him, unwelcome land aching.

"I was afraid you wouldn't wait for me." Her voice slid into him, smooth and familiar, threading through bone and blood.

"For you," he said, the lie effortless, "I would wait forever."

Her attention moved past him. Her eyes narrowed on the guardian. "Why have you brought one of your enforcers?"

"It is customary for us to have one witness." The words polished by years of diplomacy.

Her slender eyebrows rose. Her pale pink lips puckered.

She studied him for a heartbeat too long.

Then she smiled again.

The mountain breathed with her.

Her long strands of rose-colored hair lay in ringlets around her face. She wore a simple doeskin dress with no fringe, same as the women of his people.

The guardian behind him stiffened.

Jewels glimmered along her sleeves, catching the sun in brief, iridescent flashes. Her boots rose to her calves. A jeweled knife rested against her left leg.

Heat flared low in his body.

His dragon strained toward her, aching and furious all at once.

He cleared his throat and extended his hand, deliberately ignoring the quiet insult stitched into her clothing. His people did not wear the skins of animals.

"Come, my queen," he said.

She slid her hand in his, her fingers warm and delicate against his. "Queen?"

"Am I not the king of this mountain?" he teased lightly, though his dragon spirit snarled at the title. "As the mate of the alpha, that makes you my queen."

Her smile widened. A faint glimmer of triumph flashed in her eyes. It twisted in his gut like a blade.

He led her into the mountain. The air grew warmer the closer they neared entering his lair. Each step became a contest between his will and the dragon's rising fury. Stone whispered its warnings, but he ignored them, moving forward one breath at a time.

You would bring her here? His dragon snarled. *She is our mate! Mark her! Finish the bond!*

His smile did not falter, even as claws raked at the edges of his resolve. *She's not what she seems. She's a danger to us all.*

You'll see danger where I see destiny, the dragon hissed. *She is ours to protect, to cherish. You betray me by denying her!*

He gripped her hand tighter as they neared the lair's threshold. The cavernous opening loomed ahead. The cavern glowed with the orange pulse of his fire. Shadows stretched and twisted along the walls, their shapes entwined in the light.

"Are you coming?" she asked.

His heart thundered beneath his ribs. He seared her into his memory, calling upon the gift of his dragon spirit to keep this moment for the future.

Look at her, the dragon growled, thick with longing. *She is ours. The scent, the way her spirit calls to mine. You feel it /*

I feel it, he admitted, his throat tightening. *But that doesn't make her my mate. It's her magic that tricks you. I will not let her destroy us.*

Do this, and you will lose having a true mate and the part of us that makes your soul complete. His spirit growled and clawed within him. He sucked in his breath.

She reached for him.

He stepped back.

"What's wrong?"

"Nothing. I forgot to seal the lair for the ceremony. Your beauty almost made me forget."

If I don't do this, our people will suffer, he countered, steering her past the threshold without crossing it with her.

She looked up at him, her eyes alight with something that might have been hope. "This place," she murmured, "feels alive."

"It is." *Alive with the spirits protected in this mountain and the power to keep you held within.* He couldn't let the dragon's emotions, or his own, cloud his judgment. Her betrayal had already poisoned their bond.

"And the guard?" Her voice hardened slightly.

"Will stand within the entrance until I call him. I wish to have you to myself for some time before he comes to check our nest." He wiggled his eyebrows. His dragon spirit yanked at his soul.

"Will you wait for me there?" He ran his fiery gaze over her and purposely avoided her gaze.

"Shall I disrobe?" She asked, her fingers slipping toward the hem of her dress.

"Surprise me."

For he had a surprise of his own.

The dragon growled low, pain racing through his body.

I do this for our people, he told the dragon, strained to hold the spirit from forcing him to relinquish his control. *Even if it breaks us.*

She is not what you think!

He pressed a kiss to her fingers when she reached for his mouth, then gently but firmly folded her hand back against herself. Her eyes narrowed. Her touch lingered like the brush of a rose against his skin, but to his dragon it seared his spirit like a branding iron.

Her smile turned into a smirk.

She turned, her hips swaying as she walked deeper into his lair. "Don't be long, dragon. Your nest might grow cold."

He sucked in a sharp breath as the fabric of her dress fell away.

For a moment, he almost followed her.

He tore his gaze from the hypnotic sway of her retreating form and turned away. Her humming followed him, threading through the stone. His dragon spirit became frantic, clawing to return to her. He hunched, wrapping his arms against the burning sting.

Seal her if you must, but we need to return to her. Stay with her!

He stumbled outside the lair and bent forward, gripping his knees as he dragged air into his burning lungs. "Do it."

Around him, the other alphas of the mountain packs and clans stood in a semicircle. One by one, they called forth their spirit animals, and the gifts given from the Great Hunter. Against his dragon's fury, he forced his hands forward and tore fire from his spirit. Flames burst outward, slamming across the entrance in a blazing shield.

The alphas answered, commanding the spirits of their packs and clans to rise. Power sank into stone and soil, melding with flame and mountain, binding the woman and her magic within.

His dragon screamed.

Pain ripped through his soul. He collapsed onto his knees. A roar wrenched from his throat. Hands caught his shoulders, holding him upright as his strength gave out.

The ground convulsed. Stone groaned. The mountain shuddered hard enough to stagger the alphas and his brother burst into the clearing. "Fae warriors on the mountain."

Agony tore through him. The mark over his heart flared white-hot, searing until tears streamed down his face and the world fractured.

Aluk's perspective wrenched sideways, and suddenly he wasn't watching from the eyes of his ancestors anymore—

Wings tucked against his sides. The taste of smoke on his tongue.

Below, the Fae queen smiled up at him.

Beautiful. Radiant. Her hand extended in invitation.

His chest eased at the sight of her. She'd been kind. Helpful. Her people and his people had been building an alliance, after all. A bridge between realms.

He lowered his head to accept her touch.

Her fingers brushed his scales.

Cold fire laced through his skull. Aluk tried to jerk back, but his body wouldn't obey. The icy fire burrowed deeper, twisting into want. The fire spread through neural pathways, wrapped around instinct, sank hooks into the scared part of him to bond with his mate.

Issabrie's voice whispered inside his mind. You love me.

No, he didn't.

You need me.

He needed nothing except— the thought fractured.

Issabrie smiled. "There. Much better, isn't it?"

Yes. Much better. She was right. She was his love.

You would die for me.

Of course, Anything for—

No, his consciousness thrashed against invisible chains. Trying to speak. Trying to warn his human. The words that came out said instead, "My love. My mate."

Wrong. The words were wrong. But he couldn't stop them. He couldn't form truth around the barbed wire wrapping his tongue.

"That's right," Issabrie purred. "You do anything I ask, don't you?"

"Anything."

The word tasted like ash, but he couldn't swallow it back.

"Then you'll mark me and make me your mate."

Centuries slammed through him in rapid succession. Osak fought to break free. The compulsion tightened every time he tried. Fire and stone sealed Issabrie into the mountain. His relief, for one beautiful moment, but the compulsion filled him with anguish.

Free her. Find her. Need her.

A burning need intensified within him. She cursed them, wrapping her will around his soul like a python.

Naomi's face, confused and hurt.

Oska tried, strained, reached for the bond that hovered out of reach. Until Palisade.

The compulsion slammed him back. Not her. Only the queen.

Every. Single. Time.

Until he curled into himself, broken. His obsession with Issabrie was who he was, not what had been done to him.

The centuries blurred together in endless, aching wrongness.

Then—

Peaches.

The scent hit him like a bucket of ice water in the face.

Aluk jerked. Suddenly he was watching Palisade walk into the dungeon for the first time through Oska's senses. The flush in her cheeks. The way she held herself like she was ready to run or fight at any moment. And her scent.

The compulsion shuddered.

The barbed hooks retracted as if they'd touched a hot iron.

As consciousness started to slip again, Aluk went back to the meadow with Naomi. *I'm sorry I couldn't mark you. The curse stole what should have been. I'm sorry I couldn't save you.* He let her image fade away. To his dragon he vowed, *We're in this together now. No more fighting. No more separation. We choose her. We protect her. We love her.*

And for the first time since accepting the alpha dragon, the barrier between them dissolved. Man and beast synced into alignment.

Twenty-One

Palisade stared up at the ceiling, her breath shallow and uneven. Tears slid from the corners of her eyes, warm against her skin.

Trinity had removed the compulsion hours ago. The strange, suffocating haze that had once coiled around her thoughts vanished all at once, like breaking the surface of deep water.

After Alpha Vasumen collapsed, they brought her here. His tower. Her old room. Not Alpha Vasumen. His dragon spirit.

Her chest tightened until breathing hurt. Fire had torn through her muscles earlier, leaving them weak and trembling, while cold sank deep into her bones and stayed.

"I don't understand," Trinity said, somewhere beyond the room. "I removed the compulsion."

"But not the wasting illness," Conleth replied. "It may have been slowing the progress."

She turned her face into the pillow, biting back a moan. She didn't want Conleth's voice. She wanted Alpha Vasuemen's.

"What do we do now?" Trinity asked.

"She's no longer our concern," Conleth said.

"She might die."

"And so might Aluk."

A pause.

"Do we put them together?"

The voices trailed off, growing more distant.

Together?

Palisade's breath hitched. The thought of him so close again pulled at her. The way his presence made her world feel anchored. Her pulse stumbled. Would he want her near him?

A deep ache spread through her chest, all-consuming, threaded with the wasting illness gnawing at her from the inside. Alpha Vasumen surfaced in her thoughts unbidden. His stubborn resolve. She'd caught the fleeting softness only when he thought himself unobserved.

Trinity's voice drifted in and out, distant, as if carried through water. "You know what's at stake."

Breath dragged through Palisade's lungs, each inhale a battle.

"None of us has offspring, and Ben's child is female. We lose my brother, we lose the first blessing, and the curse will no longer matter."

"We're not going to lose anyone."

Yarron wouldn't stop. He'd keep sending in his elite until he found Gorak, captured Trinity, and accomplished his task. He expected Gorak to possess her, not Diaden. The end had to come from a shifter bloodline to avoid invoking a war.

If he succeeded, no one on this mountain would ever be free.

Darkness pressed in at the edges of her vision.

Warn Trinity.

Air tore into her lungs, thin and painful. She clung to the thought as the world tilted.

A voice whispered faintly, "You must become the first."

The first what? The voice vanished, leaving only silence and pain behind. Agony radiated through her chest in relentless waves, a brutal reminder of how little life remained in her body.

Palisade pushed herself upright. The room lurched. Shapes blurred and fractured, speckled with darkness that crept in at the edges of her vision. Her muscles screamed as she swung her legs over the side of the bed. Air sliced into her lungs. She hissed through clenched teeth.

Still, she stood.

Her knees buckled as she reached the door, legs trembling like a newborn deer's. Every step demanded more than she had to give. Pain flared. Breath faltered. Her body begged her to stop.

She didn't.

She forced herself forward. Alpha Vasumen would know what to do.

She needed him to understand what Yarron was planning, and why she had to stop it. Her only hope was to find him awake. Dragon or human, Aluk had the strength to summon his brothers and protect Trinity. Perhaps Trinity might understand the voice that haunted her thoughts.

You must become the first.

More than anything, Palisade needed to regain his trust. Yarron's plans were tangled and dangerous, and she could not unravel them alone. Whatever she felt for the man had to be locked away. Feelings were a luxury she could not afford.

A sound drifted up the stairwell.

Her heart slammed hard enough to steal her breath. Trace's face flashed in her mind, his cold, unyielding stare sharp with hatred. In her weakened state, she would not survive an encounter with him. He could drag her back into the lower levels, somewhere no one would hear her scream.

Trinity or Conleth were just as dangerous in their own way. One look at her shaking legs and fevered skin and they would force her back into bed, would take one look at her unsteady legs and fevered skin and insist she go back to bed, dismissing her urgency as delusion.

She could not let that happen.

She had to reach Aluk.

Palisade paused and listened. No sound. She pressed her hand to the stone wall, careful of the flames lining the corridor. They cast light without warmth. Her knees trembled as she took a cautious step forward.

The hallway stretched ahead, dim and empty. Shadows clung to the walls, crawling at the edges of her vision.

She gritted her teeth and pushed open the door to Alpha Vasumen's chamber.

The hinges creaked, and she flinched. Warm air rolled over her, heavy and suffocating, as though the room itself held its breath. Heat struck her like a blow, jolting her senses. Her strained breathing stuttered.

Her eyes adjusted to the light.

Alpha Vasumen lay on the massive bed at the center of the room, his imposing figure unnervingly still. Pain lanced through her chest.

His broad shoulders sagged into the mattress; his head tipped at an unnatural angle. Sweat glazed his brow, and the pallor dulling his vibrant skin twisted fear deeper into her gut.

Her knees buckled. She caught the doorframe, fingers digging into the wood.

Was this his dragon's doing? Had the spirit hollowed him out and left only the body behind?

She took a step toward him, then froze. The urge to shake him, to demand he fight, burned through her. What right did she have after everything?

Her heart throbbed in time with the fire racing through her legs. She forced herself forward. One step. Then another.

Conleth and Trinity stood at the end of the bed. Conleth crossed his arms tight against his chest. His face scrunched up in deep thought. Trinity hovered close, her hands twisting together.

"Palisade?" Conleth's eyes widened. "You're awake."

Trinity moved first. She crossed the room and reached for Palisade, her eyes bright with unshed tears. "Thank the stars."

She guided Palisade to sit on the edge of the bed. This time, Trinity's touch brought no visions. No strange pull.

"You should rest," Trinity said.

"I'm fine." She'd rest when she was dead.

Her gaze slid past them to Alpha Vasumen. His chest rose. Fell. Relief punched through her ribs.

"Trinity, Yarron is coming for you."

Trinity stiffened. "Me?"

"You're important in whatever he's planning. It's why we were sent to release Gorak."

Color drained from Trinity's face. "One *ohunko* trying to kill me wasn't enough, they'd send another?"

Conleth's eyes flashed, the dragon surfacing. "We'll stop him before he gets the chance."

Palisade's fingers curled into the sheets. There was more. Too much more. They needed Alpha Vasumen.

Her chest tightened as she looked at Alpha Vasumen again. "What's wrong with him?"

Conleth exchanged a look with Trinity. She put her hand on his chest. "I believe this is your department, my love," Trinity said softly.

Conleth stepped forward. His expression hardened as his gaze locked on Palisade, as if he needed her to brace for what came next.

"The dragon spirit is in turmoil. The dragon spirit is fighting for control, and Aluk is caught in the middle. It's why you're feeling the way you are—your bond with him is strong."

Pressure cinched around her ribs, tightening with his every word. *The bond.* The one thread still tied her to him, and now it could tear them both apart.

Her gaze drifted to Aluk. He looked so still, so unlike the commanding, relentless man who ran the prison. His skin went pale. His breaths came shallow, uneven. She matched them without meaning to, each one a struggle.

Trinity moved closer, brushing her fingers over her forehead. Her eyes slid shut. Her eyes fluttered shut as she concentrated.

Palisade sensed the connection linking them, a tether she could not sever. The thought of losing him to the dragon spirit sparked an ache behind her ribs. "He has to live. I need him to live. Tell me what to do. I'll do it."

Conleth gently placed a hand on her shoulder. "Right now, the best thing you can do is stay with him. He needs you."

Trinity shot Conleth a look, then turned to Palisade. "We have to prepare."

Palisade frowned. "Prepare for what?"

"We can't wait for Yarron to make the next move. If he's coming for me, we need to be ready. I'll have Pinto send guards to check the perimeter, secure the entrances, and be ready for anything," Trinity said.

Palisade's gaze dropped to Aluk. Each rise of his chest looked like effort. "Will that be enough?"

"We can contact Sia at Avalanche Ridge. He's the closest to sending more enforcers." Conleth squeezed Palisade's shoulder. "Stay with him. He needs you. We'll handle the rest."

Trinity glanced at Alpha Vasumen, then back at Palisade. "We won't be long."

Conleth and Trinity left the room, closing the door softly behind them. The faint click echoed in the quiet, but to Palisade, it sounded distant, as though muffled by the haze of pain wrapping around her.

Her fingers trembled, touching his face. The warmth of his skin met her fingertips, and a shiver ran through her like sunlight streaming through glass on a cold winter day.

"Fight this," she whispered. "Take control again. Please,"

The bond flared. Fire threaded her veins, braiding itself with the ache in her bones. "I need you."

She bent, pressing her forehead to his chest and breathed him in. The earth and spice and pine brought her comfort. Heat poured off him from the dragon lingering under his skin.

She clung to the rhythm beneath her ear. One beat. Then another.

"You're burning up," she murmured. "If you can hear me, Oska, we need Alpha Vasumen back. Whatever happens, we can fix it, but if you lose, the Fae win, and your people continue to suffer."

Her body begged for rest she couldn't afford. She traced his chest with her fingers, a plea and a prayer. The minutes stretched until his head twisted, and his body jerked.

Palisade pulled back with a gasp. His unconscious form went still again.

Panic clawed at her chest, her own heartbeat quickening into a wild rhythm. "Conleth!"

She twisted away, scrambling to leave the bed, when a low groan from Alpha Vasumen froze her. His face contorted, carved with pain.

The bond detonated.

Twenty-Two

Grief crashed through her, too big to belong to one body. It crushed the air from her lungs. Tears spilled hot and unstoppable. The pain came from him. Alpha Vasumen. His dragon spirit. Deep and endless.

It hollowed her.

She fell back against him and curled into his side, clutching his shoulders. Sobs tore through her. She pressed her face into his burning skin, her tears darkening his shirt as if she could drown the pain out of him.

Time unraveled. Breath came and went without rhythm. She clung and waited and willed.

Then a hand moved.

It slid across her back.

She jolted, sucking in a breath, and lifted her head just enough to meet his eyes.

Alpha Vasumen's eyes opened.

"Palisade?"

Tears welled in her eyes, blurring his face. Her lips trembled as she leaned closer, her heart soaring. "You're back."

His gaze softened, the stark black of his eyes fading into a rich, stunning shade of brown. "My mate."

She tried to lean back, to give him space, but his arms locked around her. Her heart slammed hard enough to hurt. "Are you alright? Your dragon?"

"I dreamed." Alpha Vasumen's hand slid up to cradle her neck, his thumb resting beneath her ear. The touch alone eased something tight in her chest. "Saw things I needed to see. Things I should have understood a long time ago."

He drew her closer, giving her a chance to pull away. "The woman in the mountain manipulated my dragon. For centuries. Her hold on him kept me and all the other alphas before me from marking a mate. They knew, and until now I didn't. I'm not making that mistake again. The woman can't mess with my instincts anymore."

"Aluk..."

His lips brushed hers, gentle, almost reverent. The kiss was soft at first, a question rather than a claim. Heat bloomed where they touched, spreading through her in a slow, aching wave. Her breath caught, and she let it out against his mouth, her hands curling into the fabric of his shirt.

A quiet hum beneath her skin went right to her toes. His lips lingered, unhurried, deepening only when she leaned into him. Her body answered him with a soft, unguarded sigh.

For a moment, the pain faded. Her illness. Even the mountain fell away, leaving only the beat of his heart beneath her palm.

Something inside her settled, clicking into place with a sense of rightness.

She pulled back, breath panting, her forehead resting against his. He followed her movement, his lips brushing her cheek, her temple, reluctant to let the space grow between them. She drew a shaky breath and lifted her head, searching his eyes.

"Who are you?"

"I'm not my dragon, if that is what you're thinking, Dr. Everett." His warmth lingered on her skin, and her body betrayed her. She leaned toward him. His half-lidded gaze, dark and intent, made it hard to think.

"A moment ago, you called me Palisade," she said.

"A moment ago, my lips were too busy kissing my mate." His gaze softened, his fingers moving to trace her face, unhurried. The red glow of his eyes had settled into a warm amber.

His fingers brushed against a loose strand of her hair, twirling it. "I'm whole. The dragon spirit and I have merged."

"Oska?" Her stomach fluttered, a mixture of unease and something far more dangerous. "Alpha Vasumen?"

"Aluk, " he corrected. His thumb brushed along her lower lip. "You have the most beautiful eyes, Peaches."

Her cheeks burned at the intimacy of his tone. "I—I should get your brother. He can assess you, ensure you're well."

"My brother can wait." Aluk's hand pressed against her back, drawing her closer. "I'm not finished with you yet."

"Oh." Palisade blinked. She fell against his chest, then caught herself and rolled away from him.

"Perhaps we should talk before... before anything else," she stammered, her hands trembling. "You kissed me." Her fingers touched her lips.

"I did." One corner of his mouth curved. "Don't say you didn't like it."

She liked it, maybe a little too much. Her stomach flipped at the truth of it. "You don't even like me."

"I never said I didn't like you." He propped himself up on his elbows. "You're the one who got all formal on me."

She opened her mouth to call him a brute, but engaging in an argument or name-calling got them nowhere. She bit her bottom lip.

"You keep doing that, and I'll have to prove you wrong another way."

Heat rushed through her, sliding and settling deep in her chest. She taught herself a long time ago that relationships didn't work for her. Survival demanded too much. Duty took priority. One kiss from this man, and she wished she had more time to explore this between them.

Her muscles loosened as she rested against him, the constant ache easing its grip. His shirt was damp beneath her cheek where her tears had fallen. The dull ache behind her eyes lessened, a small reprieve from the constant reminder of how fleeting life was.

Awareness crept back in like a blade slicing through the haze of her comfort. She remembered his wife, the ghost of her presence lingering in his life like an unspoken vow. Palisade's stomach twisted, guilt and defiance churning together until she couldn't tell which burned hotter.

"Is it true that shifters mate for life?" She didn't know whether she was stalling or testing him. Something inside her tightened, then demanded the truth before it closed and dragged him down with her.

His eyes softened. Beneath it lingered something deeper. Regret, maybe. Weariness. "When we bond with our fated mates, it's for life, Peaches."

Peaches. The nickname should've irritated her. Instead, it unsettled her. There was no venom in his voice. Only a quiet resignation.

"I thought my dragon made it clear. Mate."

"You made it clear." She searched his face for any sign of resolve. "I'm not your wife, and I can't replace her."

Her heart pounded, waiting for his reaction. Denial. Anger. Dismissal. She didn't know which would hurt most.

She bit her lip. Her fingers curled at her sides. She hadn't thought to check him for a head injury with all the blood seeping from the claw marks on his side.

"No, you'll never replace Naomi. She was not who fate chose for me. We grew up together at the resort. I knew she had always had a crush on me. Alphas have a duty. We must have a child to pass our spirits on for the next Alpha. My father had passed away the year before, and my brother Taran's dragon spirit was new to him. It was the same year Ben became the dragon guardian and Naomi agreed to become my wife. I cared deeply for her, but she made demands that even I, as an Alpha, couldn't fulfill."

Every word he spoke reverberated through her, shaking the fragile foundation of what she thought she understood.

"You've been wondering why I'm alive and she's dead."

Palisade nodded.

"When shifters bond with their mates, it's for life because our bond makes us one. When one of us dies, the other follows soon after."

A spark flared in her chest, sudden and desperate. Would their bond be enough to save her? Could she survive this illness if they became one? The thought twisted inside her. Did she want him for the bond alone? For survival?

The pain in his gaze stopped the thought cold.

What if she dragged him down with her?

"I'm sorry," she whispered. "I don't think you should tempt fate a second time. The odds..." She turned away, her chest cracking open. What strength she had summoned to make it to his room was fast depleting. "I'll go find your brother now."

"Peaches."

His voice threaded through the air, thick with command. Alpha dominance carried the single word, sliding through the invisible tether between them. It pulled at her. She turned back despite herself.

"Naomi may have been my wife long ago, but you have always been my fate. I can feel the bond between us even if you can't."

"Bond?"

"The invisible thread connecting us. I can sense where you are. Feel your emotions, or if you'll have me."

"When I die, you'll die."

"None of us knows when the Greater Hunter will call us back to his forest. Let's not waste what little time we have fighting it because of a curse given to us by the Fae."

The same curse Yarron had manipulated her, *compelled her*, into perpetuating. He had chosen her for this. Her bloodline.

"That's why you need to know something now. Yarrow knew what he was doing when he used me. He's after Trinity."

Alpha Vasumen's expression hardened. "Trinity?"

"He chose me because of my bloodline. He used my past and my illness to manipulate me into helping him." Yarron had expected her to merge with Gorak, but the bear guardian had taken Diaden instead.

Did Diaden know? Could he survive with Gorak inside him for her to uncover the truth? And Yarron. He had to know.

Fire scorched her lungs with every shallow breath.

Her parents. Had they abandoned her, or had Yarron taken her from them?

Asigwani had called her daughter. These were her people. She belonged to this world and this truth.

"Peaches?" Aluk's voice rumbled softly, cutting through the storm in her head.

"I should have told you sooner. I should have—."

"No." A deep growl rumbled from his chest. "We deal with what's in front of us. Right now, we protect Trinity and end Yarron's plans before he can act."

She didn't have the energy. This task fell on him. "You need to rest and refrain from... exerting yourself."

Her body sagged against him; the pull in her chest yanked hard. Her mind screamed at her to put distance between them. Save him.

"What kind of exertion would you prefer?" His mouth curved with teasing intent, his eyes bright with mischief.

Heat rushed to her face. "I'm getting Conleth."

"I've already spoken with Conleth." He pointed to his temple. "You don't have the strength to fetch him."

She backed toward the door, fighting the ache to stay. Tears built in the back of her eyes.

Aluk swung his legs over the bed and staggered upright. "Palisade, wait. You're trembling." His brow creased. "Oska doesn't like the vibes we're getting. What's wrong?"

"Once your brother clears you, we'll talk." She needed to lie down before she fell down. "You're confused. The merge with your dragon spirit has disoriented you."

She fled out the door. Halfway down the hall, her knees gave out. The stone floor rushed up to meet her, but the impact never came. Strong, furnace-warm arms caught her, hauling her against a broad chest before her head struck the floor.

"I've got you," Aluk rasped.

She slumped against him, her fingers feebly fisting his shirt. "I'm sorry. I just wanted to live."

"You need some rest to get your energy back."

Conleth's footsteps pounded down the hall, but Aluk didn't look up. He dropped to his knees, cradling Palisade against his lap. His face was a mask of sheer, terrified frustration.

"Conleth, fix her," Aluk commanded. "Do something."

Conleth knelt beside them, his hand hovering over Palisade's chest. He looked at Aluk, his expression grim. "Wasting illness isn't a fever. It's chronic and fatal."

Palisade forced her eyes open. Aluk's face came into focus. "Better than dying in a dungeon."

Twenty-Three

Aluk didn't laugh. His grip tightened, his head bowing until his forehead pressed against hers. She sighed, her eyes drifting closed again. He nuzzled her neck and inhaled deeply. The scent of her filled his lungs.

Peaches.

He was Oska again, lurking in the depths of their shared consciousness, watching the prison entrance through his human's eyes.

A woman stepped through the iron gate.

Strawberry-blonde hair. Green eyes. Chin lifted in false confidence.

And her scent—

Sweet summer peaches, sun-warmed and perfect, hit Oska with a rush of joy.

The compulsion shrieked.

The barbs hooked into Oska's soul burned. Like her scent poisoned them. Her very existence was antithesis to Issabrie's hold.

"You're not dying," he said, though his heartbeat raced. He tightened his hold, as if sheer will alone could hold her together. "Not like this. Not now."

The compulsion fought back. Tried to twist the bond and make it feel like the fake-need for Issabrie. It couldn't. Palisade was...clean. Pure. Real.

Maybe this time.

Conleth's voice cut through the haze. "What's going on? Dr. Everett."

"She's getting worse," Aluk's dragon's growl edged his words. "Get whatever she needs. Now."

Even as he barked orders, Aluk's gaze dropped to Palisade's face. Pale. Drawn. His throat closed hard. Flashes of Naomi's face, cold, still, and lifeless rose from the recesses of his memory.

He shut his eyes to let it wash over him rather than fight it. When he looked down again, Palisade was there. The bond between them hummed, faint. A fragile thread wove between them refusing to snap. Naomi belonged to his past. This woman was his fate.

No. The compulsion slammed down again, hooks digging deeper in punishment. Wrong female. Only Issabrie

Aluk's hand hovered over Palisade's wrist.

Mark her.

"Get her back in your room. Put her on the bed," Conleth said, his tone far too authoritative for Aluk's liking. Still, he didn't argue. There was no time.

Palisade stirred as he carried her, her fingers holding onto his shirt. The smallness of the gesture almost undid him. He lowered her onto his bed.

"Aluk...we need to stop. I can't do this...not like this."

Stop? How could they stop when she was slipping away?

"What now?" Aluk looked to Conleth.

His brother lifted one shoulder. *Keep her comfortable.*

Comfortable? Oska snarled. *She's our mate, You let her die, and I go with her. I will not lose another.*

I know! Aluk turned back to the woman on his bed.

"There has to be something you can do." His hands trembled as he cradled Palisade closer. If she died now, he'd never get the chance to prove that she was more to him than a means to an end.

"Unless you've got a spirit animal that matches her bloodline and can merge with a female, this one is beyond me," Conleth said. *I'm sorry, brother. I'm glad she brought you back, but this is beyond my knowledge.*

Aluk's dragon sank lower into the emergence of his soul. He pressed out toward their bond, offering what strength he had.

"Aluk..."

"Hang on, Peaches. We'll figure this out." He had to. He failed to reach Naomi in time because she had hidden from him. Not this time. Not ever again.

Aluk tipped his head back and shouted at the ceiling. Fire surged through his veins, heat flooding every nerve ending.

Her lashes fluttered. Green eyes clouded with pain met his. "You don't understand," she whispered. "I can't."

"Stop talking," he commanded, softer now. He brushed her hair back, his hand shaking as it lingered on her cheek. "Save your strength. We'll have that talk when you're better."

Her lips twitched, almost forming a smile, before pain pulled it away. Each flicker of her struggle carved into him.

"Aluk, please," she breathed. "I can't."

"Stop saying that." His chest locked tight around the bond between them. *Mark her.*

His tattoo burned like molten metal. Heat spread through his chest, down his arms. The tip of his tongue burned. She was his mate, and he wouldn't let her go while he still had breath to fight.

I can share the dragon spirit between us?

He lifted her trembling hand towards his mouth. "Palisade Everett, if that's even your real name, I claim you under shifter law and bind you to me in the ways of my people."

Her eyes widened. Tears spilled over, catching in her lashes.

"You can't..." she whispered.

No alpha, Conleth said in his head. *Mark her, and you condemn yourself to her fate.*

"I can. And I will." Aluk pressed his forehead to hers. "We're fated. The bond has already formed. If I can't tether you to me here, then I go with you. That's how it works."

"Aluk, you won't survive," Conleth said.

Aluk growled low, his dragon bristling at the interruption. He forced himself to turn toward his brother.

"I won't survive without her, Conleth. Don't you get it? She is my mate. My true mate. Fate gave me a second chance, and I'm not going to stand by and let her slip away."

Aluk, I know what you're feeling, but if you mark her now, when she's already this weak, she may have even less time left. You'll not only seal her fate of death, but your own.

She's already dying! Oska's fury bled straight into their link. Aluk's gaze dropped back to Palisade, fragile in his arms, her breathing shallow. "If I lose her, then I don't want to stay. I can't, Conleth."

Oska hurled a memory at him.

Naomi's laughter, bright and unguarded. The way she filled a room with stubborn warmth. Her determination to build a life with him, even knowing she was not his fated mate. The meadow. The tears streaked her face as she grabbed his hands and begged.

Why can't you love me enough to do this? To make me yours fully?

It's not love, Naomi. It's the dragon. It won't let me—

You always blame the dragon!

He had gone after her only to find her too late. The cliff. Her lifeless body. The wind stole away her last breath.

"Aluk…" Palisade's voice pulled him back to the present. Her lashes fluttered as her eyes struggled to focus on him.

"Please… don't…." Each word splintered between breaths. "You die, and the Fae win."

He tightened his hold on her hand, his thumb brushing the bare skin of her wrist. The place where his mark belonged.

"Don't ask me to let you go. I can't." He blinked several times. "You're mine, Peaches. My dragon knew it the moment you walked into the prison."

Her scent. The pull. "Fate knew it, too. That's why I could never mark Naomi. No matter how hard I tried, my dragon refused. You were always my destiny."

The truth burned through him. He had waited too long for too many things. She had no time left for hesitation. "I've waited my entire life to mark my mate. Please allow me the honor."

Tears spilled over her pale cheeks. Her hand trembled, reaching for his face. He caught her fingers, holding her hand. His dragon paced inside him.

"Aluk?" Trinity burst inside the room. "What's happening?"

"Aluk wants to mark Palisade," Conleth said.

Trinity stepped toward him. Aluk snarled. "Do not touch me."

He cut a hard glare at his brother. *Leave. Both of you.*

Conleth shook his head.

Did you let someone watch when you bonded with your mate?

"Aluk," Trinity whispered.

"I'd rather die with her than live without her."

Conleth held his gaze for a long moment. Then he took Trinity by the arm and steered her toward the door.

"What? We're leaving? You're letting him do this?" Trinity protest-ed.

"Alpha orders."

The door closed.

Aluk's tattoo flared, white-hot. Power surged through his chest as his dragon rose, lending him strength. "Where were we?"

"Aluk..."

"Let me mark you, Peaches."

Barbs threatened to break their fragile bond.

Her lips parted in protest, but Aluk silenced her with a gentle kiss, pouring every ounce of his desperation into it. Fire curled around them, the bond sparking and flaring to life between their souls.

"Please."

"I need a yes, Peaches."

Her body softened against his. With a weak breath, she whispered, "Yes."

Something inside him snapped free. Years of restraint. Longing. The hollow ache of incompleteness coiled tight, then broke open.

Aluk lifted her wrist to his mouth.

Her gasp flared against his skin as he traced the ancient sigil of his dragon into her flesh, the mark of their bond. A rush of warmth, of connection, locked into place and calmed his dragon spirit.

The burn seared into her skin. He pressed his lips there, soothing the mark with his tongue, easing the sting, anchoring her to him.

Ripped out by the roots in a cascade of golden fire, it burned through two centuries of the curse.

The bond sang between them, pure, and true and real. This. This was what fate intended.

And Palisade, his dying, human Palisade, had given it to them. Had freed them.

The cost was almost more than he could bear. His vision blurred, and darkness crept in, tugging at the edges of his mind. He thought they would have more time, that they could fight this. That he could fight for her, fight for them.

He clung to Palisade, his arms locking around her. Fight it. He needed her to fight. To stay. His strength drained fast, but he didn't loosen his hold.

Her heartbeat fluttered beneath his palm, then steadied. Her breathing slowed, each rise of her chest more even than the last. Relief crashed through him. His dragon sensed it, and shared an exhale after the brink.

"You're mine, Peaches," he whispered, putting his alpha command into the vow. "And I'm yours. Forever."

Darkness edged in, heavy and thick. His body sagged with exhaustion, but her fingers tightened around his hand, anchoring them together as he slipped under, following her into the pull of his mate's illness.

The mark tethered her bond to Aluk, his fire pulsing faintly in the depths of her soul, but her strength was slipping through her fingers like sand. She sensed the expanding space separating her from everything; the chill seeping into her extremities despite Aluk's heat.

Her body ached with a heaviness she could not fight. Breathing became a losing battle. She wanted to hold on for him, for the future they might have had, but her body no longer answered her will.

"Aluk..." She was cold, and he was warm.

"I'm here, Peaches," he murmured. His hand smoothing her damp hair. She wanted to soothe him, to promise everything would be all right, but there was nothing left to give.

The air shifted.

The temperature dropped.

A heavy stillness pressed in around them.

Daughter.

A vast shadow emerged. Silver fire burned in its eyes.

The wolf. Asigwani

You are dying, the wolf said. *The bond with your mate has bought you time, but it cannot heal what lies beneath.*

What lay beneath? A failing body? A fraying soul? She'd lived on borrowed time for most of her life. Her thoughts scattered as exhaustion pulled her under.

Deep within her fading awareness, the wolf prowled through the dark. Beside it stood a tall woman, a bow slung across her back. Palisade caught a fleeting glimpse before the woman faded again, leaving the wolf seated before her, its gaze unblinking.

The animal's glowing eyes bored into hers. *I can give you the strength to endure, but you must open your soul and merge with my spirit.*

Her thoughts flickered, fragile as embers. Merge. *I'll lose myself, and you'll gain my body.*

The wolf's voice softened, ancient and steady. *You will carry my essence within you. I will not replace you, but you will become more. Part human, part wolf—spirit and soul bound. You will be the first and the last of my heritage.*

Her life had been measured in limits. In pain, she endured. In breaths she rationed. In strength borrowed and borrowed again. She had survived by wit and endurance.

She was so tired of breaking.

"Stay with me. Fight. You hear me?" Aluk's voice pulled her back. "Stay back, wolf."

It's time, daughter. You must choose.

Her fingers twitched, searching for his.

The wolf waited.

Aluk leaned over her, eyes blazing, jaw locked like he could hold her together by force alone. The dragon churned behind his gaze, wild and unrestrained.

A tug in her chest burned. The bond. She felt it in the forest when he lay there bleeding. She had given everything she had to keep him safe from Yarron. There was nothing left to bargain with.

Behind him, at the foot of the bed, a massive shadow of a wolf crouched. Muscles coiled. Ready. Its glowing silver eyes fixed on her. *Choose.*

Her breath scraped out. Met his gaze.

Not because fate or a bond demanded it.

Because she wanted to live. She wanted *him.*

"I'll...do it."

"What?" He stared at her.

"I trust you...and I trust the wolf. This is my inheritance, this is my life, and I give it to you."

Approval rippled through her.

The spirit lunged forward, dissolving into mist that swallowed her whole. Energy crackled through the air. Fire and ice tore through her body as ancient power surged into her.

You are strong, daughter, the wolf said. Palisade whimpered as her soul splintered and reshaped. *Feel the hunt, the moonlight, the wild. You are no longer prey. You are the predator. Protect our people as the Great Hunter intended. This task I pass to you.*

Her scream ripped free. The wolf's power wove into her, stitching broken pieces together and filling the emptiness with something vast and untamed.

Memories flooded her. Running beneath endless canopies. The thrill of the chase. The quiet strength of the pack. Then human memories surfaced. Standing in a forest while flames consumed the mountain. The crashing loss of a mate. The ache lingered.

Arms wrapped around her as the world shifted. Her former self slipped away, replaced by the warrior and the wolf. The presence within her pressed close, crowding her for space.

Breathe, child, the wolf urged inside her mind.

Palisade gasped. Fresh air filled her lungs. She lay still. Her chest rose and fell in a steady rhythm. Her body no longer trembled. Strength thrummed beneath her skin.

She turned her head, taking in the room.

The world burst into brilliant clarity. Every sound. Every scent. Every detail.

"The pain... it's gone." For the first time in her life, her body was free from the gnawing ache consuming her. She paused, testing the silence within herself, the strange hollow where pain once lived. "How is this possible?" she breathed.

"*Nimitqwa ktelo,*" Aluk said, and the sound of it drew a small smile from her. *As you once were and will be again.*

You are whole now. The wolf guardian spirit assured her.

"The wolf is part of me."

Aluk gathered her against his chest, his warmth chasing away the cold in her bones. She allowed herself to simply breathe, matching the slow rise and fall beneath her cheek.

"You're alive," he whispered. "That's all that matters."

Her eyes closed. Fatigue settled deep in her muscles, but beneath it, the presence remained, silent and watchful, curled around her like a guardian. His heartbeat thrummed steadily under her ear, pulling the world inward until nothing else mattered.

Rest, the wolf murmured. We must regain our strength.

With a soft sigh, she yielded. Sleep claimed her.

Twenty-Four

Aluk stood beside the bed, his attention fixed on Palisade as she slept. Her face lay smooth in repose, lashes dark against her cheeks, but the room refused to settle.Something new had taken root, and the bond between them pulsed stronger than before.

The pulse set his dragon on edge. It prowled within him, a low snarl scraping the back of his thoughts. *A wolf? Of all the choices, fate aligned us with a wolf?*

"Not the time," he muttered, fingers tracing the worn edge of an ancient tome.

Trinity had stacked the books on the bedside table, a haphazard tower of leather and brittle pages. His brother and Trinity meant well, offering research to occupy him while Palisade recovered.

The illness had taken its toll. Her body lay frail beneath the blankets, struggling to adjust to the unfamiliar presence within her. The wolf was now as much a part of her as the blood running through her veins.

She needed time. Rest

He just didn't know how much he could give her. Gorak and Yarron roamed free on his mountain.

Aluk's dragon stirred, unease rolling through him. *The wolf. After all this time, dares to stand beside me.*

"You speak as if Aswangi is beneath you," Aluk muttered.

The wolf is a guardian, sent by the Great Hunter to protect. You know that.

A guardian, yes. And one to whom I now owe a debt.

The wolf spirit created a bond between them that carried back centuries. The first woman since the curse to carry such a blessing. A living promise to their people. And he almost died for it.

The bond hummed between them. The cost left his limbs heavy. Strength would return. The memory still burned.

"You're stronger than you know," he murmured.

The wolf answered with a low whine, smoothing the jagged edge of his dragon's temper.

What if she challenges us? Do you think Aswangi will stop with reclaiming her bloodline? She won't submit, and neither will I.

Aluk rubbed his temples. The truth pressed in anyway. His gaze drifted back to Palisade, to the slow rise of her chest. An alpha needs a strong mate. *Fate matched us for a reason.* Has she not proved her worth? *Did you not choose her when I opposed it? Without the wolf, we would have lost her, lost ourselves.*

A sacrifice I will make, the dragon grumbled.

A soft knock broke his thoughts.

"Come in," Aluk called.

"You look terrible," Conleth said, attention already on Palisade. "Is she stable?"

Aluk leaned back, the chair creaking beneath him. The movement pulled at sore muscles. He had poured everything into keeping Palisade breathing, into holding his dragon in check long enough to do it. He'd been running on fumes ever since.

"She's alive." His gaze returned to Palisade, who lay motionless, her chest rising and falling in a steady rhythm.

Conleth lifted a brow and stepped closer to the table, bracing himself against it. The wood complained under his weight. Conleth crossed his arms. His attention drifted to the scattered tomes. "The wolf ohunko claimed her?"

"Not claimed." The dragon bristled at the word.

"Blessed," Conleth corrected.

Aluk tightened his hands into fists. Firelight caught along the scars on his knuckles. Conleth's focus snapped back to Palisade.

"There's another scent," Conleth said, quieter. "What did you do?"

The air carried an unfamiliar energy. Conleth took a measured step toward the bed, breath flaring as if he could taste the change.

"I marked her before the wolf came to her."

Conleth went still. Then his mouth tightened, eyes narrowing. "The wolf came to her?"

"Yes," Aluk interrupted. "It came to her as she was dying, as we were dying. The spirit left Gwen's brother and chose Palisade instead."

"When you said wolf, I assumed..." Conleth's voice trailed off, leaving the unspoken thought hanging between them.

"What did you assume? Some random wolf spirit passing through unbound and transient?"

He met Conleth's gaze, but it was like wading through mud as his dragon rose. "The guardian chose her. She's the last of their bloodline."

"Another heartbeat." Aluk looked at Palisade, lying so still, so vulnerable. "That's all it would've taken."

Conleth's gaze flicked back to Palisade. He stood there with his arms slack at his sides, and his lips parting. "You're saying Gwen's brother is..."

"Gone."

He pictured Gwen's brother's lifeless body lying in the dungeons below.

"It left Peter and came through the enchantments? Does it mean it could've escaped all this time?"

"Apparently so," Aluk admitted. "If it found another empty host. No one else here was without a spirit, except Palisade. My dragon didn't see the wolf guardian as a threat. Not until Gorak escaped did I think anyone could get past the fire enchantments."

"So, any guardians?"

"It seems likely."

For a moment, silence filled the room. Aluk reached for the bond she shared with Taran, the faint thread reassuring his brother was moving in their direction from afar.

"You've notified Taran?" Conleth asked, cupping his jaw.

"Taran's on his way to retrieve the body. I connected with him through our bond a little while ago." Not long after his mate fell into an exhausted sleep. "We'll need to discuss our next move. Gorak is still loose, and there are Fae hiding in the mountain. We need to flush them out and send them back."

"I think it's a good idea to gather and make a plan. We need to protect our mates more than ever now," Conleth said.

Aluk leaned back in his chair, exhaustion slowing his movements. The dragon stirred in the back of his mind. "Agreed."

Conleth let out a heavy breath, his shoulders sagging slightly. "And what do we tell Gwen when she realizes her brother is gone?"

"Taran would have informed her by now." His fingers tightened against the chair. "The wolf chose Palisade. She's of the wolf bloodline. Gwen knew this arrangement was temporary."

Conleth pressed his lips into a thin line, his gaze shifting back to Palisade. The faint presence of the wolf lingered in the surrounding air, steady and strong, a contrast to her pale, fragile form.

"Can you live with it?" Conleth asked after a long silence, his voice softer. "About the wolf being part of her?"

"She's alive." Aluk's fingers dug into the armrests of his chair. "That's enough."

Aluk's dragon growled again.

Conleth studied him for a moment, then nodded slowly. "Gwen might not see it that way. She'll need time to process this, and we'd better be ready for whatever comes when she does."

"She has a right to grieve," Aluk said quietly. "And we'll deal with it, whatever it looks like."

The tension in the room was heavy as they both turned their attention to Palisade. Aluk leaned forward, rubbing his temples as his dragon's presence surged, pressing against the edges of his mind.

"A guardian as a companion," the dragon growled. "The wolf inside her must learn to stand behind her alpha."

"Not happening. Palisade is my mate. She stands beside me."

His dragon huffed.

Her guardian strength is a gift. She completes us; never forget that she is our heart, our soul, our everything.

Conleth shot him a questioning look, but Aluk waved him off, pushing himself to his feet despite the lingering weakness in his legs. "We'll tell Gwen together," he said. "But for now, we focus on keeping Trinity safe and breaking the curse. I know how it began, and I plan to see it through to the end."

Conleth nodded, though his expression remained grim. "You can see into your dragon's past? You've synced with the spirit beast."

"I'm whole, and my fated mate lives. I never thought I would see this day, and I intend to make sure our future generations no longer suffer the way we have."

"Agreed. But Aluk…" He hesitated, his eyes reddening with his dragon spirit. "Watch yourself. That wolf spirit might still have alternative motives, like the bear."

Aluk gave a slight nod, his gaze unwavering as it rested on Palisade. Her steady breathing should have comforted him, but the memory of the wolf's past actions resurfaced.

His dragon rumbled. The bond between them grew stronger. Memory followed the sensation. Not long ago, the wolf attempted to possess Gwen. She bargained with the wolf spirit to stay within her brother, Peter.

Now the sacred guardian was inside Palisade.

"Do you think it came to her out of desperation or something more?" Conleth asked.

"The wolf saved her, and for that I'm grateful, but…" His dragon rumbled inside him. "We've seen what happens to the spirits when they linger in the shadows for too long. When it tried to take Gwen, it didn't care about her life. It only cared to survive."

A guardian should have honor.

"This time is different." Aluk glanced at Palisade. "She's my mate."

Trinity filled the doorway, tension tight in her posture. She stepped inside. "Sia is gathering more enforcers, but Pinto has reported sighting Gorak south of here."

Aluk's dragon reared inside him. *Gorak.*

Aluk pushed to his feet, the effort dragging through his limbs. "Good, it narrows our hunt."

"And then what? He will not surrender. He's inside one of Yarron's enforcers. If he's here, it's because he thinks Yarron still holds his reward."

Aluk's gaze drifted to Palisade, who remained unconscious. The wolf's presence wrapped around her like a protective shield. Power hummed through the bond. Leaving her felt like abandoning half of himself, but he couldn't afford for Gorak to succeed or come after his mate again.

"We deal with him," Aluk turned back to Conleth and Trinity. "We push him back through the portal and we buy ourselves time. Enough to figure out how to break this curse and stop Yarron and his men from infiltrating our mountain."

"And her?" Conleth tilted his head toward Palisade.

"She needs to recover. The wolf is still merging and healing her. I won't risk her before she's ready."

His dragon rumbled again. *This is not her hunt.*

Aluk ignored the dragon and moved toward the door. He stopped near the threshold.

"I need you to stay here with her," Aluk said to Trinity.

Palisade's recovery came first, and Trinity was the only other person available.

"You'll watch her," he added with a push of his alpha dominance. "Keep her safe. Let me know the moment she wakes."

Trinity and Conleth exchanged a look, their eyes turning gold.

His dragon hissed as the wolf tugged on the bond. He sent waves of reassurance to his slumbering mate.

Trinity sat in the chair Aluk had vacated moments ago. "I won't leave her."

Aluk leaned closer and brushed a strand of hair from her forehead. His fingers lingered on her skin. The bond between them pulsed in response.

"Rest, Peaches. You're safe."

He pressed a soft kiss to her temple. His lips lingered longer than he had intended. It wasn't enough. Not until she opened her eyes again.

As he straightened, the tattoo on his chest glowed beneath his shirt.

"Shouldn't you rest?" Trinity asked.

"I'll rest when my mate is safe."

Then he followed Conleth out, leaving his mate to heal.

Twenty–Five

Heat rushed through her veins, waking her. Her senses sharpened, color blooming behind closed eyes, scent and sound tangling until the world pressed too close and loud.

A steady rhythm anchored her. A heartbeat not her own threaded through hers. The bond.

You are not alone. The voice pulled her from the depths of unconsciousness.

Her eyes snapped open.

Dim firelight swam into focus. Shadows crawled along the walls, cast by a low-burning flame. She sucked in a breath and froze as the scent hit her. Old wood. Spice. Lavender?

"Finally awake," a familiar voice said.

Trinity sat beside the bed, hands folded tight over a book.

"Trinity."

"Here." Trinity leaned forward, grabbing a cup on the stand and pressing it to her lips.

Palisade drank deeply, the cool liquid soothing her parched throat. When she lowered the cup, her fingers shook.

"What happened?" She remembered seeking Aluk, and their kiss. He kissed her. She touched her lips.

Trinity leaned back, her gaze studying Palisade intently. "You don't remember?"

Palisade closed her eyes. Pain slammed back into her. Aluk's voice. *Mate.* The wolf. Silver eyes burning as it lunged toward her. Her hands pressed against her heart.

"I remember the wolf."

"The wolf ohunko merged with you." Trinity's gaze softened. "It saved you."

She remembered.

"Aluk gave everything he had to make sure you survived."

He wasn't here. Her hand brushed the mark on her wrist, the skin still tender.

"He marked me, but it's not finished," she murmured.

"What do you mean?"

Palisade bit her lip, her gaze dropping to the blankets. "The bond isn't complete until he claims me." Her fingers tapped along with her heartbeat. "I feel it. It's like this hollow ache. A pull. He's inside me, but we're still separate."

Trinity laid the book down on the stack beside her.

"Where is he?" Palisade asked.

"He and Conleth left several hours ago. Gorak was spotted south of here."

"They went to intercept him before he escaped again," Palisade said.

Gorak remained a threat to her and Trinity. He may hunt for Trinity, but his intention toward Palisade chilled her. She turned her hand over, looking at the mark on her wrist. *Mate.*

She lifted her eyes to Trinity. "If Gorak gets to you…"

"He won't," Trinity said, gold flashing in her eyes. "The Vasumen brothers will stop him."

"We don't know that. Gorak's more than a shifter-blooded human now. Diaden can teleport."

"Teleportation is rare for a Fae."

"If Gorak gets a hold of you, he can portal you away in a second. The Fae will have what they need to keep the shifters in their control."

"You're not human anymore, Palisade. You're a shifter."

"And you're Fae," Palisade pointed out.

Trinity rested a hand on Palisade's arm. "I know, and now we're family."

Palisade tensed, but as the seconds passed, she relaxed. No stirring or flashes of past or future attacked her.

"Gorak will escape again."

"They won't let that happen. Aluk's an alpha and a stubborn bastard. Conleth is overprotective of me. Aluk has captured him alone before, he'll do it again."

Palisade wanted to believe her. A growl escaped her lips. *Danger is closer than you think*, her wolf spirit warned. *You cannot trust others to protect what is ours.*

Palisade swung her legs over the side of the bed. Her muscles balked at the movement.

A growl rolled up from her chest. Her hand flew to her throat.

"That's new."

Her hands curled into fists. The tips of her fingers tingled. The wolf pressed close beneath her skin. Her senses sharpened further, the room coming into even clearer focus.

"I can't stay here."

Trinity's brows knitted together. "You know Aluk wanted to be told the second you woke up, right? With the bond, he might even already know. If I let you run off, he would roast me alive."

"This isn't about Aluk."

"Is it your wolf? I can get one of the guards. They're all wolf shifters."

"It's Gorak."

Trinity stiffened.

"I helped him escape." Nor did she regret it. Survival had a cost. "I won't lie here pretending that doesn't matter."

Danger moves. The wolf murmured, *Do not wait to be hunted. Protect.*

Trinity swept her silver hair back. "And you think chasing him in this condition is a good idea?"

"No." Palisade pushed herself upright. "I think doing nothing is worse."

Trinity leaned back, arms crossed. "You're still adjusting. The wolf's presence alone makes you a beacon."

Palisade opened her mouth to argue, but Trinity held up a hand.

"Look, I get it," Trinity continued. "You're restless, but you're half-bonded, half-healed, and you're Aluk's mate, making you a target, too."

The growl slipped free before she could stop it.

Trinity didn't flinch.

"Aluk and Conleth are out there dealing with Gorak because they know what they're up against. You haven't had time to adapt to your wolf yet."

The wolf settled inside her. Separate, but the same in body.

"I need to warn them! They don't know everything Yarron is planning."

Trinity crossed her arms. "Aluk trusted me to stay with you. We wait until Aluk and Conleth are back, and you can warn them after they return."

Gorak's name alone dragged a shadow across her thoughts. It brushed against Aluk's presence at the edges of her awareness, tugging on the thin, unfinished thread between them. The mate bond pulled where it should have settled, a dull, persistent ache that refused to ease.

"I hate this," Palisade muttered.

Trinity gave a faint smile. "Yeah, well, welcome to the club. Sometimes, surviving means waiting. Trust me, Aluk would lose his mind if he came back and found you gone."

A reluctant smile tugged at Palisade's lips. "You think he would storm the entire mountain to find me?"

"In a heartbeat," Trinity said. "But for now, why don't you fill me in on Yarron's plan while we wait for the men to return?"

Palisade hesitated. The wolf spirit twisting inside her, displeased. She ignored it.

"Why not?" She slid her hand to her stomach as it growled in open betrayal. "But only if it includes food."

"Oh, you must be famished!" Trinity moved toward the door. "I've already reached out to Conleth."

She glanced back. "Does toasted cheese sound good? I've had an unusual craving for them lately."

"Perfect."

"Good." A spark lit Trinity's eyes. "They'll meet us in the war room. Shall we?"

Twenty-Six

Fire burned along the stone ledge set in the wall, casting flickering shadows across the far side of the hidden war room off Aluk's office. Maps and notes lay scattered across the heavy oak table, a few mugs of lukewarm tea abandoned where long hours of planning had ended. Aluk braced himself against the table's edge, eyes tracking the map spread before him. Smoke and leather clung to his clothes, familiar as old scars.

Conleth stood opposite him, broad shoulders rimmed in firelight. His dark hair stuck up where he'd dragged a hand through it.

"We're too exposed here." He trapped the map with two fingers. "If he moves fast, we'll lose him."

A low growl rose from Aluk, his dragon pacing in his mind.

"I've sent Sia and Pinto out with a hunting party," Aluk said, rolling his shoulders back to ease the ache lodged there. "They'll sweep back toward the prison until they pick up his trail."

"And Taran?" Conleth asked, lifting his gaze.

"With Gwen," Aluk didn't look up. "She needs him right now. The news tore the wound of losing her brother open again ."

Conleth exhaled slowly, fingers raking through his hair. "Fair." He paused. "Another dragon would help. If this involves a guardian, maybe Ben should–"

"I need Ben at the resort. If there is one Fae camp hidden on the mountain, then there are more. Now that my dragon has found one, they will shield from the sky, too."

"They could have been here all along," Conleth said, and his brother wasn't wrong. His ancestors assumed the Fae had retreated to their realm or into the human cities. All this time they had remained on the mountain in hidden camps.

"If they're smart enough to hide, they're smart enough to blend in there." Aluk's gaze hardened. "The last one glamored himself to look human."

Firelight slid over the pale scars lining his forearms and knuckles. Old failures, each one carved deeper than the last. None of them prepared him for this. A mate bound to him by fate, carrying a guardian spirit that answered to no alpha but itself.

His fingers twitched.

A tug brushed his senses.

His dragon rumbled in recognition.

She's close.

Palisade's wolf spirit brushed against his awareness like a whisper against his soul.

If enemies could vanish into forests and crowds alike, how did he shield his people? How did he protect his mate?

And would Palisade even allow it now, with the wolf coiled inside her, instincts bent toward pack and alpha before self. Assuming the wolf inside her no longer carried the taint of darkness from the past.

We can trust her. The wolf—

Is part of her.

Soft footsteps brushed the stone behind him.

Aluk drew a slow breath, letting it bleed tension from his shoulders as Trinity stepped inside. "Any updates on finding Gorak?"

Firelight caught in her platinum hair, purple tips gleaming like spilled ink. Her violet eyes held the same sharp defiance he associated with her presence, an energy that sparked and snapped against his dragon's awareness.

She unsettled him. Always had.

Her gift had once brushed too close to his dragon's past. The impulse rose to touch her, to chase whatever visions might guide them forward. He locked his hand at his side and let the moment pass.

His dragon rumbled at her proximity.

"Sia and Pinto have scouted the western forest," Conleth said, breaking the silence. He leaned onto the table, his gaze on Aluk. "They found tracks, but lost them over the ridge near here. They disappear and then show up close to the last set of tracks. It's like he's taunting us."

"He's waiting for an opening," Aluk said.

"To come back in?" Trinity scoffed.

"Or for you to come out," Conleth said.

"How close?" Palisade stepped into the light. Her hair had darkened, catching the fire like deep wine. Green eyes scanned the room, steady and assessing. The wolf prowled closer. Silver shards glinted in her gaze.

She should be resting. His dragon's disapproval rolled through him.

His lips curved in a faint smile as she approached.

Are you sure the wolf hasn't taken over? Conleth asked, the thought edged with unease.

Aluk followed the pull of the bond. *She's changed, but the wolf remains within.*

For now.

She carries herself like a guardian.

And that scared his dragon spirit more than the beast inside him would ever admit.

Trinity folded her arms. "He's not going to keep waiting forever. If we don't make a move, he will."

"And that's exactly what we're trying to avoid," Aluk said.

"Yarron intends for Gorak to capture Trinity."

"Like Pezi," Trinity breathed. "They think they can send another *ohunko* after me."

"It's the only way for the Fae to remain anonymous in upholding the curse. If we wait too long, Gorak will strike, and we'll lose our advantage."

Aluk's dragon surged hot and violent in his mind. *Gorak.*

They lost time after the attack. Whatever advantage they might have vanished with Aluk and Palisade's time in the tower.

Conleth's frown deepened as his attention went to Trinity. "Are you certain?"

"I am," Palisade said. "Yarron won't rush this. He'll wait for Gorak and set traps. He'll divide his warriors in strategic locations to increase his chances of capturing Trinity."

"We don't have time to waste. If Gorak is moving, we need to meet him head-on." Aluk's gaze caught on Palisade, on the silver of her eyes. Still healing. Still dangerous. The wolf's presence entwined through their bond.

"If the Fae like to set traps, we'll use their own tactics against them."

Trinity let out a short breath. "So, I'm bait again."

"No." Conleth's head snapped toward Aluk. "If this goes wrong—"

"If it goes wrong, we lose everything." Trinity cut in, stepping closer to the table. Gold flared in her eyes. "Do either of you have a better option?"

Silence filled the space between them.

Aluk's fist curled, fire filled his veins.

"I do."

Aluk turned slowly. She stood straight, shoulders set, her expression calm.

"No," he said. Her plan telegraphed to his mind. She might not have known she shared those thoughts with him yet. Images of Naomi, lying broken, staring up at the sky, twisted a knife in his chest. His tattoo glowed, and he pressed a palm to the spot. "You're not part of this."

She met his stare without flinching. "Gorak is hunting Trinity. If he senses me instead, he'll pivot. He wants me. It's why he possessed Diaden and not me."

"I'm not putting you at risk," Aluk said.

The wolf looked out through her eyes. Her lip curled up.

He held up a hand. "This isn't an argument, guardian. Protect Trinity."

"And I'm offering you a way to do that." Palisade didn't waver. *Stand down guardian.*

Let me do my job, Alpha.

You are my mate first and foremost. You will not put yourself in danger. I need you. Alive.

She bared her teeth at him and growled.

Trinity's lips curved down. "I don't like this. He's after me. If anyone should—"

"No," Conleth interrupted. "You're not expendable, Trinity."

"And neither is she." Aluk's gaze turned red with the heat of his dragon. His eyes locked on Palisade, daring her wolf to push him further.

She stepped closer. Silver brimming her eyes. Her chin tilted up, she said, "I know the risks. But I can do this. And I trust you to keep me safe."

His dragon spirit rankled inside him. Aluk dragged a slow breath, raking a hand through his hair.

He hated the plan.

And worse, he couldn't deny it would work.

Twenty-Seven

The forest whispered around them. Leaves rustled. Twigs snapped beneath their feet. Every sound tightened the coil in Palisade's chest.

Aluk's irritation rolled off him. A low growl cut through the night.

"This is a terrible idea."

Her wolf bristled.

"It's our best chance." Palisade stood in the clearing, shoulders squared, meeting his fire-lit gaze without flinching. The wolf paced in her mind, restless.

A storm gathered in his eyes. "You don't understand what you're offering." His jaw flexed. "Gorak isn't just some rogue shadow spirit. He's a guardian. And with the extra abilities of his Fae host, if he gets his claws into you—"

"He won't." She held his gaze. "Because you'll stop him."

He turned away, pacing. Heat hummed through the mark on her wrist. "I don't like this."

"You don't have to." She closed the distance between them. With the wolf spirit rising inside her, unsettled by his agitation, emboldened by it too. "But you know it's the only way. Gorak will be drawn to me. Whatever his reasons, we can use that against him."

Aluk froze mid-step, turning to face her. "If anything happens to you—"

"It won't." Her hand found his arm. Muscles jumped beneath her fingers. The contact cooled the mark on her wrist, even as his muscles strained under her touch. "We can do this. Together."

The bond between them pulsed. A reminder that all they hadn't made their mating permanent. His protectiveness might have overwhelmed her under different circumstances. The wolf spirit straightened her spine.

At last, he exhaled. His shoulders lowered, though the fire in his eyes held. "Fine, but I'm not leaving your side."

"I wouldn't want it any other way."

They moved into position.

Her wolf spirit's growls reverberated through her mind like distant thunder. Aluk melted into the shadows while Palisade stepped into the center of the clearing, exposed.

Gorak comes. Her wolf whispered through her consciousness. *Be ready, but do not falter.*

Palisade tilted her chin up, swallowing against the unease prickling her skin. *What's his deal, anyway? Gorak.*

Her fists clenched.

Revenge, her wolf answered.

He wants me for revenge against the alpha? Against Aluk?

Her stomach twisted, but she dragged in a steady breath. The forest held its breath with her, and the chill of Gorak's approach crawled along her skin.

Grizzlies are not the brightest, her wolf noted with wry amusement.

Let's hope you're right. We'll need every advantage we can get.

When Gorak appeared, the darkness thickened. His massive bear form emerged from the trees, muscles rippling beneath thick fur. Amber eyes locked onto Palisade, and her pulse kicked into a sprint.

The bear froze, its hulking form shimmering. Energy rippled through the clearing, crackling against her senses like static before a storm. Unease flowed from her wolf spirit.

The bear shifted. Bones cracked and reshaped, fur receding into pale, golden skin. The transformation flowed seamlessly as though nature itself bent to Gorak's will.

She'd seen him in Diaden's body before, but it never got easier. Long ago, she'd found those sharp, angular features handsome. Now, his red-tinged amber eyes blazed, setting every nerve in her body alight with the wrongness of it.

Her stomach knotted, but she held his gaze, swallowing the instinct to shrink away. He stood there, all too perfect. His presence rippled through the clearing.

Aluk's presence kept her calm. She clung to that connection, to what she fought for and what she hoped to make permanent when this ended.

Palisade drew in a deep breath. Her hands trembled. "Gorak."

"Asigwani." His lips curled into a predatory smile.

"Leave my wolf spirit out of this." She narrowed her gaze. "What does the Fae queen promise you in exchange for hunting me and my kind?"

Gorak sneered. "I make no deals with her. I don't need promises to claim what should already be mine."

His gaze swept over her. Palisade's stomach churned.

"What is it you want, then?" she asked.

"What I have always wanted. A mate." He chuckled. "You."

Her wolf recoiled, and Palisade's own horror rose to meet it. Not a captive. Not a prize. Mate. As if she'd ever—as if she could stomach—

Her wolf snarled, disgust flooding through them both. *He dares?*

Her wolf's presence swelled. The spirit paced and snarled inside her mind.

"And Trinity? The Beta's mate?" she asked.

"The girl is nothing but a loose thread to cut. Her death will settle old debts."

Ice slid down her spine. Old debts?

A bargain, her wolf whispered.

Palisade's heart hammered. "And what debts would those be?"

"The alpha stole the queen's favor. He stole her heart, her power. I was left with nothing. When the Fae woman dies, he'll lose what he holds dear, and you…" He stepped closer. "You will restore what was lost."

Her chest vibrated with the wolf's snarl. "I will do no such thing."

Groak's expression flattered, darkness flashing in his amber-red eyes.

Diaden.

Something in her chest buckled. *He's still in there?*

Yes, the wolf replied. *Buried, but alive. I sense his soul.*

She searched his gaze for Diaden. For anything resembling the Fae warrior.

Gorak blinked, and any glimmer of Diaden vanished. "We'll see."

In a blur of speed and fur, he lunged. She launched backward with inhuman grace. Her footing faltered for a heartbeat. He had saved her once. She owed him more than a lifetime trapped in his own body.

She dodged another strike and sidestepped Gorak's swipe.

Gorak's snarl filled the air, his fingers tearing through the space she'd just vacated. He lunged again. And again. Claws slashed past her shoulder, grazed her arm. Another swipe whistled past her ear. Her wolf added speed to each dodge, each pivot, keeping her at a safe distance.

"You're quick," he sneered, eyes glowing red. "But it won't save you."

Palisade didn't reply. The flicker of humanity she'd seen replayed in her mind. *If Diaden were still alive, could I save him?*

"Now!" she called, cutting through the chaos.

From the shadows, Aluk emerged, partially shifted. Black scales shimmered down his broad shoulders and arms as his claws tore into Gorak, forcing him back. Gorak stumbled, lips peeling back from his teeth, a growl tearing from his throat.

A rumble rolled from Aluk's chest, more dragon than man. "This ends now, Gorak."

"You think you can save her?" His eyes slid to her, lingering, assessing, like he was deciding which part to bite first.

Her hands tightened into fists as Gorak lunged at Aluk. The force of the attack reverberated through the ground, rattling her bones. Aluk's black scales gleamed. His claws tore into Gorak.

Gorak surged forward, impossibly fast for his size, Fae magic bending his bulk into fluid motion. His massive frame shouldn't move that fast, and shouldn't flow like water between Aluk's strikes.

She locked her gaze on the clash ahead. Gorak's bulk slammed into Aluk's dragon in a violent blur of scales, claws and tearing force. The impact shuddered through the clearing, bark exploding from nearby trees.

Careful. Her fingers itched at the palms. *One wrong move and he'll teleport.*

"Aluk! We need him alive!"

Aluk snapped his head toward her. Amber eyes burned. Frustration turned his head briefly, amber eyes blazing with frustration. "Alive? He's trying to kill us!"

"He's not the only one," she shot back.

A growl tore from his lips. He drove Gorak back by inches, herding him, forcing him to react instead of strike.

"You think you can capture me?" Gorak twisted aside with brutal speed, his hand transformed to a paw, sweeping toward her.

Palisade dropped, rolled, came up light on her feet as claws tore through empty air where her throat had been.

"You'll have to do better than that," she said, angling herself to keep his attention.

Good. Keep his focus on you. The alpha will get him.

Gorak's eyes burned as he advanced. "You think a mark makes you untouchable? You're mine, wolf. The alpha's mark won't last forever."

Claws sprouted from her fingers. "I'm not yours, and I never will be."

Aluk struck at the same time. His claws tore across Gorak's side, sending the bear shifter staggering back. His roar shook the clearing.

Now!

Palisade moved. She wrenched the enchanted cuffs from her belt and cut wide, the wolf's speed flooding her limbs. Gorak swiped for her, claws whistling through the space she'd already vacated, but Aluk drove him back with sheets of fire that scorched the earth and split bark from trees.

She circled. Waited. Counted his footing instead of her fear.

When Gorak stumbled, she lunged and snapped the cuff closed around his wrist.

The metal flared. Gorak growled as the magic bit deep, his strength bleeding away in a visible stagger. He thrashed slower; the cuffs siphoning his Fae-enhanced strength.

"Second cuff!" Aluk bellowed, his dragon claws buried in Gorak's shoulder, pinning him.

She locked the second restraint around his other wrist. The glow grew brighter, then sealed. Gorak's roar tore through the forest canopy, scattering birds across the clearing.

Aluk loomed over him, chest heaving, scales rippling beneath his skin. His dragon's golden gaze burned down at the fallen guardian. "You're not going anywhere."

Gorak spat blood and laughed. "You think the cuffs will hold me? I'll be free by nightfall, and I'll take what's mine."

They started back through the trees with Gorak bound between them. Palisade lagged a step behind Aluk, her attention drifting not to the sneer on Gorak's face, but to the memory that refused to release her.

Diaden fought to survive, and she owed it to him to free him.

Her wolf paced, restless and unsettled, brushing against the thought like a sore tooth.

"Aluk."

He stopped but didn't turn. The air around him swirled from the heat radiating off his body. "What is it?"

Palisade slowed. "Diaden... I think he's still alive."

Aluk's head tilted a fraction, acknowledging her. Beside him, Gorak growled.

"We'll figure that out later. Right now, he goes back to the prison where he can't escape and hurt anyone again."

Her wolf snarled, pacing inside her. Sweat broke out on Palisade's forehead.

The forest dimmed as they crossed into the clearing, shadows pooling between the trees. Aluk took the lead, his stride longer than hers. She had to take two strides to match his one to keep up. His shoulders stayed drawn back. His dragon pressed outward, eyes glowing red, setting the air sizzling with the heat rolling off him.

"I need to shift to fly us back."

Scales erupted along his skin, catching in the evening sun as his frame expanded. Bone realigned with a series of cracks. Wings tore free and spread wide, blotting out the stars as something old stirred awake beneath the trees.

When it was over, the dragon stood where Aluk had been.

Oska.

Her wolf pulled back, hackles raised, caught between reverence and offense.She stepped up alongside Gorak, placing a hand on his cuffs to keep him from going anywhere. His eyes turned onyx, and his shoulders slumped. "Diaden," she breathed. "If you're still there, I'll get you out."

"You'll help me escape again, mate?" Gorak's lips lifted at the corners.

"Never."

The dragon's gaze found her. Smoke drifted from his nostrils.

"Oska," she murmured.

He lowered his head until his snout hovered within reach. The wolf inside her went taut, instincts colliding, submission warring between them.

She lifted her hand. Her fingers brushed over the warm, textured surface of his scales. "Incredible," she whispered.

A low huff rolled from his chest, heat brushing her skin. The mark on her wrist blazed in response. She sensed a difference between them. This was Aluk, but at the same time it was Oska.

As we once were, her wolf swelled inside her. Tingles ran down her arms. *Soon you will be strong* enough, *and we will take my form and show this dragon mate of ours we are second only to the Great Hunter.*

Aluk's gaze snapped to Gorak.

His lips peeled back, fangs catching in the moonlight. A low rumble rolled through his chest. Her wolf's hackles rose. A prickle ran down her arms, and she had to look to see the fine hairs align her arm thickening to fur. *Not yet. She wasn't ready to become a wolf.*

Climb on. Aluk spoke in her mind.

She moved to his shoulder and hoisted herself between the ridges of his scales. A strange sense of security struck her atop the dragon.

Oska let out a deafening roar, shaking the trees and sending animals scattering into the night. With a powerful leap, he grabbed Gorak with his claws. With his wings spread wide, catching the air and flapping to gain height.

Wind whipped past her, stealing her breath. She leaned into his movement. Below them, Gorak hung bound and unmoving. She sensed more than she saw the cuffs radiating their magic. Somewhere beneath the fury and the ohunko's spirit, Diaden still lived.

Later. Her wolf rumbled. *We must grow strong first.*

The forest fell away beneath them.

Trinity was safe.

And whatever game the Fae queen had begun, they had just torn a piece off the board.

Twenty-Eight

Locked behind reinforced bars, iron cuffs biting into his wrist, the bear-shifter radiated something foul. It crawled under Aluk's skin, scraped along Oska's senses, and refused to settle. Gorak's glare followed him as they moved through the prison corridors. His muttered curses clung long after the doors sealed shut.

The cuffs stripped Gorak of his ability to open portals, and the reinforced cell kept him isolated from other prisoners, but it wasn't enough. Not yet. Not until his brother's mate, Gwen, cast Gorak back through the portal into the Great Hunter's forest and sealed him away where he belonged.

Oska rumbled in agreement, a low vibration resonating through Aluk's chest.

Avalanche Ridge rose ahead of them, the valleys spread wide and bright beneath the open sky. Summer had taken hold. Wildflowers streaked the slopes with color. Damp earth and new growth filled his lungs. The resort nestled against the lower ridges, weathered cabins blending into the land.

Taran should have been here. Oska growled at the absence, even if Aluk did not. His brother belonged beside his mate. Gwen needed him more than Aluk did.

Palisade wiggled atop him. Her hands rested on his scales. Fingers curled around one ridge along his spine. Her presence calmed his dragon in a way Aluk finally understood. Their bond, incomplete yet undeniable, left him aching for more. Marking her had deepened their connection. Strengthened the bond. Her wolf spirit solidified it. She sensed it along with him.

Once he eliminated the threats against them, he intended to finish making her his mate.

He landed thirty miles west of the resort, near a lone cabin. Grass rippled beneath the downdraft of his wings.

Palisade dismounted with fluid grace, boots sinking into soft ground. Her hair streamed loose around her face, still wind-tossed from the flight.

Aluk shifted back into human form, the lingering warmth of the change fading as the air brushed over his skin. He crossed to the supply trunk hidden at the base of a tree and pulled on the clothes his brother stored there.

Palisade's gaze swept over the resort's cabins. The lantern-lined paths swayed in the breeze.

"This place is... peaceful," she said.

"It's meant to be," Aluk replied, tugging on his shirt. "But don't mistake peace for indifference. Taran's mate might not welcome a reminder of her brother's sacrifice this soon after his loss."

Aluk reached out through the mental link between his dragon and his brothers, sending a pulse of thought toward Taran.

We're here. We need to talk.

A beat passed before Taran's acknowledgement came through their connection. He was waiting.

They approached the cabin, its rustic wooden beams blending seamlessly with the surrounding trees. Bees hummed lazily in the warmth, the scent of blooming wisteria drifting along the walls in the morning breeze. Through the wide front window, Taran's tall form stood near the fireplace, unmoving.

Aluk pushed open the door; the cool air spilled out, rich with cedar and dried herbs.

Taran straightened as they entered. "Aluk."

Taran's amber eyes glinted with concern. "I thought you'd take time to rest after capturing Gorak."

Don't worry, *brother, I'm not about to go back into hibernation.* Aluk included his head.

His gaze moved to Gwen while slipping his arm around Palisade.

"This is her?" Gwen's gaze settled on her.

"Palisade is my mate," Aluk put dominance in his words.

Gwen's face paled.

"She carries the spirit of the wolf guardian," Aluk continued. "By blood, this is her right."

Palisade stepped forward, twisting her hands. "Gwen, I'm—"

"Don't," Gwen lifted a hand, stopping her.

"You don't have to be sorry." Her gaze dropped to the floor. "I'm sorry. I'm still trying to process. I knew my brother was gone, but not until it was just his body..."

"We need your help to ensure Gorak doesn't return," Aluk said.

Gwen's eyes lifted. Dull with exhaustion. They moved to Palisade, then back to Aluk. "You've captured him?"

"Yes," Aluk said.

"He's in the body of a Fae warrior," Palisade added.

"The cuffs won't hold him forever," Aluk continued. "We need to send him back through the portal."

Gwen's lips thinned. Breath shuddered through her nose as her hands curled at her sides. "My brother died to protect us, to keep the *ohunko* locked away."

She looked at Aluk, red rimmed her eyes. "And now you're asking me to open the gate again?"

"Do you know what you are asking?" Taran said, growling.

Palisade moved closer, slow enough not to startle. She kept her voice gentle. "Your brother made a great sacrifice."

She held Gwen's attention. "Without the guardian spirit, I wouldn't be standing here. Aluk wouldn't ask you unless it was dire. We must remove Gorak from the mountain before he manipulates Daiden's Fae powers and gets his hands on Trinity."

Gwen's shoulders trembled. She turned toward the window. The light caught the edge of her face. "I don't even know if I can do it again."

Taran stayed close to her. "You can take what strength you need from me."

Gwen's shoulders eased. Her gaze turned back to Palisade. "Are we sending her through along with him?"

Aluk's dragon tattoo lit up along his skin. The mere suggestion of losing Palisade sent a fire racing through his veins, gathering at his fingertips. He clenched his hands at his sides. *No one was taking her. Not to a portal. Not anywhere.*

Easy dragon. No one is taking our mate away.

"She. Is. My. Mate." Aluk's nostrils flared.

"She's dangerous," Gwen said.

"Careful." Taran leaned closer to Gwen and whispered in her ear.

Fresh tears slid down her face. Her head shook, and he gathered in his arms. Taran looked at Aluk. *The ohunko will taint her.*

Palisade's gaze met Aluk's. Her eyes turned silver, blinking out the green. Her wolf spirit pushed forward. Aluk placed his hand on the small of her back. "The wolf ohunko exists no more. My mate is a guardian. You will respect her as such."

Gwen met his gaze and nodded.

Aluk exhaled slowly, the tension in his chest loosening. No matter what happened next, he would do everything possible to ensure that nothing threatened his family again.

❧

Palisade sat on the edge of a worn leather armchair, her wolf pacing restlessly in her mind. Aluk stood near the island separating the living space from the kitchen. Gwen lingered by the window, arms folded tight while she stared out toward the mountain ridge. Her reflection peered back from the glass.

Rourke had arrived.

Her wolf rose without thought, spine straightening, attention sharpening.

The door opened.

Rourke stepped inside and stopped. His attention snapped to Palisade.

Her wolf lifted its head before she consciously registered why.

His nostrils flared. A low whine slipped from his chest before he could stop it.

Recognition rolled through her. *Alpha.*

Palisade lifted her chin. The instinct to bare her teeth burned. She held back and bore her gaze into his.

Aluk stepped closer. Not in front of her. Beside her.

The mark on her wrist flared beneath his touch. Heat bloomed at her shoulder, sweeping down her arm. She clutched the spot. *Don't look away!*

Under her fingers, her skin burned, then cooled. The sensation rippled up her arm as she pushed her sleeve back, never breaking her stare from the wolf alpha.

Rourke froze.

His shoulders lowered by a fraction, the challenge bleeding out of his posture before it even reached her.

Taran shut the door behind him.

Silence stretched.

Rourke swallowed and inclined his head.

"Congratulations," he said at last, voice rough. "On your mating."

The room exhaled.

Palisade's gaze dropped to her arm. A wolf, inked in luminous blue, its shape winding around her arm like a living armband. Tendrils curled and overlapped; ancient markings trimmed the design.

You are getting stronger.

Her pulse thudded hard in her ears.

"Your spirit tattoo." Aluk lifted her hand and pressed a kiss to the mark on her wrist. Heat flared where his lips touched. Her wolf settled with a low, satisfied giggle.

Rourke moved to the far wall, reclaiming distance. He had tied back his long hair, and tribal tattoos were visible on the bulge of his biceps, under his sleeves. Not as intricate as hers. Although similar.

Pack, her wolf whispered.

"What's the plan?"

Aluk slipped an arm around her waist, drawing her back against him. His hand traced the new mark in slow strokes. Delicious sensations traveled along with his touch. His chest vibrated against her back with the rumble of his dragon. She resisted the urge to roll her eyes back in the sudden bliss spreading through her.

Mate.

"Now that Rourke's here, we can get this show going." Taran waved his hand and rejoined Gwen.

"How are we going to go about getting Gorak to the portal with the Fae on the mountain? Won't they follow and attack us?" Gwen rubbed her arms and leaned into Taran.

"My men will secure the route. Sia's are on patrol. How many can Pinto send from the prison?"

"Not enough. If there are more camps hidden amongst us, we're outnumbered by the Fae," Aluk said.

"We're not going into battle against them." Palisade rested her hands against his arm, soaking in the comfort of his embrace. "We just need to get Gorak to the portal without them interfering."

"Then we deal with the Fae camps loitering on my mountain."

My mountain.

Her wolf yipped with agreement. The spirit leaned outward, eager, energy rattling beneath her skin.

We go where the alpha goes.

"The pack's already positioned near the trail," Rourke said. "If Yarron's warriors move, we'll be ready."

"Good." Aluk's gaze slid to Palisade for a half breath before returning to the group. "Gorak is secured in the prison. We move fast. The longer we wait, the more time they have to plan another attempt to breach my prison."

Her focus snagged on the flex of his fingers at his side. The brief tightening of his jaw before control slid back into place. To anyone else, he stood unshaken. To her, his restraint became hers.

Warmth stirred low in her chest, unwelcome and undeniable. She pressed it down, allowing the wolf spirit to coil around it, claiming the sensation without indulging in it.

Later, the wolf promised.

"One of my rangers spotted a few at the campgrounds, blending with human campers," Taran said.

Palisade stiffened. Her wolf's hackles rose. "They're already that close?"

The idea of Yarron's warriors walking unnoticed among unsuspecting shifters living here sent a chill straight to her soul.

"How are you sure?" Rourke asked.

"The ears," Taran said, "and they lit their fire by snapping their fingers when they didn't think anyone was watching."

"We'll handle that after Gorak's gone. Ben's keeping an eye out for them at the resort," Aluk said.

"They're waiting," she murmured.

Her wolf circled the thought, teeth bared. If Yarron's forces sat this close within the mountain borders, they were waiting for a command.

Rourke scratched the shadow of scruff on his chin. "My pack is watchful of them in town. Their glamor makes it hard to detect them."

"We've swept the route between the ridge and town. No signs of them," he added.

Aluk turned Palisade to face him. "You'll stay at the resort with Trinity while we deal with Gorak."

The wolf slammed against her ribs, a full-bodied snarl reverberating through her bones.

We protect the alpha.

"I'm going with you."

Palisade crossed her arms, heat sliding under her skin. *I'm as strong as you are.*

Aluk's mouth curved, but his eyes didn't soften. He tapped two fingers against his temple and winked. "No one said you're not strong."

"Gorak and the Fae still have a purpose for you. I can't risk them getting their hands on you again."

Her wolf bared its teeth. *He locked us away once. Do not allow it again.*

Palisade tilted her head, studying him. "My wolf fears you'll lock us away like you did with Gwen's brother. You won't do that? What I did before I didn't have any control."

"Peaches."

"Yarron trained me. I'm as skilled, if not more so, than any of your wolf enforcers. I helped you catch him."

"You'll return to the prison with me when this is over. I'm not locking you away. I live there, and so do you now.

"I'm going with you."

Aluk's jaw tightened. "This isn't up for debate."

Taran folded his arms. "She has a point, Aluk. The resort doesn't put her out of reach, and her wolf outranks both pack alphas."

A low growl rolled from Rourke's chest, but it died there. His gaze flickered to Palisade, then away.

We protect the alpha.

Which one?

Mate, *then Pack.*

"I'll make sure the rangers are keeping a lookout," Taran redirected the conversation back to their plans.

"The resort is as safe as it's going to get," Rourke admitted.

Palisade's wolf huffed. *They fight a battle in the moment. We fight the war.*

Palisade took a deep breath, steadying herself. Whatever history her wolf carried with Aluk and the others would have to wait. Whatever lines had been crossed before would be reckoned with later. Right now, the mountain needed defending, and Gorak needed to be gone.

"Yarron and his warriors won't go away until the Fae have secured their hold on the mountain," Palisade said.

"The sooner he's through the portal, the better," Rourke agreed. "We should alert the local clan if Gorak hasn't already encountered them."

"Ben can contact the clan." Aluk said, his gaze distant for a moment then he focused on Palisade. "Stay with Trinity at the resort with Ben. Promise me."

"I'll protect Trinity."

As the men finalized the details of their plan, Palisade caught a flicker of movement outside the cabin.

Palisade stilled.

Her wolf rose, her sense of hearing sharpening. The presence vanished almost as soon as it appeared, too quick to track. A cold thread slipped into her gut and stayed there.

The Fae had camps on the mountain. Spying and blending in with the humans and shifter bloods. They infiltrated the state government and wanted the humans on the mountain. Better to blend in. Fewer options for the shifter bloods to defend themselves without the risk of exposure.

Her fingers curled in her palm.

If she warned them now, Aluk and Rourke might start the battle they wanted to avoid.

The Fae thrived on pushing their prey into predictable responses. They trapped them in bargains almost impossible to break or complete.

No.

Yarron sent scouts.

Her gaze slid to Aluk, then to Taran and Rourke. One thing at a time. Gorak first. Fae second. If they got the chance to walk out of here. *What are they waiting for?*

Her wolf paced, her hearing enhanced. She moved toward the window where Gwen had stood earlier. She gazed out, her eyes adjusting to spot a bug on a tree leaf a hundred yards away. Shadows crept across the grass and the stones. The trees whispered, and her heart beat in time with Aluk's.

Behind her, they discussed Gorak, the prison, and the final steps to secure Crag's Cliff.

Where would they go?

A tug on the tether between her and Aluk pulled her attention back. He lifted a brow, a silent question in his eyes. Palisade turned her gaze to the forest beyond the cabin. Shadows stretched between the trees.

The Fae weren't the only ones watching.

Yarron had taught her to read people before they ever moved. Watch their hands. Their eyes. What they avoided looking at. She'd spent years standing at the edges of rooms, learning what others thought they hid.

When Aluk turned to her one last time before they left, his gaze held onto hers. "We finish our business with Gorak. We strip the Fae of their leverage. We end this."

Her wolf crouched low inside her, a warning growl curling through her chest.

"You lock Gorak from this realm and Trinity lives, then what? How do we ensure the curse breaks?"

Ending Gorak was one feat in the battle. What if exile wasn't enough? What if the Fae found another host, another path to control the shifter bloods?"

"A centuries-old curse has to have an expiration date, right?" Taran shrugged. He grinned at Gwen, who frowned in return.

Aluk shook his head once.

He knows, her wolf growled.

Aluk slid his hand down her back to rest at her waist. "I'll take you to the resort before I return to retrieve Gorak."

Don't let him leave us.

The plea startled her, causing her to tremble.

What happened to being a strong warrior?

"I'll have Ben show you my suite there where you can rest. You're still recovering."

He would not dare call us weak. The past lingered in their shared soul. The vision of the last guardian and the darkness of the decades her spirit wandered the shadows.

"Peaches..."

"Yes," she said.

"Did you hear me, or were you too busy talking with your wolf?"

"How did you know that?" she grumbled. "The bond."

"Your eyes go blank. I was saying I'd join you for a nap and we'll take much deserved time to get to know one another as mates when this is over."

Palisade met Aluk's gaze. Fire sparked in their dark depths. Her heart pounded. She wanted to lean against him, soak in his warmth and memorize his scent. Her wolf whined.

This was something he needed to do without her.

They needed Gwen to exile Gorak. Exiling Gorak wouldn't save Diaden, but it would save Trinity.

Until then, she would protect Trinity.

She'd stop Yarron.

Twenty-Nine

The resort's main lobby hummed with quiet urgency, sunlight slanting through tall windows, and gilding the polished floors.

Aluk stood before her, his towering frame cast a shadow across the stone tiles. He went back into alpha mode the moment they arrived. His dragon brushed the edges of her senses. Her wolf pushed back with reassurance and protective vibes.

"You'll be safe here," he said.

Palisade crossed her arms. "Safe isn't the problem. Yarron needs Gorak to complete their task. His men won't stand by while you dispose of their greatest asset."

Aluk stepped closer, lifting a loose strand of hair and tucking it behind her ear. The touch lingered. Days ago, she was dying. Now she had a mate. She wandered if this was another cruel trick of Yarron's.

"I don't want to leave you. This curse has to end. After that..." His thumb brushed her skin. "We stay together. My mate."

Heat throbbed from the mark on her wrist. "Aluk..."

He didn't answer.

His hand slid to the back of her neck, firm enough to stop her breath, gentle enough to ask permission. His thumb pressed beneath her ear, right where her pulse betrayed her.

She felt him hesitate.

Then his mouth covered hers.

Not soft. Not rushed. Claiming her without possession. Promise without completion. His lips moved against hers with a quiet invitation. Heat bloomed where they touched.

Her fingers curled into his shirt.

He pulled back far enough to breathe. His forehead rested against hers, his breath warm, unsteady. His control hummed between them, taut as a wire.

"I'm coming back. We're not done yet."

He lifted her wrist, pressing a kiss to the dragon's mark branded there.

"You'd better." Her breath stuttered. "Because if you don't, I'll hunt you down myself."

Her mouth curved, slow and dangerous. "I'd expect nothing less from my mate."

He released her. "Promise me—no unnecessary risks."

"I'll try," she said, despite the knot in her throat. "I'll protect Trinity, and I'll watch for Yarron's men."

"That's what worries me." He took another step back. This time, his warmth retreated like a tide. At the door, he glanced over his shoulder before leaving.

Outside, the mountains stood tall, cloaked in pine and dusted with snow. Beautiful. Unforgiving.

Deep inside the mountain, the greatest threat to their future waited.

A hum of ancient energy, prickled along her skin.

"Palisade? Dr. Everett?"

She turned.

A man in the polo shirt moved toward her. "I'm Ben."

The wolf inside her lifted its head. Something old stirred, nameless and restless. Her pulse slowed. A prickle climbing up her spine.

Guardian.

She sensed something coiled beneath this calm. Heat without flame. A spirit similar to Aluk and his brothers.

Dragon.

Pressure built behind her eyes. Her vision sharpened. The room narrowed to the space between them.

Ben's eyes turned red.

The wolf bared its teeth, a growl vibrating through her chest. The dragon didn't blink.

"Looks like our spirits know each other," Ben said.

Palisade crossed her arms. "They seem to have some unresolved history."

"History's irrelevant. What matters is what's ahead." He jerked his chin toward the exit. "Trinity is safe at the clinic with Conleth. Aluk notified Conleth and I of the plan."

Palisade didn't move right away. Her wolf paced, unsettled by the dragon's restraint. She studied him, searching for a fracture in that calm veneer.

Nothing.

Her wolf scoffed.

"Then we make sure she stays safe."

The walk to the clinic passed in silence.

Inside, the antiseptic stung the air mixed with the faint trace of lavender. Conleth's voice drifted from the back talking to a patient.

Trinity sat in a small office off the main hall, laptop light washing her features pale. She looked up as they entered, a smile gracing her face.

"Palisade." Trinity rose. "Conleth said you'd be spending time with us today. I'm glad you're here."

Ben took up the doorway, broad shoulders blocking half the hall. "She didn't come for tea."

Trinity's mouth curved up further. "Perhaps Kaya would like to join us?"

"My mate is occupied preparing this evening's dinner." Ben folded his arms in front of his chest. "You can find refreshments at the coffee shop."

Palisade stepped past without looking his way. "Tea sounds perfect." Her gaze swept the hallway, lingering on reflections in the glass, the way a pair of voices dipped when she passed. "And a better place than cooped up with all this antiseptic." She waved a hand in front of her nose.

"Still getting used to all those heightened senses, are you?" Trinity asked.

Her senses stretched at the mention of them, tuning to movement and sound,

The wolf nudged her to circle and test them.

"I've been working here for hours. A change of scenery is due," Trinity closed her laptop and stretched. She moved closer to Palisade. "What are we really up to?"

"People watching," Palisade whispered.

Ben rolled his eyes. "You know I can hear you."

"Shoo!" Trinity waved him off and turned back to Palisade. "Anyone particular?"

Palisade hesitated, glancing at Ben. He gave a slight nod, though his posture remained guarded. "My old benefactor Yarron or his men. There might be other Fae who have infiltrated the resort under disguise and glamor."

Trinity frowned. "We've all been on the lookout. I have seen humans. Shifters. No Fae beside myself and Gwen."

"I need you to touch me." Hopefully, then she'd get over the unsettling feeling of her wolf spirit since meeting Ben. Whatever spooked her wolf, slipped from memory.

"Please."

She needed *something*. A direction. A truth that had been circling beyond her reach.

The wolf spirit pushed fragments of memories at her. A shadow moving through trees. Fear braided with rage with no clear beginning or end.

Trinity went still. "You're asking for a vision."

"There's something my wolf spirit needs me to see. It might open another piece of my past as the last one did."

Her wolf huffed within her.

Choose carefully who you trust.

Trinity exchanged a glance with Ben. He lifted one shoulder.

"Spirits don't reveal what we ask for. Only what they decide we see," Ben said.

"Are you certain?" Trinity's eyes filled with gold.

"You did it before, so you can do it again?"

Trinity hesitated. "It's different now that you have a spirit. Will the wolf not tell you?"

"It's complicated."

"It might take some time to distinguish your feelings from your wolf. It takes years to understand and become one with your spirit," Ben said.

"Once we open this door, I can't control what you'll see," Trinity warned.

"I'm okay with that," Palisade said.

Trinity studied Palisade for a moment longer. "Alright. Come with me."

Trinity turned down the hall, already half elsewhere. She paused, glanced back and smiled. "We can grab coffee on the way."

Ben kept pace a few steps behind her. His dragon spirit brushed against her wolf spirit, wary and coiled, waiting to strike.

Trinity slowed near the bend in the hall where the spa and boutique shops opened into a wide corridor. Warm light spilled from glass storefronts. Laughter drifted from somewhere ahead. Just beyond them sat a coffee shop, dark wood tables polished smooth by use, black metal fixtures catching the light.

"We can have lunch sent to my suite," Trinity said, angling toward the counter. "But I prefer the London Fog here with an extra pump of vanilla."

Ben closed the distance between them. "You're sure this is a good idea?"

"It's not about good or bad. It's about necessity," Trinity replied without breaking stride.

Palisade's wolf snorted. *Since when is coffee a necessity?*

Palisade might have shared the sentiment, but the moment they crossed the threshold, her humor vanished.

The smell of roasted beans and sugar wrapped around her. Yet, beneath it slid something wrong, threading through the air like burnt metal.

Her steps shortened. Her gaze swept the room.

Soft instrumental music filled the space. A handful of patrons occupied the tables. Not far from the counter, a couple leaned close, sharing a pastry while a man scrolling on his phone sat on a couch in the far corner.

At the counter, a woman lifted her cup and turned. A smile curved on the woman's lips. Her vivid blue eyes swept over Palisade. Pale silver flashed around the woman's neck, the glamor blinked in, then out.

A low chill crawled up Palisade's spine.

The woman's fingers tightened around the cup. Her smile came late, practiced.

Palisade kept her posture relaxed. She focused on the drink menu as the woman stepped past her.

She peered around, catching subtle movements of the other patrons. Two women at the table to their left, engaged in quiet conversation, their voices too controlled. A man on his phone sipping tea a lazy sort of patience.

All Fae.

They're watching us.

Palisade's pulse slowed.

And she wants us to know.

The Fae had positioned themselves at the resort. She counted three women and four men. Yarron was getting impatient.

Her wolf let out a low growl in her mind. *We should rip them apart before they have the chance to act.*

Not yet. They needed to know how many warriors Yarron sent and what their task was here. How long ago did they arrive? If Yarron's men were here, then maybe Aluk and the others had a chance of getting Gorak through the portal.

She and Trinity weren't as safe as Aluk believed.

"What will it be?"

Palisade turned to the barista. "Iced chai, please."

Her hand dipped toward her pocket and stilled. No wallet or cash.

"She's the alpha's mate." Ben said from behind her.

She whirled around. He'd snuck up on her this close.

"The alpha and his family own this resort. Even if you had money, it has no value here," Ben said.

"You mean it's not my royal blood that grants me free tea?" Trinity put her hand to her chest, grinning.

A smile of her own tugged at Palisade's mouth. Her wolf snapped her attention to the man seated near the window.

Ben's gaze turned more amber than brown. A foreign voice said in her head. *Fae.*

Palisade's eyes widened. *Ben?*

Asgiwani has much to teach you.

Ben gave the barista his order.

We're guardians. We are connected like the pack is to the alpha, but to each other. Our mate connection grows, and once our mate finishes the claim, we'll communicate the same, her wolf assured her.

A strange ache bloomed in her chest.

Ben lowered his chin, his gaze locked on her.

Wait.

How do you know?

Ben's dragon huffed. *Gold eyes when their gift is in use. Slender, shorter than most humans, with stiff personalities. Their ears are the first to lose their glamor, and they're crazy attractive to other bloods.*

As if summoned by the thought, a woman crossed the shop and slid into the chair across from the counter. She lifted her coffee, a phone in the other hand. Her attention drifted back to Ben again and again.

See?

Ben's eyes flared, red bleeding through the brown.

What deal do you have with them?

"Hey," Trinity moved back into their space, holding an iced coffee and her tea. "Whatever you two have going on, take it somewhere else."

They stole and hid my bloodline, her spirit said to Ben's dragon. *I never betrayed my alpha.*

A deep ache rippled through Palisade. Love. For the past alpha.

Palisade took a sip of the latte she had ordered. There was something in the past her wolf hadn't shown her yet. Something buried that mattered.

They couldn't wait.

Her gaze returned to the man by the window, to the woman leaning too close, to the way the air around them crackled with static.

Yarron sent a team to extract Trinity. Or had they come for her?

They'd officially run out of time.

Thirty

Trinity's suite was a sanctuary of muted tones and functional elegance. Soft beige walls accented the space with dark wood trim, and a faint scent of lavender lingered, calming with an undercurrent like the charge in the atmosphere before a storm.

Palisade glanced around as she entered, her wolf restless within her. The room was organized. However, the desk in the corner sat cluttered with papers and an open laptop showing rows of data.

"Sit," Trinity motioned toward the small sofa near the window.

Ben lingered near the door, his arms crossed over his chest, a silent sentinel. His eyes tracked Palisade's every movement, though his expression betrayed nothing.

Palisade's wolf let out a low huff, ears flattening in irritation. *A guardian does not need a dragon's shadow.*

"You can leave now," Trinity said to him without looking up.

Palisade didn't like Ben's presence. Aluk sent him to watch over them, and Ben wouldn't disobey his alpha. But another part of her bristled at the unspoken implication that she needed his protection.

He frowned, but didn't move. "My dragon says we'll stay."

Her wolf paced. *He does not trust us.*

Palisade pressed her lips thin. She didn't need a babysitter, and she certainly didn't need Ben standing over her while she opened herself to a vision she couldn't control. Sending him away would create unnecessary conflict, and right now, unity was more important than pride.

"Let him stay," she said. *If he sees something he doesn't like, maybe then he'll finally understand.* Her wolf stretched out inside her.

"Fine. Just stay out of the way," Trinity said, resigned.

As the door clicked shut behind him, the room seemed to grow smaller, the weight of what was coming pressing down on Palisade's chest.

Her wolf growled softly in the back of her mind. The vision could expose more than she or her wolf was ready to face—truths about the past, secrets she wasn't sure she wanted to uncover. What if it revealed something that would change everything? What if it exposed their vulnerabilities or showed them a path they weren't prepared to walk?

She took a deep breath, settling on the couch. "What do I need to do?"

Trinity held out her hand. "Just focus on what you need to know. The vision will find the rest."

Palisade hesitated for a moment before reaching for Trinity's hand. Whatever was to come, there was no turning back now.

The moment her hand touched Trinity's, a rush of cold shot through her, and light pulled Palisade into a vision of the past.

When her senses settled, she found herself in the shadow of towering pines. The earthy scent of moss and damp leaves filled her lungs, and the chill of the air prickled her skin. She crouched low in the underbrush, her heart pounding.

Ahead, through the tangled branches, the mountain's peak rose like a sentinel against the sky. On a rocky outcrop, she saw him—the alpha of the past—standing tall and commanding, his silhouette stark against the blinding light of the sun.

Her wolf stirred within her, pacing restlessly as if it, too, sensed the pull.

Beside the alpha stood another figure, one she instantly recognized despite the unfamiliarity of the vision. The dragon guardian. His dark hair caught the fading light. He exuded a calm authority that contrasted with the alpha's raw intensity.

Palisade's attention snapped back to the alpha as he turned, his powerful voice carried by the wind. "Take her. She cannot stay here."

Her gaze shifted to where the Fae queen emerged into view, her beauty otherworldly, and her expression glowing with happiness. The force of it reached her, even through the layers of time and memory, and slammed into her.

Her chest tightened. The warrior whose eyes she saw through wanted to move, to run to him, to stop him from taking the woman into his lair. The alpha was her everything, her anchor, her reason for breathing.

But the wolf within her growled, a warning that cut through the haze of emotion. Her instincts screamed to keep him from choosing another. She needed to warn him about the woman's deception before they all came under the queen's control.

Before she could act, a warm breath touched the back of her neck. She spun, her hand instinctively reaching for a blade in her belt. The dragon guardian stood behind her, his amber eyes piercing, knowing.

"Why haven't you stopped him?"

He gazed up at the mountain. "The queen's charms have captivated our alpha, but the man sees the truth and rebels."

"She cannot be harmed." She turned to the guardian. "Those we love will be hunted."

"You must not interfere," he said. "The others have already fallen for the Fae's plan."

"No," she whispered, her voice breaking. She glanced back through the trees, her heart aching as the Fae queen disappeared into the mountain's shadows. The alpha's shoulders were rigid; his pain etched into the very air around him. "You do not have as much to lose as the rest of us. I will kill her before he can claim her."

She raced toward the lair, yanking her bow from her shoulder. She found a tree and leaned against it to pull an arrow.

A sharp, burning pain struck her side. She glanced down, stumbled, and fell to her knees. Her wolf whined as she pressed her hands to the knife embedded in her flesh. She looked up as someone approached. She fell forward, one hand holding her up. Her wolf growled as she turned her head toward the figure.

The vision blurred. The sound of her own breathing filled her ears, mingling with a woman's cries and the whisper of a prayer to the Great Hunter to save those she loved.

Palisade's wolf stirred restlessly inside her, a deep growl vibrating through her chest. The raw, unbridled anger burned within her, a flame reigniting as memories of the vision played out in her mind. *He stopped us,* the wolf snarled, the words filled with bitter fury. *He blocked us when we had to act. The dragon guardian betrayed us.*

Palisade gritted her teeth. The wolf's rage pulsed against her skin, a violent, guttural noise rising within her. It was the same fury that had ignited in the past, the same emotion that had burned her every time she remembered the way he had blocked her path, stopping her from reaching the alpha.

Palisade closed her eyes for a moment. Her hand rested on her chest, covering the heartbeat of her wolf. She could still sense the anger inside her, but there was confusion too. Her wolf was furious, but it didn't understand why the dragon had prevented them from acting.

He. Stopped. Us. The wolf's voice was relentless, almost unhinged. *We could have ended it all then. We could've stopped the curse! The Great Hunter blessed us as mates. Oska has always been mine!*

Palisade's breath quickened, her pulse racing in sync with the wolf's fury. A primal force of the wolf spirit's anger surged. Her lungs burned. The wolf wanted to strike, to punish the dragon guardian for what it perceived as a betrayal, and it wasn't stopping.

Ben's presence flared suddenly, as strong and commanding as ever, his dragon energy pressing in from all around her. *Palisade,* his voice reached out, trying to calm her. *Don't do this. Listen to me.*

The wolf's hackles rose, snarling, refusing to listen. *He stopped us when we needed to act. He was the enemy!*

Ben stepped forward, his energy pressing in like a steady pulse.

"Palisade," he commanded, reaching her through the chaos of the wolf's rage. "I need you to listen to me."

"What's happening?" Trinity asked.

"He betrayed us!" Palisade's hands balled into fists, nails biting into her palms as the wolf spirit surged again. *He stopped us when we had the chance to save him.*

"Ben?" Trinity stepped back. "Your dragon was in the vision. You... you took out the wolf guardian. I saw it too."

Ben drew a slow breath. "My dragon had no choice. My ancestor made a vow to my alpha and to the Great Hunter to protect. Unlike the others, he did not fall prey to the Fae. Nothing would ever make us break our vow."

"I could have saved our people from the curse," she spoke for the wolf.

"I knew if you went after the alpha, Asigwani, you would have condemned yourself to the shadows forever." He held her gaze, unflinching.

The wolf inside her hesitated. The furious snarl collapsed into a low rumble as the truth sank in.

She would not have had a hold on him any longer, the wolf huffed.

The ache came sharp and sudden, slicing deeper than Palisade expected. Betrayal. Loss. Unhealed wounds clawed their way up her spine.

The voice of Ben's dragon grated against her thoughts. *You let the jealousy of your human blind you.* "I did as the Great Hunter commanded. If not our alpha, then she would have turned to Gorak. I saw how she manipulated them both. She pulled them both under her compulsion."

"How do you think we captured Gorak? He hunts and desires the alpha's mate."

"Revenge," Ben said.

"Wolf," Trinity said gently, "you need to hear him out. You need to calm down. Conleth is on his way."

The prospect of Trinity's mate arriving did little to settle her wolf.

Ben took another step toward her. His gaze softened. "I didn't know where you had run."

He set his hand on her shoulder. His energy spread through her, almost soothing. "I shifted to fly over you, knowing you intended to take out the queen, but it was not my dragon who took your warrior's life."

"Truth," Trinity said, "I would sense if he lies. We Fae cannot, but we know when someone else is."

Palisade closed her eyes and inhaled. The anger drained, quieting her spirit. She didn't know whether to feel angry or grateful. Her wolf had been so sure of the dragon guardian's actions.

Do not trust those you don't know.

Why would they have any reason to lie to me? She'd been their enemy not too long.

Ignoring her, the wolf spirit continued through their mental link with Ben.

I had to stop her, the wolf growled, though her guardian spirit sounded less certain now. Her question forgotten, the wolf rambled on. *The queen lives, and the curse slowly takes us out. Our people will not survive another decade without mates or young. The Great Hunter blessed you for being a coward.*

I followed the plan, Ben's dragon murmured, *none of us saw the curse coming. We are all after the same goal, just on different paths, which have led us here. Where the others have failed, you have a second chance.*

"Ben," Palisade tried to interrupt. "If it wasn't your dragon guardian to take out the wolf guardian. Would the others have attacked?"

The glow in Ben's eyes dulled. "Possible, but the guardian would have sensed them nearby. Asigwani was there because of our bond. The others were not close."

"How long after the queen became trapped inside the mountain did the Fae attack?" Palisade's hand went to her side, the haunting memory of the vision still fresh in her mind. "The blade had a bone handle."

The vision replayed through her consciousness like shards of a broken mirror. She'd come too close to dying recently to welcome the reminder.

"Yes," he confirmed. "It was the Fae who attacked you. Not me. The moment the queen realized she was trapped, they struck. The next memory my dragon has is from twenty years later."

The realization hit Palisade like a wave. The Fae had attacked her—had stabbed her—right after the dragon had shifted to return to the alpha. Palisade's wolf growled low in her chest, its fury simmering again, but this time it wasn't directed at the dragon.

We were misled. The wolf finally relented, though the anger was still present. *We were deceived.*

"The queen had planned to take control either way."

Palisade's breath trembled as she met Trinity's gaze.

"The Fae were the ones who tried to destroy us. They turned us against each other. A wise combat move. Create chaos within the enemy and they won't resist when you jump in the middle to take out more at once," Palisade whispered, the truth settling heavily in her mind.

Ben's dragon exhaled in relief.

"Sounds like you know their battle strategies," Ben said, his eyes and voice fully back to human.

"I lived with Yarron all my life, and trained with his elite. He figured I would be dead, since the plan was for Gorak to possess me. I wouldn't have been a threat to him, but I am now."

She was a threat now, and her knowledge and experience with Yarron's elite fighters gave her a sense of control she hadn't had before. The wolf inside her stirred in approval.

"You recognized some of them down in the coffee shop. There must be more. If Gorak is through the portal, and I'm still alive, then what else do we do to keep them from starting another war?" Trinity asked.

"We break the curse and keep them from stealing our spirit animals. Without them, pure-blooded Faes can't stay in this realm for more than a few weeks without becoming deathly ill," Palisade said, surprised Trinity didn't know this.

"Which is why the Fae queen needed to mate with a shifter blood to go between the realms, and she'd need a strong one to take control without question. She must not have considered the alpha having access to her Fae abilities as part of the mate exchange," Trinity tapped her lips thoughtfully with a finger.

The wolf growled once more, then settled. The spirit's anger tempered with the knowledge of the true enemy. *We will stop them,* Palisade promised, then asked Trinity, "Do you think she's still alive?"

Ben looked at Trinity, then back at Palisade. "Conleth and I have spent years trying to find information on the curse. One of our theories is that she finally died, and so the curse is fading."

The queen's death made sense. The curse had weakened, like a crack in a wall finally crumbling. By the way the Fae and the spirits behaved, Palisade could find no other explanation. If the queen was dead, the Fae could no longer draw from her power inside the heart of the mountain. They needed the spirit animals under their control, which meant keeping the curse on the shifter bloods.

"We need to round up the Fae on our mountain and exile them, too." Palisade suspected they'd been hiding on the mountain for years.

Trinity nodded, her expression less convincing than her words. Palisade sensed the worry lingering beneath her calm facade. The Fae remained a threat. The queen's death may have weakened the curse, but that didn't mean the Fae would simply vanish.

Thirty-One

An unseen force pulsed against the boundaries of the clearing. Aluk scanned the tree line, the dragon's awareness tightening against the unnatural silence. Beside him, Taran lowered into a crouch, shoulders set, attention locked on the woods ahead.

Behind them, Rourke, his men, and two prison guards held a tight formation around Gorak. At the break in the trees where the path narrowed, Gwen dropped to her knees.

"Hurry, *Solanu*," Taran urged. Her fingers trembled as she reached for the shimmering veil of energy. The cuffs on her wrists glinted in the fading light.

Aluk's focus snapped to Gwen. She needed those cuffs off. "Rourke!"

Rourke stalled, his attention cutting to Gwen.

Aluk's dragon rumbled toward the wolf alpha.

Gwen's head snapped up, eyes widening. "Something is wrong?"

"Shhh," Taran leaned close to his mate. "Focus on the portal."

Rourke glanced at his men before stepping forward. With a sharp twist of his hand, he unlocked the enchanted cuffs. The metal clattered to the ground. Gwen rubbed her wrists and turned back to the portal.

"I'll get it open, but you need to keep them away from me," Gwen said.

As if on cue, the forest erupted with movement. Yarron's warriors emerged from the shadows, their eyes glowing gold with their gifts.

Aluk swore under his breath. He stepped in front of them. Oska roared to the surface.

"Here they come," Rourke muttered, already shifting into his wolf form. His two men followed suit, their massive forms sprouting fur.

Gorak turned slowly, his eyes changing. He smirked. "Might get what I came for after all."

"Take it up with the Great Hunter." The bear ohunko escaped the portal once, but not this time. Not again.

Taran shifted into his dragon, his massive body shielding Gwen. The first wave of attackers descended, and the clearing erupted into chaos.

"Keep them back!" Aluk roared, flames bursting at his palms and scales rippling down his shoulders and arms. His dragon rose, ready to burn through anything in his path.

Rourke and his men lunged into the fray, their claws and teeth tearing through Fae warriors clad in camouflage, blending with the dense forest. Aluk charged forward, unleashing a stream of fire that forced a group of advancing Fae back. They scattered, dodging the flames.

Behind them, Gwen's hands glowed with faint blue light as the portal's energy pulsed in response, its swirling patterns growing more erratic.

A warrior lunged at him from the side, twin daggers gleaming in motion. Aluk ducked the first strike and caught the second with a swift, crushing grip around the Fae's wrist. With a snarl, he twisted, snapping bone, then sent the warrior flying into a tree with a brutal kick.

"Faster, Gwen!" he barked, stepping back just enough to shield her from an incoming attack.

Fire flared again, Oska bristling in his soul, demanding release. Aluk forced another Fae warrior to retreat, his muscles coiled to strike again. They were losing ground.

"I'm trying!" she snapped, her hands trembling as she fought to control the Fae magic in her blood. The portal flickered, its swirling energy unstable, the strain evident in the tightness of her jaw.

A piercing cry rang out. Aluk turned just in time to see one of Yarron's warriors heading straight for Gorak.

Heat burned up his throat. *We must not let Gorak get free again!*

"Rourke!" Aluk bellowed, his voice shaking the ground.

The wolf shifter was already moving, launching himself at the attacker. They collided mid-stride, crashing into the earth in a brutal tangle of claws and teeth.

Gorak, still bound but observing with sharp eyes, sneered. "You think this will stop them? You remember the battles of the past. They have others waiting and will keep coming. You're finished, alpha. Let me go and I might let you see her once more."

Aluk's dragon snarled. *He will not touch our mate!* "Gwen, how much longer?"

"Almost... there," she gritted out, the portal's energy now swirling faster, its light growing brighter.

Aluk glanced at the tree line, where another wave of warriors prepared to charge. "We're out of time."

"We get Gorak through now," Rourke growled, blood staining his skin as he shifted back into his human form. "Gwen, can you hold it open?"

"Yes," she hissed through gritted teeth.

"Taran, help Rourke," Aluk ordered, grabbing Gorak by the arm and dragging him toward the portal, the ohunko hissing curses under his breath.

As Aluk shoved Gorak toward the portal, the bear ohunko's demeanor shifted abruptly. His posture sagged, his breathing grew labored, and the wild rage in his eyes flickered. For a moment, specks of gold shone in the dark orbs, faint but unmistakable.

"Wait..." The voice that emerged wasn't Gorak's guttural snarl. It was softer, broken, pleading.

Oska growled a low warning in Aluk's mind. *Be careful. It could be a trick.*

Aluk hesitated, his grip tightening on the restraints.

The golden flicker in Gorak's eyes pulsed, growing stronger with each passing second. His breath came in ragged gasps.

"Listen to me," the voice insisted, trembling with urgency.

Aluk's grip tightened.

Unnatural heat radiated from Gorak's body.

"That's enough." Aluk yanked the man closer to the portal.

Gwen stood rigid at its edge, sweat trailing down her temples, her lips forming whispered incantations. The portal wavered, its energy straining against her control. Taran shifted, planting himself firmly between her and Gorak, his scales rippling and steam rolling from his nostrils.

His sweet mate had been right. Diaden was still there, fighting for his soul.

"This won't save you," the voice said.

Diaden. It was the name Aluk had nearly forgotten, the man Gorak had been before the curse twisted him.

The Fae's golden gaze locked onto Aluk's, a faint, pained smile touching his lips. "The queen... is the cure. But she'll destroy all three of you first." His breath hitched. "You're the one she wants, dragon. The one she's waiting for."

Aluk's blood chilled.

Taran's voice rang sharply in his mind. *What are you waiting for? Now!*

Diaden's expression twisted in agony, his body trembling as he struggled to speak. "Don't let her die," he gasped, golden light blazing in his eyes. "She's the key, but not alone. You'll need—"

Gorak's roar cut through the moment like a blade, his body convulsing violently. The golden light vanished, replaced by black rage as the *ohunko* regained control.

"You'll regret this," Gorak spat, thrashing against his restraints. "None of you are strong enough to stop what has already been set in motion. Yarron's already won."

As Aluk shoved Gorak toward the portal, the bear ohunko's posture sagged.

"Wait..." A soft plead, from the man Gorak possessed.

Aluk hesitated, his grip tightening. This man mattered to his mate, not the beast, but the warrior within had once helped her.

"Diaden?"

The man's eyes pulsed with a brilliant, steady gold. He looked at the swirling vortex of the portal and back at Aluk.

"Send me back," Diaden rasped, his breath coming in ragged gasps as if he were drowning in the mountain air. "It's the only way."

Aluk saw the truth in the way the man's pupils grew.

"The queen is the cure," Diaden choked out, his eyes flickering as the black rage of the ohunko bled through. "She'll destroy all of you first. You're the one she's waiting for, dragon. Then she'll go after Sade. Protect... Fire..."

Gorak's roar rumbled in his chest, his jaw unhinging in a terrifying snarl. The gold almost gone, swallowed by the black.

Aluk's grip slackened. Diaden leapt toward the portal. Aluk shoved him forward. Blue light from the portal flared as it sucked in the Fae warrior. The roar of the bear cut short as the threshold snapped shut behind him.

. Silence settled over the clearing, heavy and oppressive.

Yarron's warriors howled in rage. One of them shouted, "Fall back!"

Aluk retreated for Oska to take over, shifting smoothly to fly overhead to track their retreat. *Get your mate to safety!*

Taran scooped up Gwen, taking flight high into the mountain range. Rourke and two of the guards took chase from the ground.

You're the one she's waiting for...

His dragon tried to change direction, distracted by the thought, but Issabrie would have to wait. The warriors disappeared into the thick of the woods. He fixed the location in his mind for later. Right now, he needed to get back to his mate, Palisade.

Thirty-Two

Trinity and Palisade walked in from the dining area, the lingering taste of hurried sandwiches doing little to settle the unease in Palisade's stomach. Lunch had been an afterthought as they grabbed food from the cafe when their room service never arrived.

Ben had excused himself over an hour ago and hadn't returned.

"I'm starting to think he's avoiding us," Palisade muttered, scanning the lobby.

Something is off. Too quiet.

Her wolf spirit agreed.

"He's probably hiding in the clinic."

Trinity gazed out toward the windows, her fingers tightening around her shirt sleeves. "Can you blame him? None of this is easy to process. For any of us."

Before Palisade could respond, movement by the fireplace caught her attention. Gwen sat on the edge of a chair near the lobby's centerpiece, her posture rigid, fingers gripping the armrest as if bracing herself.

"Is that... Gwen?" Palisade asked, nodding toward her.

Trinity followed her gaze, her expression tightening. "Looks like it. And she's not wearing the cuffs."

Palisade bit her lip, unease creeping through the faint connection of her bond with Aluk. It tugged at her, letting her know he was still farther away than the bond liked. She pressed the heel of her palm against her heart. The mark on her wrist throbbed.

Trinity's eyes changed for several seconds. "Conleth says Taran is with him, and the others are still out in the woods. A group of warriors attacked them at the portal."

Palisade's wolf stirred, hackles rising. "That explains Ben's desertion. Do you think he's with Aluk?"

"I don't know," Trinity exhaled, her fingers twitching at her sides. "Let's check on Gwen."

As they approached, Gwen sat stiffly, her expression hollow. She looked like someone forcing herself to blend in, to act normal when everything inside her was unraveling.

Palisade recognized that look because she, many times, had sat and looked out at the world the same way, but the warm glow of the fireplace did little to soften the ache in her chest. The scent of roasted coffee and polished wood hung in the air, but beneath it, her heightened wolf senses picked up something else.

A presence that didn't belong.

Her wolf's ears flattened, her vision sharpening as she scanned the room.

A young boy stood near Gwen, clutching a folded piece of paper.

Cat. Her wolf growled, and Palisade recognized the young boy had the spirit of a mountain lion. So young. How?

But it didn't matter now, not as much as the knowledge that the Fae were here. And so was Gwen.

Protect.

"Did you draw that?" Gwen asked.

The blond-haired boy nodded enthusiastically and held up the paper. "It's a dragon! Do you like it?"

Gwen's lips curved into a faint, hesitant smile, but her body remained rigid, her fingers curling into the fabric of her pants. "It's... nice."

The boy leaned closer, an innocent gesture yet Gwen flinched, her breath catching. Her gaze darted to the boy, then away, her shoulders hunched forward as if bracing for something.

"Hey there," Trinity said, stepping forward with a warm smile. "That's an amazing drawing. Your mom must be proud of you."

The boy turned, beaming at the praise. "I made it for Gwen."

Trinity crouched to his level, a grin tugging at her lips. "You shaded it well. The red eyes are outstanding. If I didn't know better, I'd say you captured Taran very well. Maybe smaller than his dragon."

Gwen barely reacted, her eyes unfocused, fingers pressing against her thigh.

Palisade followed her line of sight—past the boy, past the fireplace—to the entrance.

Her stomach clenched.

Two men dressed in hiking boots and with satchels over their shoulders entered. The tips of their ears pointed. How many of them were here?

A couple lingered near the doors, while others spread out amongst the guests. A man near the concierge desk spoke on his phone. A woman stirring sugar in her iced tea for far too long. Another perched near the windows, he watched them from the corner of his vision.

Trinity straightened. "I think it's time for lunch. Have you eaten?"

Palisade's pulse quickened. The boy hesitated, glancing at Gwen, before dashing off toward a nearby table where a woman waved him over.

Gwen exhaled shakily, her head dropping into her hands for a moment before she straightened. "Thank you," she whispered. "It's hard to deny him when he's such a great kid."

"What happened out there? Did you and the others send Gorak through the portal?" Palisade asked.

Trinity reached out, keeping Palisade from approaching Gwen any closer.

Gwen bent her head into her hands for a moment then straightened.

"Yes," she murmured. "We got him through, but it wasn't easy. The Fae–"

"Are Aluk and Taran okay?"

"They're alive, but the Fae ran off after Gorak was exiled. Aluk thinks they might be regrouping," Gwen said.

Palisade stiffened, her wolf snarling inside her. "They're here."

Gwen let out a bitter laugh, rubbing her arms. "I know. I can sense them."

She lifted her gaze. "Without the cuffs, being near anyone is painful. It seems to have amplified, or maybe it's because I no longer have the tolerance I once did since wearing the cuffs."

"Painful? How?" Palisade asked.

Gwen's fingers twitched against her arms. "Touch mostly, but it's unbearable since I got here. It's like static crawling under my skin, like a thousand tiny needles pressing down, trying to remind me what I am."

Gwen's gaze flickered toward the far end of the lobby. "They haven't taken their eyes off me since I walked in."

Palisade followed her gaze, taking in the figures lingering near the windows and seating areas.

"How many?" Palisade asked, keeping her voice low.

"At least a dozen," Gwen muttered. "And those are just the ones in this area."

She lifted her wrists, revealing the open cuffs dangling from her hands. "I can't activate them myself, and as my mate, neither can Taran. Rourke took off in a rush after the attack."

"Was anyone hurt?" Palisade's wolf bristled at the thought of Aluk still out there, hunting down the Fae who had trespassed on their mountain. Every instinct screamed that they needed to move, to find him, to make sure he wasn't walking into a trap. But first, she promised Aluk to protect Trinity.

Gwen hesitated for half a beat. "Two guards," she admitted. "Conleth is tending them. Ben met us here, but he and Taran are debriefing."

"And Aluk?" Oska had closed his connection to her wolf. The spirit inside her huffed at another failed attempt.

"He hasn't returned, if that's what you want to know. He tossed Gorak into the portal and chased after the men who attacked us."

Palisade's wolf surged forward, causing her arms to tingle and fur to coat her skin.

Trinity's eyes widened. She slipped out of her jacket and hurriedly tossed it over Palisade's shoulders. "Humans," she whispered. "Get your wolf under control."

She focused on Aluk. He was still out there.

He has Oska; she assured her wolf. *He is as strong as we are. We must protect Trinity.* Slowly, she rescinded the wolf. Her arms tingled, and the fur disappeared.

"I'm not sure how much longer it's safe to wait here for the men," Gwen whispered, her gaze fixed beyond them.

"I would offer to help you with the cuffs, but my Fae blood is stronger than yours and they won't lock for one of us." Trinity glanced at Palisade.

"So, you want someone to lock the cuffs again? Don't they use them on the prisoners at the fortress?"

Gwen scoffed. "You don't know what I could do to you without my cuffs. That wolf inside you? I could force it from you, then you'd die like my brother."

Could she really do that? Just rip the wolf from her like it was nothing?

She spent her whole life not knowing who she was, what her wolf meant to her. The idea of someone severing that connection, of forcing it away, twisted low in her stomach.

The truth lodged in her throat. If Gwen had the ability to do it, then Palisade's willpower wouldn't matter. She'd seen the aftermath of what the Fae could do. She'd watched the way they manipulated, twisted, and controlled. Was that what Gwen meant? Was it something conscious, something deliberate, or simply a part of what she was, something she couldn't stop?

Her gaze landed on the cuffs around Gwen's wrists. Palisade swallowed, her mouth suddenly dry. She didn't trust Gwen, not completely. Inside her, the wolf growled. But she believed her. And that was far more terrifying.

"If you can do that to me, you can do it to any of them. If the Fae get to you first–."

"They won't," Gwen cut in, but her hands trembled where they rested on her lap.

"You don't know that," Trinity said. "And neither do we. If you lose control, if they force you to turn against us…" She trailed off, chewing on her lip.

Gwen didn't argue. Her eyes dulled, pain settling into her expression.

"I'll do it. We need you, and my wolf is strong. We don't stand a chance against Yarron's men if we keep standing here. Trinity is in danger."

Palisade's fingers worked quickly, clicking the cold metal cuffs around Gwen's wrists. Each snap of the buckle echoed in the hushed lobby. Gwen stiffened, a flash of wild magic sparking behind her eyes, and Palisade braced herself—her wolf spirit dug into her soul.

Gwen blinked, focus snapping back, as if she were only just hearing them. "Need me for what?"

"To go to the mountain," Palisade said. "We need to see if the queen is alive—or if her spirit remains."

Palisade cast a glance toward the far side of the lobby, where one guest stood, stretching with exaggerated ease before making his way toward the fireplace. Toward them. Another abandoned his drink and sauntered toward the front desk, his posture deceptively relaxed.

"Do the men know about this?" Gwen leaned back away from them.

Palisade held back the sharp retort her wolf placed on her tongue. The men would never let them go without a fight. But that was exactly the problem. The men would try to shield them. They couldn't afford their protectiveness right now. They needed answers before Yarron made his next move.

If the Fae queen had perished, if the curse was fading, then Yarron's warriors would be desperate. Desperation made people reckless.

The man at the front desk exchanged a glance with someone out of sight, then nodded. Palisade's stomach twisted.

"If we can draw her out, maybe we can use her to stop Yarron and his warriors," Trinity said, Gwen's question ignored. If Aluk found out, he would insist on coming, and if things went wrong… She couldn't think about that right now.

A woman in a hotel uniform emerged from behind the front desk, her expression placid, too smooth. Her hands folded neatly in front of her, but Palisade wasn't fooled. "We need to find her. Now."

The scent of something too sweet clung to the air, thick and cloying. Her wolf whispered, *Fae magic.*

"She may have answers about the curse," Trinity said, tilting her head and glancing around. Her violet eyes sparked with gold. "They're moving," she murmured, barely moving her lips.

Palisade stiffened beside Trinity, her fingers twitching for a weapon she didn't have.

Gwen's gaze darkened as she finally took in their surroundings. Her fingers curled around her cuffs. "What if we get there and this Fae queen is alive and tries to escape before we get the information we need?"

Her eyes flickered toward the boy and his mother at the table. His mother ruffled his hair, oblivious to the danger creeping closer.

Palisade followed Gwen's line of sight, her stomach twisting. One by one, the guests around them positioned themselves around them. A man lounged near the fireplace, his head tilted as if lost in thought, but Palisade sensed his focus pressing against her skin. *They're closing in.*

"We don't let her escape," Palisade said. "But we're out of options. Yarron's already set his plans in motion."

Movement near the entrance caught her eye. Another Fae stepping inside, his gaze sweeping the room before settling on them. The man from the front desk turned and headed toward their best path to exit the lobby doors.

Trinity inhaled sharply, moving closer to Gwen. "If we don't leave now, we won't get another chance."

Gwen's grip on her cuffs tightened, her expression torn. But there was no more time for hesitation.

"We have to stop Yarron before more people get hurt," Palisade pressed. "And they can't have Trinity."

Her wolf twisted inside her, class scraping at her chest, a deep ache spreading through her ribs. *If she lives and you free her, she'll seek the alpha.*

If they didn't act now, their people would perish. Palisade understood helplessness all too well. She wouldn't wish it on her worst enemy.

Gwen hesitated, pressing her hands to her stomach. Then she exhaled sharply, resigned. "Fine. But if the queen is dead, then what?"

"The heart of the mountain holds our answers. I'm sure of it," Trinity said.

"You've seen this in one of your visions?" Gwen asked.

Trinity's eyes flashed gold. "If we are going to go, we go now."

Gwen's amusement faded as her head tilted slightly toward the entrance. "Taran says Aluk is on his way back, and I see our company is getting restless."

Palisade turned her head, spotting two humans and two Fae heading toward them. Their pale eyes swept over the group, probing every move. Her wolf spirit bared its fangs, heat flaring along her skin.

"They're blocking the entrance," Trinity murmured.

One lunged, and Palisade twisted her stance as his hand shot out, magic crackling in the palm. She dodged, twisting away just as the second Fae grabbed for Trinity.

Gwen slammed her foot into the first Fae's chest, sending him stumbling back. "Through the dining room kitchen. It leads out toward the hiking trails."

Palisade snarled, dropping low and sweeping the woman's legs out from under her as she drew a blade. She crashed to the floor. A figure moved from the bar, drawing a second blade.

"We have to go!" Trinity shouted, throwing up her hands. Golden energy flared around her, shoving one of the Fae back.

Six additional Fae warriors appeared, advancing quickly.

Palisade grabbed Gwen's wrist and shoved toward the kitchen doors. "Run!"

She bolted, weaving between tables as shouts and crashing footsteps echoed behind. The back exit was their only chance. If they didn't reach it —

A figure stepped into their path.

Palisade skidded to a stop as another Fae suddenly appeared in front of the kitchen doors, his pale, glacial eyes locked onto her. He smirked and lifted a hand. Sickly green power crackled between his fingers like lightning.

Palisade shoved Gwen behind her as the green light lanced toward them.

A blur of motion cut between them. Ben.

He slammed into the Fae, sending them both crashing into a nearby table. Wood splintered and drinks flew in every direction.

Relief and adrenaline flooded Palisade in equal measure as more figures rushed in—Conleth, Ben, and three others, weapons glinting in the dim light.

Steel met steel as the room erupted into chaos.

Another Fae lunged. She twisted under his grasp, but he was faster than she expected. His hand closed around her arm, and pain ignited through her nerves as his magic flared.

Her wolf howled inside her, a primal scream that burned through her chest.

She gasped, vision blurring, fire tearing through her from the inside out, ripping apart everything she thought she was.

No, not like this.

Pain twisted, sharpened, then exploded outward.

Her chest clenched, fire snapping through her nerves. She doubled over, vision swimming, muscles tearing and reshaping, bones snapping. Pain exploded outward as her body reformed.

She landed on all fours.

The Fae stumbled back, eyes widening.

Palisade growled, a deep vibration rolling through her chest. Then she launched forward.

She hit the Fae with the full weight of her wolf form, knocking him to the ground. Her teeth sank into his arm, and he screamed as she tore into him.

Someone shouted her name—Ben? Trinity?

The Fae crumbled beneath her as Asigwani tucked Palisade safely back in her mind to allow the guardian to take the lead. Blood coated her tongue, coppery and thick. More Fae surged toward. Wolves snarled, claws raked, teeth snapped as other wolves and shifters joined the fray.

A massive gray wolf lunged at a warrior, hurling him into a table that splintered under the force. A shifter swung a chair at another, dodged mid-air, fur rippling as they landed, sprinting straight into the fight.

"We have to go! Now!" Gwen shouted.

Asigwani pivoted, her gaze locked onto Trinity and Gwen. Back-to-back, the two braced against a circle of Fae dressed to go on a hike. Trinity's gold-burning gaze met hers. "We need a path out. Can you clear one?"

The guardian yipped, muscles coiling. With a powerful leap, Asigwani slammed into a Fae, sending him sprawling. A blade swiped toward her neck. She veered away, teeth bared.

Gwen seized Trinity's wrist. "Go!"

Golden light arced from Trinity's hands, slamming into a cluster of Fae and throwing them back. Wolves snapped and tore at their enemies, fur bristling as they worked together to drive the Fae back. The Fae pressed forward, relentless.

We must get them out. Protect.

Palisade agreed with her wolf.

The front doors. Their only way out. Fae swarmed from inside the resort, spilling into the lobby.

Asigwani spun, eyes locking on Trinity and Gwen, a low snarl vibrating through her chest, then barreled toward the exit, knocking over Fae and shifters in her wake.

Ben flanked her. A Fae warrior leaped at her, but Ben intercepted him midair, slamming the Fae into the floor with bone-shaking force.

"Stay close!" Trinity yelled, golden sparks dancing from her fingertips.

Asigwani plowed forward, carving a path through the remaining Fae.

Sunlight hit them as they burst through the doors, warm and sharp against their skin. The scent of pine and damp earth swept in, bracing and fleeting. No time to stop.

Gwen and Trinity sprinted, lungs burning, hearts hammering. Wolves spun behind them, forming a protective barrier as they surged down the trail.

Asigwani slowed at the edge, front legs bending, head swinging toward the mountain path. She yipped at the women to get on. Gwen and Trinity climbed onto Asigwani's back.

"We ride," Trinity said.

Asigwani took off. Wind whipped past, tangling hair and carrying the scent of pine and damp earth. Chaos faded behind them, replaced by the wild of the trail ahead.

Where are we heading? Palisade asked.

The trail wound upward through dense groves, narrowing between gnarled roots and moss-covered stones. Asigwani slowed, her lungs burning, muscles still trembling from the run and the fight at the resort. She couldn't carry them much farther.

Trinity and Gwen slid from her back, landing lightly despite the uneven ground. Asigwani caught her breath, paws pressed to the dirt. Her chest throbbed; her claws scraped against the trail. She used too much energy too fast.

Too many shadows. Too many secrets. Yarron's traps could be anywhere. Asigwani's ears twitched, nostrils flaring at the faintest rustle in the underbrush. Every snapped twig, every whisper of wind made her pulse spike.

Trinity adjusted the straps of her cloak, eyes sweeping the trees. "Are you okay?" she asked, voice tight with concern.

Palisade forced a nod, though her body ached. *We can't stop. Not yet.* She watched the two women move ahead a few steps, their shoulders tense. *If they fall, the queen, the curse... everything we're risking could vanish.*

We have no room for mistakes. Asigwani's claws dug into the earth, grounding her, drawing strength from the mountain itself.

No matter what lies ahead, we keep moving. Protect Trinity. Protect Gwen. Protect the queen.

The path twisted upward. Asigwani inhaled deeply; a breeze ruffled through her fur. *We press on. Nothing will stop us from keeping them safe.*

Asigwani led the way along the narrow trail, her pace slowing as the trees thickened and the ground steepened. Branches brushed against her fur, needles catching, tugging her attention toward the open wild beyond the path. The urge to veer off and run hit her hard.

Trinity and Gwen stumbled behind her, breath ragged, boots scraping over roots and loose stone. Palisade felt Asigwani's struggle press heavier than the mountain air in her lungs. She couldn't carry on much further.

Not now, Palisade insisted, pushing back against the force of Asigwani flooding her senses. The wolf's awareness stretched outward. The higher they climbed up the trail, the more the thread between herself and Aluk strained. His dragon tugged at their bond.

Asigwani ignored it. The rush of becoming a wolf, of running, and the scents of the earth distracted the wolf spirit. The comfort of her place in the wolf's mind became constricting.

I can take it from here. Palisade reached inward, grasping for control.

Asigwani didn't stop.

I want my body back!

A growl vibrated through the wolf, but her pace slowed. *I know this mountain better than you. It is my right to face the lair. He is my mate!*

Mine! Palisade corrected. *It's my right. You will yield, wolf, or I will find a way for Gwen to rip you from my soul.*

You'll die without me. Asigwani kept walking. Her tongue rolling out the side of her mouth, panting.

And so will you. Did you save me only to use me for revenge? Palisade asked.

Asigwani came to a halt. The forest stilled around them. Slowly, reluctantly, the wolf loosened her grip.

Palisade's balance shattered. Her legs buckled as the world lurched, bones grinding and shrinking beneath her skin. Fur receded in a painful ripple, muscle tearing and reforming as the wolf withdrew. Her lungs burned as breath tore from her chest. Human again.

She hit the ground hard, one knee slamming into the earth. Her hands followed, palms sinking into cold soil and pine needles as the last echo of claws faded from her limbs. Her skin prickled, oversensitive, with the ghosts of fur still buzzing beneath it.

The clothes she had worn earlier were gone, leaving her bare to the mountain air.

Before she could react, Gwen and Trinity moved.

"Here. Take this." Gwen's expression softened as she shrugged out of her sleeveless hooded cardigan and draped it around Palisade's shoulders. The fabric whispered against her skin.

Trinity produced a sturdy belt from her satchel and wrapped it around Palisade's waist to secure the garment. "That should keep it closed."

We must go deeper into the mountain. Asigwani's voice stirred in the back of her mind. *If we find the queen, we can uncover the truth of the curse, and free our people.*

"The heart of the mountain," she muttered.

"What did you say?" Gwen asked, her breathing steady despite the incline.

Palisade lifted her head, meeting both their gazes. "We need to leave the trail. The lair is north."

"How are you so sure?" Gwen asked.

"My wolf knows. I've seen it in my vision. Trinity has too."

"She's right. This is where we're supposed to go," Trinity said.

They crested a ridge together. The land fell away before them, revealing the imposing peak of the mountain against the sky. Palisade fixed her gaze on the summit as a faint, almost imperceptible hum filled the air.

That peak...

The hum of the air stirred her spirit's memories, a resonance that brushed against her spirit's memories. Hope and fear collided in her chest, twisting together until she was unable to tell them apart. She pointed through the trees toward a distant ridge beyond the dense canopy.

"That's where we need to be."

Trinity's life, her own future, and the survival of their people propelled her to keep going.

Trinity moved to her side, gaze fixed ahead. "It's calling us."

Gwen's breath hitched. She clamped a hand over the mark on her wrist. "Taran is looking for me. He wants to know where I am. We won't make it there on foot before he finds us."

"Conleth is getting restless. Aluk is on his way back to the resort," Trinity confirmed.

A soft rustle in the underbrush behind them caught Palisade's attention. Her wolf spirit tensed as she strained to listen. After a few seconds, Palisade growled low in her throat. "Keep moving. I'll handle it."

"No. We stay together."

"Can you sense what is there?" Gwen whispered.

Fae. Palisade's nostrils flared with the scent.

"Taran is on his way. And so is Aluk." Gwen touched the cuffs on her hands. "If we are doing this, we have to be fast."

The wolf surged at the invitation, heat blooming beneath Palisade's skin. "I'll shift again, and my wolf can take us."

Gwen put herself between Palisade and the trees. "I don't trust your wolf."

"You trusted her to get us here," Trinity pointed out.

Gwen's lips pressed together.

"Asigwani wants the same as you do. Family. Pack. Is everything." Palisade stepped back, the burning under her skin taking her breath away.

"Wait!" Trinity caught her arm. She loosened the belt and helped Palisade shrug out of the borrowed clothes. "You'll need these again."

Cool air brushed bare skin. Palisade closed her eyes. *You better shift back when I say so.*

The wolf huffed.

Palisade let go.

Thirty–Three

Aluk landed hard in the clearing outside the resort, the impact sending small rocks skittering across the ground. His dragon form shimmered, collapsing into human shape as mist curled thick around the towering evergreens and veiled the resort ahead in an eerie haze.

She's not here. We need to go back to the mountain.

Oska's fury rolled through him. The pull of Palisade's presence was light, stretched thing, tugging him away from the resort and toward the mountain's shadowed spine. Something was wrong. Her silence through the bond set his nerves on edge. She had gone too far for him to detect her emotions.

He needed to find her. Now.

Taran emerged from the side of the resort lodge. His eyes turned dark and storm-heavy. His usual relaxed demeanor vanished. "They're gone."

"What do you mean, 'gone'? Who's gone?"

Peaches and who else?

"Trinity, Gwen, and Palisade," Taran replied.

His dragon growled low in his chest. *Go to her. Find her. Now.*

"Where would they go?"

The wolf. They seek Issabrie.

"Ben says Palisade had a vision. The others wouldn't have let her go alone. Do you think they'll try to find the lair?" Taran asked.

Asigwani. "They know where it is." Aluk cupped the back of his neck. "Too much time has passed, even for a Fae. All they'll find is her ghost or a spirit."

His jaw locked, breath burning as Oska stirred. *It has to be you…*

Aluk muttered a harsh curse under his breath, then fixed a steely glare on the tree line. "And no one thought to stop them?"

Ben strode out in Aluk's line of sight, his expression as grim as the gathering clouds overhead. "The Fae are moving. Yarron's men are here. They attacked at the resort."

Taran's brow furrowed. "The resort? Why would they care about the resort?"

Ben's gaze swept over the lodge. "Strategic location, maybe. Or they're trying to cut off reinforcements. Either way, Sia and his wolves are here, and more shifters are on their way. But it won't stay contained for long. The humans are noticing things, and if this keeps up, our world won't be a secret much longer."

Aluk's fists clenched at his sides. *Too many witnesses.* The human government wouldn't tolerate this kind of exposure. If more humans found out about them, more hunters would come. Their battle would be with more than the Fae. Aluk growled, torn between the urgency of finding his mate and the escalating chaos at the resort. "Where's Conleth?"

He reached into his mind for his brother. *Where are you?*

Clinic inside the resort. I've got a badly injured enforcer needing a leg set before it heals. I'm almost done and headed to join Trinity. She and the others planned to head toward the village when the fighting broke out. I lost their trail.

Use your senses, brother. She's gone without you toward the mountains, Taran intervened.

Conleth cursed in his head.

Stay. Help Ben defend the resort. The Fae are there. I will bring back our mates.

Conleth growled. *She's in danger.*

We all are. Defend the resort. Shift if you must.

Humans?

Let them see. We can't let the Fae take control.

"We'll have to split up. Ben, you stay and defend the resort. Conleth, you help him. Shift if you must. Keep the Fae away from the humans. We've had too many close calls in the past months. Taran and I will head for the mountain and bring the women back."

Ben hesitated, his jaw working as though he wanted to argue. But he nodded, his expression resigned. "Fine. But be careful. We don't know how many more are out there."

Aluk gave a curt nod, his gaze directed toward the mountain. Palisade's presence, distant yet undeniable, remained tethered to him like a lifeline. She had become his anchor, and he couldn't bear the thought of her facing this alone. Wolf guardian or not, he would find her. Put his body between her and whatever waited on that mountain.

If he failed her, if fate took them away... He swallowed hard, the taste of regret and determination mingling on his tongue. *Not again,* Oska growled. *Not again.*

Yarron wanted the throne. He'd been too distracted to see it before now.

If Yarron reached the queen's resting place first, the curse would be the least of their worries. The veil itself would tear. Worlds would bleed together.

Aluk's dragon had seen what happened when power went unchecked. Bloodlines erased. Survivors bent until obedience was all they had left.

And humans–blind, fragile humans–would become playthings in a war they didn't even know existed. A war born of spirit animals desperate enough to flee their own realm.

Aluk's dragon surged, refusing to let history repeat itself. They vowed long ago to protect the people of this mountain. This was their mountain, and the Fae had no place here.

Before he and Taran could shift, a low growl rumbled from the trees. Sia stepped forward, his golden eyes gleaming with feral intensity. Behind him, a group of wolf shifters emerged, their movements fluid and predatory.

"Palisade's wolf alerted us about the Fae at the resort," Sia said, his voice steady. "We're here to show them the way out."

Ben stepped forward, his shoulders squaring. "They will not leave willingly. Protect and defend our territory, wolf. We have human guests, but shift if you must. The Fae have no rights to this land or our people."

Aluk's gaze lingered on his brothers and the wolves. He trusted them to hold the line. What waited on the mountain twisted his gut.

"Taran," Aluk commanded. "We're leaving. Now."

In an instant, the two brothers shifted, their massive dragon forms towering over the trees. Aluk's wings unfurled with a powerful snap, the force of it sending a gust of wind rippling through the clearing.

As they launched into the sky, the resort grew smaller beneath them, its lights flickering like beacons against the encroaching darkness. Aluk's focus narrowed, the pull of Palisade guiding him like a lodestar.

The mountain loomed in the distance, shrouded in mist and shadow. Aluk's jaw tightened. He didn't know what they would find there, but he knew one thing with certainty: he wouldn't let Yarron win.

Not while Palisade's life—and the fate of their people—hung in the balance.

Thirty-Four

The wind tore through the trees, carrying the icy bite of the coming storm. Dark clouds churned overhead, blotting out the faint light of the sun and casting the mountain in a foreboding gloom. Palisade's wolf surged forward, her consciousness clinging to the edge of a roaring current. Her paws struck the rocky terrain with a relentless rhythm, driven by Asigwani's instinct. Each breath burned in her chest, cold air biting as she climbed higher, drawn by an ancient pull that no longer belonged to just one of them. The alpha's lair. Her mate's lair. A dragon's place of claiming.

Aluk promised to complete their bond. To claim her. Is this why he hesitated? Was this another reason for his dragon to prevent him from marking a mate?

Mine. Her wolf growled, the sound reverberating through her body like thunder. *The queen must die.*

What if she already has? Palisade thought, forcing reason against the wolf's hunger. Whatever waited ahead, the mountain held answers. Answers that could end the curse.

She's dangerous.

She's our only hope, Palisade shot back, the tension between them snapping like a taut wire.

A jagged streak of lightning split the sky, illuminating the dense forest and the jagged rocks ahead. The distant roll of thunder followed, growing louder with every passing second.

Trinity's voice rose faintly above the wind. "Palisade, wait! Slow down!"

Foolish, the wolf snarled inwardly. *So close.* Palisade registered the warning, but the wolf's blood sang with anticipation. *No time for caution.* They were close. The wolf broke through the trees. The ledge rose ahead.

Then, she sensed the shift in the air.

The storm was no longer just nature's fury—it carried something unnatural, laced with magic and malice. *Yarron.* The scent of him, acrid and sharp from his magic, burned in her nostrils. She was trapped between the wolf's single-minded pursuit and the growing foreboding trickling through her invisible tether to Aluk.

Palisade slowed, her wolf's gaze narrowing as she scanned the mist-shrouded forest path. The path ahead was barely visible, swallowed by the dense fog. But her new wolf's senses cut through it. She could see the subtle disturbances in the undergrowth, the broken twigs, the faint tracks in the mud. The path wasn't just obscured by mist. It was *deliberately* hidden.

Her wolf's growl rumbled, louder now, sending a chill down her spine. Her ears caught the faintest sound—footsteps, deliberate and synchronized, crunching on the frosted ground. The acrid scent of Fae magic reached her nose, sharp and bitter like scorched earth.

The storm seemed to pause; the world holding its breath.

Yarron stepped out of the swirling mist, his figure imposing and otherworldly against the darkened forest. His pale skin shimmered in the dim light; his gold eyes fixed on her with predatory focus. Behind him, four Fae warriors moved into position, their weapons glinting with glowing runes that pulsed like a heartbeat.

"Ah, the wolf. You've led me right where I wanted you," Yarron said.

Palisade's wolf bristled, its fur standing on end as a low growl escaped its throat. Trinity and Gwen wiggled atop her, their pounding hearts loud in her ears.

Her wolf lowered to the ground, allowing the two women to slide off. Palisade forced the wolf to yield. Pain shot through her bones. Heat flared through her blood as her fur receded, and Palisade gasped. When she opened her eyes again, the wolf paced in her mind, and she stood bare before them. From behind, Trinity draped the cardigan over her shoulders. Palisade slipped it on without looking back.

Palisade stepped between her friends and the Fae. "What do you want, Yarron?"

Yarron's smile deepened, cold and calculating. "Only what I've always wanted—to claim what is rightfully mine. You turned against me, but I see you are not entirely useless after all. You, dear wolf guardian, are about to help me complete this mission."

Palisade's fingers curled at her sides. Heat pressed under her skin as the guardian paced inside her head. The queen was close. Close enough to taste. Whether the pull came from instinct or jealousy, she couldn't tell.

Thunder rolled overhead, closer now. The first icy drops of rain struck her bare legs, then her shoulders.

Yarron stepped forward. His warriors fanned out, quiet and precise, closing the distance.

Her wolf surged, a warning snarl vibrating through her ribs. *Shift. Now.*

No.

Lightning split the sky, bleaching the forest white for a heart-beat. Palisade held her ground, breath locked in her chest, every instinct screaming to tear through him and every scrap of reason holding her still.

We have to fight.

Not yet.

Her breath hitched. The wolf surged against her skin, teeth and muscle coiled to strike, while her feet stayed rooted to the ground.

Yarron's eyes gleamed as he spoke, his voice sliding into her thoughts, warm and invasive. "You've felt it, haven't you? The power inside you. The strength that could end all of this."

A low growl rose from her chest before she could stop it. The rain thickened, cold and relentless, soaking through her cardigan and dragging her hair into her eyes.

Yarron stepped closer. His warriors moved with him, tightening their circle until the air.

"You're the key, Palisade. The queen's power has bound us all. You can finish what the ohunko could not. I assumed wrong. I was wrong about you. I thought it was bear blood in your veins." He smiled. "Now I see the wolf and the power to end this. Here. Now."

A pulse of magic radiated from him, subtle but invasive, brushing against the edges of her mind. Her jaw locked as the pressure slid deeper, threading through instinct and fear, tugging at the wolf's need to protect. To eliminate the threat.

Her eyes flicked to Trinity. Her golden gaze unwavering despite the rain streaking down her face. Yarron's magic tried to twist

Take her out. The command whispered like a serpent, curling around her consciousness.

Palisade staggered forward. The compulsion pressed harder, a sharp pain behind her eyes as if Yarron's magic were trying to split her apart from within.

"Fight it," Trinity said.

Palisade forced a smile, letting her wolf snarl rise. She glanced back at Gwen. Her gaze dropped to the iron cuffs on her wrists. A plan formed through the haze of Yarron's magic.

Pretend.

Yarron's smile widened as he sensed her shift, mistaking her intent. "That's it," he coaxed. "You know what must be done. Free yourself from this torment. Take what's yours. Finish it."

Palisade stepped closer to Trinity, slowly so Yarron believed she was succumbing to the compulsion. Rain dripped from her lashes. Inside her, the wolf slammed and snarled, held back by a leash of will.

She reached out. Her fingers brushed Trinity's shoulder, then slid down to her arm.

"It'll be okay," she murmured, letting her voice shake enough to sound broken.

Trinity's brow furrowed. "Palisade—"

"Trust me," Palisade said, raising her voice over the storm.

She turned and gathered herself to strike. At the last moment, her hand slipped from Trinity and landed on Gwen's cuffs instead. Cold bit into her palm. The iron burned, threaded with magic that stung like a dozen wasps.

"Don't—" Gwen started.

The cuff clicked open. Magic snapped loose. She flinched back as the contact with Gwen's skin sparked through her. Her wolf rushed forward, drawn to Gwen.

"Do it now, wolf. End her," Yarron commanded.

The compulsion cracked across her mind, white-hot. Pain bloomed behind her eyes. Palisade bared her teeth and held.

Fingers shook as she reached again for Gwen.

The second cuff fell away.

Yarron's warriors closed in. Rain dripped from their weapons. The faint glow of their runes cast eerie shadows on the ground.

"Palisade," Gwen said harshly.

Palisade didn't look back. She tilted her head toward Yarron and mouthed, *Grab him.*

Gwen flexed her wrists and stepped forward.

The storm changed with her. For a heartbeat, the rain thinned, droplets hanging longer in the air before striking the ground, as though something unseen had turned its attention to her.

Palisade straightened. The wolf pressed close to the surface, teeth bared in silent triumph. She lifted her chin and met Yarron's gaze. "Did you know this one is the *hehewuti* the shifters whisper about? They say she can pull spirits from warriors. Perhaps even control the queen for you."

Yarron's smile thinned. "Ah, yes. Indeed."

He moved closer to Gwen, his golden eyes narrowing as if calculating her strength. Thunder rolled low above them. One of his warriors changed his stance, weapon poised.

Gwen narrowed her eyes. Under those lashes, something burned in her eyes, bright enough to evaporate the rain.

"You're a gift," Yarron said. She held still at his approach. "With your power, we could restore this world."

Inside Palisade, the wolf snarled.

Wait, she told it.

The wolf paced.

Just wait.

Yarron shot Palisade a warning glare before smoothing it away. His focus slid back to Gwen. He extended a hand toward her. Silver and gold threads unwound from his palm, drifting toward her like living filaments.

"Join me. Together, we can restore what was lost," Yarron said.

Gwen tilted her head. Rain traced the line of her cheek. Her lips curled into a faint, dangerous smile.

"Restore?" she echoed. "You mean like you restored Gorak? Or tried to destroy Trinity?"

Yarron's eyes hardened. His hand fell, fingers curling as the silver threads of magic pulled back and tightened around him.

The gold tendrils of his magic stayed with Gwen. "Do not confuse necessity with cruelty," he said. "Every future worth having demands sacrifice."

Gwen's smile didn't waver. "You're right about one thing."

"And what's that?" he asked.

"Sacrifices are necessary."

Gwen lunged. Her hands locked around his arm. The storm broke open above them, thunder cracking so close it shook the ground. Yarron screamed as the magic ripped free, gold light surging out of him and flooding into her.

His warriors froze.

Trinity moved, stepping between them, her hands held out, palms out. "I can't hold them long."

Palisade staggered back. Her blood sang, wild and electric, her wolf clawing at her ribs as Gwen drew deeper. Yarron thrashed, terror blowing his pupils wide.

"No!" he gasped. "You can't—"

His body jerked once.

Then again.

The gold in his eyes guttered, flickered, and went dark. He collapsed at Gwen's feet, empty as a husk.

Silence swallowed the clearing.

The warriors backed away from Gwen.

Gwen drew the essence of Yarron's magic into herself. "Leave and never return to this mountain," she said. "Or stay and face the dragons."

As if summoned by the storm itself, a distant roar came through the storm. The mark on Palisade's wrist warmed and glowed.

The warriors stiffened. Glances flicked sideways. Feet shuffled in the wet leaves.

Wings thundered overhead, driving rain outward in violent spirals. Shadows swept across the clearing as a large black dragon and another with a blue underbelly dropped through the storm, blotting out what little light remained.

Aluk's big black dragon form landed first. The impact cracked the ground. Steam rose from his scales as he lifted his head, eyes burning as they locked on the remaining Fae.

The warriors broke. One by one they vanished into the trees, dissolving into the forest as if the mountain itself had swallowed them.

Only then did Gwen release a long breath. The faint glow clinging to her skin dimmed, leaving her swaying on her feet.

"You okay?" Palisade asked.

Gwen huffed a tired laugh. "I am so lit I am surprised I don't glow."

Relief hit Palisade like a delayed impact.

Aluk shifted mid-stride, scales folding into skin as he crossed the clearing. He caught Palisade and hauled her against his bare body.

"You're reckless," he muttered into her hair, his heart thudding loud to her wolfs heightened hearing.

Palisade smirked, pressing her forehead to his chest, and grounding herself in his scent of pine and smoke. "But effective."

Taran joined them, rain sliding down his shoulders as his gaze lingered on Gwen. Relief warred with caution in his expression.

"What now?" Trinity asked, glancing at the sky. Palisade followed her gaze. Another dragon on his way.

Aluk's gaze turned toward the mountain. "I told him to stay and help Ben."

"They haven't finished the fighting at the resort?" Palisade's pulse jumped, her wolf pacing inside her mind.

Aluk closed his eyes, then opened them. The red sheen of his dragon receded. "There weren't as many as we thought. Our enforcers have captured most of them."

"I'm sending the rangers to track the rest." Taran moved toward Gwen. He studied her face, his brow reading. "What happened to you, *Solanu*? Your eyes have changed."

Gwen held out her uncuffed hands. The golden light in her gaze flickered with the remnants of Yarron's power. Taran walked over to the Fae warrior's body. He crouched and reached for a pulse.

"He's dead," Gwen said.

Taran nodded and backed away.

"You didn't stay at the resort," Aluk said.

Palisade growled low, her attention still locked on Yarron.

"Peaches," Aluk said, drawing Palisade's attention back.

She lifted her gaze. Her stomach did a crazy flip at the hint of vulnerability there. She searched his eyes.

"Diaden," she asked. "Did you...is he free?"

"He chose the portal, Palisade. He said, 'Protect' and 'Fire'. Do you know what he meant?"

She saw the truth in Aluk's eyes. She'd given Diaden back his will. "You're a dragon. Protect and Fire make sense."

"He also said 'The queen is the cure.'"

"Well then, you can be mad at me later. Right now, we need to speak to this queen your dragon sealed in his lair. She's the cure, and don't even try to talk us into going back."

Thirty-Five

"Will you lead, or shall I, Alpha?" Her chin tilted up.

Heat flared beneath his skin. She should not be standing here in bare feet. She should have been behind him, protected, safe. Instead, her eyes glinted with a promise of challenge, and she would bleed before she ever backed down.

For a heartbeat too long, he didn't move. Didn't respond.

Trinity broke the silence. "We cannot delay. We have to find the entrance and face the queen."

Issabrie.

Oska stirred, drawn toward the mountain with a pull that had nothing to do with the woman standing closest to them. The same pull that had haunted him long before Palisade ever existed.

"You won't make it far barefoot," Aluk said, because if he didn't say something practical, he might say something reckless.

Palisade squared her shoulders, her gaze hardening. "I'm not going back. How long have our people suffered from the curse? I won't let Yarron or the Fae win. I want a future. I want…us."

Us.

Her words wound around his heart. She placed her hands on his chest. Heat answered, the mark beneath his skin flaring from their bond.

Mine. Protect. Claim.

For too long, he wore the cold armor his dragon forced on him to protect old secrets. His hand curled around her wrist with his mark. Beneath his touch, it glowed.

Her breath caught. "Aluk."

He didn't trust his voice. Not with the war with his spirit rising inside him. If he chose wrong, he would lose her one way or another.

He wouldn't live in a world where the bond between them remained unfinished.

Our people look to us, Alpha. We cannot falter now. Her wolf's voice brushed against his thoughts through the unsealed bond.

"Very well."

Aluk didn't release Palisade's wrist at once. Heat lingered where he held her, the mark beneath his skin pulsing as if it recognized what he was about to surrender. He forced himself to step back.

Oska, Aluk said internally, *It's time.*

A surge of heat answered him, sealing the choice.

Aluk stepped away from his mate, and shifted.

Scales and fire tore through flesh as Oska surged free, massive wings unfurling with a force that bent the air. He lowered his body, head dipping toward Palisade in silent command.

Trinity's golden eyes snapped skyward. "He's here."

The air split with a rush of wind.

Conleth descended fast, silver and black flashing between clouds as his dragon form broke through the mist. He dropped straight towards them, wings snapping wide at the last possible moment before landing with a force that sent loose stone skittering down the slope.

Grab your mates and follow. Aluk instructed his brothers.

Trinity took an involuntary step forward.

Conleth's massive head lowered toward her, his breath washing over her in a rush of heat and ozone. With one leg bent, he nudged her to climb onto him.

Taran was at Gwen's side. "Wait!"

Aluk tilted his head toward her. She held out her hands.

Palisade rushed under his neck. "I got this."

Gwen swallowed. "I hate this part."

"Me too." Palisade closed her hands around the glowing cuffs at Gwen's wrists. Biting her lip, she snapped them together. The runes dimmed; the cuffs locked with a click.

Taran shifted in a rush of heat and wind, his dragon form unfurling around them. A massive claw scooped Gwen up with practiced care, tucking her close against his chest where she could not see the drop, or the heights above.

Aluk turned to Palisade.

She didn't wait for him to offer again. She stepped into his space, chin lifted, and grabbed hold of her mate's scales. He plucked her up and slid her onto his back.

Hold on. Once he felt her settled, he lurched off the ground.

"We're moving," Aluk said through their minds. "Now."

Conleth launched after him, Trinity on his back.

Taran circled and followed behind them with Gwen.

Aluk led them higher up the mountain, circling once, twice, scanning for movement before turning toward his lair.

His heart thudded in time with the low hum of magic as the lair came into sight. Each beat tightened the knot in his chest. His brothers landed along the narrow shelf of stone and secured their mates before shifting back to men.

He followed, Oska surrendering the sky with reluctant heat. Stone slammed beneath his bare feet. Cold air cut across his skin, and the mountain answered him with a low, resonant thrum that vibrated through bone and blood alike.

Palisade slid off and took several steps away from him.

For a breath, Oska resisted.

"Aluk?" Their sweet mate's voice tugged at him.

The dragon withdrew inside him, fire licking at his trembling sides. *Mine*, the ancient presence rumbled, the memory of sealing stone and screaming magic rising hot and bitter in Aluk's chest.

Enough, Aluk pressed back, teeth clenched as the shift settled over him.

The heat collapsed inward. Flesh replaced scale. He staggered one step, naked and breathing hard, the cold biting deeper as memory pressed close. Centuries had not dulled it.

Palisade was beside him.

Her presence steadied the fracture inside his chest. Trust flowed through their unsealed bond. He reached for her without thinking, angling his body enough to shield her from the other's eyes.

She was his. Not yet claimed. Standing with him at the mouth of the place where everything went wrong.

He was bare before her in every way that mattered.

The cave mouth rose before them, sealed beneath layers of stone and ancient intent. Time had scarred the surface, but the enchantment remained intact. Markings etched into the rock stirred as Aluk stepped closer, their glow blooming faint and alive, pulsing in rhythm with the deep drumbeat thrumming through the mountain.

"Stand back." Trinity moved forward, wet silver hair catching the pale light. She pressed her hands to the stone, tracing the symbols with careful precision as soft words slipped from her tongue in the flowing cadence of her ancestors.

The markings did not answer.

"Those symbols may resemble Fae work, but it was not your people who bound her." Conleth studied the markings.

Trinity pressed her palm flat against the stone once more, then withdrew it. "I thought since I was the key to bringing the queen back, I could unlock it." She pulled back wet strands of hair from her face. "The magic has layers. Woven beyond my reach. Whatever sealed this was not meant to be undone by Fae hands."

"Let me try." Gwen laid her palms against the stone. Her lips moved in a whisper too quiet to follow. The air thickened around her. Sweat beaded along her temples as the markings flared brighter, resisting her pull. "Maybe I need to take off my cuffs."

"No." Taran caught her before her knees buckled, hauling her back against his chest.

Even with the hehewuti's gift and the stolen power still lingering in her veins, the barrier did not yield.

Silence settled in the aftermath.

The mountain waited.

The pause lingered, a chasm filled with echoes of their past trails and the taunting of a future withheld from them. Aluk's dragon spirit teetered on the brink of curling deeper inside him as every possible outcome branching from one simple decision rested in his hands.

Palisade, Trinity, Gwen, and his brothers... They were all looking at him.

With the force of a promise carved into the bedrock of his being, his dragon spirit opened the memories suppressed from him.

Palisade took his hand. "Can your dragon remember? Please Oska, what did you and the others do to trap her here in the first place?"

Aluk approached the barrier. Oska rose inside him, as Aluk shared his sight with the spirit. The markings on the stone seemed to awaken at his presence, sensing Oska within him. He placed his hands on the cool surface of the stone. The roughness of the ancient symbols pressed into his skin. He closed his eyes, searching through the memories.

The runes flared to life under Aluk's touch. A warm, golden glow spread from his palms, illuminating the intricate patterns and causing them to pulse under his touch. The light intensified, its brilliance throwing stark shadows across the faces of the others.

Oska's energy merged with his, the dragon's ancient wisdom seeping through the cracks of his human restraint. Together, they united their strength against the barrier, pushing, willing it to yield to the rightful heir of the lair within.

The magic coursed through the stone, responding to the call of blood and spirit, the pulsating glow syncing with the thrumming of his heart. His spirit grunted against the effort to move the stone away from the entrance. His hands heated, pouring fire into the stone.

A symphony of crackles echoed through the mountain pass as the boulder crumbled under his pressure. A ripple, like a disturbed pond, vibrated with released magic, the scent of ozone mingling with the crispness of the alpine breeze.

Palisade pressed her hand to the middle of his back. Her touch caused subtle tremors to travel through him, like pleasant zings of electricity.

The world held its breath as man and dragon stood ready to face the woman who stood beyond the crumbling boulder of the lair within the heart of the mountain.

Thirty-Six

Palisade broke away from Taran. Oska moaned, and light tore around him. Aluk's human form stood amid the smoke and charred earth at his feet, shoulders tight, breath uneven. Burning leaves drifted from several trees against the mountainside. The scent of electricity hung heavy in the air. Above them, the storm crackled and sizzled, gathering strength. The wind kicked up from the far side of the ledge, lifting the fine hairs along her neck.

Palisade curled her fingers. Fire raced through her veins, bright against the growing darkness.

"Aluk?" she called softly.

He turned his head, his eyes still glowing red with an inner inferno. Palisade pressed her palm to his back and leaned in.

As the wind swept away the smoke and ash, the figure of a woman shimmered beneath the dark rain clouds. Her body blurred with bending light, edges doubling and slipping when Palisade tried to fix her gaze.

"Alpha," she whispered.

The ghost's eyes flared with a cold, otherworldly light, each flicker locking her form into place. As the spectral queen gathered into focus, her face contorted, lips peeling back as heat burned through her gaze. She lunged. Shimmering hands reached for Palisade.

A searing gust of spectral energy slammed into Palisade's flank, sending her skidding sideways. Her wolf snarled, prickling against her flesh.

Trinity darted forward, arms outstretched. Her magic crackled as she summoned a shimmering barrier. It flickered under the strain, edges dissolving as the spirit's power pressed against it.

A whisper of Asigwani's will brushed Palisade's mind. She rushed toward the spectral queen, her wolf spirit pulling her left, then driving her forward.

"No!" Gwen cried.

The ghost spirit slipped past Trinity's tenuous hold. The clearing erupted in a crackling burst of energy as the spirit broke free. Leaves shivered on their branches, and the air snapped with sudden static as if lightning had brushed the world awake.

Gwen's hands trembled, reaching for the spirit. "I can't hold both the Fae magic and the spirit. It's too much."

"Don't release that magic!" Trinity lunged forward.

"Let go!" Taran moved to reach his mate, but the wind slammed into him and Conleth, sending them scrambling at the ledge's edge.

"Taran!" Gwen shouted, frozen in place. Gold flared in her eyes.

Trinity appeared beside her. "We have to trap her. Now!" She tightened her grip. "All three of us."

Trinity caught Gwen's hand and reached for Palisade. She glanced over her shoulder at Aluk. He stalked toward the spectral queen, eyes burning blood red.

Still reeling from the spirit's strike, Palisade forced herself forward. "Gwen, Trinity. Focus on trapping her."

Adrenaline burned through her as she positioned herself where the queen would strike again. Gwen's hand locked around hers. Trinity reached across and seized Palisade's other hand.

The spectral queen lunged.

A shimmering shield snapped into place, trapping the spirit and holding her just beyond reach.

The ghost spirit circled, a whirlwind of shimmering energy and bitter malice. She lunged repeatedly, hammering at her containment. Gwen released threads of golden magic, letting them weave into Trinity's.

Gwen struggled to keep her focus. Her attention fractured between her mate climbing back over the ledge of rocks and the spectral queen slamming against the shield in front of them. Ghostly fingers raked at Palisade's face, skidding uselessly across the barrier. Asigwani growled low, the sound reverberating through Palisade's bones.

"Gwen, hold on!" Palisade roared, her voice echoing over the storm's rising wail. The spectral queen shrieked. The sound shattered through the air like breaking glass, as the energy binding her tightened.

Palisade bared her teeth in a snarl. "Don't let go!"

The spectral queen writhed as the bindings constricted; her fiery eyes flashed with fear. "Oska... alpha.... Help me."

"Issabrie..." Aluk said, his glowing red eyes dulled.

"I've waited all this time for you!" the spectral whined.

Her form thickened, flesh knitting until she stood solid as any living woman. The queen's gaze drifted among all three women. A smirk lifted on her lips as her gaze landed on Trinity. "You have my brother's eyes. He still lives then? You must take me to him. We are family."

Palisade stiffened as Aluk's commanding voice cut through the swirling chaos. Standing just behind her, he demanded, "Tell us how to break the curse."

Heat rolled from him. His dragon spirit surged, rage braided tight with regret. Aluk's chest bumped against Palisade's back.

"You put this curse upon yourself."

The spectral queen's voice was a venomous hiss, echoing off the mountain's craggy walls.

Gwen cut in. "Would you like us to put you back on the mountain?"

The spectral queen laughed, sending a shiver through Palisade's bones.

The ghost turned her gaze from Gwen and fixed it on Aluk. Her lips curled into an exaggerated pout as she purred, "Come now, dragon. You belong to me. You can't escape where you came from. Unless your kind refills the forest with its gifts, the curse will slowly consume you and the foolish humans who bonded with you. They wanted you because they are weak. They took what is ours. You will return to me."

Protectiveness flared within Palisade. She tightened her grip on Gwen and Trinity's hands.

"You're dead," Palisade's voice braided with the rising spirit of her wolf guardian, a vow etched into every taut muscle. "And he's mine. He's always been mine." Her voice braided with the rising spirit of her wolf guardian; a vow etched into every taut muscle.

The spectral queen's head tilted back. Long white hair billowed like a phantom's veil as her eyes narrowed on Palisade. "Ah, wolf guardian. You have escaped the shadows. Too bad I intend to send you back, and this time, I will ensure you have no heirs to which to return."

The spectral queen dived straight for Trinity.

Trinity screamed, her body arching as the ghost's shimmering form sank into her skin. Trinity's eyes flashed a terrifying, frozen white. "The vessel," Issabrie's voice hissed, vibrating through Trinity's throat. "I take the blood of my blood to walk the earth again!"

"Trinity!" Gwen's golden magic lashed out, but it passed through Trinity's body

"Aluk, help her!" Palisade cried, not having enough energy to shift into her wolf.

Aluk froze. As Issabrie's power flared within Trinity, a primal, ancient tether snapped tight between the Queen and the Dragon. Aluk's eyes bled a dark, molten gold. He gasped, his knees hitting the earth.

"Come to me, Dragon," the possessed Trinity purred, her hand reaching out. "The curse is a hunger only I can feed. Leave the wolf. Return to the throne." She turned to look out into the distance. "And it would seem I get two for the price of one. Let's make that three dragons, shall we?" She turned back and smiled at Gwen.

Palisade felt the bond between her and Aluk fraying. The mountain pulsed in time with the Queen's heartbeat. Aluk looked up, and for a second, Palisade saw the dragon's ancient, weary soul wanting to surrender.

"Aluk, look at me!" Palisade stepped between him and the ghost. She seized his face, the heat from his skin blistering her palms. "She's the past. The curse. I am the life you chose!"

The Queen shrieked, a shockwave of spite that sent the trees groaning. "She is a flicker of fur and bone. I am eternal!"

Aluk's hands locked onto Palisade's wrists. He turned his gaze to the Queen, his voice vibrating with the weight of the mountain. "You are not my mate. You are the shadow of a grave I've already stepped out of."

He stood, pulling Palisade with him. "Gwen! Now!"

Palisade didn't let go. She reached out and grabbed Gwen's hand, while Gwen seized Trinity's shoulder. The circle wasn't just a shield anymore. It was a circuit.

"Out!" Aluk thundered, his command shaking the foundations of the ledge.

The queen snarled, her face a distorted mask over Trinity's pale features. "You think your word is enough to banish me? I am your queen. You will obey me, Dragon!"

Trinity's eyes turned gold. Her fingers sparked with violet light along her fingertips. Tears poured down her face.

The air grew unnaturally cold; the rain turned to hail.

"She's siphoning her magic," Gwen shouted above the roar of the wind.

Palisade let go of Aluk. She grasped Trinity's hand. Her palm burned, not with the steady heat of Aluk's dragon fire, but with a violet pulse. Through their joined palms, Palisade sensed the bond between Trinity and Conleth. "You want dragons?" Palisade shouted. "Trinity, hold on!"

"Peaches, what are you doing?"

"Where's Conleth and Taran?"

Trinity's power flared a jagged, electric violet, snapping upward like a defensive viper. It hummed with a frequency so high Palisade almost let go. Her wolf howled in her head at the sound.

The queen screamed. Two powers gnashed together like rusted gears in a failing machine. Palisade watched as sparks of violet and sickly silver sprayed forth, scorching the earth at their feet.

The metallic scent of ozone bit at Palisade's nostrils, warring with the suffocating smell of ancient dust and grave dirt kicked up by the Queen's presence. The pressure in the circle mounted, a build-up of kinetic energy that made the fine hairs on Palisade's arms stand on end.

The Queen contorted Trinity's face as the violet shield pushed back. Her possession of Trinity slipped. Trinity's magic surged, wrapping her in a golden aura. With a final, ear-piercing screech of magical metal on metal, the shield buckled outward; the backfire throwing the Queen's spectral form backward.

Palisade caught Trinity on the downfall. Gwen crouched down beside her. The rain and hail pelted them, and they used their bodies to shield Trinity from the worst of it. Palisade glanced back over her shoulder. Her breath caught as the brothers moved to trap the spectral queen between them.

The impact rippled through the air in a violent pulse. The wind hushed.

Two massive forms erupted from below the ledge, their scales shimmering like polished obsidian and molten copper.

Aluk rushed forward, one stride a man, the next a dragon. As he shifted, the sheer force of his draconic aura surged through Palisade's bond, knocking her on her butt beside Trinity.

The queen's spectral form hovered in the air, a tattered shroud of silver malice, screaming in a language lost to time.

"Issabrie!" Aluk's voice now came from the massive throat of the dragon behind Palisade. "You are the past. We are the dawn."

The three dragons opened their maws in unison.

A synchronized blast of dragon fire blasted the queen. Trinity sat up, grabbing Gwen's arm by the cuff. A stream of gold and violet hit the spectral queen. The flames swallowed the queen's screams until there was nothing left but a handful of pale sparks whisked away into the night by the storm.

The mountain's roar died into a thick silence. Palisade's fingers finally uncurled from the death-grip she had on Trinity and Gwen. Her palms buzzed with a phantom electrical hum that made her skin twitch.

Beside her, Trinity began to fall.

Before Palisade could catch her, a blur of motion cut through the settling steam. Conleth hit the ground, barely human; his skin still shimmered with the ghost of obsidian scales. He caught Trinity mid-air, his arms locking around her with a force that locked like it might crush her.

"Trinity!"

Palisade's breath hitched as Conleth dragged Trinity into his arms. His hands trembled as they moved over her face and shoulders. He buried his face in the crook of her neck, letting out a low, guttural sound—half sob, half growl—that vibrated through the ground Palisade stood on.

"I'm here," Trinity gasped, her gold eyes fading to violet as she clung to his forearms. "Con, I'm okay. She's gone."

"She was inside you," Conleth rasped, pulling back to frame her face, his thumbs stroking her cheeks as if trying to rub the Queen's mask off her skin. "I felt your spark go dark. The bond turned cold."

The mention of their bond hit Palisade like a wave, but a different heat anchored her from behind.

Aluk's arms wrapped around Palisade's waist, pulling her back against his chest. His was radiating a furnace-like heat, his heart thudding a heavy, rhythmic tattoo against her spine. Palisade leaned her head back against his shoulder, her adrenaline finally ebbing into a bone-deep exhaustion. Rain slicked back her hair and soaked her clothes.

His jaw tightened against her temple, his breath coming in ragged, relieved hitches.

To her left, the circle had dissolved into pairs. Taran had Gwen hauled against him, his hand cupped over the back of her head, shielding her as if the storm might sweep her up at any moment. Gwen was shaking; the golden Fae light absorbed from Yarron flickered like a dying candle around her.

Movement stirred at the edge of the clearing, drawing her attention away.

Her wolf was silent and watchful in the back of her mind. Palisade straightened in Aluk's arms as dark silhouettes gathered at the mouth of the lair and between the gnarled trunks of the storm-battered trees.

"Shadow spirits..." Trinity said from Conleth's arms.

Velvet shadows shaped like mountain lions paced the prominent ridges. Wolves with eyes like distant stars blended into the stone, their forms shifting like smoke. One wolf took a single, deliberate step forward. It lowered its massive, translucent head in silent acknowledgement that sent more shivers tracking down Palisade's spine. One by one, the other spirits followed suit.

"They recognize you as their guardian," Aluk murmured.

"They're free."

He turned her in his arms, forcing her to look up at him. The corner of his mouth curved, a look of weary, profound peace softening the hard lines of his face. The blood-red fire in his eyes turned to a sunset amber.

"There's only one way to find out if the curse is broken," he said, his breath warm against her ear. His arms tightened, anchoring her to the earth and to him. "I believe we still have a bond to complete."

A spark lit within Palisade, catching and taking hold. She looked at Trinity walking toward the edge of the ledge with Conleth, then at Gwen and Taran behind them.

The Queen was dead. The rain had lessened, and the mountain loosened its hold on her secrets.

Palisade lifted her gaze to his. "I'm ready."

Thirty-Seven

The wind carried away the last remnants of the night as the first light of dawn spilled over the mountain. Palisade's nerves still hummed beneath her skin. She moved through the resort lobby, where people bustled about, lifting broken furniture and setting nails with ringing blows.

The scent of fresh paint mingled with the earthy bite of wood shavings. Beyond the tall glass windows, the village stirred awake.

Her gaze caught on Ben as he moved among the workers with a calm authority. Dust motes drifted through the morning light as he surveyed the damage, his tight smile like a beacon amid the ruins.

"Keep it tight, folks!" Ben called, clapping a burly man on the back. His laughter carried through the space, easing some of the strain that still clung to the battered walls.

Aluk looked for her, and Palisade threaded through the chaos toward him. As she approached, the lines on Ben's face eased. He paused, wiping dust from his cheek with the back of his hand.

"Palisade," he said, cautious but warm. "It's good to see you standing and whole."

She managed a tired smile. "It's good to be alive."

"And mated," Ben added with a chuckle.

Heat crept into her cheeks, the memory of Aluk's presence settling deep and sure beneath her skin.

Aluk stepped forward from a few paces back and joined them.

"Speaking of mates," Aluk asked, glancing around. "Yours?"

"In the kitchen, as always," Ben replied with a broad grin. "Organizing a feast with the others." He clapped Aluk on the arm. "Feels like a good day to celebrate, doesn't it?"

Palisade let her gaze drift. Faces streaked with grime bent over broken tables and shattered beams. Laughter surfaced in small bursts, tentative gestures, as ruin gave way to repair. The room pulsed with a stubborn, living energy.

"It's hard to imagine we'll ever be the same," she said.

Ben's smile softened. "Maybe that's not such a bad thing. We're stronger now."

Aluk looked at her then, his expression gentler than she had ever seen it. "Strength is built on hardship, Palisade. Every mark of damage is just a reminder of how far we've come, and how much further we can go."

Ben gestured toward a group of workers replacing broken windows, pane by pane. "We needed to remodel, anyway. It's been decades since this place got a proper upgrade."

Aluk's gaze lingered on Palisade. "Places. Things. They're replaceable. You, Peaches, are not. Cursed or not, I could not live without you."

The sincerity in his voice tightened her chest until she had to breathe through it.

Ben clapped his hands together. "I've got things handled here. Go get some rest while you can. We've got a busy day ahead, and I know you've got many other duties calling."

Nearby, Rourke coordinated a team to clear debris from the lobby. A brief exchange and a steady nod between him and Ben said enough. For now, the resort was secure. The murmur of voices, the clatter of tools, and the steady rhythm of rebuilding wrapped the space in a quiet reassurance.

Standing there, enveloped by the warmth of familiar voices and the resilience of a community reborn, the weight of the night's horrors lifted. Yet beneath the relief, a quiet question gnawed at the edges of her thoughts. How would they truly know if they'd broken the curse?

Her wolf stirred, unsettled by the lingering scent of ash and magic.

It will take root in the next generation, her wolf murmured.

Life will come forth and claim what was nearly lost, and the land will know when the bond is restored.

Her hand drifted to her abdomen, fingers brushing lightly over the fabric of her shirt as warmth bloomed deep inside her. The thought hit her all at once. A new generation. That would be their answer.

When life took hold, when the cries of newborns rose where silence once ruled. When wolves, dragons, and Fae alike welcomed children into a world no longer bound to the past.

She turned and found Aluk's gaze on her. A slow smile curved his mouth, heat and promise woven into it, and anticipation slid down her spine.

Her lips parted, a teasing remark ready, but he was already there. His arms closed around her, solid and warm, and when his mouth met hers, the kiss drove the air from her lungs. Her hands fisted in his shirt as heat unfurled low and aching inside her. For a heartbeat, there was nothing else. No curse. No mountain. Just him, the promise held in his touch.

"Geez, aren't there any rooms in this place for that?"

Aluk's head jerked up.

Taran and Gwen stood a few paces away. Dark circles clung beneath Gwen's eyes. She wore yesterday's clothes, and Taran a simple shirt and jeans.

"It's done," Conleth said, rolling his shoulders as if shedding the last of the fight as he and Trinity joined them. "The Fae are gone. The ones who escaped us have scattered. Sia and his men are hunting them down. Those who linger will spend time in the old fortress for a while."

"The walls are infused. Yarron's donation to the cause. He's a true benefactor now. Gwen made sure of it. No Fae blood will ever be able to create portals inside the fortress or here again," Trinity said, brushing a stray lock of hair from her face.

Gwen let out a long breath, rubbing her temples. When she met Palisade's gaze, a flicker of something unreadable in her eyes. "They can't hurt us anymore."

Taran stretched, arms lifting overhead. "It's about time we ended this so we can all start living." He glanced at Aluk. "Are you planning on celebrating with the rest of us?"

Aluk's hand slid to Palisade's waist. His mouth curved as his gaze dropped to hers. "Oh, I've got my own ways of celebrating."

Palisade's cheeks warmed, but she didn't look away.

Conleth gave a low hum of approval, crossing his arms as he surveyed the battered lobby. "Maybe now someone will finally listen to me and rip up these wood floors. Leave the warm stone beneath."

"It's only warm from Aluk's bad temper," Taran said, ribbing his brother.

Gwen leaned close to him, murmuring, and he nodded. He lifted his chin and slid his arm around her shoulders. "I need to walk with my mate to our suite, then I'll return to help with the cleanup."

"Stay with her," Conleth said, gesturing to Trinity as he took her hand. "We'll be in the clinic here if you need us, and you, brother," he added to Aluk, "should I find you in your lair or the tower?"

Aluk shook his head. "We'll stay here until the cleanup is done."

Palisade leaned into Aluk's warmth, fitting against the solid rise and fall of his breath anchoring her. Their surroundings faded. His hand settled on the small of her back. For the first time, the path ahead felt open.

For My Readers

Thank you for taking a chance on this series. I can't believe it's come to an end, but not *the* end, for there are plenty more stories to tell n the Warrior's Mark world. This series started out under a different pen name and with shorter novels, but it had so much more it needed to expand. It has grown as I have grown as an author. I added the Fae and the curse and gave it layers of complications. Sometimes I thought I'd gone too far, and sometimes I wondered if it was enough. But all this is to say, I loved writing it. I hope you enjoyed reading it and discovering the mountain. Please leave a review or rating on your preferred retail site for your fellow reading besties. Take a photo and share it on your Instagram and follow me@author_selower for updates in this and other upcoming story worlds.

Every review, every post, makes a difference in helping other readers discover books they'll love.

Suz E. Lower

P.S. Trace's story isn't over yet. He's left Crag's Cliff and headed home to Sentinel Peak. You'll be able to find out what's next for the wolf guard in *Marked by a Wolf*.

Sign up for my email list for early access to all sorts of digital goodies, deleted scenes, and advanced peeks of upcoming books. You can also find the link on my website at www.selower.com.

Also by S. E. Lower

<u>Warrior's Mark: Dragons</u>

Marked by Loyalty (Novella)

Marked by a Vow

Marked by an Oath

Marked by a Curse

About the author

S.E. Lower writes urban fantasy, paranormal romance, and epic fantasy, bringing readers into worlds filled with magic, hidden realms, and supernatural intrigue. Whether it's dragon shifters, fae, or the forces of darkness and destiny, her stories are packed with immersive adventure. When she's not writing, she loves thrifting for hidden gems, walking through the woods, and spending time with her kiddos and husband, riding on motorcycles and looking for her next adventure.

www.ingramcontent.com/pod-product-compliance
Lightning Source LLC
Chambersburg PA
CBHW051209190726
48288CB00006B/1871